MARKET FORCES

RICHARD
MORGAN
MARKET FORCES

GOLLANCZ
LONDON

The right of Richard Morgan to be identified as the author
of this work has been asserted by him in accordance with
the Copyright, Designs and Patents Act 1988.

First published in Great Britain in 2004 by

Gollancz
An imprint of the Orion Publishing Group
Orion House, 5 Upper St Martin's Lane,
London WC2H 9EA

A CIP catalogue record for this book
is available from the British Library

ISBN 0 575 07512 0 (cased)
ISBN 0 575 07567 8 (trade paperback)

Typeset at The Spartan Press Ltd,
Lymington, Hants

Printed in Great Britain by
Clays Ltd, St Ives plc

ACKNOWLEDGMENTS

Market Forces has had a long and varied evolution, from nasty idea to short story, to screenplay, to the novel you now hold in your hands. Along the way, it (and its author) has incurred a few debts. In chronological order, then, so near as I can recall:

Thanks to Simon Edkins for the original thought-provoking sneer: *they think they live in a jungle, don't they?*, and to Gavin Burgess for sharing his knowledge of some of the more feral business training procedures out there. Thanks to Sarah Lane for seeing the potential in a moth-eaten unpublished short story, for pushing me into building a screenplay around it, and for all the unflagging enthusiasm and hard work she poured into the project along the way – great movie producers are made of this, or should be. Thanks also to Alan Young for substantial anecdotal inspiration over the years, and for reading the raw product with an economics consultant's beady eye. Thanks, as always, to my agent, Carolyn Whitaker, and my editor, Simon Spanton, for excellence in the field of making me pay attention to detail. Thanks to everyone on the Gollancz team for making the fifth floor a great place to hang out. And finally, most of all, thanks to my recently acquired wife, Virginia Cottinelli, for her patience in sharing with me the contents of a Master's programme in Development at the University of Glasgow, the getting of which was already costing her more grief than any paying student should have to put up with.

A list of books that proved inspirational during the writing of *Market Forces* is appended at the end of the novel, should the reader be interested. They are too many to list or talk about here, but they are too important not to mention at all. On a lighter note, *Market Forces* also owes a rather obvious debt of inspiration to the ground-breaking movies *Mad Max* and *Rollerball*, both of which made a massive impact on me at an age when legally I shouldn't have been watching either.

Market Forces is dedicated, with love, to my earliest fan,
my sister Caroline – because she's waited long enough

It's also dedicated to all those, globally, whose lives have been
wrecked or snuffed out by the Great Neoliberal Dream and
Slash-and-Burn Globalisation.

I know – that the cannibals wear smart suits and ties
And I know – they arm-wrestle on the altar
And I say – don't leave your heart in a hard place

Midnight Oil – *Sometimes*

If (I asked) the commercial banks, the official creditors, the Bank, the
IMF, the TNCs, the money managers and the global elites were happy,
who were we to complain?

Susan George – *The Lugano Report*

PROLOGUE

Checkout.

The shiny black plastic swipes through.

Nothing.

The machine fails in its habitual insectile chittering and the screen blinks, as if outraged at what it has been fed. The checkout girl looks up at the woman who has handed her the card and smiles a little too widely. It's a smile that contains as much genuine emotion as there is fruit juice in a carton of Five Fruit D-Lish.

'*Are you sure you want to use this card?*'

Up to her arms in bagged shopping, the woman sets down the two-year-old she has been propping against the checkout flange and looks back to where her husband is still unloading the last of the brightly coloured tins and bags from the trolley.

'*Martin?*'

'*Yeah, what?*' *Voice irritable with the household task they've just completed.*

'*The card doesn't . . .*'

'*Doesn't what?*' *He meets her eyes and reads the distress there, then switches to the checkout girl. His voice comes out tight.* '*Run it again, please. Must have glitched.*'

The girl shrugs and swipes the card a second time. The screen flickers with the same disdain.

TRANSACTION DENIED.

The girl takes the card and hands it back to the woman. A small pocket of quiet expands around the action, bubbling out past the conveyor belt to the boy at the next checkout unit and to the three customers waiting behind Martin. In a few more seconds it will dissolve into the slither of whispering.

'*Would you like to try another card.*'

'*This is ridiculous,*' *snaps Martin.* '*That account had funds as of the first of the month. I've just been paid.*'

'*I can run the card a third time,*' *offers the girl with studied indifference.*

'*No.*' *The woman's knuckles have gone white around the small piece of black plastic.* '*Martin, try the Intex.*'

'*Helen, there's money in that acc—*'

'*Some problem,*' *asks the man behind him, tapping his own plastic significantly against the pile of shopping he has assembled so close to the*

3

Next Customer divider that it's in danger of tumbling over into Martin's space.

Martin's mouth shuts like a trap.

'No problem.'

He hands over the blue flecked Intex card and watches at least as intently as the people behind him as the checkout girl swipes it.

The machine chews it over for a couple of moments,

And spits it out.

The girl hands it back and shakes her head. Her smooth, plastic politeness is beginning to degrade.

'Card's blocked,' she says dismissively. 'Terminal audit.'

'What?'

'Terminal audit. I'm going to have to ask you to put those purchases back on the far side of the counter and leave the store.'

'Run the card again.'

The girl sighed. 'I don't have to run the card again, sir. I have all the information I need right here. Your rating is invalidated.'

'Martin,' Helen presses forward at his side. 'Leave it, we'll come back when it's cleared u—'

'No, goddamn it.' Martin shrugs her off and leans over the counter, into the checkout girl's face. 'There is money in that account. Now swipe the card again.'

'Better do as she says,' says the pushy customer behind him.

Martin swings on him, tensed.

'This got something to do with you?'

'I am waiting.'

'Well, wait some fucking more.' He snaps his fingers in the man's face, dismissing him, and the pushy customer flinches back. Martin turns back to the checkout girl. 'Now, you—'

The prod hits him in the side like a rude elbow. A heartbeat later the charge shocks him off the counter and into a seemingly immense clear space. He hits the floor, smelling burnt fabric.

He hears Helen shriek. Sees confusedly from floor level. Boots in front of him and a voice that sounds like tearing cardboard at a great height.

'I think you'd better leave the store, sir.'

The security guard hauls him to his feet and props him against the counter again. A big man, swelling at the waist but watchful and hard around the eyes. He's been doing this for a long time, probably cut his teeth on cordoned zone clubs before he got this gig. He's shocked men before and Martin is out of office clothes at four-thirty on a Wednesday afternoon, casual in faded jeans and a well-worn crew-neck pullover that doesn't show what it was once worth. The security guard thinks he has the measure of this one. He doesn't know, can't know.

4

Martin comes off the counter.

The palm heel strike smashes the guard's nose flat. The knee goes in at groin level. As the guard falls, Martin drives into the base of his skull with one clenched fist.

The guard hits the ground a dead weight.

'Stand where you are!'

Martin reels around and comes face to face with the guard's smaller, female partner just as she clears a pistol from her holster. Still scrambled from the cattle prod, he lurches the wrong way, towards her, and the guard blows his brains out all over his wife and son and the checkout and the checkout girl and all the shiny packaged items on the belt that they can no longer afford.

FILE#1:
INITIAL INVESTMENT

ONE

Awake.

Jackknifed there in sweat.

Fragments of the dream still pinning his breath in his throat and his face into the pillow, mind reeling in the darkened room . . .

Reality settled over him like a fresh sheet. He was home.

He heaved a shuddering sigh and groped for the glass of water beside the bed. In the dream he'd been falling to, and then through, the tiles of the supermarket floor.

On the other side of the bed Carla stirred and laid a hand on him.

'Chris?'

''sokay. Dream.' He gulped from the glass. 'Bad dream, s'all.'

'Murcheson again?'

He paused, peculiarly unwilling to correct her assumption. He didn't dream about Murcheson's screaming death much any more. He shivered a little. Carla sighed and pulled herself closer to him. She took his hand and pressed it onto one full breast.

'My father would just love this. Deep stirrings of conscience. He's always said you haven't got one.'

'Right.' Chris lifted the alarm clock and focused on it. Three-twenty. Just perfect. He knew he wouldn't get back to sleep for a while. *Just fucking perfect*. He flopped back, immobile. 'Your father has convenient amnesia when it comes to clearing the rent.'

'Money talks. Why'd you think I married you?'

He rolled his head and butted her gently on the nose. 'Are you taking the piss out of me?'

For answer she reached down for his prick and rolled it through her fingers.

'No. I'm winding you up,' she whispered.

As they drew together he felt the hot gust of desire for her blowing out the dream, but he was slow to harden under her hand. It was only in the final throes of climax that he finally let go.

Falling.

It was raining when the alarm sounded. Soft hiss outside the open window like an untuned TV at very low volume. He snapped off the

9

bleeper, lay listening to the rain for a few moments and then slid out of the bed without waking Carla.

In the kitchen he set up the coffee machine, ducked into the shower and got out in time to steam milk for Carla's cappuccino. He delivered it to her bedside, kissed her awake and pointed it out. She'd probably drift off to sleep again and drink it cold when she finally got up. He lifted clothes from the wardrobe – plain white shirt, one of the dark Italian suits, the Argentine leather shoes. He took them downstairs.

Dressed but untied, he carried his own double espresso into the living room with a slice of toast to watch the seven o'clock bulletins. There was, as usual, a lot of detailed foreign commentary and it was time to go before the Promotions & Appointments spot rolled around. He shrugged, killed the TV and only remembered to knot his tie when he caught himself in the hall mirror. Carla was just making waking noises as he slipped out of the front door and disabled the alarms on the Saab.

He stood in the light rain for a long moment, looking at the car. Soft beads of water glistening on the cold grey metal. Finally, he grinned.

'Conflict Investment, here we come,' he muttered, and got in.

He got the bulletins on the radio. They started Promotions & Appointments as he hit the Elsenham junction ramp. Liz Linshaw's husky tones, just a touch of the cordoned zones to roughen up the otherwise cultured voice. On TV she dressed like a cross between a government arbitrator and a catered-party exotic dancer, and in the last two years she had graced the pages of every men's lifestyle magazine on the rack. The discerning exec's wet dream, and by popular acclaim the AM ratings queen of the nation.

'—very few challenges on the roads this week,' she told him huskily. 'The Congo bid play-off we've all been waiting on is postponed till next week. You can blame the weather forecasts for that, though it looks from my window as if those guys have blown it again. There's less rain coming down than we had for Saunders/Nakamura. Still nothing on the no-name orbital call out for Mike Bryant at Shorn Associates. Don't know where you've got to Mike, but if you can hear me we're anxious to hear from you. And so to new appointments this week – Jeremy Tealby makes partner at Collister Maclean; I think we've all seen that coming for a long time now; and Carol Dexter upgrades to senior market overseer for Mariner Sketch, following her spectacular performance last week against Roger Inglis. Now back to Shorn again for word of a strong newcomer in the Conflict Investment division—'

Chris's eyes flickered from the road to the radio. He touched up the volume a notch.

'—Christopher Faulkner, headhunted from investment giants Hammett McColl where he's already made a name for himself in Emerging Markets. Regular Prom & App followers may recall Chris's remarkable string of successes at Hammett McColl, commencing with the swift elimination of rival Edward Quain, an exec some twenty years his senior at the time. Vindication of the move came rapidly when—' Excitement ran an abrupt slice into her voice, 'Oh, and this just in from our helicopter team. The no-name call out on Mike Bryant has broken, with two of the challengers down past junction twenty-two and the third signalling a withdrawal. Bryant's vehicle has apparently sustained minimal damage and he's on his way in now. We'll have in-depth coverage and an exclusive interview for the lunchtime edition. Looks like the start of a good week for Shorn Associates then, and I'm afraid that's all we've got time for this morning, so back to the Current Affairs desk. Paul.'

'Thank you, Liz. First up, the falling rates of production in the manufacturing sector threaten a further ten thousand jobs across the NAFTA territories, according to an analysis by the Glasgow-based Independent News Group. A Trade and Finance Commission spokesman has called the report "subversively negative". More on the—'

Chris tuned it out, vaguely annoyed that Bryant's no-name scuffle had knocked his name off Liz Linshaw's crimson lips. The rain had stopped and his wipers were beginning to squeak. He switched them off and shot a glance at the dashboard clock. He was still running early.

The proximity alarm chimed.

He caught the accelerating shape in the otherwise deserted rearview and slewed reflexively right. Into the next lane, brake back. As the other vehicle drew level, he relaxed. The car was battered and primer-painted in mottled tan, custom-built like his own but not by anyone who had any clue about road-raging. Heavy steel barbs welded onto the front fenders, bulky external armouring folded around the front wheels and jutting back to the doors. The rear wheels were broad-tyred to provide some manoeuvring stability but it was still clear from the way the car moved that it was carrying far too much weight.

No-namer.

Like fifteen-year-old cordoned zone thugs, they were often the most dangerous because they had the most to prove, the least to lose. The other driver was hidden behind a slat-protected side window, but Chris could see movement. He thought he made out the glimmer of a pale face. Along the car's flank was flashed the driver number in luminous yellow paint. He sighed and reached for the comset.

'Driver Control,' said an anonymous male voice.

'This is Chris Faulkner of Shorn Associates, driver clearance

260B354R, inbound on M11 past junction ten. I have a possible no-name challenger number X23657.'

'Checking. A moment please.'

Chris began to build his speed, gradually so that the no-namer would soak up the acceleration without tripping into fight mode. By the time the controller came back on, they were pacing each other at about one hundred and forty kilometres an hour.

'That's confirmed, Faulkner. Your challenger is Simon Fletcher, freelance legal analyst.'

Chris grunted. *Unemployed lawyer.*

'Challenge filed at 8.04. There's a bulk transporter in the slow lane passing junction eight, automated. Heavy load. Otherwise no traffic. You are cleared to proceed.'

Chris floored it.

He made a full car length and slewed back in front of the other vehicle, forcing Fletcher to a split-second decision. Ram or brake. The tan car dropped away and Chris smiled a little. The brake reflex was instinctive. You had to have a whole different set of responses drilled into you before you could switch it off. After all, Fletcher should have *wanted* to ram him. It was a standard duel tactic. Instead, his instincts had got the better of him.

This isn't going to last long.

The lawyer accelerated again, closing. Chris let him get within about three feet of his rear fender, then hauled out and braked. The other car shot ahead and Chris tucked in behind.

Junction eight flashed past. Inside the London orbital now, almost into the zones. Chris calculated the distance to the underpass, nudged forward and tapped at Fletcher's rear. The lawyer shot away from the contact. Chris checked his speed display and upped it. Another tap. Another forward flinch. The automated haulage transport appeared like a monstrous metal caterpillar, ballooned in the slow lane and then dropped behind just as rapidly. The underpass came into sight. Concrete yellowed with age, stained with faded graffiti that pre-dated the five-metre exclusion fencing. The fence stuck up over the parapet, topped with springy rolls of razor wire. Chris had heard it carried killing voltage.

He gave Fletcher another shove and then slowed to let him dive into the tunnel like a spooked rabbit. A couple of seconds of gentle braking, then accelerate again and in after him.

Shutdown time.

Beneath the weight of the tunnel's roof, things were different. Yellow lights above, two tip-to-tail rows of them like tracer fire along the ceiling. Ghostly white 'emergency exit' signs at intervals along the walls. No breakdown lane, just a scuffed and broken line to mark the edge of the metalled road and a thin concrete path for maintenance workers. A sudden first-person-viewpoint arcade game. Enhanced sense of speed, fear of wall impact and dark.

Chris found Fletcher and closed. The lawyer was rattled – telegraphed clear in the jerky way the car was handling. Chris took a wide swing out into the other lanes so that he'd disappear from Fletcher's rearview mirror and matched velocities dead level. One hundred and forty on the speedo again – both cars were running dead level and the underpass was only five miles long. Make it quick. Chris closed the gap between the two cars by a yard, flicked on his interior light and, leaning across to the passenger side window, raised one hand in stiff farewell. With the light on, Fletcher couldn't fail to see it. He held the pose for a long moment, then snapped the hand into a closed fist with the thumb pointing down. At the same time, he slewed the car one-handed across the intervening lane.

The results were gratifying.

Fletcher must have been watching the farewell gesture, not the road ahead and he forgot where he was. He jerked his car aside, pulled too far and broadsided the wall in a shower of sparks. The primer-painted car staggered drunkenly, raked fire off the concrete once more and bounced away in Chris's wake, tyres shrieking. Chris watched in the mirror as the lawyer braked his vehicle to a sprawling halt, sideways across two lanes. He grinned and slowed to about fifty, waiting to see if Fletcher would pick up the challenge again. The other car showed no sign of restarting. It was still stationary when he hit the upward incline at the far end of the underpass and lost sight of it.

'Wise man,' he murmured to himself.

He emerged from the tunnel into an unexpected patch of sunlight. The road vaulted, climbing onto a long raised curve that swept in over the expanses of zoneland and angled towards the cluster of towers at the heart of the city. Sunlight struck down in selective rays. The towers gleamed.

Chris accelerated into the curve.

TWO

The light in the washroom was subdued, filtering down from high windows set in the sloping roof. Chris rinsed his hands in the onyx basin and stared at himself in the big circular mirror. The Saab-grey eyes that looked back at him were clear and steady. The bar-code tattoos over his cheekbones picked up the colour and mixed it with threads of lighter blue. Lower still, the blue repeated in the weave of his suit and on one of the twisted lines in his Susana Ingram tie. The shirt shone white against his tan and, when he grinned, the silver tooth caught the light in the room like an audible chime.

Good enough.

The sound of splashing water ran on after he killed the tap. He glanced sideways to see another man washing his hands two basins down. The new arrival was big, the length of limb and bulk of trunk habitually used to model suits, and with long fair hair tied back in a ponytail. An Armani-suited Viking. Chris almost looked for a double-bladed battle axe resting against the basin at the man's side.

Instead, one of the hands emerged from the basin and he saw, with a sudden, visceral shock, that it was liberally stained with blood. The other man looked up and met his gaze.

'Something I can help you with?'

Chris shook his head and turned to the hand-dryer on the wall. Behind him, he heard the water stop in the basin and the other man joined him at the dryer. Chris acknowledged the arrival and gave a little space, rubbing away the last traces of moisture on his hands. The dryer ran on. The other man was looking at him closely.

'Hey, you must be the new guy.'

He snapped his fingers wetly. There was still some blood on them, Chris saw, tiny flecks and some in the lines of his palm.

'Chris something, right?'

'Faulkner.'

'Yeah, Faulkner, that's it.' He put his hands under the flow of air. 'Just come in from Hammett McColl?'

'Right.'

'I'm Mike Bryant.' A hand offered sideways. Chris hesitated briefly, eyeing the blood. Bryant picked up on it. 'Oh, yeah. Sorry. I was just in a no-namer, and Shorn policy is you've got to recover their plastic as proof of the kill. It can get messy.'

'Had a no-namer myself this morning,' said Chris reflexively.

'Yeah? Where was that?'

'M11, around junction eight.'

'The underpass. You take him down in there?'

Chris nodded, deciding on the spur of the moment not to mention the inconclusive nature of the engagement.

'Nice. I mean, no-namers don't get you anywhere much, but it's all rep, I guess.'

'I guess.'

'You're up for Conflict Investment, aren't you? Louise Hewitt's section. I'm up there on the fifty-third myself. She was batting your résumé about a few weeks back. That stuff you did at Hammett McColl way back was some serious shit. Welcome aboard.'

'Thanks.'

'I'll walk you up there if you like. Going that way myself.'

'Great.'

They stepped out into the broad curve of the corridor and a glass-wall view of the financial district from twenty floors up. Bryant seemed to drink it in for a moment before he turned up the corridor, still scratching at a persistent speck of blood on his hand.

'They give you a car yet?'

'Got my own. Customised. My wife's a mechanic.'

Bryant stopped and looked at him. 'No shit?'

'No shit.' Chris held up his left hand, the dull metal band on the ring finger. Bryant examined it with interest.

'What's that, steel?' He caught on and grinned suddenly. 'Out of an engine, right? I've read about this stuff.'

'Titanium. Got it off an old Saab venting chamber. Had to resize it, but apart from that—'

'Yeah, that's right.' The other man's enthusiasm was almost childlike. 'Did you do it over an engine block, like that guy in Milan last year?' The finger snap again. 'What was his name, Bonocello or something?'

'Bonicelli. Yeah, like that, pretty much.' Chris tried to keep the annoyance out of his voice. His engine-block altar marriage pre-dated the Italian driver's by some five years, but had gone almost unnoticed in the driving press. Bonicelli's ran for weeks, in full colour. Maybe something to do with the fact that Silvio Bonicelli was the hellraising younger son of a big Florentine driving family, maybe just that he had married not a mechanic but an ex-porn star and blossoming manufac-tured pop singer. Maybe also the fact Chris and Carla had done it with a minimum of fuss in the backyard at Mel's AutoFix, and Silvio Bonicelli had invited the crowned heads of corporate Europe to a ceremony on a cleared shop floor at the new Lancia works in Milan. That was the trick with the twenty-first century's corporate nobility. Family contacts.

'Marry your mechanic.' Bryant was grinning again. 'Man, I can see where that would be useful, but I've got to tell you, I admire your courage.'

'It wasn't really a courage thing,' said Chris mildly. 'I was in love. You married?'

'Yeah.' He saw Chris looking at his ring. 'Oh. Platinum. Suki's a bond trader for Costerman's. Mostly works from home these days, and she's probably going to quit if we have another kid.'

'You got kids?'

'Yeah, just the one. Ariana.' They reached the end of the corridor and a battery of lifts. Bryant dug in his jacket pocket while they waited and produced a wallet. He flipped it open to reveal an impressive rack of credit cards and a photo of an attractive auburn-haired woman holding a pixie-faced child. 'Look. We took that on her birthday. She was one. Nearly a year ago already. They grow up fast. You got kids?'

'No, not yet.'

'Well, all I can tell you is don't wait too long.' Bryant flipped the wallet closed as the lift arrived and they rode up in companionable silence. The lift announced each floor in a chatty tone and gave them brief outlines of current Shorn development projects. After a while Chris spoke, more to drown out the earnest synthetic voice than anything else.

'This place have its own combat classes?'

'What, hand to hand?' Bryant grinned. 'Look at that number, Chris. Forty-one. Up here, you don't go hand-to-hand for promotion. Louise Hewitt'd consider that the height of bad taste.'

Chris shrugged. 'Yeah, but you never know. Saved my life once.'

'Hey, I'm kidding.' Bryant patted him on the arm. 'They've got a couple of corporate instructors down in the gym, sure. Shotokan and Tae kwon do, I think. I do some Shotokan myself sometimes, just to stay in shape, plus you never know when you might wind up in the cordoned zones.' He winked. 'Know what I mean? But anyway, like one of my instructors says, learning a martial art won't teach you to fight. You want to learn that shit, go to the street and get in some fights. That's how you really learn.' A grin. 'Least, that's what they tell me.'

The lift bounced to a halt. 'Fifty-third floor,' it said brightly. 'Conflict Investment division. Please ensure you have a code seven clearance for this level. Have a nice day.'

They stepped out into a small antechamber where a well-groomed security officer nodded to Bryant and asked Chris for ID. Chris found the bar-coded strip they'd given him at ground-floor reception and waited while it was scanned.

'Look, Chris, I've got to run.' Bryant nodded at the right hand corridor. 'Some greasy little dictator's uplinking in for a budget review at ten and I'm still trying to remember the name of his defence minister. You know how it is. I'll catch you at the quarterly review on Friday. We usually go out after.'

'Sure. See you later.'

Chris watched him out of sight with apparent casualness. Beneath was the same caution he'd applied to the no-name challenger that morning. Bryant seemed friendly enough, but almost everyone did under the right circumstances. Even Carla's father could seem like a reasonable man in the right conversational light. And anyone who washed blood off their hands the way Mike Bryant did was not someone Chris wanted at his back.

The security guard handed back his pass and pointed to the twin doors straight ahead.

'Conference room,' she said. 'They're waiting for you.'

The last time Chris had been face to face with a senior partner was to hand in his resignation at Hammett McColl. Vincent McColl had a high windowed room, panelled in dark wood and lined along one wall with books that looked a hundred years old. There were portraits of illustrious partners from the firm's eighty-year history on the other walls, and on the desk a framed photo of his father shaking hands with Margaret Thatcher. The floor was waxed wood, overlaid with a two-hundred-year-old Turkish carpet. McColl himself had silvery hair, buttoned his slim frame into suits a generation out of date and refused to have a videophone in his office. The whole place was a shrine to hallowed tradition, an odd thing in itself for a man whose primary responsibility was a division called Emerging Markets.

Jack Notley, Shorn Associates' ranking senior in Conflict Investment, could not have been less like McColl if he'd been on secondment from an inverted parallel universe. He was a stocky, powerful-looking man with close and not especially well-cropped black hair that was just beginning to show a seasoning of grey. His hands were ruddy and blunt fingered, his suit was a Susana Ingram original that had probably cost as much as the Saab's whole original chassis, and the body it clothed looked fit for a boxing ring. His features were rough-hewn and there was a long jagged scar under his right eye. The eyes were keen and bright. Only the fine web of lines around them gave any indication of Notley's forty-seven years. Chris thought he looked like a troll on holiday in Elfland as he moved across the light-filled pastel-shaded reception chamber.

His handshake, predictably, was a bonecrusher.

'Chris. Great to have you aboard at last. Come on in. I'd like you to meet some people.'

Chris disentangled his fingers and followed the troll's broad back across the room to where a lower central level housed a wide coffee table, a pair of right-angled sofas and a conspicuously unique meeting leader's armchair. Seated at either end of one sofa were a man and a woman, both younger than Notley. Chris's eyes focused automatically on the woman, a second before Notley spoke and gestured at her.

'This is Louise Hewitt, divisional manager and executive partner. She's the real brains behind what we're doing here.'

Hewitt unfolded herself from the sofa and leaned across to take his hand. She was a good-looking, voluptuous woman in her late thirties, working hard at not showing it. Her suit looked Daisuke Todoroki – severe black, vented driver's skirt to the knees and square-cut jacket. Her shoes had no appreciable heel. She wore long dark hair gathered back in a knot from pale features and minimal make-up. Her handshake wasn't trying to prove anything.

'And this is Philip Hamilton, junior partner for the division.'

Chris turned to face the deceptively soft-looking man at the other end of the sofa. Hamilton had a weak chin and a fat bulk that made him untidy, even in his own charcoal Ingram, but his pale blue eyes missed absolutely nothing. He stayed seated, but offered up a damp hand and a murmured greeting. There was, Chris thought, a guarded dislike in his voice.

'Well now,' said Notley, in jovial tones. 'I'm not really much more than a figurehead around here so I'll hand over to Louise for the moment. Let's all take a seat and, would you like a drink?'

'Green tea, if you've got it.'

'Certainly. I think a pot would be in order. Jiang estate okay?'

Chris nodded, impressed. Notley walked up to the large desk near one of the windows and prodded a phone. Louise Hewitt seated herself with immaculate poise and looked across at Chris.

'I've heard a lot about you, Faulkner,' she said neutrally.

'Great.'

Still neutral. 'Not entirely, as it happens. There are one or two items I'd like to clear up, if you don't mind.'

Chris spread his hands. 'Go ahead. I work here now.'

'Yes.' The thin smile told him she hadn't missed the counterblow. 'Well, perhaps we could start with your vehicle. I understand you've

18

turned down the company car. Do you have something against the house of BMW?'

'Well, I think they have a tendency to overarmour. Apart from that, no. It was a very generous offer. But I have my own vehicle and I'd rather stick with what I know, if it's all the same to you. I'll feel more comfortable.'

'Customised,' said Hamilton, as if naming a psychological dysfunction.

'What's that?' Notley was back, settling predictably into the armchair. 'Ah, your wheels, Chris. Yes, I heard you're married to the woman who put it together. That is right, isn't it.'

'That's right.' Chris took a flickered inventory of the expressions around him. In Notley he seemed to read an avuncular tolerance, in Hamilton distaste, and in Louise Hewitt nothing at all.

'That must give you quite a bond,' Notley mused, almost to himself.

'Uh, yes. Yes, it does.'

'I'd like to talk about the Bennett incident,' said Louise Hewitt loudly.

Chris locked gazes with her for a beat, then sighed. 'The details are pretty much as I filed them. You must have read about it at the time. Bennett was up for the same analyst's post as me. Fight lasted to that raised section on the M40 inflow. I swiped her off the road on a bend and she stuck on the edge. Weight of the car would have pulled her over sooner or later; she was running a reconditioned Jag Mentor.'

Notley grunted, a used-to-run-one-myself sort of noise.

'Anyway, I stopped and managed to pull her out. The car went over a couple of minutes later. She was semi-conscious when I got her to the hospital. I think she hit her head on the steering wheel.'

'The hospital?' Hamilton's voice was politely disbelieving. 'Excuse me. You took her to the *hospital*?'

Chris stared at him.

'Yeah. I took her to the *hospital*. Is there a problem with that?'

'Well,' Hamilton laughed. 'Let's just say people around here might have seen it that way.'

'What if Bennett had decided to have another crack at the post?' asked Hewitt gravely, detached counterpoint to her junior partner's hilarity. Chris thought it rang rehearsed. He shrugged.

'What, with cracked ribs, a broken right arm and head injuries? The way I remember it, she was in no condition to do anything but some heavy breathing.'

'But she did recover, right?' Hamilton asked slyly. 'She's still working. Still in London.'

'Back at Hammett McColl.' Hewitt confirmed, still detached. The jab, Chris knew, was going to come from Hamilton's corner.

'That why you left, Chris?' The junior partner was right on cue, voice still tinged lightly with derision. 'No stomach to finish the job?'

'What I think Louise and Philip are trying to say,' Notley interposed, the kindly uncle at a birthday-party dispute, 'is that you didn't *resolve* matters. Would that be a fair summary, Louise.'

Hewitt nodded curtly. 'It would.'

'I stayed at HM two years after Bennett,' said Chris, keeping his temper. He hadn't expected this so early. 'She honoured her defeat as expected. The matter was resolved to my satisfaction, and to the firm's.'

Notley made soothing gestures. 'Yes, yes. Perhaps, then, this is more a question of corporate culture than blame. What we value here at Shorn is, how shall I put it? Well, yes. Resolution, I suppose. We don't like loose ends. They can trip you, and us, up at a later date. As you see with the embarrassment the Bennett incident is causing us all here and now. We are left in, shall we say, an ambiguous situation. Now that couldn't have happened had you resolved the matter in a terminal fashion. It's the kind of ambiguity we like to avoid at Shorn Associates. It doesn't fit our image, especially in a field as competitive as Conflict Investment. I'm sure you understand.'

Chris looked around at the three faces, counting the friends and enemies he appeared to have already made. He manufactured a smile.

'Of course,' he said. 'Nobody likes ambiguity.'

THREE

The gun sat, unambiguously, in the middle of the desk, begging to be picked up. Chris put his hands in his pockets and looked at it with wary dislike.

'This mine?'

'Heckler and Koch Nemesis Ten.' Hewitt strode past him and filled her hand with the black rubber butt. 'The Nemex. Semi-automatic, double action hesitation lock, no safety necessary. Just pull it out and start shooting. Standard Shorn issue. Comes with a shoulder holster, so you can wear it under a suit. You never know when you'll have to give a coup de grâce.'

He fought down a smirk. Maybe she saw it.

'We've got a way of doing things here, Faulkner. If you call someone out, you don't take them to the hospital afterwards. You go in and you finish the job. With this if necessary.' She pointed the pistol one-handed at the datadown unit built into the desk. There was a dry click as she pulled the trigger. 'If you can, you bring back their plastic. Speaking of which.' She reached inside her jacket pocket with her free hand and produced a small grey rectangle. Light flashed on the entwined red S and A of a Shorn Associates hologo. She tossed the card onto the table and laid the gun down beside it. 'There you are. Don't get separated from either. You never know when you'll need firepower.'

Chris picked up the card and tapped it thoughtfully on the desk-top. He left the gun where it was.

'Clips are in the top drawer of your desk. It's a jacketed load, should go through the engine block of a bulk transporter. You actually used to drive one of those things, didn't you? Mobile Arbitrage or something.'

'Yeah.' Chris pulled out his wallet and racked the card. He looked back up at Hewitt expectantly. 'So?'

'No, nothing.' Hewitt walked past him to the window and looked out at the world below. 'I think it was an inspired idea, selling commodities from a haulage base. But it's not quite the same thing as driving for an investment bank, is it?'

Chris smiled a little and seated himself on the corner of the desk, back to the window and his new boss.

'You don't like me very much, do you Hewitt?'

21

'This isn't about like, Faulkner. I don't think you belong here.'

'Well someone evidently does.'

He heard her coming back to the desk and turned his head casually towards her as she arrived. Behind her, he suddenly noticed how bleak the undecorated office was.

'Well, look at that,' she said softly. 'Got me back here, didn't you? Is that the kind of powerplay you're used to? You won't cut it here, Faulkner. I've seen your résumé. Big kill eight years back with Quain, nothing much since. You got lucky, that's all.'

Chris kept his voice mild. 'So did Hammett McColl. They saved about fifteen mil in bonus payments when Quain went down. And I haven't *needed* to do much killing since. Sometimes it's just enough to do the work. You don't have to be proving yourself all the time.'

'Here you do. You'll find that out.'

'Really.' Chris pulled out the top drawer and looked in at the contents as if they interested him marginally more than the woman in front of him. 'You got some toy boy lined up to call me out for this office?'

For just a moment he had her. He caught it in the way her frame stiffened at the upper edges of his peripheral vision. Then she drew a long breath, as if Chris was a new flower she liked the scent of. As he looked up, she smiled.

'Cute,' she said. 'Oh, you're cute. Notley likes you, you know that? That's why you're here. You remind him of him, back when he was young. He came out of nowhere just like you, riding one big kill. He had a tattoo, just like you. Stream of currency signs, like tears down from one eye. Very classy.' Her lip curled. 'He even dated his mechanic for about five years. Little zone girl, with a smudge of grease across her nose. They say she even turned up to a quarterly dinner once with that smudge. Yeah, Notley likes you, but you notice something about that tattoo? It's gone now. Just like that little zone girl. See, Notley gets sentiment attacks sometimes, but he's a professional and he won't let it get in the way. Hold that thought, because you're going to disappoint him, Faulkner. You don't have the grit.'

'Welcome aboard.'

Hewitt looked at him blankly. Chris gestured with one open hand.

'I thought one of us should say it.'

'Hey.' She shrugged and turned to leave. 'Prove me wrong.'

Chris watched her go, face unreadable. As the door closed, his eyes fell on the matt black Nemex pistol on the desk and his own lip twisted derisively.

'Fucking cowboys.'

He swept the gun ceremonially away with the clips and slammed the drawer closed.

There was a list of induction suggestions on the datadown: people to call, when to call them, and where they could be found. Procedures to implement, the best time to access the areas of the Shorn datastack necessary for each procedure. A selected overview of his caseload for the next two months, flags to indicate which needed attention first. The p.a. package had phased everything into a suggested convenience sequence which got the work done as efficiently as possible and told him he would find it most convenient to go home at about eight-thirty that evening.

He toyed briefly with the idea of loading up the Nemex with its jacketed ammunition and repeating Hewitt's target practice on the datadown.

Instead, he punched the phone.

'Carla, this is Chris. I'm going to be late tonight, so don't wait up. There's still some chilli in the fridge, try not to eat it all, it'll give you the shits and I'd like some myself when I get in. Oh, by the way, I'm in love.'

He put down the receiver and looked at the datadown screen. After a long pause, he prodded the bright orange triangle marked Conflict Investment and watched as it maximised like an opening flower.

The backglow lit his face.

It was past eleven by the time he got home. He killed his lights at the first bend in the drive, though he knew that the crunch of his wheels on the gravel would probably wake Carla as surely as the play of high beams across the front of the house. Sometimes she seemed to know he was home more by intuition than anything else. He parked beside the battered and patched Landrover she ran, turned off his engine and yawned. For a moment he sat in the still and the darkness, listening to the cooling tick of the engine.

Home for six hours' sleep. Why the fuck did we move this far out?

But he knew the answer to that.

This place is no different to HM. Live at work, sleep at home, forget you ever had a relationship. Same shit, different logo.

Well, that's where all the money comes from.

He let himself into the house as quietly as he could and found Carla in the lounge, watching a TV screen tuned to the soft blue light of an empty channel. Ice clicked in her glass as she lifted it to her lips.

'You're awake,' he said, and then saw how far down the bottle she was. 'You're drunk.'

'Isn't that meant to be my line?'

'Not tonight, it isn't. I was wired to the fucking datadown until quarter to ten.' He bent to kiss her. 'Rough day?'

'Not really. Same old shit.'

'Yeah, done some of that myself.' He sank into the chair beside her. She handed him the whisky glass just a fraction of a second before he reached out for it. 'What you watching?'

'Dex and Seth, 'til the jamming got it.'

He grinned. 'You're going to get us arrested.'

'Not in this postcode.'

'Oh, yeah.' He glanced across at the phone deck. 'Did we get any this morning?'

'Any what?'

'Any mail?'

'Bills. Mortgage repayment went through.'

'Already? They just took it.'

'No, that was last month. We're over the line on a couple of cards as well.'

Chris drank some of the peat-flavoured Islay whisky, tutting learnedly over the sacrilege of ice in a glass of single malt. Carla gave him a murderous look. He handed her back the glass and frowned at the TV screen. 'How'd we manage that?

'We spent the money, Chris.'

'Well.' He stretched his suited legs out in front of him and yawned again. 'That's what we earn it for, I guess. So what same old shit did you do today?'

'Salvage. Some arms supply company just moved into premises out on the northern verge lost a dozen of their brand new Mercedes Ramjets to vandals. Whole lot written off.'

Chris sat up. 'A *dozen*? What did they do, park them in the open?'

'No. Someone dropped a couple of homemade shrapnel bombs through a vent into their executive garages. Boom! Corrosives and fast-moving metal in all directions. Mel got a contract to assess the damage and haul every write-off away gratis. Paid to clear it, and he gets to keep whatever salvage we can strip out of the wrecks. And here's the good bit. Some of these Mercs are barely scratched. Mel's still out celebrating. Says if the corporates are going to insist on this urban regeneration shit, we could have a lot more work like that. He must have put a good metre of NAME powder up his nose tonight.'

'Shrapnel bombs, huh?'

'Yeah, ingenious what kids can wire together out of scrap these days. I don't know, maybe Mel even set them up to do it. Connections he's got in the zones. Jackers, drugs. Gangwit stuff.'

'Fuckers,' said Chris vaguely.

'Yeah, well.' An edge crept into Carla's voice. 'Amazing what you'll get up to when you've got nothing to lose. Nothing to do but stand at the razor wire and watch the wealth roll by.'

Chris sighed. 'Carla, could we have this argument some other time, please? Because I haven't rehearsed in a while.'

'You got something else you want to do?'

'Well, we could fuck by the light of the TV screen.'

'We could,' she agreed seriously. 'Except that I always end up on top and I've still got carpet burns on my knees from the last time you had that bright idea. You want to fuck, you take me to a bed.'

'Deal.'

After, as they lay like spoons in the disordered bed, Carla curled around his back and murmured into his ear.

'By the way, I'm in love.'

'Me too.' He leaned back and rubbed the back of his head against her breasts. She shuddered at the touch of the close cropped hair and reached instinctively for his shrunken prick. He grinned and slapped her hand away.

'Hoy, that's your lot. Go to sleep, nympho.'

'So! You just want to fuck me and leave me. Is that it?'

'I'm,' said Chris, already sliding headlong into sleep. 'Not going anywhere.'

'Just use me, and then when you've used me you go to sleep. Talk to me, you bastard.'

A grunt.

'You haven't even told me how it went today.'

Breathing. Carla propped herself up on one arm and prodded at the springy muscle in Chris's stomach. 'I'm serious. What's Conflict Investment like?'

Chris took her arm, folded the offending finger around his own and tugged Carla back into the spoon configuration.

'Conflict Investment is the way forward at a global level,' he said.

'Is that right?'

'It's what the Shorn datadown says.'

'Oh, it must be true then.'

He smiled reflexively at the scorn in her voice and began to drift away again. Just before he slept, Carla thought she heard him speak again. She lifted her head.

'What?'

He didn't respond, and she realised he was muttering in his sleep. Carla leaned over him, straining to catch something. She gave up after a couple of minutes. The only sense she succeeded in straining out of the soup of mumbling was a single, repeated word.

checkout

It took a long time to find sleep for herself.

FOUR

'Conflict Investment is the way forward!'

Applause rose, and clattered at the glass roofing like the wings of pigeons startled into flight. Around the lecture theatre, men and women came to their feet, hands pumping together. The entire CI contingent of Shorn Associates were gathered in the room. The youngest, Chris noticed, were the most fervent. Faces gashed open with enthusiasm, teeth and eyes gleaming in the late afternoon sun from roof and picture window. They looked ready to go on applauding 'til their hands bled. Sown in amongst this crop of pure conviction, older colleagues clapped to a slower, more measured rhythm and nodded approval, leaning their heads together to make comments under the din of the applause. Louise Hewitt paused and leaned on the lectern, waiting for the noise to ebb.

Behind his hand, Chris yawned cavernously.

'Yes, yes,' Hewitt made damping motions. The room settled. 'We've heard it called risky, we've heard it called impractical and we've heard it called immoral. In short, we've heard the same carping voices that free-market economics has had to drag with it like a ball and chain from its very inception. But we have learnt to ignore those voices. We have learnt, and we have gone on learning, piling lesson upon lesson, vision upon vision, success upon success. And what every success has taught us, and continues to teach us, again and again, is a very simple truth. Who has the finance.' A dramatic pause, one slim black clad arm holding a clenched fist aloft. 'Has the power.'

Chris stifled another yawn.

'Human beings have been fighting wars as long as history recalls. It is in our nature, it is in our genes. In the last half of the last century the peacemakers, the *governments* of this world, did not end war. They simply *managed* it, and they managed it *badly*. They poured money, without thought of return, into conflicts and guerrilla armies abroad, and then into tortuous peace processes that more often than not left the situation no better. They were partisan, dogmatic and inefficient. Billions wasted in poorly assessed wars that no sane investor would have looked at twice. Huge, unwieldy national armies and clumsy international alliances; in short a huge public-sector drain on our economic systems. Hundreds of thousands of young men killed in parts of the world they could not even pronounce properly. Decisions based on political dogma and doctrine alone. Well, this model is no more.'

Hewitt paused again. This time there was a charged quiet that carried with it the foretaste of applause, the same way a thick heat carries with it the knowledge of the storm to come. In the closing moments of the address, Hewitt's voice had sunk close to normal conversational tones. Her delivery slowed and grew almost musing.

'All over the world, men and women still find causes worth killing and dying for. And who are we to argue with them? Have we lived in their circumstances? Have we felt what they feel? No. It is not our *place* to say if they are right or wrong. It is not for us to pass judgment or to interfere. At Shorn Conflict Investment, we are concerned with only two things. Will they win? And will it pay? As in all other spheres, Shorn will invest the capital it is entrusted with only where we are sure of a good return. We do not judge. We do not moralise. We do not waste. Instead, we assess, we invest. And we prosper. *That* is what it means to be a part of Shorn Conflict Investment.'

The lecture theatre erupted once more.

'Nice speech,' said Notley, pouring champagne into the ring of glasses with an adept arm. 'And press coverage too, thanks to Philip here. Should profile us nicely for license review on the eighteenth.'

'Glad you liked it.' Hewitt lifted her filled glass away from the ring and looked round at the gathered partners. Excluding Philip Hamilton at her side, the five men and three women watching her accounted for fifty-seven per cent of Shorn Associates' capital wealth. Each one of them could afford to acquire a private jet with less thought than she gave to shopping for shoes. Between the eight of them, there was no manufactured object on the planet that they could not own. It was wealth she could taste, just out of reach, like bacon frying in someone else's kitchen. Wealth she wanted like sex. Wanted with a desire that ached in her gums and the pit of her stomach.

Notley finished pouring and raised his own glass. 'Well, here's to small wars everywhere. Long may they smoulder. And congratulations on a great quarterly result, Louise. Small wars.'

'Small wars!'

'Small wars.' Hewitt echoed the toast and sipped at her drink. She surfed the polite conversation on autopilot and gradually the other partners began to drift back to the main body of the hotel bar, seeking out their own divisional acolytes. Hamilton caught her eye and she nodded almost imperceptibly. He slipped away with a murmured excuse, leaving her with Notley.

27

'You know,' she said quietly, 'I could have done without Faulkner falling asleep in the front row. He's too impressed with himself, Jack.'

'Of course, you never were at his age.'

'He's only five years younger than me. And anyway, I've always had these.' Hewitt set her glass aside on the mantelpiece and cupped her breasts as if offering them. 'Nothing like a cleavage for reducing professional respect.'

Notley looked embarrassed and then away.

'Oh, come on Louise. Don't give me that tired old feminist rap agai—'

'Being a woman around here makes you tough, Jack.' Hewitt let her hands fall again. 'You know that's true. I had to claw my way up every centimetre of the way to partnership. Compared to that, Faulkner got it handed to him on a plate. One big kill, catch the imagination of App and Prom and he's made. Just look at him. He didn't even shave this morning.'

She gestured across the bar to where Chris appeared to be deep in conversation with a group of men and women his own age. Even at this distance, the dusting of stubble on his face was visible. As they watched, he masked another yawn with his glass.

'Give him a break, Louise.' Notley took her shoulder and turned her away again. 'If he can do for us what he did for Hammett McColl, I'll forgive him not shaving occasionally.'

'And if he can't?'

Notley shrugged and tipped back his champagne. 'Then he won't last long, will he.'

He put down the glass, patted her on the shoulder again and walked off into the press of suited bodies. Hewitt stayed where she was until Hamilton appeared noiselessly at her side.

'Well?' he asked.

'Don't ask.'

On the other side of the room, Chris was in fact deep in nothing other than the classic party nightmare. He was becalmed at the edges of a group he had only passing acquaintance with, listening politely to conversations he had no interest in about people and places he did not know. His jaws ached from trying not to yawn and he wanted nothing more than to bow out quietly and go home.

Five days into the new job? I don't think so, pal.

Out of boredom he went to the bar for a refill he didn't want. As he was waiting, someone nudged him. He glanced round. Mike Bryant, grin on full beam, with a Liz Linshaw clone in tow and a tray full of drinks in his hands.

'Hey, Chris.' Bryant had to raise his voice above the crowd. 'How did you like Hewitt? Talks up a storm, doesn't she?'

Chris nodded noncommittally. 'Yeah, very inspiring.'

'You're not kidding. Really gets you in the guts. First time I heard her speak, I thought I'd been personally selected to lead a holy fucking crusade for global investment. Simeon Sands for the finance sector.' Mike did a passable burlesque of the satellite-syndicated demagogue. '*Hallelujah, I believe!* I have *faith!* Seriously, you look at the productivity graphs following each quarterly address she gives. Spikes through the roof, man.'

'Right.'

'Hey, you want to join us? We're sitting back on the window flange there, see. Got some of the meanest analysts in creation gathered round those tables. Isn't that right, Liz?'

The woman at Bryant's side chuckled. Shooting a glance at her, Chris suddenly realised this was no clone.

'Oh, yeah, sorry. Liz Linshaw, Chris Faulkner. Chris, you know Liz, I guess. Either that or you don't have a TV.'

'Ms Linshaw.' Chris stuck out his hand.

Liz Linshaw laughed and leaned forward to kiss him on both cheeks. 'Call me Liz,' she said. 'I recognise *you* now. From the App and Prom sheets this week. You're the one that took down Edward Quain in '41 aren't you.'

'Uh, yeah.'

'Before my time. I was just a stringer on a pirate satellite 'cast in those days. Quite a kill. I don't think there's been one like it in the last eight years.'

'Stop it, you're making me feel old.'

'Will you two stop flirting and grab some of these drinks,' demanded Bryant. 'I've got a dozen thirsty animals back there to water. What do you want in that, Chris?'

'Uh, Laphroaig. No ice.'

'Yyyeurgh.'

They carried the glasses over to the tables between the three of them and unloaded. Bryant pushed and shoved at people, joking and cajoling and bullying until he had space for Chris and Liz to sit at his table. He raised his glass.

'Small wars,' he said. 'Long may they smoulder.'

Approval, choral in volume.

Chris found himself squeezed in next to a tall, slim executive with steel-rimmed glasses and the air of a scientist peering down a microscope lens at everything. Chris felt a ripple of irritation. Affected eyeware had always been one of Carla's pet hates. *Fucking poverty chic*, she invariably

29

snarled when she saw the ads. *Fake fucking human imperfection. It'll be cool to ride around in a fucking wheelchair next. It's fucking offensive.* Chris tended to agree. Sure, you could run a datadown uplink projected onto the inside of the lenses, but that wasn't it. Carla was right, it was zone chic. And why the fuck pretend you couldn't afford corrective surgery when everything else you were wearing screamed the opposite.

'Nick Makin,' said the narrow face behind the lenses, extending a long arm sideways across his body. The grip belied his slender frame. 'You ah Faulkner, ahn't you?'

'That's right.'

Mike Bryant leaned across the table towards them. 'Nick was our top commission analyst last year. Predicted that turnaround in Guatemala over the summer. Went against all the models for guerrilla conflict that we had. It was a real coup for Shorn.'

'Congratulations,' said Chris.

'Ah.' Makin waved it off. 'That was last season. Can't live off things like that indefinitely. It's a whole new quarter. Time for fesh meat. Another new appoach. Speaking of which, Chris, ahn't you the guy that let a pomotion challenger off the hook at Hammett McColl last year?'

Probably imagination, the way the whole table was suddenly listening to this sharkish young man with the carefully masked speech impediment. Probably. Chris's eyes flickered to Bryant. The big blond was watching.

'You heard about that, huh?'

'Yeah.' Makin smiled. 'It seemed kind of. Odd, you know?'

'Well,' Chris made a stiff smile of his own. 'You weren't there.'

'No. Lucky for Elysia Bennett that I wasn't, I'd say. Isn't she still awound somewhere?'

'I assume so. You know, Nick, I tend not to worry too much about the past. Like you said, it's a whole new quarter. Bennett was two years ago.'

'Still.' Makin looked around the table, apparently to enlist some support. 'An attitude like that must make for a lot of challengahs. Shit, I'd dive against you myself just for the expewience if I thought you'd have a sentiment attack like that after the event. If I lost, that is.'

Chris realised abruptly that Makin was drunk, alcohol-fuelled aggressive and waiting. He looked at his glass on the table.

'You would lose,' he said quietly.

By now it wasn't his imagination. The buzz of conversation was definitely weakening as the executives lost interest in what they were discussing and became spectators.

'Big words.' Makin had lost his smile. 'Fom a man who hasn't made a kill in nearly four years.'

Chris shrugged, one eye on Makin's left hand where it rested on the table top. He mapped options. Reach down and pinion the arm. Snap the little finger of that hand, take it from there.

'Actually,' said a husky voice. 'I think they're quite small words from the man who took down Edward Quain.'

The focus of attention leapt away across the table. Liz Linshaw sat with one long-fingered hand propping her tousled blonde head away from the back of her seat. The other hand gestured with a cigarette.

'Now that,' she continued, 'Was the mother of all exemplary kills. No one ever thought Eddie Quain was coming back to work. Except maybe as lubricant.'

Somebody laughed. Nervous laughter. Someone else took it up, more certainly and the sound built around the table. Bryant joined in. The moment passed. Chris gave Makin one more hard look and then started laughing himself.

The evening spread its wings under him.

FIVE

An unclear space of time later, he was relieving himself in a scarred porcelain urinal that reeked as if it hadn't been cleaned in a week. Yellowed plaster walls crowded round him. Sullen, gouged graffiti ranged from brutal to incomprehensible and back.

PLAISTOW GANGWITS IN YER SOUP
YOUR RAGS SUIT THEM
FUCK OFF MARKEY CUNT
MONEY MAKES THE WORLD GO BROWN
EMMA SUCKED MY PRICK HERE
U SUCKED IT USELF
ZEK TIV SHIT
BRING THE OMBUDSMEN
FUCK THE U.N.
PISS ON YOU TOO
MEAT THE RICH

It wasn't always clear where one message ended and the other began. Either that or he was very drunk.

He *was* very drunk.

Bryant's idea, as numbers in the hotel bar began thinning; carry the party over into the cordoned zones.

'They may be shit-poor over there,' voice blurred as he leaned across the table. 'But they know how to have a good time. There's a couple of places I know you can buy all sorts of interesting substances over the counter, and they've got floor shows you wouldn't believe.'

Liz Linshaw wrinkled her sculpted features. 'Sounds strictly for the boys,' she said. 'If you gentlemen will excuse me, I'm for a cab.'

She kissed Bryant on the lips, causing a small storm of whoops and yells, and left with a sideways grin at Chris. A couple of other women excused themselves from the group in her wake and Mike's expedition began to look in danger of fizzling out.

'Oh, come on, you bunch of *pussies*,' he slurred. 'What are you afraid of? We've got guns.' He yanked out his Nemex and brandished it, 'We've got money, we've got this city by the balls. What the fuck kind of life is it when we own the fucking streets they walk on and the blocks they live in and we're still fucking scared to go there. We're supposed to be in *charge* of this society, not in hiding from it.'

It wasn't speech-making of Louise Hewitt's calibre, but Mike managed to rope in a half dozen of the younger men round the table and a couple of the harder-drinking women. Ten minutes later, Chris was in the passenger seat of Bryant's BMW, watching the emptied streets of the financial district roll by. In the back seat sat a nameless young male executive and an older woman called Julie Pinion – macho sales talk snarled back and forth between them. In the wing mirror, the following lights of two other cars. Shorn was descending on the cordoned zones in force.

'Okay, you two keep it down,' said Mike over his shoulder as they turned a corner. Up ahead the lights of a zone checkpoint frosted the night sky. 'They won't let us through here if they think there's going to be trouble.'

He brought the BMW to a remarkably smooth halt at the barrier and leaned out as the guard approached. He was, Chris noticed, chewing gum to mask the alcohol on his breath.

'Just going down to the *Falkland*,' Bryant called cheerfully, waving his Shorn Associates plastic. 'Take in the late show.'

The guard was in his fifties, with a spreading paunch beneath his grey uniform and broken veins across his nose and cheeks. Chris saw the cloud of vapour he made when he sighed.

'Have to scan that, sir.'

' 'course.' Bryant handed over the card and waited while the guard ran it through his hipswipe remote and handed it back. The unit chimed melodically, and the guard nodded. He seemed tired.

'You armed?'

Bryant turned back into the car. 'Show the man your peacemakers, guys.'

Chris slid the Nemex out of its shoulder holster and displayed it. Behind him he heard the two backseat disputants doing the same. The guard flashed his torch in the windows and nodded slowly.

'Want to be careful, sir,' he told Bryant. 'There's been layoffs at Pattons and Greengauge this week. Lot of angry people out getting drunk tonight.'

'Well, we'll stay out of their way,' said Bryant easily. 'Don't want any trouble. Just want to see the show.'

'Yeah, okay.' The guard turned back to the checkpoint cabin and gestured to whoever was inside. The barrier began to rise. 'I've got to check your friends as well. You want to park just past the gate till we clear them?'

'Be glad to.' Mike beamed and drove the BMW through.

The second car passed muster but with the third there was some trouble. They peered back and saw the guard shaking his head while suited forms craned from the windows front and back, gesturing.

'The fuck is going on back there?' muttered Julie Pinion. 'Couldn't they even act sober for a couple of minutes.'

'Stay here,' Bryant said, and climbed out into the night air. They watched him walk back to the third car, lean down and say something to those leaning out. The heads disappeared back into the vehicle, as if on wires. Bryant put his hand on the guard's shoulder and dug in his pocket. Something passed between them. The guard said something to the driver of the third car. A clearly audible whoop of delight bounced out of the windows. Bryant came back, grinning.

'Gratuities,' he said as he got into the car again. 'Ought to be compulsory, the shit they pay those guys.'

'How much did you give him?' asked Pinion.

'Hundred.'

'*A hundred!* Jesus.'

'Ah, come on Julie. I've tipped waiters better than that. And he's going to take a lot more heat than a waiter if this dinner party goes awry.'

The little convoy pressed on into the cordoned zone.

It was an abrupt transition. In the financial district, street lighting was a flood of halogen, chasing out shadows from every corner. Here, the street lamps were isolated sentinels, spilling a scant pool of radiance at their feet every twenty metres of darkened street. In some places, they were out, lamps either fused or smashed. Elsewhere they had been destroyed more unambiguously, rendered down to jagged concrete stumps still attached to their trunks by a riot of cables and metal bands.

'Look at that,' said Pinion disgustedly. 'What a bunch of fucking animals. It's no wonder nobody wants to spend money fixing these places up. They'd just tear it all down again.'

Even the street beneath their wheels changed. Within a hundred metres of the checkpoint the ride turned bumpy and Bryant had to slow down and negotiate rain-filled potholes the size of small garden ponds. On either side, the houses huddled. Here and there, for no visible reason, one had been taken down, sprawling smashed brick and spilled interior in the space in which it had stood. There were no other vehicles on the streets, moving or parked. A few figures moved on the pavements on foot, but they grew immobile as the twilight-blue armoured saloons with their Shorn Associates logos rolled by. Most turned up their collars or simply sank back into the shadows.

'Fucking creepy,' said the young executive behind Chris. 'I mean, I knew it was bad out here but—'

'Bad,' Julie Pinion coughed laughter at him. 'You think this is bad? Mike, you remember the suburbs in that shithole we got seconded to for Christmas last year.'

'Muong Khong, yeah.' Bryant looked in the rearview. 'Gives you a whole new perspective on what real poverty is, man. Chris, you ever been on secondment? With Emerging Markets, I mean?'

'Couple of times, yeah.'

'Pretty awful, huh?'

Chris remembered the call of a muezzin in the warm evening air, smells of cooking and a small child prodding three goats homewards. Later, he'd been walking past a stone-and-thatch dwelling when a young girl of about fourteen came out and offered him fruit from their dinner table because he was a guest in the village. The unlooked-for kindness, with its hints of an antique and alien culture, had pricked tears out on the underside of his eyes.

He never told anyone.

'It wasn't somewhere I would have wanted to live,' he said.

Pinion smirked. 'No shit,' she agreed.

The *Falkland* – a squat brick building at the intersection of two streets still boasting a picturesque scattering of car wrecks. The vehicles looked old enough to have burnt leaded fuel when they were alive. Mike Bryant's little convoy swept to a disdainful halt and disgorged suits.

'No cars,' said the young executive, wonderingly. 'I only just noticed.'

'Of course, no cars,' said Pinion, rolling her eyes in Chris's direction. 'Who, outside of criminals, do you suppose can afford a tank of fuel around here? Or a licence, come to that?'

'Price of the green agenda,' said Mike as he alarmed the car. 'You guys coming or what?'

The door of the *Falkland* was beaten steel. Two black men in coveralls stood outside, one dangling a sawn-off shotgun negligently from his left hand, the other, older, watching the street, arms folded impassively across his chest. When he spotted Mike Bryant, he unwrapped and his face split into a huge grin. Mike lifted a hand in greeting as he crossed the street.

'Hey, Troy. What're you doing on the fucking *door*, man?'

'Protectin' my investment.' The rich treacle of a Jamaican accent. 'Bein' seen. It's more than I can say for you, Mike. 'Ave not seen you in a fuckin' long time. What's the matter? Suki not let you out to play any more?'

'That's right.' Mike winked. 'Chopped it off and locked it in the bedroom dresser. That way she can take it out and play with it while I'm at work. Which, by the way, is all the fucking time.'

'That is the motherfuckin' truth.' He looked at the entourage Bryant had brought to the bar. 'These are friends of yours?'

'Yep. Julie, Chris. Meet Troy Morris. He owns this shithole. Among others. Troy, Julie Pinion, Chris Faulkner. The rest I don't remember.' Bryant waved back at the entourage he was trailing. 'Just sycophants, you know how it is when you're an important man.'

The Jamaican reeled off a deep chuckle. 'Faulkner,' he rumbled. 'No relation of William, right?'

Chris blinked, confused. Before he could ask, Mike Bryant broke in again.

'They're all carrying, Troy. Left mine in the car, but these guys are new and they don't know the rules. Bear with us. You got a bag for the hardware?'

With the dozen-odd pistols dumped into a greasy holdall clearly reserved for this specific purpose, they pushed inside. Quiet slammed down through the smoke-hung bar. Even the girl on the stage stopped in mid writhe, one doped boa constrictor gripped in each fist. Music thumped on behind her, suddenly unchallenged by voices. Mike nodded to himself, took a chair to the centre of the bar and climbed onto it.

'As you may have noticed,' he said, pitching his voice above the music. 'We are zek-tivs. I know that may pass for a crime around here, but we don't want any trouble. All we want is to buy a drink for every-one in the house, and have a few ourselves. Anyone who has a problem with that can come and have a word with me, or my friend Troy Morris, and we'll sort your problem out. Otherwise, it's open bar for the next ten minutes and the drinks are on me.' He turned to the girl on the stage. 'Please. The show must go on. It looks like we got here just in time.'

He climbed down and went to talk to the barman. Conversations resumed slowly. The dancer went back, a little stiffly, to what she was doing with the two boas. People drifted to the bar, a few at first, then the bulk of those present. Bryant appeared to know a couple of them. Chris was introduced, promptly forgot names and cornered Mike.

'What did Troy mean about being related to William?'

Bryant shrugged. 'Search me. Troy knows a lot of people. What are you drinking?'

And so it went on, the night swelling with noise and hilarity for a while, and then paring down again as people left. Chris's high began to flatten into something more reflective. Julie Pinion went home in a cab, the young executive she'd been arguing with in smug tow. The driver of one of the other cars announced his imminent departure around three a.m. and most of the remaining Shorn crew went with him. By four the party was down to one table – Chris and Mike, an off-duty Troy Morris and a couple of the floorshow dancers, now dressed and divested of most of their garish make-up. One introduced herself as Emma and lurching into the toilets, Chris had to wonder if she was the object of the fellatio-inspired graffiti gouged there amidst the political commentary.

When he got back to the table, Emma had gone and Troy was leaving with her colleague. The gun bag from his doorman duties was dumped on the table, the sawn-off and Bryant's Nemex nestling together in the canvas folds. Chris joined in the round of farewells and there was much drunken promising to keep in contact. 'Yeah,' said Troy, pointing at Chris. 'You should write, Faulkner.'

He left, chortling inexplicably, with the shotgun slung over one shoulder and his other arm around the dancer's waist. At that moment Chris found himself possessed of a powerful desire to be Troy Morris, walking out of the *Falkland* into an entirely simpler and, to judge by the black man's laughter, more joyous existence.

He slumped into the chair opposite Bryant.

'I,' he pronounced carefully, 'Have drunk far too much.'

'Well, it's Friday.' Bryant's attention was focused on heating a stained glass pipe. 'Switch horses, try some of this.'

Chris's eyes tightened on what the other man was doing.

'Is that—'

Bryant's eyes shuttled sideways above the pipe and lighter. Narrowed irritably. 'Ah, come on, man. Lighten up. Just a little drive-right.'

The contents of the pipe smouldered and Mike inhaled convulsively. A shudder ran through his suited form. He made a deep grunting sound and his voice came out squeaky as he offered the pipe.

'So. How does it feel?'

Chris frowned, confused. 'What?'

'Conflict Investment, a week in. Go on, take it. How's it feel?'

Chris waved the pipe away. 'No thanks.'

'Pussy.' Bryant grinned to defuse the insult, and drummed impatiently on the table. 'So tell me. How's it feel?'

'What?'

'Conflict fucking Investment!'

'Oh.' Chris marshalled his sludgy thoughts. 'Interesting.'

'Yeah?' Bryant seemed disappointed. 'That all?'

'It's not so different to Emerging Markets, Mike.' Trying to think was hard work. Chris began to wonder if he should have accepted the pipe. 'Longer-term outlook, but basically the same stuff. Yeah, I like it. Apart from that bitch Hewitt.'

'Ah. I wondered how that was going. Had a run-in, have we?'

'You could say that.'

Bryant shrugged. 'Hey, don't let it get you down. Hewitt's been that way as long as I can remember. It's always been harder to cut it as a woman in this field, so they come out twice as tough. They have to. See, these days Hewitt practically *is* Conflict Investment. Big reorganisation about five years back, austerity measures. Division got cut to the bone. There's a lot of pressure to make good, and most of that pressure falls on Hewitt's shoulders.'

'Notley's senior partner.'

'Notley?' Bryant piped more smoulder. 'Nah, it was his baby in the beginning, but once he went senior he downloaded everything onto Hewitt and Hamilton. There was another guy, Page, but Hewitt called him out just before profit share last year. Rammed him right off the Gullet. Believe that?

'The Gullet?'

'Yeah, you know. Last section as you come up over the zones on the M11. The two-lane narrows. Where you took out that no-namer, well, just after, after the underpass. Where it goes elevated. Hewitt let Page get ahead there, knew he'd have to either slow down or turn around to face her. No chance of just being first to work these days, you've got to turn up with blood on your wheels or not at all. So yeah, she lets him go, waits, he's not good enough to make the 180 turn on a piece of road that narrow, so he slows up, tries for a side-to-side, she won't let him, just rams him off on a corner. Bam!' Bryant gripped the pipe in his teeth and slammed fist into open palm. 'Page goes through the barrier, falls right into a low-rise, goes through seven levels of zone housing like they were paper. Gas supply ripped open somewhere in one of the flats on the way down. Boom. Adios muchachos, everybody in black.'

'Jesus.'

'Yeah, pretty fucking impressive, huh.' Mike squinted at the pipe, tried the lighter again. 'See, now what Hewitt did, that's okay, but now she's got to prove that she doesn't need two junior partners to help her run CI. If she can't, it means she made a bad call. Pure greed call. No one round here minds greed, just so long as it's good for the company as well. If it works out for Hewitt, she's saved Shorn the expense of a junior partner, and she and Hamilton get bigger equity. It's the free-market trade-off. Something for us, something for them. But if it doesn't work out, she's dead in the water and she knows it.'

'Well, Ms Conflict Investment doesn't have a whole lot of confidence in me,' said Chris gloomily. 'Not bloody enough for her, apparently.'

'That what she said?' Bryant shook his head. 'Shit, after what you did to Quain? That doesn't make any sense.'

'Well, let's just say that not all my challenges have been that uncompromising. This kill-or-be-killed stuff is strictly for the movie-makers. It's crude, man. You *don't* always need a kill. *That's* crude.' Chris leaned forward as his enthusiasm kindled. 'You ever see any of those old samurai movies?'

'Bruce Lee? Shit like that?'

'No, no. Not those. This is other stuff. Older. More subtle. See, these two guys, they're about to have a duel. So they both stand there, swords out.' Chris thrust with an imaginary sword and Bryant jerked back in reflex. His eyes narrowed momentarily, and then he laughed.

'Whoops. Scared me there.'

'Sorry. Wasn't intentional. So yeah, the two of them stand there, and they stare into each other's eyes.'

He locked gazes with Bryant, who emitted another snort of laughter.

'They just stare. Because they both know that the one who blinks or looks away first, that's the one who would have lost that fight.'

Bryant's laughter dried up without fuss. He set the pipe aside. Both men were leaning on the table now, drilling their gazes into each other's eyes with chemically altered concentration. The shared stillness of the moment stretched. The sounds of the bar receded into a backdrop, surf on a distant beach. Time ran on like a train they had both just missed. The pipe smouldered quietly to itself on the scarred wooden table. Vision wired their stares over it, eyeball to eyeball. From somewhere, an internal silence leaked into the world.

Mike Bryant blinked.

Mike Bryant laughed and looked away.

The moment blew away like an autumn leaf and Chris sat back with a look of tipsy fulfilment on his face. Bryant grinned, a little intensely. Chris was too drunk to catch the upped voltage. Bryant made a pistol of thumb and forefinger. He pointed at Chris's face.

'*Bang!*'

The laughter bubbled up again, this time from both men. Bryant made a sound between a snort and a sigh.

'There you are. You stared me out.'

Chris nodded.

'But I blew your fucking head off.'

'Yeah.' Chris leaned back across the table. Enthused. Oblivious to the edge sheathed in the other man's voice. 'But you see, there was no need for that. We'd already established the winner. You blinked. I would have won.'

'Bullshit. Maybe I had a hair in my eye. Maybe all these samurai guys walked away from fights they could have won just because they had a jumpy eye muscle that day. Where'd you read all this shit, anyway?'

'Mike, you're missing the point. It's about total control. It's a duel between two whole people, not just two sets of skills. We could have a fist fight and you could turn up with a gun. We could have a gun fight and you could come with an armoured car and a flame-thrower. That's not what a duel's about.'

Bryant picked up the pipe again. 'Duel's about winning, Chris,' he said.

Chris wasn't listening.

'Look at China, a couple of centuries ago. There were cases there where two warlords sat down on the battlefield and played chess to decide the outcome of a battle. Chess, Michael. No death, no slaughter, just a game of chess. And they honoured it.'

Bryant looked sceptical. 'Chess?'

'Just a game of chess.' Chris was staring off into a corner. 'You imagine that?'

'Not really, no.' Bryant stuffed the pipe into a pocket and started to get up. 'But it makes a good story, I'll give you that. Now, how about we get the car and get out of here before the sun comes up? Because Suki's going to fucking take me apart if I don't get back soon. And she's not into chess.'

SIX

They came out of the *Falkland* through a side door and onto a different street. Cold night air like a slap in the face, and for a couple of moments Chris reeled. He wondered how Bryant was dealing with the pipe high.

'Where's the fucking car?'

'This way.'

Bryant grabbed him by the arm, dragged him round the corner and started across the deserted street. Halfway there, he jammed to an abrupt halt.

'Ooops,' he said softly.

The BMW sat on the far side of the street under one of the few working street lamps. Sitting on the car: four men and one woman, all dressed in oil-smeared jeans and jackets. The grime was a uniform, the pale silent faces style-coordinated accessories. Heads shaven and tattooed, feet heavily booted. Hands filled with a variety of blunt metal implements.

None of them looked over eighteen.

They stared at the two suited men on the other side of the street and made no move to get off the car.

'You've got to get your contact stunner fixed, Mike,' Chris sniggered, still drunk. 'Look at the shit you get all over it if you don't have it powered up.'

'Shut the fuck up,' hissed Bryant.

The female contingent of the car-jackers levered herself off the hood of the BMW with sinuous grace.

'Nice car, Mister Zek-tiv,' she said solemnly. 'Got the keys?'

Bryant clutched automatically at his pocket. The woman's eyes flickered to the move and locked on. She nodded in satisfaction.

'Get off my fucking car!' Bryant barked.

The remaining four jackers obeyed in unison, arms spread and hands holding their makeshift weapons. Chris glanced sideways at his companion.

'Bad move, Mike. You carrying?'

Bryant shook his head almost imperceptibly.

'In the car, remember. You?'

'Yeah.' Chris paused, embarrassed. 'But it's not loaded.'

41

'*What?*'

'I don't like guns.'

'See, it's like this.' The woman's voice jerked Chris back from the disbelieving expression on Bryant's face. 'Either you can give us the keys. And your wallets. And your watches. Or we can take them from you. That's our best offer.'

She lifted thumb and little finger solemnly to ear and mouth, making a child's telephone.

'Sell, sell, sell.'

Bryant muttered something out of the corner of his mouth.

'What?' Chris muttered back.

'I *said*, back the way we came and *fucking run*!!!'

Then he was gone, sprinting flat out for the corner they had just rounded. Chris went after him, flailing to stay upright in the Argentine leather shoes. Behind him, the incentive – sounds of yells and booted pursuit. He levelled with Bryant and found, incredibly, that the other man was grinning.

'All part of a night out in the zones,' he said through gritted teeth. 'Try to keep up.'

Behind them, someone ran a metal wrecking bar along a concrete wall. It made a sound like a gigantic dentist's drill.

They looked at each other and put on speed.

Three streets away from the *Falkland*, the neighbourhood plunged from run-down to rotted-through. The houses were suddenly derelict, unglassed windows gaping out at the street and tiny gardens full of rubble and other detritus. Chris, brain abruptly adrenalin-flushed and working, grabbed Bryant and yanked him sideways into one of the gardens. Over piles of junk, scrambling. In past a front door that someone had kicked in long ago. Weeds grew up waist-high in the gap it had left. Beyond, a narrow, darkened hallway ran parallel to a staircase with half the banisters torn out. At the end, a tiled room that breathed stench like a diseased mouth.

Chris leaned cautiously against the staircase and listened to the yells of the car-jackers as they ran past and down an adjacent street.

Bryant was bent over, hands braced on his knees, panting.

'You mind telling me,' he managed hoarsely after a while. '*Why* you're carrying an unloaded gun around with you?'

'I told you. I don't like guns. I don't like Louise Hewitt telling me what to do.'

'Man, after five days that's a bad attitude to have. I wouldn't go telling anybody things like that, if I were you.'

'Why not? I told you, didn't I?'

Bryant straightened up and looked hard at him.

'Anyway, where's your gun, hotshot?'

'At least it's *loaded*.'

'Alright, old piece of folk wisdom coming up.' Chris gulped his breath back under control. 'A gun in the hand is worth *half a fucking million locked in the car*.'

'Yeah, you're right.' Bryant's grin flashed in the gloom. 'But I wasn't expecting this kind of trouble. We're only a couple of klicks inside the zones. Those guys are out of their territory.'

'You think they know that?' Chris nodded out towards the street, where voices were coming back. Some of the jacker gang, at least, were retracing their steps. He jabbed an urgent finger upward and Bryant took the creaking stairs into the darkness at the top. Chris slid back along the hallway towards the tiled room and sank into the shadows there. The stench enveloped him. The floor was slimy underfoot. He tried not to breathe.

A moment later two of the jackers were standing where he had just been. Both were armed with long crowbars.

'I don't see why we need the keys anyway. Why not just smash the fucking window.'

'Because, moron, this is a BMW Omega series.' The other jacker cast a doubtful glance up the stairs. 'State-of-the-fucking-art corporate jam-jar. These mothers have alarms, engine immobilisation locks and a broadcast scream to the nearest retrieval centre. You'd never move it a hundred metres down the fucking street before they got you.'

'We could still smash it, anyway. Rip it up.'

'Ruf, you got no fucking ambition, man. If it weren't for Molly, you'd still be smashing up telephone points and throwing stones at cabs. You got to think *bigger* than that. Come on. I don't think they came in here. Too much chance of getting their suits dirty. Let's—'

Chris's foot slipped. Knocked against something that rolled on the tiled floor. Clink of glass. Chris gritted his teeth and inched one hand down to the butt of his empty gun. The two jackers had frozen by the door.

'Hear that?' It was the ambitious member of the duo. Chris saw a silhouetted wrecking bar raised in the faint light from the doorway. 'Okay, Mister Zek-tiv. Game over. Come out, give us your fucking keys, and maybe we'll leave you some teeth.'

The two jackers advanced down the hall. They were about halfway when Mike Bryant dropped through a gap in the banister rail above. He landed feet first on the head of the gangwit bringing up the rear. The two of them tumbled to the floor. The lead jacker whipped round at the noise and Chris exploded from his hiding place. He punched hard, driving high for the face and low for the guts. The jacker turned back

43

too late. Chris's high punch broke his nose and then he folded as the solid right hook sank into his midriff. Chris grabbed the gangwit's shoulders and ran his shaven head sideways into the staircase wall. Up ahead, he saw Bryant reel to his feet and stamp down hard on the other jacker's unprotected stomach. The gangwit moaned and curled up. Bryant kicked him again, in the head.

'Mother *fucker*! Touch my car, you fucking piece of *shit*!'

Chris laid a hand on his shoulder. Bryant hooked round, face taut.

'Whoa, it's all over.' Chris stood back, hands raised. 'Game over, Mike. Come on. There's only three left now. Let's try for the car again.'

Bryant's face cleared of its fury.

'Yeah, good. Let's do it.'

The street outside was quiet. They checked both ways, then slipped out and loped back towards the *Falkland*, Bryant navigating. Less than five minutes to relocate the corner pub, and the BMW sat gleaming pristinely under the street lamp as if nothing had happened.

They circled the vehicle warily. Nothing.

Bryant produced his keys and pressed a button. The alarm disarmed with a subdued squawk. He was about to open the door when the shaven-headed woman stepped out of the shadows of a doorway less than five metres away, a piece of iron railing raised in ironic greeting. She put her fingers to her mouth and whistled shrilly. Another jacker, similarly armed, stepped out of another doorway up the street and ambled down to meet them. The woman smiled at Bryant.

'Thought you'd be back. Now, you want to throw me those keys?'

In the moment that her eyes were fixed on Bryant, Chris produced his empty gun and levelled it at her.

'Alright, that's enough,' he snapped. 'Back off.'

The other jacker took a step forward and Chris swung the gun to cover him, willing him to believe.

'You too. Back off, or you're dead. Michael, get in the car.'

Bryant opened the door. Chris was feeling for the door handle on the other side when the woman spoke.

'I don't think that gun's loaded.'

She took a step forward, followed by her companion. Chris brandished the Nemex.

'I said, back off.'

'Nah, you would have shot us by now. You're bluffing, Mr Zek.'

She raised her piece of railing, took another step forward and Mike Bryant stood up from his side of the car, Nemex in hand.

'I'm not bluffing,' he said mildly and shot her three times in the chest and stomach.

Boom, boom, boom.

The sound of the gun in the quiet street. Echoes off houses.

Chris saw and heard it in fragments.

The woman, kicked back two metres before she dropped. The railing, out of her hand and flying, clattering and rolling across the camber of the street into the gutter.

The other jacker, hands raised, placatory, backing away.

Face implacable, Bryant put the next three shots into him.

Boom, boom, boom.

He reeled and spun like a marionette, crashed into the wall and slid down it, leaving gouts of blood on the brickwork.

'Mike—'

The sound of pounding feet.

The final member of the gang, summoned by the gunshots, sprinting across the street towards the fallen bodies. He seemed oblivious to the two men in suits. He hit the ground on his knees next to the woman, disbelieving.

'Molly! *Molly!*'

Chris looked across at Bryant. 'Mike, let's—'

Bryant made a sideways hushing gesture with his free hand and lowered his aim.

Boom, BOOM.

The kneeling boy jolted as if electrocuted, and then keeled slowly over on the woman on the ground. Blood ran out over the street and trickled down to join the crowbar in the gutter.

The echoes rolled away into the predawn gloom like reluctant applause.

They drove back to the checkpoint in silence, Chris wrapped in numb disbelief. The guard let them through with a cursory glance. If he smelled the cordite from Mike's gun, he said nothing. Bryant waved him a cheerful goodnight and accelerated the big car away into the well-lit canyons of the financial district. He was humming quietly to himself.

He glanced across at Chris as they were approaching the Shorn block.

'You want to sleep over at my place? Plenty of space.'

The thought of the hour-long drive back home was abruptly unbearable. Chris mustered a dried-out voice.

'Yeah. Thanks.'

'Good.' Bryant speeded up and cornered west.

Chris watched the towering blocks begin to thin out around them. As the BMW picked up the main feeder lane for the London orbital, he turned slightly in his seat to face Bryant.

'You didn't have to kill them all, Mike.'

'Yeah, I did.' There was no animosity in Bryant's voice. 'What else was I supposed to do. Fire warning shots? This symbolism of combat shit you talk about doesn't work with people like that. They're gangwit scum, Chris. They don't know how to lose gracefully.'

'They'd already lost. And they were kids. They would have run away.'

'Yeah, yeah. Until the next time. Look, Chris. People like that, civilised rules don't apply. Violence is the only thing they understand.'

Outside the hurrying car, the sky was brightening in the east. Chris's head was beginning to ache.

SEVEN

Chris awoke with the horrified conviction that he had been unfaithful to Carla. Liz Linshaw was sitting up in bed beside him, buttering a piece of toast and wiping the knife casually on the sheets.

'Breakfast in bed,' she was saying authoritatively, 'is *so* sexy.'

Chris looked down at the stains she was making and felt a hot lump of mingled guilt and sadness swelling in the base of his throat. There was no way he could hide this from Carla.

He opened his eyes with a jolt. Daylight strained through chintz curtains just above his head. For a moment the chintz hammered home the dream – Carla hated the stuff with a passion. He really had gone home with Liz Linshaw, then. He turned on his side with the blockage of unshed tears still jammed in his throat and—

He was in a single bed.

He propped himself up, confused. Matching chintz quilt and pillow-case, massive hangover. Close behind this sensory surge, the events of the previous evening crashed in on him. The street. The jackers. Bryant's gun in the quiet night. The relief made him forget the pain in his head for a couple of moments. Liz Linshaw was a dream.

He hauled up his wrist and looked at his watch which he had evidently been in no state to remove the previous night. Quarter past twelve. He spotted his clothes hanging on the door of the tiny guest room and groped his way out of bed towards them. The door was open a crack – beyond, he could hear kitchen sounds. The smell of coffee and toast wafted under his nose.

He dressed hurriedly, stuffed his tie in his jacket pocket and picked up his shoes. Outside the guest room, a white-painted corridor hung with innocuous landscapes led to a wide, curving staircase. Halfway down, he met a woman coming up. Auburn hair, light eyes. He made the match with Michael's wallet photo. Suki.

Suki had a cup of coffee, complete with saucer, in her hand and there was a tolerant smile on her perfectly made-up face.

'Good morning. It's Chris, isn't it? I'm Suki.' She offered one slim, gold-braceleted arm. 'Nice to meet you at last. I was just bringing you this up. Michael said you'd want to be woken. He's in the kitchen, talking to work, I think.'

Chris took the coffee, balancing it awkwardly in his free hand. His head was beginning to pulse alarmingly.

'Thanks, uh. Thanks.'

Suki's smile brightened. Chris had the disturbing impression that his hands and face could have been painted with blood and she would have smiled the same way.

'Had fun last night, did you?' she asked maternally.

'Uh, something like that. Would you excuse me?'

He slipped past her and found his way down into the kitchen. It was a large, comfortable room with wooden furniture, and tall windows along one wall letting in the sun. The scrubbed wooden table was laid for three and covered with an assortment of edible breakfast items. At the far end a two-year-old child sat in a high chair, belabouring a plate of unidentifiable sludge with a plastic spoon. Over by the window, and well out of splash range, Mike Bryant watched her with a tender expression on his face and drank coffee out of a mug. There was a mobile pinned between his ear and shoulder and he appeared to be listening intently. He nodded and waved as Chris came in.

'They certainly were. What, you think I imagined it? Who says that? Right, get him on the line.'

Bryant cupped a hand over the phone.

'Chris, call your wife at work. She's been screaming down the Shorn switchboard since eight this morning. You sleep well?'

He pointed at a videophone hung on the wall near the door. Chris put down his coffee, picked the phone up and dialled from memory. He waved at Ariana, who regarded him in silence for a moment and then grinned and started bashing her breakfast again. Bryant went back to his conversation.

'Yes, this is Michael Bryant. No I'm not, I'm at home, which is where I'm likely to stay until you can promise a little more safety on the streets. I don't care, we don't pay you people to stand around scratching your balls. We were less than three, don't shout me down detective, three klicks inside the cordon. Yes, you're fucking right I shot them.'

The screen in front of Chris lit up with a grimy, gum-chewing face.

'Yeah, Mel's AutoFix.' He caught sight of Chris. 'Need a tow?'

'No,' Chris cleared his throat. 'Could I speak to Carla Nyquist please.'

'Sure. Be a moment.'

Behind him, Bryant went on with his tirade. 'They were just about to take me and my colleague to pieces with machetes. What? Well, I'm not surprised. Probably got scavenged by someone last night. Listen, there were five of them to two of us. Hardcore gangwits. Now if I can't claim that as self defence then—'

Carla appeared, knuckling grease across her nose. There was a fairly obvious scowl under the black marks. 'What happened to you, then?'

'Uh, I stayed over at Mike's place. There was some, uh.' He glanced at Bryant who was listening to the other end of his own call with a face like thunder. 'Trouble.'

'Trouble? Are you—?'

'No, I'm fine.' Chris forced a grin. 'Just a headache.'

'Well, why didn't you call me? I was worried sick.'

'I didn't want to worry you. It was late, and I was going to call first thing this morning. Must have overslept. Look,' he turned to Bryant again. 'Mike, are you going in to Shorn today?'

Bryant nodded glumly, covering the phone mouthpiece again. 'Looks like it. I've got to fill out half a hundred fucking incident reports, apparently. Say an hour?'

Chris turned back to Carla's waiting face. 'I'm going in to pick up the car with Mike in about an hour. I'll pick you up from the garage and tell you all about it then. Okay?'

'Okay,' It was grudging. 'But this had better be a fucking good story.'

'Deal. By the way, I'm in love.'

Mike Bryant shot him a peculiar glance across the kitchen.

On screen, Carla kept her scowl. 'Yeah, yeah. Me too. See you at four. And don't be late.'

She reached for the phone and the image faded. Chris turned just in time to catch the last of Bryant's call.

'Yes, I am aware of that, detective. Well next time I'm attacked on the street, I'll be sure and remember it. Goodbye.'

He snapped the phone shut angrily.

'*Asshole*. Get this, the corporate police, *our* fucking police want to conduct an investigation into whether this was an unlawful shooting. I mean.' He gestured helplessly, lost for words. 'Defend yourself, and you're fucking breaking the law. Meanwhile, some piece of shit gangwit cracks a fingernail in a back alley and you've got Citizens' Rights activists screaming for someone's neck. What about us citizens? Who's looking out for us? What about *our* rights?'

'Michael!' Suki appeared in the kitchen doorway, a coffee cup in each hand. 'How many times have I told you, don't use that language in front of Ariana. She just comes right out with it at the playgroup, and I get dirty looks from the other mothers.' She put the coffee cups on the table and went to clean some of the surplus food from around her daughter's mouth. Ariana made half-hearted protests, all the time squinting shyly at Chris. 'That's right, don't you listen to Daddy when he talks like that.' She turned a fraction of her multi-tasked attention in the same direction as her daughter. 'Take no notice, Chris. He's always moaning

49

about citizens' rights. This'll be the second time he's been in trouble, *there*, is that better darling, the second time he's been in trouble with the police this year. Use of undue force. *Yes*, who's a *clean* girl? I think he just likes living dangerously.'

Bryant made a disgusted noise. Suki went to him and put an arm round his waist. She kissed him under the chin.

'Maybe that's what I see in him. You're married, aren't you Chris? Was that her on the vid?'

'Yeah.' To Chris, his own voice sounded unfairly defensive. 'She's a mechanic. Got to work most Saturdays.'

He sipped his coffee and watched for a reaction, but Suki either didn't care one way or the other or had been trained to black belt in social graces. She smiled as she unfastened Ariana from the high chair.

'Yes, Michael said. You know, one of the Shorn partners had a girlfriend who worked in auto reclaim. Now what was his name?' She snapped her fingers. 'I met him at the Christmas bash.'

'Notley,' said Bryant.

'That's it, Notley. Jack Notley. Well, you must both come over for dinner, Chris. What's your wife's name?'

'Carla.'

'Carla. Lovely name. Like that Italian holoporn star Mike gets so turned over on.' She put a playful hand over Bryant's mouth as he protested. 'Yes, ask her to come over. In fact, why don't you come over tonight? We've got no plans, have we, Mike?'

Bryant shook his head.

'Well, then. I'll cook sukiyaki. You're not vegetarian, either of you?'

'No.' Chris hesitated. There had been some notion of going to visit Carla's father today, and in the whirl of the week just gone, he wasn't sure quite how solidified the plan was. 'Uh, I'm not sure if—'

'Not to be missed, that sukiyaki,' said Michael, draining his coffee and setting down the mug. 'Beef direct from the Sutherland Croft Association herds. Hey, you reckon Carla'd like a look at the BMW? Seeing as she's a mechanic and all. That's the new Omega Injection series under the bonnet. State of the art, not even on general release outside Germany yet. I bet she'd love to watch it turn over.'

Chris, aware suddenly of the exact depth to which he did not want to visit his father-in-law, made a decision.

'Yeah, she'd like that,' he said.

'Good, that's settled then,' said Suki brightly. 'I'll get the beef this afternoon. Shall we say about eight-thirty?'

Mike insisted on dropping Chris right beside his car. The underground parking decks beneath the Shorn block were largely deserted and the level Chris had parked on showed only three other vehicles. Bryant slewed to a halt across the battery of empty spaces opposite, killed the engine and got out.

'Hewitt's,' he said, nodding at the nearest of the isolated vehicles. 'Audi built it for her to spec when she made partner. Fancy seeing that coming up in your rearview?'

Chris looked at it. Broad black windscreen, heavy impact collision bars that jutted from the end of the raked hood.

'Not much,' he admitted. 'But I thought Hewitt was a BMW fan.'

Mike snorted. 'Hewitt's a fan of money. Back when she made partner, Shorn had this deal with Audi. They supplied all our company cars and hardware, and the partners got special edition battlewagons thrown in for free. Two years ago BMW made Shorn a better offer and they went with it. As a partner, Hewitt can opt for any vehicle she likes but when this baby gets written off or superseded, you can bet she'll just take a top-of-the-line Omega with all the armour options, free to partners of BMW clients. To her, it's all just a cost-benefit analysis.'

'So what does Notley think of all this?'

'Notley's a patriot.' Mike grinned. 'I mean, in the real, uncut sense of the word. Last of the diehard anti-Europeans. Anti-American too, come to that. He actually believes in the cultural superiority of England over other nations. Shit like that. I mean, you'd think he'd be able to see a little more clearly from the fiftieth floor, wouldn't you. Anyway, when *he* made partner, he didn't want to know about the German makes. He had Landrover build him a customised battle-wagon from scratch. And he's still driving it ten years later. Fucking thing looks like a tank but it'll do nearly two hundred kilometres an hour. Except he won't use metric, so that'd be . . . what, about a hundred and twenty-something? Miles an hour? Whatever. That's what his speedo reads in.'

'Yeah, right.'

'No, really. He made them fit an imperial speedo. Miles per hour. Ask him to let you look at the dashboard some time.'

'He's not here today?'

'No way. You won't catch Notley working weekends. Calls it the American disease, working all the hours God sends you.' Bryant's eyes flicked away with recollection. 'I remember one quarterly do, I ran into him in the men's room, we were both pretty pissed and I was asking him if being a partner was really worth all the extra shit, the weekend work, the all-nighters and he looked at me like I was insane. Then he says, still treating me like I'm a headcase, talking very slowly, you know, he says, *Mike, if you make partner and you're still working weekends then there's*

51

something wrong somewhere. You make partner so they can't tell you to do that shit any more. Otherwise, what's the point? You believe that?'

'Sounds like a decent philosophy.'

'Yeah, not like the rest of these fucking wannabes.' Mike gestured around dismissively. He wandered across to Chris's car. 'So what have we got here? This looks Scandinavian to me.'

'Yeah.' Chris laid a proprietorial hand on the car's flank. 'Saab combat chassis. Carla's family are Norwegian, but she did her apprenticeship in Stockholm. Been around Saabs and Volvos all her life. She says the Swedes were building cars for road-raging decades before anybody even thought of it.'

Bryant nodded. 'It looks pretty mean. But I reckon you'd still lose on speed to an Omega.'

'She's faster than she looks, Mike. A lot of that bulk's Volvo spaced armouring. Strut-braced stuff. It isn't solid, and the slipstream channels through flues on the outer edges for stability, but by Christ you'd still know if it hit you. Volvo've crash-tested the struts at aeroplane speeds, and they hold.'

'Spaced armouring, huh?' Bryant looked thoughtful for a couple of moments, and Chris had the unsettling sensation that he had given something important away to the big man. Then another grin swept the calculating expression out of his eyes. He clapped Chris on the shoulder. 'Remind me to divorce Suki and get a Swedish mechanic to shack up with.'

The parking deck was filled with a soft chime. The Shorn elevator voice announced two o'clock for the whole building. Mike glanced reflexively at his watch.

'That's me,' he said sourly. 'Look, Chris, I'd better run. Corporate police can be a real drag when they're determined to do something by the book. See you tonight, alright?'

'Yeah.' Chris watched him stride away towards the double doors that led upwards into the Shorn tower. 'Hey, Mike.'

'Yo.'

'Good luck.'

Bryant raised a hand and waved it sideways. 'Ah, don't worry about it. Piece of piss. Be out of here by three. See you tonight.'

'He said *what?*'

Carla paused in the act of fastening one earring and stared disbelievingly at Chris in the mirror. Chris looked back at her, confused.

'He said it'd be a piece of piss and they'd—'

'No, before that. That stuff about divorcing Suki.'

'He said to remind him to get a divorce so he could shack up with a

Swedish mechanic.' Chris saw the look on her face and sighed, feeling the edge of the row they were teetering on. 'He's just trying to be friendly, Carla. It's a kind of compliment, you know.'

'It's a load of sexist shit is what it is. Anyway,' Carla finished with the earring and came away from the mirror. 'That's not the point.'

'No? Then what is the point, Carla?'

This time it was Carla that sighed. 'The point,' she said heavily, 'is that I'm not some curiosity for you to show off. This is my wife, by the way she's a mechanic. I'm sure it's fun to say. The shock value. The looks you get. I know you get a kick out of taking me to these corporate functions, showing everyone what a rebel you are.'

Chris stared at her.

'No, it's because I love you.'

'I—' She'd been about to raise her voice. Something broke in the effort. 'Chris, I know that. I *know*. You just, you don't have to prove it against overwhelming odds all the time. It's not a-a battle or a quest. It's just, living.' She saw the pain flit across his face and went to him. Her hands, scrubbed clean with aromatic oil, cupped his downturned face. 'I know you love me, but I'm not here just to *be* loved. You can't use me as a statement of how strongly you feel about everything, how loyal you are.'

He tried to turn his head away. She held it in place.

'Look at me, Chris. This is me. I'm your wife. Mechanic is just a job, just a statement of financial disadvantage. I don't let it define me, and I don't want you doing it behind my back. We're more than what we do.'

'Now you sound like your father.'

She paused for a moment, then nodded and let go of his head. 'Yeah, you're right.' She touched her throat. 'Should be fucking miked up, huh? And that reminds me, you said we'd go and see him this weekend. Whatever happened to that promise?'

'I didn't think we'd—'

'Oh, forget it. I don't really want to go anyway. I don't feel up to the refereeing. Once you two get at each other's throats . . .' she sighed again. 'Look, Chris, about this mechanic thing. How would you like it if I dragged you over to see Mel and Jess and said you'd just love to have a look at their tax returns.'

Chris's eyes widened with outrage. 'I'm not a fucking accountant.'

Carla grinned and dropped into a defensive boxing stance. 'Want to bet? Want to fight about it?'

The bravado ended in a shriek as Chris hurled himself at her and rugby-tackled her back onto the bed. The brief tussle ended with Chris straddling Carla's body and struggling to hold her flailing arms at bay. He could feel the strength leaking out of his grip in giggle increments.

'Sssh, sssh, stop it, stop it, behave yourself. We're going out.'

'Fucking let go of me, you piece of shit.' She was laughing as well, breathlessly. 'I'll claw your fucking eyes out.'

'Carla,' Chris said patiently. 'That's not really an incentive. You've got to learn the art of negotiation. Now—'

An incoherent squeal. Carla tumbled him. They grappled at each other across the bed.

EIGHT

Out, driving through Hawkspur Green in the waning light of evening, while Carla tried to do something with her dishevelled hair. The sex had taken half an hour, and it still lurked in the grins at the corners of their mouths.

'We're going to be late,' said Chris severely.

'Ah, bollocks.' Carla gave up on her hair and settled for pinning it untidily up. 'I don't know why we're doing this anyway. Going out to dinner with some guy you're going to wreck in a couple of years' time. It doesn't really make sense, does it?'

Chris glanced across at her, the implied confidence in the remark warming him inside. There was always an intimacy to the conversations they had while driving, maybe born out of the secure knowledge that the car was clean. Carla swept for bugs on a regular basis, and her knowledge of the Saab meant they were sure of their privacy in a way they never quite could be at home.

'You know it might not come to that,' Chris said, feeling his way through his own thoughts. 'A wreck. We don't have to run for the same promotions.'

'No, but you will. Like at Hammett McColl. It always works out that way.'

'I don't know, Carla. It's strange. It's like he's just decided he's going to be my friend and that's it. I mean, there's a lot about him I don't like. That stuff in the zones was pretty extreme—'

'No shit. The man sounds like a fucking crackhead psycho to me, Chris. Whatever you say.'

Without actually lying to his wife about anything specific, Chris had somehow managed to omit Bryant's execution-style dispatch of Molly and her jacker colleagues. The way it came out, it really had been self defence against armed and violent attackers. In retrospect, Chris was almost starting to believe it himself. The gangwits had wrecking bars. Not much doubt they would have used them if Chris's unloaded gun had given them the chance. Carla remained unimpressed.

'He's just like a lot of the guys at Shorn—'

'Well, I certainly believe that.'

Chris shot her an irritated glance. 'He's worked hard for what he's got, Carla. He just got angry because someone was trying to take it away from him. That's a natural reaction, isn't it? How do you think Mel'd react if someone turned up and tried to trash the workshop.'

'Mel doesn't make his money the way you people do,' Carla muttered.

'What?'

'Nothing. Forget it.'

'Mel doesn't make his money like me and Mike Bryant?'

'I said, forget it, Chris.'

'That's right, he doesn't, does he? Mel doesn't do what we do. He just makes a living fixing our cars for us, so we can go out and do it again. Jesus fucking Christ, don't you take the high moral ground with me, Carla, because—'

'Al*right*.' Her voice caught on the second syllable. 'I said forget it. I'm sorry I said it, so just forget it.'

The air between the two front seats frosted with silence. Finally, Chris reached across the chill and took Carla's hand.

'Look,' he said wearily. 'In the First World War fighter pilots used to toast each other with champagne before they went out and tried to shoot each other out of the sky. Did you know that? And the winners used to drop wreaths on their enemies' airfields to commemorate the men they'd just killed. That make any sense to you? And we're talking about less than a hundred and fifty years ago.'

'That was war.'

'Yeah.' Chris made his voice stay calm. 'A war for what? Lines drawn on a map. Can you honestly say that those men were fighting for anything that made any kind of sense? Anything that makes more sense than a competitive tender or a promotion duel?'

'They had no choice, Chris. If they laid wreaths it was because they hated what they had to do. This is different.'

He felt his anger twist and jump like a fish in a net: this time it was an effort to hold it down. It looked as if Carla was going to pull her favourite trick and they were going to arrive at the Bryants' front door in the brittle silence of an interrupted row.

'You think we have any more of a choice than they did? You think I like what I do for a living?'

'I don't think you dislike it as much as you say.' Carla was digging in her bag for cigarettes, a bad sign on the row barometer. 'And if you do, there are other jobs. Other companies. Chris, you could go and work for the fucking *ombudsmen* with what you know. They'd take you. UNECT, or one of the others. The regulatory bodies are screaming for people with real commercial experience.'

'Oh, great. You think I want to be a fucking bureaucrat. Playing at

56

international social democracy with a fucking placard and a zone-level salary.'

'Ombudsmen make a lot of money, Chris.'

'Says who?'

'My mother used to know some of the guys from UNECT in Oslo. Their field agents pull down near two hundred grand a year.'

Chris snorted. 'Not bad for fucking socialists.'

'Al*right*, Chris.' It was cold and even, a flip side of her anger he hated worse than the shouting. 'Forget the fucking ombudsmen. You could get a job with any other investment firm in the city.'

'Not any more.' He hunched his shoulders as he said it. 'Have you got any idea how much Shorn paid to get me out of Hammett McColl? Any idea what they'll do to protect that investment?'

'Break your legs, will they?'

The sneer hurt, not least because it sounded like something Mel might have said in workshop banter. Jealousy flared. He hid it and worked at calm.

'Not mine, no. But the word will be out there, Carla. Every executive search company in London will have been warned off me. Anyone who chooses to ignore it, they'll find strung up under Blackfriars Bridge.'

She exploded smoke across the car. 'Come off it.'

'No? You don't remember Justin Gray, then?'

'That was petrol-mafia stuff.'

'Yeah, right. A recruitment consultant with a flat in Knightsbridge and a house in St Albans is really going to get mixed up with those clowns. *Everybody* believed that one.'

'Wearing a suit doesn't make you smart, Chris. It just makes you greedy.'

'Thank you.'

'That's not what I meant, and you know it.'

'Look. Two weeks before he died, Gray was instrumental in moving two senior cutting-edge technologies execs out of Shorn and into Calders UK. He told the police he'd been receiving death threats throughout the run-up to that deal. Conveniently enough, they failed to investigate.'

'I think you're talking wine-bar dramatics and a coincidence, Chris.'

'Suit yourself. Gray's not the only one. There was that guy they found floating in his swimming pool in Biarritz last year. Another one a couple of years before that in a car smash. Mistaken duel call-out, they said, like *that* happens all the time. Both chasing candidates at Shorn. Coincidence? I don't think so, Carla. Over the last five years, there've been at least a dozen executive search personnel who've ended up dead or damaged while, *coincidentally*, they were trying to prise candidates away from Shorn.'

'So why'd you go to work for them?' she snapped.

Chris shrugged. 'It was a lot of money. Remember?'

'We didn't need it.'

'We didn't need it, *right then*. These days, that means nothing. You can't ever be backed up too much. Besides, Shorn aren't the only ones to play rough with the reckies.' He found he was smiling faintly. 'They're just better at it than most. More prepared to go to the asphalt, quicker to floor it when they do. Just a harder crew, that's all.'

'Yes, and that's really it, isn't it Chris.' There was ice in her voice – she'd caught the smile. 'It wasn't the money, it was the rep. You couldn't wait to get in the running with the hard crew, could you? Couldn't wait to test yourself against them.'

'All I'm saying is when you talk about choices, face the facts. Be realistic. *Realistically*, what choice do I have?'

'You always have a choice, Chris. Everyone does.'

'Yeah?' Finally, his anger slipped its leash. 'Have you listened to any fucking thing I've said, Carla? What fucking choice do I have?'

'You could resign.'

'Oh, *good* idea.' This time there was a break in his voice that he couldn't iron out. 'And then we could go and live in the zones. And when your father gets threatened with eviction again, instead of paying off what he owes, we could just be poor and helpless, and maybe go and help him pick his possessions up off the street where they throw them. Maybe you'd like that better.'

Carla flicked ash off her cigarette and stared out of the side window. 'I'd like it better than waiting to see this car on fire on the six o'clock news.'

'That isn't going to happen.' He said it reflexively.

'Isn't it?' Now he could hear the unshed tears in her throat. She drew hard on the cigarette. 'Isn't it? Why is that, Chris?'

Silence. And the sound of the Saab engine.

Mike grinned. Laughter erupted around the table.

Two hours earlier, Chris would have been willing to bet that he wouldn't hear Carla or himself laugh for the whole weekend. But here he was, seated in soft candlelight, watching across a food-laden, black wood table top as his wife broke up in peals of genuine hilarity. Against all the odds, the evening with the Bryants had taken off like a deregulation share issue.

'No, really.' Suki fought her own laughter down to a smirk. 'He actually said that. Can you believe it? Would you have gone out with a man who said that to you?'

'No, I wouldn't.' Carla was still laughing, but her answer was absolutely serious.

'Oh,' Suki reached across the table and took her husband's hand. 'I'm being horrible, aren't I. Tell us how you met Chris, Carla.'

Carla shrugged. 'He came in to get his car fixed.'

The laughter rekindled. Chris leaned forward.

'No, it's true. You know, she was standing there, in this. T-shirt.' He made vague female body gestures with both hands. 'With a spanner in her hand, grease on her nose. And she says, *I can give you the best road holding in Europe*. And that was it. I was gone. Falling.'

Carla lost a little of her mirth. 'Yeah, what he doesn't tell you is, he was beaten up from some fucking stupid competitive tender. He *was* falling. He could barely stand. Torn suit, blood on his hands. Down his face. Trying all the time to make believe he wasn't hurt.'

'Mmm,' Suki grinned. 'Gorgeous.'

Carla's smile faded slightly. 'No, not really.'

'Oh come on, Carla. I bet that's when you fell for him as well. Noble savage and all that caveman stuff. Just like that Tony Carpenter flick, you know, the one where he fights off all those motorcycle thugs. What's it called, Michael? I can never remember the names of these things.'

'*Graduate Intake*,' said Mike Bryant, eyes intent on Carla's face.

Chris nodded. 'Seen it. Great movie.'

'That kind of macho shit doesn't turn me on,' Carla said flatly. 'I see too much of the results, working salvage. See, they haven't always finished pulling the bodies out by the time we get there.'

'Carla's boss spends a lot of time separating losers from their vehicles,' said Chris, miming a pair of salvage shears. 'Literally.'

'Chris!' Suki laughed again, then put one elegantly varnished set of fingernails over her mouth in mock mortification as if she'd just realised what she was laughing at. 'Please.'

'Okay, here's a joke.' Chris ignored the look Carla was giving him. 'Who are the lowest-paid headhunters in the city?'

'Oh, I know this one.' Suki wagged a finger at them. 'Don't tell me, don't tell me. The guys at Costermans were telling this a couple of months ago. Ohhh, I can't remember, Chris. Go on, then.'

'Paramedic crews on the orbital after the New Year playoffs.'

Suki's brow creased in fake pain. 'Oh, that's awful.' She sniggered, winding up to another full-blown laugh. 'That's *horrible*.'

'Isn't it just,' said Carla unsmilingly, staring across the table at her husband.

Mike Bryant coughed. 'Ah. Would you like to see that Omega now,

Carla? It's just through the kitchen to the garage. Bring your glass if you like.'

He got up and flashed a glance at Suki, who nodded on cue.

'Yes, go on. I'll clear these away.'

'I'll help you,' said Chris, standing automatically.

'No, it's just loading the machine. You can help me make the coffee later. Go on, I don't know the first thing about engines. Michael's been dying to show it off to someone who understands what he's talking about.' Suki reached across and kissed Bryant. 'Isn't that right, darling?'

'Well, if you're sure—' Chris broke off as Carla tugged at his sleeve, and the three of them trooped out after Bryant, leaving Suki at the table. They crossed the kitchen space and Bryant threw open a door that let in a wave of cold air and a view of a wide, concrete-floored garage. The BMW stood gleaming in the light from overhead neon tubes. They filed through the door and stood around the hood end of the vehicle while Mike Bryant reached in and popped the locks. Then he set aside his wineglass on a workbench and lifted up the hood. Service lights sprang up in the engine space and the Omega Injection was revealed in all its matt grey glory.

'Ain't that a beautiful sight?' Bryant burlesqued, some mutilated sub-Simeon Sands idea of an American accent.

'Very nice.' Carla walked around the engine, peering down into the clearance on either side. She pressed down hard with one hand on the engine block and nodded to herself. She looked up at Bryant. 'Cantilevered support?'

'Got it in one.'

'Looks like they've mounted the weight a long way back this time.'

'Yeah, well, you probably remember the Gammas.' Bryant came to lean into the engine beside her, leaving Chris feeling suddenly unreasonably isolated. 'Never drove one myself, but that was the big complaint, wasn't it? All that nose armour and the engine too.'

Carla grunted agreement, still groping around down the side of the engine. 'Yep. Handled like a pig. This one doesn't, I imagine.'

Bryant grinned. 'You want to take it for a spin, Carla? Put her through it?'

'Well, I . . .' Carla was clearly taken aback. She was saved an answer by Suki, who appeared in the door with her hostess smile and a silver foil packet in one hand.

'How many for coffee, then?'

'Leave it, Suki.' Bryant went to her and took the packet away. 'We're all going to go for a ride.'

'Oh no, Michael.' For the first time that Chris could detect, he saw a crack in Suki's social armour. 'You've drunk too much, you're just going to get someone killed.'

'No, Carla's going to drive.'

'Oh, I'll believe that when I see it. Carla, honestly, the number of times he's let me behind the wheel, then yanked me out again at the first serious sign of—'

'Don't listen to her, Carla. Suki, it's the weekend, it's nearly midnight, there's nothing on the roads. Just out on the orbital, as far as the M11 hook up. Carla drives there, I'll drive back. C'mon, it'll be *fun*.'

True to Mike's prediction, the orbital was a ghost highway. Nothing more substantial than waste paper stirred beneath the march of gull-winged sodium lamps. There was no sound other than the rush of their tyres on the asphalt and the comfortable growl of the Omega Injection engine. Carla drove with a rapt expression on her face at a rock-steady hundred and fifty kilometres an hour, occasionally swerving from lane to lane as chunks of decaying surfacing flashed towards them. A faint rain fell on the big oval windscreen, cleaned off meticulously by the gapped speed wipers.

'Crawler,' said Mike Bryant from the passenger seat, as the tail lights of a transporter appeared on the sweep of motorway ahead of them. 'Looks like it's automated; only a machine drives in the slow lane with this much road to play with. Pass him close, see if you can trip the collision systems.'

Next to Chris in the back, Suki sighed. 'You are *such* a child, Michael. Carla, just ignore him.'

The BMW flashed past the transporter, giving it a wide berth. Mike sighed and shrugged. Up ahead, the lights of a junction glowed like a UFO landing site. A massive metal sign announced the M11 ramp. Carla pulled across into the filter lane and eased off the accelerator, letting the BMW's speed bleed away on the approach slope. They cruised to a gentle halt at the summit, just short of the roundabout. Carla sat for a moment, listening to the engine run, then nodded.

'Very smooth,' she said, almost to herself.

'Isn't it.' Mike Bryant cracked open his door. 'Swap places. There's a couple of things I want to show you.'

Carla met Chris's eyes in the rearview mirror for a moment, then she got out and walked round the front of the car, passing Bryant halfway. Bryant high-fived her, came round and fastened himself into the driving seat with a broad grin. He waited until Carla had also belted herself in, then dropped the car into gear and revved hard against the parking brake. Chris heard the wheels spin and shriek for a moment as the

BMW held position, then Bryant knocked off the brake and they leapt forward.

'Always forget that bit.' Bryant shouted above the engine and he grinned in the mirror. The car plunged down the ramp opposite, gathering speed and hit the main carriageway of the orbital at nearly a hundred and twenty. Bryant let them cover about half a kilometre, then slapped his forehead.

'Wait! This isn't the way home!'

He grinned again, then hauled on the wheel. Chris heard his feet hit the pedals at the same moment and was just too late to brace himself and Suki as the BMW executed a perfect U-turn dead stop in the centre lane.

'Michael,' said Suki severely. 'Stop it.'

'Let's try that again,' said Bryant and kicked the BMW into another wheel-spinning takeoff. They flashed back towards the intersection, swerving into the slow lane on the slight incline under the bridge. Bryant turned round to look at Chris and Suki.

'Now, you know that—'

They trampled him down with their voices.

'Michael!'

'Look at the fucking r—'

'Don't tur—'

In the time it all took to begin saying, Bryant had turned back to a more conventional driver's posture and they were under the bridge and climbing the incline up on the other side.

'Shit, sorry,' he said. 'I was just going to say, you know that truck we passed a couple of klicks back—'

The interior of the car flooded with light as the automated transporter cleared the crest of the rise ahead and bore down on them. Suki, Chris and Carla uttered another multiple yell and this time Bryant yelled with them, louder than anyone. The transporter's robot brain blasted them with an outraged hoot from the collision alert system and bands of orange hazard-warning lights lit up on the cab. Mike's burlesque Sands accent reappeared, cut with wide-eyed, breathless psycho.

'I'm sorry, honey. I guess I. Just shouldna. Taken all those drugs.'

He laughed maniacally and, at the last moment, he yanked the wheel and the BMW swung violently to the left. They slid out of the path of the oncoming juggernaut and past the high side of the transporter's wagon, so close that through the side window Chris saw individual dents in the metal surface of the freight container. He heard the hissing explosion of brakes across the night air, and knew that Bryant had just gone ahead and done what he'd asked Carla to do earlier. He'd deliberately tripped the transporter's collision systems. He'd been playing chicken with the machine's reflexes. For fun.

Much later, back in his own car, he watched the same stretch of road again while Carla drove them home. Had he been a little more aware of his immediate surroundings, he would have seen Carla open her mouth to speak several times before she finally made up her mind.

'I'm sorry, that was my fault. I didn't—'

'No, it wasn't.'

'I didn't think he'd force it like—'

'He was just making things clear,' said Chris distantly.

They rode in silence.

'He's good, isn't he,' said Carla after a while.

Chris nodded wordlessly.

'Even drunk, even like that, he's the best I've seen.' She laughed without humour. 'And to think I said you were going to wreck him in a couple of years' time. Jesus, irony or wha—'

'Carla, I'd really prefer not to talk about it, alright.'

Carla looked sideways at him, eyes narrowed, but if she'd planned to be angry, what she saw in his face drained the anger out of her. Instead, she reached across to take his hand in hers.

'Sure,' she said very quietly.

Chris took up the offered clasp, squeezing her fingers tightly. A faint smile twitched at his mouth, but his eyes never left the road ahead.

NINE

In architectural echo of service pyramid theory, the Shorn block had rented out its bottom two levels to a series of shopping and eating units that collectively went under the name *Basecamp*. According to the Shorn promotional literature that Chris had read, *Basecamp* provided employment for over six hundred people and, together with the Shorn-owned vehicle repair shops in the basement, was a working embodiment of the virtues of trickle-down wealth creation. Prosperity spread out from the foundations of the Shorn block like vegetation from an aquifer, said the literature warmly, though the metaphor that occurred to Chris was water leaking from the cracked base of an old clay flowerpot. Wealth, in his experience, was not something the people who had it were at all keen to see trickling anywhere.

On the street opposite the Shorn complex the prosperity had blossomed – or leaked – into the form of a tiny corner restaurant called *Louie Louie's*. Originally set up in the previous century to serve the butcher's market that had once stood where the Shorn complex now loomed, the place had closed down briefly during the domino recessions and then reopened under new management, supplying coffee and snacks to the post-recessional influx of workers in *Basecamp*. This much Chris had gleaned from Mike Bryant when they went across for coffee one morning. What he noticed on his own was that the place never seemed to close and that, whether through inverted snobbery or genuine quality, the execs in the Shorn tower sent out to *Louie Louie's* in preference to almost any other eating establishment in the district.

The coffee, Chris was forced to admit, was the best he'd had in the UK, and he derived a further, ridiculously childish, satisfaction from drinking it out of the tall styrofoam canister while he stood by the window of his office and gazed down fifty-odd floors to the dimly illuminated frontage of the place it had been made. He was doing exactly that, and bluffing his way through an audiophone local-agent call from Panama, when Mike Bryant came to call.

'Well, you go and tell El Commandante that if he wants his Panthers of Justice to have bandages and mobile cover next month he'd better reconsider that stance. All the phones—'

He broke off as someone banged on the half-open door. Turning from the window, he saw Bryant shouldering his way into the office. In the big man's arms were two packages wrapped in fancy black and gold paper. The bottom package was wide and flat and about the width of Bryant's shoulders, the top one about the size and shape of two hard-copy dictionaries taped together. Both looked to be heavy.

'I'll call you back,' Chris said and clicked the audiophone off.

'Hi, Chris.' Bryant grinned. 'Got something for you. Where do you want it?'

'Over there.' Chris gestured at a small table in the corner of the still minimally furnished office space. 'What is it?

'Show you.'

Bryant put down the packages and ripped back the wrapping on the flat package to reveal the chequered surface of a marbled chess board. He grinned up at Chris again, freed the board from the wrapping entirely and set it straight on the table.

'Chess?' Chris asked stupidly.

'Chess,' agreed Bryant, working on the wrapping of the other box. It came loose and he tipped the box sideways, spilling carved onyx pieces across the board.

'You know how to set this up?' he asked.

'Yeah.' Chris came forward and picked up some of the pieces, weighing them in his hand. 'This is good stuff. Where'd you get it?'

'Place in *Basecamp*. They were having a sale. Two for the price of one. I've got the other one set up in my office. Here, give me the white ones. You do the black. Who was that on the phone?'

'Fucking Harris in Panama. Got problems with the Nicaraguan insurgents again, and of course Harris won't take a fucking decision on his own because he's five hundred klicks off the action. He's not sure of the angles.'

Bryant paused in mid-action. 'He said that?'

'More or less.'

'So he called someone who's five thousand klicks off to decide for him? You ought to call in the audit on that guy. What's he on anyway, three per cent of gross?'

'Something like that.'

'Audit the fucker. No, better yet, call a retender. Let's see him fight for his fucking three per cent like we have to.'

Chris shrugged. 'You know what it's like out there.'

'What, better the scumbag that you know?'

'You got it.' Chris put the final black pawn in place and stood back. 'Very nice. Now what?'

Bryant reached out to the white files.

'Well, I don't know much about this game, but apparently this is a fairly good way to start.'

He moved the white king's pawn forward two squares and flashed another grin.

'Your move.'

'Do I have to decide now?'

Bryant shook his head. 'Call me with it. That's the idea. Oh, and listen. That thing with Harris. I had the exact same shit with him over Honduras last year. Wish I'd called the retender then, but it was a sensitive time. Is this a sensitive time?'

Chris thought about it for a moment.

'No. They're plugged up in the jungle somewhere, nothing going to happen till the rain stops.'

Bryant nodded. 'Call the retender,' he said, pointing a cocked finger pistol downward, execution-style. 'I would. Get that motherfucker Harris either dead or jacked up and working properly for you. You ever been to Panama?'

'No. Emerging Markets stuff was all further south. Hammett McColl were into Venezuela, the NAME, bits of Brazil.'

'Yeah, well, let me tell you about Panama.' Bryant offered his grin again. 'Just for your information. The place is stuffed full of agents who'll do Harris's job twice as well for half the money. You offer one and a half, maybe two per cent of total, they'll rip his fucking heart out and eat it. Down there they do the tendering in converted bullrings, gladiator-style.' The American burlesque came on full. '*Real* messy.'

'Delightful,' muttered Chris.

'Fuck it, Chris, he deserves it.' Bryant's brow creased with good-humoured exasperation. He held out his hands, palms up. 'That's our investment he's fucking with. If he can't cut it, well, get someone who can. Anyway, not my account, not my call. Speaking of which, I've got some calls to make. You coming out to play tonight? Up for the *Falkland* again?'

Chris shook his head. 'Promised Carla we'd eat out in the village. Maybe some other time.'

'Okay. What about cutting work early, coming down to the firing range with me. Just for an hour or so, before you go home. Get the feel of that Nemex, in case you ever decide to put bullets in it.'

Chris grinned reluctantly. 'That's not fair. At least I was carrying mine. Alright, alright. I'll come down and play in the arcade for an hour. But that's all. After that, I'm off. Meet you down there at six, say.'

'Done.' Bryant shot him with the finger pistol and left.

Chris stood and looked at the chessboard for a while, then he moved the black king's pawn hesitantly out two spaces, so it was faced off against its white counterpart. He frowned over the move, shifted the piece back a space, hesitated some more then pulled an irritated face and restored the pawn to the face off position. He went back to his desk and stabbed rapidly through a number from memory.

'Panama Trade and Investment Commission,' said a Hispanic woman's voice in English. The speaker swam into focus on the screen and recognised him.

'Señor Faulkner, how can we help you?'

'Get me Tendering,' said Chris.

'I don't know,' he told Carla that evening over margaritas and fajitas in the village Tex-Mex. 'I thought after that shit on the orbital last week, the battle lines were drawn. I felt like a fucking idiot for all that stuff I'd been saying to you about us staying friends. But I was right. He *wants* to be my friend.'

'Or he's scared of you.'

'Same difference. I seem to remember someone telling me once that same-sex friendships are just a way of negating competition. Now who was that?'

'I didn't say that. I said that's what Mel thinks. I didn't say I agreed with him.'

Chris grinned. 'Well, he'd know about same-sex friendships, I suppose. From a real in-depth point of view.'

'Don't be a wanker, Chris.'

'Hey, come on. It was a joke.' Chris hung onto his smile, but there was a tiny feeling of slippage somewhere inside him. There had been a time, he was sure, when Carla could read him better than this. 'You know I've got nothing against Mel or Jess. A whole stack of the people I worked with at HM were gay. Jesus Carla, before I met you I was sharing a *flat* with two gay guys.'

'Yeah, and you used to make jokes about them.'

'I—' But the oozing sense of unfairness was already setting in, like cold mud, chilling his mood and tugging his smile away. 'Carla, they used to make jokes about me too. They called me the household het, for fuck's sake. It was all part of the banter. I'm not homophobic. You know that.'

Carla looked at her food, then up at him.

'Yeah, I know.' She mustered a small smile. 'I'm sorry. I'm just tired.'

'Who fucking isn't?' Chris took an overly large pull at his margarita and said nothing more for a while.

Fajitas are not a dish to be eaten in resentful silence, and neither of them did much more than pick at the food. When the waiter stopped by he sensed the mood radiating out from the little table and took the cooling dishes away without comment.

'Any dessert?' he asked carefully when he returned.

Carla shook her head, mute. Chris drew a deep breath.

'No thanks.' He made a sudden decision. 'But you can bring me another margarita. In fact, make it another pitcher.'

'I don't want any more, Chris,' said Carla sharply.

He looked at her with a blank expression he knew would hurt her. 'Who asked you? Pitcher's for me.' He nodded at the waiter, who withdrew with obvious relief. Carla put on her disdainful face.

'You're going to get drunk?'

'Well, looking at the logistics, I would think so. Yes.'

'I didn't come here to get drunk.'

'I didn't ask you to.'

'Chris . . .'

He waited, going nowhere near the opening the forlorn fade in her voice had left him. Her shoulders slumped.

'I'm going home,' she said.

'Okay. Want them to call you a cab?'

'I'll walk,' she said coldly. 'It isn't far.'

'Fine.' He buried himself in the margarita glass as she got up. She hesitated towards him for just a second, barely leaning, and then something stiffened in her carriage and she walked away from the table. Chris very carefully did not look round to watch her leave and when she stalked past the window of the restaurant, he busied himself with his drink again. Out of the corner of his eye, he saw that she did not look in at him.

He worried for a while about her walking home alone, but then stopped himself, recognising the feeling for guilt over the fight. Hawkspur Green was a hamlet, made ludicrously prosperous by the influx of driver-class professionals and their families. It had crime levels appropriate to a playgroup, nothing beyond occasional vandalism and even that mostly graffiti tagging. Plus Carla could look after herself and the house was barely fifteen minutes away. He was just manufacturing excuses to go after her.

Fuck that.

The pitcher came.

He drank it.

68

TEN

South-west zone. The Brundtland.

The decaying concrete bones of the estate squatted mostly in darkness. A handful of unsmashed lights cast sporadic stains of sodium orange on walkways and stairstacks. Isolated lit windows stamped the darkened bulk of buildings in black and yellow code. Child-sized shadows scurried away from Carla's headlights as she parked the Landrover. Once outside the protection of the vehicle, it was worse. She could feel professional eyes watching her set the anti-theft systems, professional ears listening to the quick, escalating whine of the contact stunner charging from the battery. She walked as rapidly as she could without showing fear, away from the vehicle and into the lobby.

Miraculously, the lifts appeared to be working.

She had stabbed at the button more to vent frustration than anything else, and was almost alarmed when the lights above the battered metal doors blinked and the downward arrow illuminated. She blinked a little herself, wiped angrily at a tear that had leaked out from under one eyelid, and waited for the lift to arrive. Her right hand was wrapped tightly around the stungun Chris had bought for her and there was a can of Mace in her left. The lobby at her back was coldly lit by grating-protected halogen bulbs and starkly empty, but the wired glass portals she'd come through were cracked and pushed in at a height suggesting kicks, and the damage looked recent.

FUCK YOU ZEK-TIV CUNTS said a wall to her left in daubed red lettering. Pointless rage; no self-respecting executive was going to be seen dead in the Brundtland.

The lift arrived, but when the doors opened the stench of urine was so thick she gagged. She deliberated for a moment, then compressed her lips and headed for the dimly-lit stairwell to her right. Holding the Mace, hand extended, and keeping the stungun hidden behind her back, she climbed the five double flights of stairs and marched down the corridor with steps intended to convey to anyone who might hear her that she was at home in this stinking pit.

She stopped at number fifty-seven and hammered on the door with the bottom of the Mace can. There was the sound of slow, slurred movement inside and a light sprang up under the door.

'Who's there?'

'Dad, it's Carla.' She tried to keep her voice even, partly out of pride, but more out of a desire not to alarm. Only a year ago, her father had told her, one of the local edge gangs on the estate had forced an elderly woman to open her door by holding a gun to her daughter's head on the doorstep. Once in, they'd ransacked the flat, raped the daughter while her aged mother was forced to watch and then beaten both women into unconsciousness. Apparently, they hadn't bothered to kill either of their victims. They knew there was no need. The police attitude to the zones was containment, not law enforcement. Raids were infrequent and unrelated to actual crimes committed. The estate was gangwit-run. Rape and burglary were not considered transgressions of gang law.

'Carla?' There was the snap of the lock being unfastened, the solid thunk as the security-bolt system she and Chris had paid to have installed was disengaged, and then the door was thrown wide. Her father stood in the doorway, a pool cue hefted in his right hand.

'Carla, what are you doing here at this time of night?' He switched to Norwegian. 'And where's Chris? You didn't come up here alone, did you? For Christ's sake, Carla.'

'Hello, Dad,' she managed.

He ushered her inside, slammed the door shut and engaged the bolt system again. Only then did he relinquish his grip on the cue, dropping the makeshift weapon into an umbrella stand by the door and opening his arms to hug her.

'It's good to see you, Carla. Even if it is half past midnight. What the fuck happened? Oh, don't tell me.' He nodded as the repressed tears began to leak out and she trembled against him. 'Not another fight? Is he downstairs?'

She shook her head against his shoulder.

'Good. I won't have to be diplomatic then.' Erik Nyquist stepped back from his daughter a little and took hold of her chin. 'Why don't you come and have a whisky coffee with me and we can bitch about him in his absence.'

She choked a laugh. He echoed her with a gentle smile.

'That's better,' he said.

So they sat in front of an antique electric fire in the threadbare living room with mugs of cheap coffee and cheaper whisky steaming in their fists and Erik stared into the reddish glow of the heating element while his daughter talked. The tears were under control now, and Carla's voice was firm, an analytical tool sifting through the settled sediment, first of the last few hours, then of the last few weeks, finally of the last few years.

'It's just,' she said. 'I'm sure we didn't always used to fight this much. Did we? You must remember.'

'Well, you never drove across the cordoned zones in the middle of the night alone because you'd been fighting,' Erik admitted. 'That's a first, at least. But if I'm honest? I think you've been having rows with Chris about as long as you've known him to any appreciable depth. Certainly as long as you've been married. I couldn't say if you have more now than you used to, but that's not really the point.'

Carla looked up, surprised. 'It isn't?'

'No, it isn't. Carla, marriage is an artificial state. Invented by the patriarchy to ensure that fathers know who their children are. It's been going on for thousands of years but that doesn't make it right. Human beings were never designed to live like that.'

'I think I've read this somewhere before, Dad.'

'The fact that it was written by your mother,' said Erik severely, 'does not invalidate the argument. We are tribal, not matrimonial.'

'Yeah, yeah. Let's see if I remember how it went. The basic human social unit would have been a matriarchal tribe; a female, child-rearing and knowledge-keeping centre with a protective outer shell of warrior males. Uh, how does it go, children held in common by the tribe, reproduction only understood by the females and—'

'The point is, Carla, exclusive pairing is unnatural. Two people were never meant to be so exclusively much to each other.'

'That's a pretty fucking poor excuse,' she said, then bit her lip.

Erik gave her a reproachful look. 'That isn't what I meant. Look, even in the recent past you had extended families to soak up some of the strain. Now we live in isolated couples or nuclear families, and either both partners are working so hard they never see each other, or they're not working and the stress of living on the poverty line tears them apart.'

'That's a simplification, Dad.'

'Is it?' Erik cradled his mug in both hands and looked back into the red glow from the bar fire. 'Look at where you live, Carla. A village neither of you knew the name of three years ago. No friends living close, no family, not even a workplace social life unless you're prepared to drive for an hour and a half at the end of the evening. All these things put a huge strain on you both, and rows are the result. The natural result. It wouldn't be natural not to fight with someone you share your whole sleeping and waking life with. It's healthy, it provides release, and if you don't hold grudges it shouldn't damage the relationship.'

Carla shivered despite the fire.

'This is damaging us,' she said.

Erik sighed.

'You know what your mother said to me before she went back to Tromsö?'

'Fuck you and that English bitch?' She regretted it as soon as the words left her mouth, surprised that the anger was still there on tap nearly two decades later. But Erik only smiled wryly and if there was pain behind that, it didn't show. She reached across to him with one hand. 'I'm sorry.'

'Don't be.' The smile flickered but held. 'You're right, she did say that. More than once. But she also said that it was high time, that she wasn't really surprised because we didn't have fun together any more. She said that. *We have no fun any more, Erik.*'

'Oh, come on!'

'No, she was right, Carla.' He looked across at her and this time there was pain in his face. 'Your mother was usually right about these things. I was always too busy being political and angry to spot the emotional truths. She hit the nail on the head. We didn't have fun any more. We hadn't had any real fun for years. That's why I ended up with Karen in the first place. She was fun, and that was something your mother and I'd stopped trying to do years ago.'

'Chris and I still have fun,' Carla said quickly.

Erik Nyquist looked at his daughter and sighed again. 'Then you hold onto him,' he said. 'Because if that's true, if it's really true, then what you've got is worth any amount of fights.'

Carla shot him a surprised glance, caught by the sudden gust of emotion in his voice.

'I thought you didn't like Chris.'

Erik chuckled. 'I don't,' he said. 'What's that got to do with it? I'm not sleeping with him.'

She smiled wanly and went back to watching the fire.

'I don't know, Dad. It's just.'

He waited while she assembled her feelings into a coherent shape.

'Just since he went to work at Shorn.' She shook her head wearily. 'It doesn't make any sense, Dad. He's making more money than he ever has, the hours aren't so different to what he used to clock at Hammett McColl. Fuck it, we *ought* to be happy. We've got all the props for it. Why are we falling out more *now?*'

'Shorn Associates. And is he still in Emerging Markets?'

She shook her head. 'Conflict Investment.'

'Conflict Investment.' Erik smacked his lips, then got up and went to the bookcase set against the wall opposite the fire. He dragged a finger across the tightly packed spines of the books on a lower shelf, found what he was looking for and tugged the volume out. Flicking through the pages, he came back to the fire and handed it to her.

'Read that,' he said. 'That page.'

She looked at the book, turned it to see the title. '*The Socialist Legacy.* Miguel Benito. Dad, I'm not in the mood. This isn't about politics.'

'*Everything* is about politics, Carla. Politics *is* everything. Everything in human society anyway. Just read the passage in highlighter.'

She sighed and set down her coffee mug at her feet. Clearing her throat, she picked up the line with one finger and read aloud. ' "Revolutionaries throughout the twentieth century had always been aware"?'

'Yes. That one.'

' "Revolutionaries throughout the twentieth century had always been aware that in order to bring about a convulsive political change".'

'Actually, I meant, read it to yourself.'

She ignored him, ploughing on with the edge of singsong emerging in her voice. ' "In order to bring about a convulsive political change, it was essential to intensify the existing social tensions to the point where all would be driven to choose sides in what would thus be established as a simplistic equation of class conflict. Marxists and their ideological inheritors described this as sharpening the contradictions of society. In populist recog—" Dad is there a point somewhere in all this bullshit?'

'Just finish it, will you.'

She pulled a glum face. ' "In populist recognition of this underlying truth, the cry during the latter half of the the last century became *if you're not part of the solution, you're part of the problem.*" Aaaagh, new paragraph. "What any survivor of late Marxist ideology would be forced to recognise in the politics of the twenty-first century is that the contradictions are now so heavily disguised that it would be the work of decades simply to reveal them, let alone sharpen them into anything resembling a point." A bit like this prose style, huh? Alright, alright, nearly there. "An overall problem is now no longer perceived, therefore an overall solution no longer sought. Any distasteful elements within the world economic order are now considered either candidates for *longer term fine tuning* or worse still an irrevocable by-product of economic laws supposedly as set in stone as the laws of quantum physics. So long as this is believed by the vast majority of the populace in the developed world, the contradictions identified by Marxism will remain hidden and each individual member of society will be left to resolve for themselves the vaguely felt tensions at an internal level. Any effort to externalise this unease will be disdained by the prevailing political climate as discredited socialist utopianism or simply, as was seen in chapter three, *the politics of envy.*" ' She laid down the book. 'Yeah, so what?'

'That's your problem, Carla.' Erik had not sat down while she was reading. He stood with his back to the fire and looked down at her as if she were one of his students. She felt suddenly fifteen years old again. 'Unresolved contradictions. Chris may still be the man you married but he's also a soldier for the new economic order. A corporate samurai, if you want to adopt their own imagery.'

'I know that, Dad. That's nothing new. I know what he does, I know how his world works. I help build and repair the vehicles they use to kill each other, in case you'd forgotten. I'm just as involved in it all, Dad. What?'

He was shaking his head. He crouched to her level and took both her hands gently in his own.

'Carla, this isn't about you and Chris. It's barely about you at all. Benito's talking about *internal* contradictions. Living with what you are, with what your society is. At Hammett McColl, Chris could do that because there was a thin veneer of respectability over it all. At Shorn, there isn't.'

'Oh, bullshit. You've read what these people are like. Dad, you used to write about what they were like, back when there was anyone with the guts to publish it. The only difference between Conflict Investment and Emerging Markets is the level of risk. In Emerging Markets, they don't like conflict or instability. The guys in CI thrive on it. But it's the same principle.'

'Hmm.' Erik smiled and let go of her hands. 'That sounds to me like Chris talking. And he's probably even right. But that's not the point.'

'You keep saying that, Dad.'

Erik shrugged and seated himself again. 'That's because you keep missing it, Carla. You think this is about a rift between you and Chris, and I'm telling you it's not, it's about a rift inside Chris. Now you're saying there's no difference in what he used to do and what he's doing now, and aside from a few semantic quibbles that may be true. But Chris hasn't just changed what he does. He's changed where he does it, and who he does it for, and that's what counts. Along with Nakamura and Lloyd Paul, Shorn Associates is the most aggressive player in the investment field. That applies to their Arbitrage and Emerging Markets divisions just as much as to Conflict Investment. They're the original hard-faced firm. No gloss, no moral rationalisations. They do what they do, they're the best at it. That's what they sell on. You go to Shorn because they're mean motherfuckers, and they'll make money for you, come hell or high water. Fuck ethical investment, just give me a fat fucking return and don't tell me too much about how you got it.'

'You're making speeches, Dad.'

There was a taut silence. Carla stared into the fire, wondering why she found it so easy to sink these barbs into her father. Then Erik Nyquist chuckled and nodded.

74

'You're right, I am,' he said cheerfully. 'Sorry about that. I miss seeing myself in print so much, it all just balls up inside me. Comes out whenever I have someone to talk to.'

'I don't mind,' she said distantly. 'I just wish . . .'

'Wish what?'

She had a vivid flash of recall, toothpaste-white. She would have been about six or seven at the time, staying with grandparents in Tromsö and cocooned in the cold outside/warm inside security the visits there always brought. She remembered Erik and Kirsti Nyquist on skis, propped against each other for support on the hill behind Kirsti's parents' house and laughing into each other's faces. Having fun in the definitive Nyquist fashion that she, as a child, had always imagined would characterise her future married life, the way it would always characterise her parents'.

The flash faded, into the dull red glow of the electric fire. She reached for her father's hand.

'Nothing.'

ELEVEN

'Drink?'

Mike Bryant shook his head. 'Still dealing with a hangover, thanks, Louise. Just water, if you've got it.'

'Of course.' Louise Hewitt closed the steel-panelled door of the office drinks cabinet and hefted a blue two-litre bottle from the table beside it instead. 'Sit down, Mike. Drinking – or whatever – mid week, that can be a pretty lethal mistake.'

'Not lethal,' said Bryant, massaging his temples a little as he sank onto the sofa. 'But definitely a mistake at my age.'

'Yeah, must be hell being thirty-four. I remember it vaguely.' Hewitt poured water into two glasses and sat on the edge of the sofa opposite. She looked at him speculatively. 'Well, I won't toast you with water, but congratulations do seem to be in order. I just got off the phone to Bangkok. That sketch on Cambodia you dropped last time you were out there finally landed on the right guerrilla head.'

Bryant sat up straighter, and forgot his hangover.

'Cambodia? The smack-war thing?'

Hewitt nodded. 'The smack-war thing, as you so elegantly define it. We've got a guerrilla coalition leader willing to deal. Khieu Sary. Sound familiar?'

Bryant drank from his water glass and nodded. 'Yeah, I remember him. Arrogant motherfucker. Had ancestors in the original Khmer Rouge or something.'

'Yeah.' There was the slightest hint of mockery in Hewitt's echo of the grunted syllable. 'Well, it looks like this Sary needs arms and cash to hold the coalition together. The Cambodian government's on the edge of offering an amnesty to any of the heroin rebels who want to come in and disarm. If that happens, the coalition's gone and Sary loses his powerbase. But if he can hang on, our sources in Bangkok reckon he's in line to march on Phnom Penh inside two years.'

'Optimistic.'

'Local agents always are. You know how it is, they pitch rosy so you'll bite. But this guy's been on the money in the past. I'm inclined to go with it. So you'd better break out your copy of Reed and Mason, because this one's yours, Mike.'

Mike Bryant's eyes widened. 'Mine?'

'All yours.' Hewitt shrugged. 'You made it happen, you've got the executive experience to cover it. Like I said, congratulations.'

'Thanks.'

'The proposal is not uncontested,' said Hewitt casually.

Bryant grinned. 'What a surprise. Nakamura?'

'Nakamura and Acropolitic both. Nakamura must have parallel information on Sary, they're offering him essentially the same deal you put together in Bangkok, and the bastard's smart enough to know that forcing us all to tender will bring the prices down.'

'And Acro?'

'They've got the status quo mandate. Official economic advisers to the Cambodian regime. They're in it to squash the proposal before it gets off the ground. It's all already cleared with Trade and Finance.'

'What's the ground?'

'North. Three-hundred-kilometre duel envelope, contracts to be signed in conference auditorium six at the Tebbit Centre. Turn up with blood on your wheels or don't turn up. The word is Nakamura have pulled Mitsue Jones for this one. Flying her in to head up the UK team. Acropolitic don't have anyone in her league, but they'll no doubt be sending their finest. Against all of that, you get a team of three including you. Suggestions?'

'Nick Makin. Chris Faulkner.' There was no hesitation in Bryant's voice.

Hewitt looked dubious. 'Your chess pal, huh?'

'He's good.'

'You don't let personal feelings get in the way of professional judgment around here, Mike. You know that. It's bad for business.'

'That's right, I know that. And I want Faulkner. You said this was mine, Louise. If you don't—'

'Makin doesn't like Faulkner,' said Hewitt sharply.

'Makin doesn't like anyone. That's his secret. The problem here, Louise, is that *you* don't like Faulkner. And it isn't much of a secret, either.'

'May I remind you that you're speaking to the executive partner of this division.' Hewitt's voice stayed level, just a shade cooler all of a sudden. She poured herself more water while she talked. 'For your information, Mike, personal feelings have nothing to do with this. I don't think Faulkner is up to a tender of this magnitude. I also think that you're letting a friendship cloud your professional judgment and I'm going on record with that. This is going to go badly wrong if you're not careful.'

'Louise, this is going to go like a dream.' Bryant grinned wolfishly.

'Makin and Faulkner are both proven hard men on the road and as far as I'm concerned that's the bottom line. We don't have anybody better and you know it.'

There was a pause in which the loudest sound was Louise Hewitt swallowing water. Finally she shrugged.

'Alright, Mike, it's your call. But I'm still going on record against it. And that makes Faulkner one hundred per cent your responsibility. If he fucks up—'

'If he fucks up, Louise, you can fire him and I'll hold the door open.' Bryant flashed the grin again. 'Or the window.'

Hewitt took a disc out of her pocket and tossed it onto the table between them.

'If he fucks up, you'll all be dead,' she said shortly. 'And Shorn'll be out of a medium-term CI contract worth billions. That's the briefing. Route blow-ups, road-surface commentaries. Make sure they both get copies. Make sure Faulkner understands what he's got to do. Blood on the wheels, Mike, or there's no deal.'

'I remember a time,' Bryant let just a hint of his American burlesque tinge the words. 'Used to be enough just to *get* there first.'

Hewitt smiled despite herself. 'Bullshit, you do. You just heard Notley and the others talk about it. And even they barely remember when it was that cuddly. Now get out of here, and don't disappoint me.'

'Wouldn't dream of it.' Bryant picked up the disc and got up to go. At the door, he paused and looked back to where she was still sitting at the desk, sipping her water.

'Louise?'

'Yes.'

'Thanks for giving me this.'

'Don't mention it. Like I said, don't let me down.'

'No, I won't.' Bryant hesitated, then took the plunge. 'You know, Louise, you go on record against Faulkner now and you run the risk of looking very silly when he works out.'

Hewitt gave him an icy, executive-partner smile.

'I'll run that risk, thank you, Michael. Now, was there any other advice you'd like to give me on running the division?'

Bryant shook his head wordlessly and left.

He stopped by Chris's office and found the other man standing at the window, staring out at the hail. Winter was hanging on unseasonably long in London and the skies had been gusting fistfuls of the stuff for weeks.

' 's happening?' he asked as he stuck his head around the door.

Chris jerked visibly as Bryant spoke. Clearly he'd been a long way off.

Coming across the office to the window, Bryant was hard put to see anywhere visibly more attractive than the fifty-third floor of the Shorn tower, and was forced to conclude that Chris had been daydreaming.

'Mike.' Chris turned away from the view to face his visitor. His eyes were red-rimmed and angry with something not in the immediate vicinity. Bryant backed up a step.

'Whoa, Chris. You've got to lay off the crystal edge.' It was only half a joke, he admitted to himself. Chris looked like shit. 'Remember Rancid Neagan. Just say *No, not 'til the weekend.*'

Chris smiled, a forced bending of the lips, as he rolled out the time-honoured Dex and Seth comeback.

'Hey, I don't do that shit no more.'

'What, weekends?'

Reluctantly, the smile became a grin. 'You come up with a move or what?'

'Not yet. But don't worry, the turnaround is in sight.'

This time they both grinned. The match, currently their fifth, was well into the endgame, and, barring a brain haemorrhage, Chris couldn't lose. Which would make it four to one against Bryant, a score that the big man didn't seem to mind as much as Chris had thought he might. Bryant played a flamboyant, queen-centred game and when Chris inevitably worked out a fork and took that piece away from him, Bryant's strategy usually went to pieces. Chris's cautious defensive earthworks stood him in good stead every time and Bryant continued to be perplexed when his assaults broke on the battlements of pawns while a pair or a trio of innocuous pieces chased his exposed king around the board and pinned it to an ignominious checkmate. But he was learning, and seemed content to pay the price of that process in defeats. His calls at weekends came far faster than they had in the beginning, and Chris was taking longer to respond each time. This last match, at over two weeks, had already lasted twice as long as the preceding games. Chris thought it might be time to go up in the loft and bring down some of the battered strategy books his father's brother had given him as a child. He needed to sand off the rust if he was going to hold his lead.

Maybe in return, Mike was teaching him to shoot. They were down to the Shorn armoury a couple of times a week now, firing off Nemex rounds at the holotargets until Chris's gun hand was numb with the repeated kick of the big gun. To his own surprise, he was turning out to have some natural aptitude. He hit things more often than he missed, and if he didn't yet have Mike's casual precision with the Nemex, he was certainly making, in the midst of the crashing thunder on the firing range, a quiet kind of progress.

He wasn't sure how he felt about that.

'Got something for you,' said Bryant, producing the briefing disc from his pocket with a conjuror's flourish. He held it up between index and ring fingers. The light caught it and opened up a rainbow-sheened wedge on the bright silver circle. Chris looked at the colours curiously.

'And that is?'

'Work, my friend. And this season's shot at the big time. TV fame, as many drive-site groupies as you can handle.'

Chris ran the disc at home.

'Look it over,' Bryant told him. 'Kick back and relax, take off your tie and shoes, pour yourself a shot of that iodine-flavoured shit you drink and just let it wash over you. I'm not looking for feedback for at least forty-eight hours.'

'Why can't I just run it now?' Chris wanted to know.

'Because,' leaning closer, with a secret-of-my-success type air, 'that way you're keyed up with anticipation and you eat it up at a deeper level. Your brain really sucks it in, just like the forty-eight-hour wait after gives it time to really stew, and by the time we meet to talk about it, you're ready to boil over with insight.' He winked conspiratorially. 'Old consultancy trick from way back.'

'This just you and me?'

Bryant shook his head. 'Three-man team. You, me, Nick Makin.'

'Oh.'

'Is there a problem with that?' Bryant's eyes narrowed. 'Something I should know about?'

'No, no.'

Watching the closing sequences of the briefing disc, Chris turned it over in his head and tried to work out why he did feel there was a problem with Nick Makin. Makin hadn't exactly come across as friendly, but neither had Hewitt, or Hamilton for that matter, and a lot of Shorn execs had probably heard the story of Elysia Bennett and Chris Faulkner's sentiment attack.

The disc ended with the Shorn Associates logo engraved into a metallic finish on the screen, then clicked off. Chris shelved his thoughts, picked up his drink and went to look for his wife.

He thought for a moment she'd gone to bed with a book, but as he passed the kitchen he saw that the connecting door to the garage was open and the lights were on. Led by the clinking sounds of tools, he walked through, and around the bulk of the Saab, which was jacked up on one side. Carla's coverall-clad legs and hips protruded from under the car beside an unrolled oilskin cloth full of spanners. As he watched she must have stretched out to one side for something, because the angle of her hips shifted and the plain of her stomach changed shape beneath the coveralls. He felt the customary twinge of arousal that her more sinuous movements still fired through him.

'Hey,' he kicked one of her feet. 'What're you doing?'

She stayed beneath the car. 'What does it look like I'm doing. I'm checking your undercarriage.'

'I thought you'd gone to bed.'

There was no response other than the creak of something metallic being tightened.

'I said I thought you'd gone to bed.'

'Yeah, I heard you.'

'Oh. You just didn't think it was worth answering me.'

From the stillness he knew she had stopped work. He didn't hear the sigh, but he could have cued it, accurate to milliseconds.

'Chris, you're looking at my legs. Obviously I haven't gone to bed.'

'Just making conversation.'

'Well, it's not the most engaging conversational gambit I've ever heard, Chris. I'm sorry I didn't pick up on it.'

'Jesus! Carla, sometimes you can be so—' Anger and dismay at the idea of having a row with his wife's feet gave ground in a single jolt to mirth. It was such a ludicrous image that he suddenly found himself smirking and trying to stifle a snort of laughter.

She heard it and slid out from under the car as if spring-loaded there. One hand knuckled across her nose and left streaks of grease.

'What's so funny?'

For some reason, the irritation in her voice combined with her rapid ejection from under the car and the grease on her nose drove the final nail into the coffin of Chris's seriousness. He began to cackle uncontrollably. Carla sat up and watched curiously as he leaned back on the wall and laughed.

'I said what's so . . .'

Chris slid down the wall, spluttering. Carla gave up as a reflexive smile fought its way onto her face.

'What?' she asked, more softly.

'It was just,' Chris was forcing the words out between giggles and snorts. 'Just your legs, you know.'

'Something funny about my legs?'

'Well, your feet really.' Chris put his glass down and wiped at his eyes. 'I, just.' He shook his head and waved a hand with minimal descriptive effect. 'Just thought it was funny, talking to them, you know. Your feet.' He snorted again. 'It's. Doesn't matter.'

She got up from the floor with an accustomed flexing motion and went to crouch beside him. Turning her hand to present the ungrimed back, she brushed it against his cheek.

'Chris . . .'

'Let's go to bed,' he said suddenly.

She held up her hands. 'I've got to wash up. In fact, I need a shower.'

'I'll come with you.'

In the shower, he stood behind her and ran soaped hands over her breasts, down across her belly and into the V of her thighs. She chuckled deep in her throat and reached back for his erection, hands still gritty with the last of the engine grime. For a while it was enough to lean in the corner of the shower stall together, locked in an unhurried kiss, rubbing at each other languidly in the steam and pummelling jets of hot water. When the last of the dirt and soap had cascaded off them and swirled away, Carla swung herself up and braced her upper body in the corner while her thighs gripped Chris around the waist and her hips ground against this.

It was an inconclusive coupling, so Chris shut off the water and staggered with Carla's arms and thighs still locked around him into the bedroom, where they collapsed giggling onto the bed and set about running through every posture in the manual.

Later, they lay on soaked sheets with their limbs hooked around each other and faces angled together. Moonlight fell in through the window and whitened the bed.

'Don't go,' she said suddenly.

'Go?' Chris looked down in puzzlement. He had slid out of her some time ago. 'I'm not going anywhere. I'm staying here in this bed with you. Forever.'

'Forever?'

'Well, till about six-thirty anyway.'

'I'm serious, Chris.' She lifted herself to look into his face. 'Don't go on this Cambodia thing. Not up against Nakamura.'

'Carla.' It was almost a reprimand the way he said it. 'We've been over this before. It's my job. We don't have any choice. There's the house, the cards, how are we going to cover those things if I'm not driving?'

'I know you've got to drive, Chris, but at Hammett McColl—'

'It's not the same, Carla. At HM I already had my rep. I've got to carve it out all over again at Shorn, or some snot-nosed junior analyst is going to call me out, and once that starts you're watching your tail forever. If they think you're easing up, going soft, they're on you like fucking vultures. The only way to beat that is to stay hard and keep them scared. That way you make partner, and from then on it's a Sunday afternoon spin. They can't touch you. No one below partner status is allowed to call you out.' A vague disquiet passed over him as he remembered what Bryant had told him about Louise Hewitt and the partner called Page. 'And partner challenges are few and far between. You see them coming. You can negotiate. It's more civilised at that level.'

'Civilised.'

'You know what I mean.'

Carla was silent for a while. Then she rolled away from him and huddled herself into the pillow.

'The disc says Nakamura are going to send Mitsue Jones.'

Chris shifted a little and tucked in behind her. 'Yes, probably. But if you'd stayed to watch the rest of it, you would have seen that Jones hasn't duelled in the last six months. And it won't be her home turf. There's a good chance they won't even use her because of that. Not knowing the road can get you killed a lot faster than going up against a better driver. And anyway, driving on the same team as Mike Bryant and this other guy Makin, I've got nothing to worry about. Really.'

Carla shivered. 'I saw a profile of Jones a couple of years ago. They say she's never lost a tender.'

'Nor have I. Nor has Bryant as far as I know.'

'Yes, but she's driven over two dozen challenges, and she's only twenty-eight. I saw her interviewed, and she looks scary, Chris. Really scary.'

Chris laughed gently against the skin at the nape of Carla's neck. 'That's just camerawork. In the States, she's done centrefolds for Penthouse Online. Pouting lips, the works. She's a fucking pin-up, Carla. It's all hype.'

For a moment, he almost believed it himself.

'When is it?' she asked quietly.

'Wednesday next week. Dawn start. I've got to sleep over at the office Tuesday night. You want to come in and stay in the hospitality suites with me?'

'No. I'll go across to Dad's.'

'You could always ask him to come and stay here for a change.' Chris frowned and nuzzled at her back. 'You know I don't like the thought of you sleeping in that shithole. I worry about you.'

Carla turned round to face him again. It was hard to tell which was uppermost in her expression, affection or exasperation. 'You worry about me? Chris, listen to yourself, will you? Next Wednesday you're out on the road, duelling, and you're worried about me sleeping in some substandard housing. Come on.'

'There's been a lot of violence on that estate,' said Chris doggedly. 'If I had my way—'

He stopped, not entirely sure what he wanted to say next.

'You'd what?'

He shook his head. 'Doesn't matter. Forget it. I just think, why can't Erik come and stay here with us for a change?'

'You know why.'

Chris sighed. 'Yeah, because I'm a fucking suited parasite on the lives of honest working men and women.'

'Got it in one.' Carla kissed him. 'Come on, I'll be alright. You just worry about keeping my spaced armour intact. If you come back with the wings all chewed up like last time, you really will see some violence.'

'Oh yeah?'

She jabbed him in the ribs. 'Oh yeah. I didn't put in all that work to have you broadside and stick like a fucking no-namer. You drive like it matters what happens to your wheels, or that'll be the last blowjob you see this year.'

'Have to go to my usual supplier then. Ow!'

'Fucking piece of shit! Usual supplier did you say? Who else are you getting blowjobs from, you piece of—'

'Blowtorch! I thought you said blow*torch*.'

Their mingled laughter penetrated the glass of the window and sounded faintly, in the still of the garden beyond. Had Erik Nyquist been there in the darkness, he would have been forced to admit that what he could hear was, indisputably, the sound of his daughter and the man she had married having fun. He might even have been glad to hear it.

Unfortunately, Erik Nyquist was nearly a hundred kilometres south-west of the laughter, listening instead through paper-thin walls to the sounds of an edge dealer beating his girlfriend to pulp. In the garden, the only witness to the noise of Chris and Carla's hilarity was a large tawny owl who watched the window unwinkingly for a moment, and then turned its attention back to the more pressing matter of dis-embowelling the half-dead field mouse in its talons.

TWELVE

Apparently, it was a long-standing Shorn tradition to do final briefings down among the variously stripped and jacked-up bodies of the company workshops. Chris could see where the custom originated. Nominally, it gave the executives the opportunity to do some corporate bonding with the mechanics overseeing their final vehicle checks. Far more importantly, the scattered flare of welding torches and the stink of scorched metal put the hard edge of reality on what might have otherwise seemed very far removed from the air-conditioned civility of a more conventional briefing room. In Shorn parlance, it avoided any potential ambiguity.

Accordingly, Hewitt kept it brutally short. Keep it tight, don't fuck up. Come back with the contract. Leave the others in pieces on the road. She thanked the chief mechanic personally for his team's hard work, and walked away.

After she'd gone, Bryant went for Indian carry-out and Chris sat in the open passenger doorway of the Saab, leafing absently through the background printout on Mitsue Jones, while two mechanics in logo-flashed company coveralls strove in vain to find anything worth doing to the engine that Carla had not already done.

'Chris?' It was Bryant, somewhere off amidst the clang and crackle of the body shop. 'Chris, where are you?'

'Round here.'

There was the sound of stumbling, a clatter and cursing. Chris repressed a grin and did not look up from the printout. Ten seconds later Bryant appeared round the opened hood of the Saab, cartons of take-out food in his arms and a huge naan bread jammed into his mouth. He seated himself without ceremony on a pile of worn tyres opposite Chris and started laying out the food. He took the naan bread out of his mouth and gestured with it towards two of the cartons.

'That's yours. Onion bhaji, and dhansak. That's the mango chutney. Where'd Makin go?'

Chris shrugged. 'Toilet? He looked pretty constipated.'

'Nah, Makin always looks like that. Anal-retentive.'

A shadow fell across the food cartons and Bryant looked up, biting on the naan again. He talked through the mouthful.

'Nick. Your tikka's in there. Rice there. Spoons.'

Makin seated himself with a wary glance at Chris.

'Thanks, Michael.'

There was silence for a while, broken only by the sounds of chewing. Bryant ate as if ravenous and finished first. He cast glances at both men.

'Make your wills?'

'Why? I'm not going to die.' Makin looked across at Chris. 'Are you?'

Chris shrugged and wiped his fingers, still chewing.

'See how I feel.'

Bryant coughed laughter. Makin allowed himself a small, precise smile. 'Vewy good. It's good to have a sense of humour. I hear they ah big on it at HM. Must make losing more beahable.'

'Yeah.' Chris smiled gently back. 'It can make winning pwetty wadical too, you should twy it.'

Makin tensed. His glasses gleamed in the overhead arc light.

'Does the way I speak amuse you?'

'Not weally.'

'Hey, you guys,' Bryant protested. 'Come on.'

'You know, Chwis,' Makin looked down at his open right hand as if considering using it as a fist. 'I'm not a chess player. Not much of a game player at all. Oh, I know you like symbolism. Games. Humour. All good ways of avoiding confontation.'

He tossed his fork into the cooling sauces of Chris's carton.

'But tomorrow is a confontation. You can't laugh it away, you can't turn it into a game. Mitsue Jones won't play chess with you. She'll hit you with evything she's got and she'll hit you *fast*.'

On the last word he clapped his hands violently and his eyes pinned Chris from behind the rectangular-paned screens of his glasses.

'There'll be no time to consider your moves out there. You must see it coming.' He snapped his fingers. 'And act. Nothing else.'

Chris nodded and looked down at his food for a moment. Then his hand whiplashed out and snatched Makin's glasses from his nose.

'I think I see what you mean,' he said brightly.

'Chris.' There was a warning in Mike Bryant's voice.

Without his glasses, Makin looked a lot less sharkish, for all his clear lack of vision defects. The narrowly watchful face now looked simply thin. When he spoke, his voice had gone thick and slow with rage, but there was nothing to back it up.

'Michael, I don't think I want to dwive with this clown.'

Chris held out his hand. 'Would you like your glasses back?' he asked innocently.

Oddly, it was Bryant who snapped.

'Alright you two, that's enough. Nick, you asked for that, so don't act so fucking superior. And Chris, give him back his glasses. Jesus, I'm going up against Nakamura with a pair of fucking kids.'

'Michael, I don't think—'

'No, you *didn't* think, Nick. You just opened your fucking mouth. Louise asked me to head up this team. When she asks you, you can pick who drives with you. Until then, just get in line and keep a lid on it.'

The small circle of space between the three men rocked with silent tension. Behind them, the two mechanics looking over the Saab had stopped what they were doing to watch the action. Nick Makin drew in a compressed breath, then took his glasses back without a word and stalked away.

Bryant prodded at the food cartons for a while. Finally he glanced up and met Chris's gaze.

'Don't pay any attention to him. He'll have calmed down by morning.' He brooded a little. 'I think this chess thing might be backfiring. Symbolic conflict isn't what you'd call a popular concept around here.'

'What, no game-playing? Come on, you're winding me up.'

'Yeah, there's *games*, sure. Some of the other Shorn guys I know are into those alliance games on the net. The *Alphamesh* leagues, stuff like that. But chess.' Bryant shook his head. 'Just not cool, man. Makin isn't the first to mention it. I don't think it'll be catching on.'

Chris picked an onion bhaji out of a carton and bit into it reflectively. 'Yeah, well. Always happens when you challenge someone's world view. Means they have to re-evaluate. Most people don't like to think that hard.'

Bryant forced a chuckle that loosened up audibly as he produced it.

'Yeah, me included. Still, Makin should know better. No way you start this shit at a time like this.'

'Going to be bloody tomorrow, huh?'

'You heard of Jones?'

'Me and the rest of the Western world, yeah.'

Bryant looked at him. 'There's your answer, then.'

'Well,' Chris tossed the half-eaten bhaji back into the carton. 'I always wondered what the big bonuses were for.'

'You keep your mind on that bonus tomorrow,' grinned Bryant, regaining some of his good cheer. 'And everything will work out just fine. You'll see. Easy money.'

The Acropolitic car caught the central reservation barrier head-on, flipped effortlessly into the air and came down on its back, wheels still spinning. A figure slumped broken and still within. Chris, who'd been expecting a prolonged dogfight with the other car, whooped and slammed a fist against the roof of his own vehicle as he swept past.

'Acropolitic, thank you and *goodnight!*'

'Nice,' said Mike Bryant's voice over the intercom. 'Now form up and stay tight. Those guys were in pristine condition, which to my way of thinking means Nakamura aren't on this stretch.'

'Conforming,' said Nick Makin crisply. Chris smirked, raised his eyes to the roof and, saying nothing, tucked into the wedge behind Mike.

Behind them, the wrecks of the Acropolitic team lay strewn across three kilometres of highway, like the abandoned toys of a child with emerging sociopathic tendencies. Two of them were burning.

'Conforming.'

Chris wasn't the only one smirking at Makin's fighter-pilot pretensions. Thirty kilometres up ahead, Mitsue Jones grinned disbelievingly as the voice crackled out of her car radio. She grasped the edge of her open door and hinged herself out of the Mitsubishi Kaigan. The wind came and battered at her two-hundred-dollar Karel Mann tumbling spike cut.

Oh well.

The face beneath the jagged hair was pin-up perfect, tanned from a month on the Mexican Pacific coast and made up to accent her Japanese heritage. In keeping with Nakamura duel tradition, she went formally suited, a black Daisuke Todoroki ensemble whose sole concession to the driving was the flared and carefully vented skirt. There were flat-heeled leather boots on her feet, sheer black tights on her legs.

'Looking *good*, Mits.'

She cranked round in the direction of the shout. Behind the long sunken lines of the Kaigan, her colleagues' own shorter, blunter Mitsubishi cruisers were parked with raked precision along the overgrown curve of the intersection roundabout. The two Nakamura wedge men were cutting up lines of edge on the sleek black hood of the closest car. One of them waved at her.

Jones pulled a face and turned to the motorway bridge railing on the other side of the road. Beyond the bridge, the green of the landscape rose in a series of granite flecked interlocking spurs that blocked out the view of the road at about five kilometres distance. She crossed the road and prodded at the feet of the fourth Nakamura team member, who sat with his back to the rails, checking the load on his Vickers-Cat shoulder-launcher. He glanced up as Jones kicked him and grinned through his beard.

'Ready to rock 'n' roll.' It came out surfer-drawled. His English, like hers, was West Coast American. The association ran back a couple of years. He nodded across at the other two men and their edge ritual. 'You cool with that?'

Jones shrugged. 'Whatever works. New York says they're the best we've got around here, and they should know.'

'They should.' The missileer laid his weapon aside and got up. Standing he was a giant, towering over Jones's diminutive frame. 'So what's the disposition?'

'Acropolitic are out of the game.' Jones leaned on the bridge rail. 'Shorn did the shit work for us, just like we figured. All we have to do is sweep them up.'

The missileer leaned beside her. 'And you're sure this is going to work?'

'It worked at Denver, didn't it?'

'It was new at Denver.'

'On this side of the Atlantic it's still new. Total press blackout until US Trade and Finance thrash out the precedent.' A cold smile. 'Which, I'm reliably informed by our government liaison unit, is going to take the rest of the year. The report won't be out till next spring. These guys aren't going to know what hit them.'

'It could still be disallowed.'

'No.' She seemed lost in the southward perspectives of the road below them. 'I had the legal boys check the rulings back as far as they go. No discharge of projectile weaponry from a moving vehicle, no substantial destruction to be inflicted with a projectile weapon. We'll get through the same loophole we used in Colorado.'

Out of the open door of the Kaigan battlewagon, the radio crackled again. The voices of the men they were waiting for wavered as the set strained to pick up and decode the scrambled channel. There was a sudden increase in volume and clarity as the Shorn team cleared some geographical obstacle in amongst the rising land behind the bridge. Mitsue Jones straightened up.

'Better get in position, Matt. Feels like showtime.'

Mike Bryant saw the intersection bridge up ahead as they cleared the last spur and he let a fraction of his speed bleed off.

'Watch the bridge,' he said easily. 'Watch your peripherals till we're past. Keep it tight.'

On the northside ramp, Mitsue Jones heard him and grinned as she slipped her driving glasses on. In the rearview mirror, she saw Matt settle into a firing stance with the Vickers-Cat. She let off the parking brake and the Mitsubishi shifted on the hard shoulder.

The missile leapt out, trailing a thin vapour thread as it went.

As they hit the bridge, Bryant saw it. Through the windscreen a column

89

of greasy smoke lifted from the hills up ahead. A muffled crump rolled in to accompany the explosion.

'See that?' He braked a little more, puzzled. 'They must be in trouble up ahead.'

'I don't know, Mike.' Chris's voice crashed into the cabin. 'Trouble with who? Tender was all over the news this week. No one'll be out here who doesn't have to be.'

'Maybe one of those fancy Mits' fuel feeds blew up on them,' suggested Makin.

'Could be.' Chris's tone said he thought it was a stupid idea, but since they'd started the run both he and Makin had shut down the bullshit. 'I still don't like, *go right!! Right!!!*'

The yell came too late. They were under the bridge and past the access ramp and the sleek black shapes on the left came spilling directly down the grass slope like commandos breaching a wall defence. The lead Nakamura car hit the highway at reckless speed, bounced and slammed into Mike Bryant's BMW.

'Fuck!'

Bryant hauled on the wheel, too slow. The second Nakamura vehicle scuttled through the gap behind him and came up on his right flank. There was a long grating clang as the two Mitsubishi cruisers sandwiched him. Bryant caught a flash of a third vehicle, longer and lower, pulling ahead and knew what was going to happen. He wrestled desperately with wheel and brakes, but the clinch was set. The Nakamura wingmen had him.

'Can you get these motherfuckers off me,' Bryant tried for a nonchalant tone, but sweat was beading on his face. Every move he tried to break free was matched. 'They're going to head-to-head me.'

A side impact jarred through Bryant.

'No fucking way.' Chris yelled his results. 'They're locked on tight, Mike. You've got to crash-stop.'

'Can't afford to lose the momentum, Chris. You know that.'

'You can't afford to stay in theah, Mike.' The crisp edge of control in Makin's tone made him sound almost prissy. 'Chwis is wight. Dwop out, pick it up after.'

'No fucking way.'

Up ahead, the long, low Mitsubishi battlewagon whipped around on shrieking tyres and came back up the highway towards the locked-up Shorn leader.

'Nick,' Bryant's voice was strained. 'That's Jones up ahead. Get out there and see if you can't derail her.'

'On it.' Makin's BMW flashed on the edge of Bryant's vision as it accelerated away from the three-vehicle clinch. Bryant blew out breath, hard and fast, and settled into his speed.

'What about me?'

'You hang back, Chris. This doesn't work, I'm going to need you.'

Up ahead, he watched as Nick Makin drove hard at what had to be Mitsue Jones's vehicle. A hot knot of hope pulsed through his guts in defiance of the icy knowing that told him Jones would not be stopped. The Nakamura team had set him up with consummate skill, and they'd left him with only two options. Slam stop and lose the duel inertia; in effect drop out of the combat, admit Nakamura's tactical superiority and have to drive catch up for the next two hundred kilometres—

An image of Chris's chessboard flashed through his mind.

Symbolic defeat.

Or—

The Mitsubishi flinched aside and left Makin stalled across the highway. Bryant grimaced and floored his accelerator. The two Nakamura vehicles matched it effortlessly. The battlewagon came on.

'Chris, this is going to be messy,' he gritted. 'Get yourself clear.'

Seconds from the chicken head-to-head, the two Nakamura wingmen peeled away as if their vehicles were under the command of a single driver. Bryant caught a face grinning at him from the left-hand vehicle and a hand lifted in farewell. Jones's car was almost on him. The radio crackled at him.

'Sayonara, Bryant-san.'

Mitsue Jones must have jerked the wheel at the last possible moment. Bryant misread it and stayed on line, but Jones had left the rear of the Mitsubishi in his path. The BMW hit at speed and the front left wing of the car kicked into the air. Bryant yelled, incoherent with shock as his vehicle left the road. The Omega turned lazily in the air and came down on its side, trailing a carpet of sparks across the asphalt. Three seconds into the skid, it ploughed into the central reservation.

Jones heard the yell but had no time for anything other than fighting her own vehicle back under control. The Mitsubishi whipped about on the impact and staggered sideways. For three seconds the wheel was like a live thing under her hands, and then she had it back. She braked the cruiser towards a smoking halt, facing back the way she'd come.

Bryant's BMW lay on one side, jammed into the central barrier and leaning jauntily. The vehicle's roof faced out, windscreen showing spiderweb cracked in the weak spring sunlight. Bryant was pinned in clear view, struggling with his belt. Jones snarled a grin and came off the brake, slamming in the gear as the cruiser freewheeled backward, accelerating hard against the inertial drag. The Kaigan's engine shrilled and the cruiser sprang forward.

Trapped and twisted against his own seatbelt, Mike Bryant heard the sound and flailed about to look. By the time he had forced his head round far enough to see, the Mitsubishi was almost on him.

He just had time to scream.

'*Ah, fu—*'

And the cruiser was gone, jolted past, and there was a titanium-grey Saab crunched to its tail. Two engines in savagely low gear, roaring against each other, and the shriek of steel under stress.

'Chris?'

Chris's voice drifted into the upturned space, laconic.

'Be right back.'

Metal tore down one wing of the Nakamura car and ripped clear, exposing the driver's side rear wheel. Jones shrieked abuse in Japanese, her English abandoned in momentary fury. Chris was already past, yelling into his mike with sudden urgency.

'Makin, where are you?'

'Up ahead.' There was a tight edge of panic in the other man's voice. 'I've got both these motherfuckers on my tail. I think they're going to lock me up same as Mike.'

'On my way.'

Chris spotted the Nakamura wingmen a pair of seconds later, dancing spirals behind and alongside Makin's BMW. As he watched, the left-hand car slipped in and struck the Shorn car a glancing blow. Makin jerked sideways and the other Mitsubishi rammed him from the rear. It was consummate teamwork, Chris had time to reflect briefly, something that the young guns at Shorn could learn from and probably never would. Then he was on the left-hand car. He hit it at full acceleration and felt the impact down to the roots of his teeth.

'Right,' he muttered.

The Nakamura car tried to pull away but didn't have the power. Chris gave up a hand's breadth of space, then floored the pedal and hit again. This time the wingman tried to skate sideways right. Chris matched the move. He gave up the hand's breadth again and when the Nakamura driver slewed to the left, he let him. He went with the move and forced it. Another jolt and he was jammed onto the rear fender, driving the other car towards the grass bank that lined the left-hand hard shoulder.

It could have been better – could for example have been the drop on the other side of the carriageway – but it would have to do.

Something flashed in his peripheral vision, the glossy black of the other Nakamura car. The other wingman was coming to his comrade's aid. Chris fought down the urge to let go and face the new threat. His voice went gritted into the mike.

'Makin, get rid of this fucker, will you?'

'Done.'

The BMW was there, twilight blue jostling with the black for position. The two cars peeled away as the Nakamura driver fled. Chris turned his full attention back to killing the man in front of him.

The rapid rumble as they crossed the cats-eye line of the hard shoulder and the wingman finally panic-braked as he neared the bank. It was far too late. Chris hit the overdrive on the Saab's gear box and drove his opponent hard up the fifty-degree incline. As soon as the other vehicle was fully off the road, he braked savagely and dropped back. Denied the power of the Saab's pushing, and subject to his own desperately applied brakes, the wingman slithered back down the grass, hit the road surface with an overload of kinetic energy to shed and tumbled across the three lanes into the crash barrier.

The Mitsubishi exploded.

'Bonus,' said Chris to nobody in particular, and threw the Saab into a U-turn crash-stop.

A kilometre back along the highway, he saw what he'd been expecting. Mitsue Jones's battlewagon heading directly for him, trailing wreckage from one wing like a shark with prey in its jaws. Chris engaged the Saab's launch gear. The rear wheels squealed on the road, scrabbled for purchase and found it. The Saab leapt forward.

Past the egg-yolk yellow and billowing black smoke of the crashed and burnt wingman, back down the slope towards the bridge where the duel had kicked in. The hungry roar of the engine seemed to recede as he plunged back towards the Nakamura car. He had time to notice the marred lines of the other vehicle as it ballooned in his windscreen, time to notice the pewter cloud formations smeared across the sky behind, time even to see the gusting wind blowing the grass flat along the embankment to his right—

At the last possible moment, Jones flinched left, covering the torn wing damage as he guessed she would. He ploughed into her right-hand rear side with brutal precision. The Saab spaced armouring held and opened a huge gap over the Mitsubishi's rear tyre. Chris hit the brakes and at the relatively low speed he'd developed the U-turn came comfortably. He was back on Jones's tail before she'd made five hundred metres of road away from him.

The Mitsubishi was crippled, limping at barely a hundred. He matched speeds and glanced across at the other car. Polarised glass hid Jones from view.

Finish it.

He slewed sideways, caught the exposed rear tyre on the leading edge of his front fender and braked. Textbook manoeuvre. The tyre ripped and exploded with a muffled bang. He felt the front fender unstitch along half its length with the force of the impact, but the rest held.

Yes! Carla, you fucking beauty!

The Kaigan jerked and began to skid. Chris worked his pedals, gunned the engine and rammed into the rear of the Mitsubishi as it floated past ahead of him. The skid built, the car wallowed on the road and Chris steered back across and around. Another sharp jab at the retreating side of the car. The driver's side door dented inward, and Mitsue Jones was irretrievable. The Nakamura battlewagon skated a figure of eight in towards the bank and hit with an audible crump.

Chris brought the Saab to a screeching halt, braking clouds of rubber smoke off the asphalt as he slid past Jones's wreck. A three-sixty sweep showed no other vehicles in either direction. He engaged the reverse and backed up gingerly to check on his handiwork.

'Chris?' It was Bryant's voice, distorted over the comset.

'Yeah, Mike. I'm here.' The strange calm was back, the sky and windswept landscape pressing down on his consciousness like a thumb on an eyeball. He gave the status report through lips that felt slightly numb. 'One wingman down, flamed out. Think Makin got the other. You okay?'

'I will be as soon as someone comes and cuts me out of this fucking wreck. What about Jones?'

He stared at the wrecked battlewagon. The sleek bodywork was torn and crumpled, sunk on tyres that had blown out somewhere in the crash. Steam curled up from the gashed radiator grille like smoke, was whipped away by the wind. And in amidst all that calm, it looked as if Jones was trying to kick the driver's side door open. The buckled metal quivered but didn't shift.

Finish it.

'Jones is out of the game,' he said.

Mike's whoop came through, bristling with static and overload distortion. Chris dropped his hand to grasp the gear lever, and with the motion a small ripple arose in the pit of his stomach. It was nothing much, the feeling of having eaten too much sweet food, but as his hand touched the lever, he was suddenly slightly sick of the whole thing.

Then finish it!

Burn her up. The thought belched abruptly up from the deepest mud-geyser recesses of his being, and it gripped him like claws. It was the sickness of the moment before, turned up to full. The edgy thrill of rollercoaster exhilaration as he turned the sticky new idea over in his mind. *Ram the tank and barbecue that bitch. Go on! If it doesn't blow when it ruptures, you can go and light her from close up. Like—*

He shook himself free of it with a shiver. Impossible to believe he'd even been considering it. After all, what if the tank blew when he hit—

They almost never do.

'Too risky.' He heard himself talking out loud to the hot mud-thing in his head and what he heard sounded too much like whining. He grimaced and dropped the car into reverse again. Much better just to—

He backed up another twenty metres, aligned the nose of the Saab and then crushed the accelerator smoothly to the floor. The Saab leapt across the the short gap and slammed into the driver's side door. Metal crunched and the Mitsubishi rocked on its springs. The glass in the side window cracked and splintered. He backed up and watched carefully to see if there was any movement.

Do it again! Finish it!

She is finished.

Hewitt, with the Nemex in her hand. *You bring back their plastic.*

He heard his own voice in the Shorn conference chamber two months ago.

Nobody likes ambiguity.

Yeah, and this is real fucking ambiguous, Chris. So either you go for the burn, or you take that pistol in your pocket and go and recover Jones's fucking plastic right now.

'Chris, are you okay?' Bryant, sounding concerned. His voice ruptured the ominous quiet on the comlink, and every second that Chris left without replying was a stillness that prickled.

'Yeah. I'm fine.' He unlatched the door and pushed it open. The Nemex had already somehow found its way into his hand. 'Be right back.'

He climbed out and advanced cautiously towards the Mitsubishi, gun-hand extended and trembling slightly. Steam was still boiling from the engine space, hissing as it went, but there was no scent of petrol. The car's fuel system, classic weakness in most Mitsubishi battlewagons, had apparently not ruptured.

Chris stopped less than a metre away from the smashed glass of the polarised window and peered in over the sight of the Nemex. Mitsue Jones lay, still strapped into the driver's seat, face bloodied and right arm hanging slackly at her side. She was still conscious and as Chris's pale shadow fell across the car window she looked up. Blood had run into her right eye and gummed it shut, but the other eye was desperately expressive. Her left hand came up and across her trapped body in a futile warding gesture.

Finish it!

Chris shielded his face with one hand and levelled the Nemex on Jones's face.

Nobody likes ambiguity.

The shot echoed out flatly across the pewter-smeared sky. The blood splattered warm on his fingers.

THIRTEEN

'Would you say that this tender was excessively bloody?'

Chris's face felt stretched tight under the make-up. Studio lights made his eyes ache with glare. Beside him, Bryant betrayed no discomfort as he tilted his head back at an angle and swivelled slightly on his chair.

'That's a tricky question, Liz.'

He paused. Pure theatrical bullshit, the bloodshed question was a staple of all business news post-tender interviews. Bryant had had nearly a full day to think about his answer.

Liz Linshaw waited. She crossed long, tanned legs and readjusted the datadown clipboard on her short-skirted lap. From where he was sitting, slightly to the left of Bryant's centre-stage, Chris could see liquid crystal sentences spilling down the clipboard screen. Her next set of cues from the studio control room.

From where he was sitting, he could also see the swell Liz Linshaw's left breast made where it squeezed up in the open neck of her blouse. He shifted his gaze uncomfortably, just as Bryant launched into his answer.

'The thing is, Liz, any competitive tender is bound to involve a certain degree of conflict. If it didn't, then the whole market ethos of what we're doing here would be lost. And in the case of a tender of this magnitude, obviously the parties involved are going to play hard. That, sadly but necessarily, means bloodshed. But that's exactly the way it should be.'

Liz Linshaw made out she was taken aback. 'There *should* be bloodshed? You're saying that it's *desirable*?'

'Desirable, no.' Bryant put on a schoolmasterly smile that looked Notley-derived. Beside him, Louise Hewitt nodded sober agreement. 'But consider. The situation in Cambodia is extreme. These people are not part of some theoretical economic model. They are involved in a life-and-death struggle to determine the future of their nation. At Shorn, we've just been appointed their financiers. We are supposed to fund and advise these people and, I might add, take a fair chunk of their GNP as a fee. Now, if you were a Cambodian, what kind of exec would you want? A suited theoretical economist with computer models he says define your reality half a world away? Or a warrior who has put his own life on the line to earn his place beside you?'

'You call yourself a warrior.' Linshaw made an elegant gesture that might have been acceptance. 'And obviously the fact that it's your team here at the Tebbit Centre this evening proves your credentials in that department. Alright. But does that necessarily make you the best economist for the job? Does a good economist have to have blood on his hands?'

'I'd say a practising free-market economist has blood on his hands, or he isn't doing his job properly. It comes with the market, and the decisions it demands. Hard decisions, decisions of life and death. We have to make those decisions, and we have to get them right. We have to be determined to get them right. The blood on our hands today is the blood of our less determined colleagues, and that says something. To you, Liz, to our audience, and most of all to our Cambodian clients, that blood says that when the hard decisions come, we will not flinch from them.'

'How do you feel about that, Chris?' Liz Linshaw swivelled abruptly to face him. 'You eliminated Mitsue Jones today. What do you think the Nakamura team lacked that gave you the edge?'

Chris blinked. He'd been drifting.

'I think, ah. Ah, they were very polished, but . . .' He scrambled after the answer they'd worked out earlier when they ran the question check-list with the programme's producer. 'But, ah, there didn't seem to be much flexibility of response in the way they played as a team. Once they'd sprung the trap and it failed, they were sluggish.'

'Was this the first time you'd driven against Nakamura, Chris?'

'Yes. Ah, well, apart from a few informal skirmishes, yes.' Chris got his act together. 'I drove against Nakamura junior execs in two con-sortium bids when I was working at Hammett McColl, but it's not the same. In a consortium bid, people tend to get in each other's way a lot. They usually haven't had a lot of time to train. It's easy to break team wedges. This was a whole different engine.'

'Yes.' She smiled brilliantly at him. 'Was there any point where you were afraid Shorn were going to lose to Nakamura?'

Hewitt sat forward, bristling.

'I don't think we ever came that close,' said Bryant.

'Yes, but you were trapped in wreckage for most of the duel, Michael.' There was just a hint of acid in Linshaw's voice. 'Chris, you were the one who actually took Jones down. *Was* there ever a critical point?'

'I—' Chris glanced across at Bryant who was wearing a rather thin smile. The big man's shoulders lifted in the barest of shrugs. Beyond him, Hewitt showed as much emotion as a block of granite. 'I think the missile ploy caught us the way it was intended to – and the jury's still out on whether that was a legal manoeuvre or not – but after Nakamura actually engaged, we were never really up against it.'

'I see.' Liz Linshaw leaned forward. 'This is a great moment for you, isn't it Chris. The hero of the hour. And coming so soon after your transfer. You must be over the moon.'

'Uh, yes.' He shrugged. 'It's my job.'

'A job you enjoy?'

Mindful of Hewitt's gaze, Chris manufactured a smile. 'I wouldn't be in this line of work if I didn't like it, Liz.'

'Of course.' Linshaw seemed to have got what she wanted. She turned her attention to Hewitt. 'Now, Louise, you made all this happen. How do you feel about the way your team performed?'

Chris switched off again as Hewitt began to mouth the viewer-consumable platitudes.

'What was that all about?'

He asked Bryant the question later, as they sat in front of whisky tumblers in the hotel bar of the Tebbit Centre. Outside, wind-driven rain lashed impotently at big glass panels that gave a view out onto drenched and darkened hills. Makin had cried off early, pleading tomorrow's crack-of-dawn start. It was pretty obvious he was choked about Chris's guest spot on the Liz Linshaw evening special. Standard practice in post-tender reports was to interview only the team leader and the divisional head, but Bryant had been crowing about Chris's performance from the moment they cut him out of the wreckage of his BMW. Makin had gone conspicuously unmentioned.

'That?' Bryant gave him a wry grin. 'Well, let's just say I'm not flavour of the month with Ms Linshaw at the moment.'

Chris frowned. His nerves were still a little shot from the duel and he found his mind tended to skitter when he tried to concentrate. At the same time, as if compensating for its poor performance in other areas, it spat chunks of memory at him with near total recall. Now, as if listening to it on tape, he heard the words Liz Linshaw had used over the radio that first morning as he drove in to the new job at Shorn: *Still nothing on the no-name call out for Mike Bryant at Shorn Associates, don't know where you've got to, Mike, but if you can hear me we're anxious to hear from you.* He strained to remember Bryant and Linshaw's body language the evening of the quarterly review party, but his recall was too alcohol-damaged to trust.

'Were you two, ah . . . ?'

Bryant grinned and sank half his whisky. 'If, by that delicate *ah*, you mean *fucking*, then yes. Yes, we were fucking.'

Chris sat still, remembering Suki.

As if reading his mind, Bryant said, 'It was no big deal. Scratching an itch, you know. She gets off on drivers the way some guys do on Italian holoporn. It was back when Suki was, you know, off sex. Just after Ariana was born.' He shrugged. 'Like I said, no big deal.'

Chris tried to think of an appropriate question to fill the space. In the background, something insipid lilted from the bar's sound system.

'So how long did it last?'

'Well,' Bryant turned to face him, getting comfortable. 'In the initial stages, about eight months. I'm telling you, Chris, she was hot. We both were. She was doing this in-depth study of Conflict Investment, for a series and then, you know, that book, *New Asphalt Warriors*. So we saw a lot of each other without anyone wondering. She used to do these interviews and then we'd get off camera and fuck like rabbits wherever there was a lockable door. I used to get hard-ons just talking to her on camera. Even after the series was wrapped, we were fucking two or three times a week in hotels around the city, or the car. She really liked that, the car. Then it sort of cooled off. Once a week, sometimes not even that. And Suki came back on line, so there was that as competition. I'd missed Suki, you know, and that whole pin-up buzz thing was fading anyway. There was about six months when Liz and I didn't see each other at all.' Another grin. 'Then she made, like, this amazing come-back. She asked me out to the studio one night, after everyone had gone home. I wasn't going to go at first, but I was curious, you know. Man, I'm glad I went.' Bryant leaned closer, still grinning. 'We fucked on the interview set and she filmed the whole thing with one of those big studio cameras. Then she *mailed me the fucking disc at work*. You believe that? I mean, I didn't know at the time she was doing it, otherwise I'd never have agreed. Then suddenly there's this Studio Ten disc on my desk with *Souvenir* written on it.'

'Jesus.'

Bryant nodded. 'I thought at first she was going to send it to Suki. Fact, I thought she already had when I got my copy. But when I rang her she just asked how I'd liked it and if I wanted a repeat performance. So the last six months we've been repeat-performing a couple of times a month and it's still as hot as ever.'

'And Suki?'

'She doesn't know. You know, the weird thing is, you'd think I'd go back to Suki too tired to perform but it's not like that. I'm more buzzed when I get home from a session with Liz than I would be if I hadn't had sex all week. It's that fucking disc, man. It makes you feel like a fucking porn star.'

'So what's the problem now?'

'Ah, nothing really. We had this big row the last time we met up to fuck.' Bryant's gaze floated off into the corners of the bar. The carnal shine faded from his face. He seemed disinclined to go on.

'What about?'

Bryant sighed. 'Ah, shit. Chris, do you think I was right to shoot those gangwit motherfuckers that night at the *Falkland*?'

'Yeah, sure.' Chris heard himself and stopped. 'I mean—'

'See that's what I think.'

'They were—'

'Fucking going to trash us, right?'

Chris gestured. 'Uh, yeah.'

'Right, that's what I said. It's what Suki says, it's what the fucking corporate police enquiry says. So, what's the big deal?'

'She doesn't buy it?'

Bryant glanced at him. 'What's to buy? I told her the truth.'

'What about the machetes?'

'Machetes? Wrecking bars? What's the fucking difference. I don't even remember which thing I told her.' Bryant swallowed more whisky and waved his glass laterally. 'Didn't matter. She said I was a fucking animal. Get that. I, *I* was an animal. Never mind the fuckers with the crowbars. *I* was a fucking animal. You understand that?'

Chris crowded Carla's voice out of his head with a pull at his own drink. 'She wasn't there, man.'

'That's right, she wasn't.' Bryant stared broodingly at the bottles behind the bar. 'Fucking reporters.'

Chris snapped his fingers and the liveried barman arrived as if on rails. Bryant didn't look at him. Chris indicated their glasses.

'Fill us up.'

The liquor drizzled down, catching the light.

'Got work to do tomorrow,' said Bryant gloomily. 'Makin's right, you'll see. They'll want twenty-five fucking drafts of that contract before it's put to bed. Bentick from the DTC, I know that motherfucker and he wants every 'i' double-dotted, just in case his precious minister runs into embarrassing questions on civilian casualties or some such shit.'

'Worry about it tomorrow.' Chris raised his glass. 'Here. Small wars.'

'Yeah, small wars.'

Crystal chimed between them. Bryant knocked back the whisky in one and signalled the barman again. He watched the glass fill up.

'*I'm* an animal,' he muttered with bitter disbelief. '*I'm* a fucking animal.'

They kicked it in the head about an hour later, when it became clear that no amount of drinking was going to extract Bryant from his sudden puddle of gloom. Chris half-carried his friend to the lift and along the corridor to his room, where he propped him against the wall while he fumbled with keys. Once inside the room, he hauled Mike most of the way onto the pristine expanse of king-size bed and set about unlacing his shoes. Bryant began to snore. Chris took off the shoes and shovelled Mike's unshod feet up onto the bed with the rest of him.

As Chris bent over him to remove his tie, the other man stirred.

'Liz?' he queried blearily.

'Not a chance,' said Chris, loosening the knot on his tie.

'Oh.' Bryant heaved his head up and made an attempt to focus. 'Chris. Don't even think about it, man. Don't even think about it.'

'I won't.' Chris finished unknotting the tie and stripped it from around Bryant's neck with a single hard tug.

'That's right.' Bryant's head fell back on the bed again and his eyes rolled sluggishly closed. 'You're a good guy, Chris. That's you. You're a. Fucking good guy.'

He drifted off to sleep again. Chris left him there snoring and let himself quietly out of the room. He slipped into his own room like a thief and went to his hotel bed, where he lay awake a while, masturbating to the thought of Liz Linshaw's tanned thighs and cleavage.

It was very quiet inside the limo now. The torrential rain of the storm had died back to a persistent drizzle that smeared the windows but no longer drummed on the roof. The limo's Rolls Royce engine made slightly less noise than the rush of its tyres on the wet asphalt outside. The loudest sound in the rear cabin was the chirrup of Louise Hewitt's laptop as it processed data.

Maps and graphs came and went, summoned and dismissed by the deft ripple of Hewitt's hands across the deck. Projections for the Cambodian conflict, altered minutely as new potential elements were factored in. Crop failures, *what if*? Typhoon impact, *what if*? Hong Kong federation cuts diplomatic ties, *what if*? Bryant's preliminary work was an inspired piece of modelling, but Hewitt believed in tracking her subordinates and pushing for potential weaknesses until they emerged. It was an exercise in basic security. As with any alloy, you didn't know the material well until you knew what would break it.

The car mobile purred up at her from where it was curled on the seat like a red eyed cat. She killed the phone's video option and picked up the handset, eyes still fixed on the Hong Kong federation variant.

'Yes?'

A familiar voice crackled in her ear. She smiled.

'On my way to Edinburgh, why?'

Crackle crackle.

'No, I didn't think there was any point. I've got breakfast with a client in the Howard at eight and contracts to go over before that.'

Crackle crackle SNAP. Hewitt's smile broadened.

'Oh, is that what you thought? Well, sorry to disappoint you, but I wouldn't have come all the way up here just for that. Good enough to eat though you looked.'

The phone crackled some more. Hewitt sighed and hoisted her gaze to the roof. Her voice became soothing.

'Yes, media exposure's a powerful thing. But I was sitting there, remember. I really wouldn't worry about it if I were you.'

The voice in her ear grew agitated and Hewitt's good-natured exasperation hardened. She sat forward.

'Alright, listen. You just let me worry about Faulkner. You leave him alone.' The crackling stopped on a sharp interrogation mark.

'Yes, I know. I was there, remember. It's no big surprise, to be honest. Look, it's just an angle.'

Snap, crackle. Incredulous.

'Yes, I do.'

Snap, question.

'Because that's what they pay me for. I don't have the details worked out yet, but it shouldn't take much leverage.'

Crackle, crackle, crackle.

'Mike Bryant will do as he's told. That's the difference between them, and you need to remember that. Now, we've talked about this enough. I'll be back in London day after tomorrow, we can meet and discuss it then.'

Sullen *crackle*. Silence.

Hewitt cradled the phone and grinned to herself in the quiet gloom.

FOURTEEN

'Seen enough?'

Erik Nyquist got up and held the cracked remote closer to the screen. The red active light winked feebly a couple of times and the programme credits continued to scroll down, superimposed over an aerial view of Nakamura wreckage. Finally, Erik gave up on the failing remote and snapped on the blue standby screen manually. In the glow it cast, he turned back to face his daughter. Carla sat, glass in hand, and stared at the place where the images had been.

'The hero of the hour,' Erik grunted. 'Jesus, the irony of that. Butcher a couple of fellow human beings to maximise neo-colonial profiteering half the globe away and you're a goddamn hero.'

'Dad,' Carla said tiredly.

'You heard her. *This is a great moment for you, Chris*. And your beloved husband sitting there grinning like a Mormon. *I wouldn't be in this line of work if I didn't like it, Liz*. Christ!'

'He had no choice. The woman on the left was his boss, and from what I hear she already doesn't like him. What was he supposed to do? If he stepped out of line the way you want, he'd probably lose his job.'

'I know that.' Erik went to the table that served him as an open-plan drinks cabinet and began to mix himself another vodka and orange. 'Been there, bought the T-shirt. But sometimes you have to stand by the odd principle, you know.'

'Yes, I know,' Carla snapped, surprising herself. 'And where did that get you in the end, standing by your much-vaunted principles?'

'Well, let's see.' Erik grinned down into the glass he was pouring. Having provoked her, he was now cheerfully backing down again. It was one of his favourite drinking games. 'I was arrested, held without trial under the Corporate Communications Act, shunned by my so-called friends and colleagues, blacklisted by every news editor in the country and refused a credit rating. I lost my job, my home and any hopes for the future. Nothing that a young man of Chris's calibre couldn't take in his stride. The trouble is, he just lacks the vision to make it happen.'

Carla smiled, despite herself.

'Liked that one, did you?' Erik lifted his glass in her direction. 'For once, it's something I just made up. Cheers.'

'Cheers.' She barely sipped at her own neat vodka. It had taken her the whole news report to get three fingers down the drink, and now it was warm.

'Dad, why do you stay here? Why don't you go back to Tromsö?'

'And meet your mother in the high street every day? No thanks. I'm living with enough guilt as it is.'

'She isn't there most of the time and you know it.'

'Okay, I'd just see her every time she comes back from some particularly successful book launch or lecture tour.' Erik shook his head. 'I don't think my ego's up to that. Besides, after all these years, who would I know?'

'Alright, you could move to Oslo. Write a column back there.'

'Carla, I already do.' Erik gestured at the battered computer in the corner. 'See that. It's got a wire in the back that goes all the way to Norway. Marvellous what they can do with technology these days.'

'Oh, shut up.'

'Carla.' The mockery drained from his tone. 'What am I going to change, moving back there now? It isn't as if the costs are prohibitive here. Even with the zone tax on top, email is so cheap you can't realistically cost it on the number of articles I mail out in a month. And even if you could, even if I was *walking* my work to the editors in Oslo to save money, I'd spend what I saved on winter socks.'

'Don't exaggerate, it's not that cold.'

'I think you're forgetting.'

'Dad.' Her voice grew very gentle. 'We were there in January.'

'Oh.' She heard, in that single gruff syllable, how much it hurt him. He made a point of looking her in the face. 'Visiting your mother?'

She shook her head. 'There wasn't time, and anyway, I think she was in New Zealand. Chris took me to the Winter Wheels show in Stockholm, and we went across to see Sognefjord on the way back. He'd never been there.'

'And it wasn't cold? Come on, Carla. I may not be able to afford flights on a whim, but it hasn't been so long.'

'Alright, it was cold. Yes, it was cold. But, Dad, it was so—' She gave up and gestured around her. 'Dad, look at this place.'

'Yeah, I know I haven't tidied up for a while, but—'

'You know what I mean!'

Erik looked at her in silence for a while. Then he went to the window and tugged back one of the ragged curtains. Outside, something had been set on fire and it painted leaping shadows on the ceiling above where he stood. Shouts came through the thin glass pane. 'Yes,' he said softly. 'I know what you mean. You mean this. Urban decay, as only the

British know how to do it. And here I am, fifty-seven years old and stuck in the middle of it.'

She avoided his eyes.

'It's just so civilised back there, Dad. There's nobody sleeping on the streets—'

'Just as well, they'd freeze to death.'

She ignored him. '—nobody dying because they can't afford medical attention, no old people too poor to afford heating and too scared to go out after dark. Dad, there are no gang zones, no armoured police trucks, there's no *exclusion* like there is here.'

'It sounds as if you should be talking to Chris, not me.' Erik knocked back a large portion of his drink in one. It was an angry gesture, and his voice carried the ragged echo of the emotion. 'Maybe you can persuade him to move up there if you like it so much. Though it's hard to see what you'd both do for a living without anybody to kill on the roads.'

She flinched.

He saw it and reined himself in.

'Carla—'

She looked at her lap. Said nothing. He sighed.

'Carla, I'm sorry. I. I didn't mean to say that.'

'Yes, you did.'

'No.' He set down his drink and came to crouch in front of her. 'No, I didn't, Carla. I know you're just doing what you have to get by. We all are. Even Chris. I know that. But can't you see. Any argument for me going back to Norway is an equally valid argument for you. How do you think *I* feel, looking at *you*, stuck in the middle of this?'

The thought stopped her like a slap. Her hands tightened on his.

'Dad—' She swallowed and started again. 'Dad, that's not it, is it? You're not staying because of me?'

He chuckled and lifted her chin with one hand.

'Staying because of you? Staying to protect you, with all the money and influence I've amassed? Yeah, that's right.'

'Then tell me *why*.'

'Why.' He stood up and for a moment she thought she was in for another lecture. Instead, he went to stand at the window again, staring out. The flames were stronger now and they stained his face with orange. 'Do you remember Monica Hansen?'

'Your photographer?'

Erik smiled. 'I'm not sure she'd like the possessive pronoun, but yes, Monica the photographer. She's back in Oslo now, taking photos of furniture for some catalogue. She's bored, Carla. The money's okay, but she's bored to screaming.'

'Better bored than sleeping in the streets.'

'Don't exaggerate, Carla. I'm not sleeping in the streets. And, no, listen to me a moment, think about it. You said yourself there's no exclusion there like there is here. So what would I write about. Back in the comfort and safety of my own Scandinavian social system? No, Carla. This is the front line – this is where I can make a difference.'

'No one wants you to make a difference, Dad.' She got up from the chair, suddenly angry again, and faced him. She jerked back the other curtain and glared angrily down at the fire below. 'Look at that.'

The source of the flames, she saw as she gestured, was an overturned armchair. Other items lay scattered around, unrecognisable in the darkness and as yet untorched. A shattered window directly above suggested an origin. Someone had been in one of the first-floor flats, throwing down what it contained. Now figures in baggy, hooded sportswear stood gathered around the fire, making Carla think of menacing negative-image Disney dwarves out of some nightmare where it all definitely did not end happily ever after.

'Look at it,' she hissed again. 'You think those people care what you write? You think most of them can even read? You think people like that care about you making a difference?'

'Don't be so quick to judge, Carla. Like Benito says, don't make 3D judgments of what you can only see on your TV screen.'

'Oh, for—' Her expletives evaporated in an exasperation too old and deep for words. She rapped hard on the glass. 'This isn't a TV, Dad. It's a fucking window, and you live here. You tell me what we're looking at, community night barbecue maybe?'

Erik sighed. 'No, it's probably gang retribution for something. Someone they thought informed on them, someone who spoke out of turn. They did the same thing to Mrs McKenny last summer because she wouldn't let her son run balloons for them. Of course, then he had to, just to buy some new furniture. You can't fault the gangwits on psychology.' He turned away from the window, and suddenly, in the motion, she saw how tired he had become. The vision only fanned the flames of her anger again. Up from the pit of her stomach, a licking, gusting sickness.

Erik appeared not to sense it coming. He was freshening his drink again, working on an ironic grin to match it. 'Of course, it could just be kids having fun. Random stuff. A lot of those first-floor flats have been empty for longer than I've been here. They just break in and—'

He shrugged and drank.

'And throw the stuff out the *window!*' Suddenly she was yelling at him, really yelling. 'And set fire to it! For *fun!* Jesus fucking *Christ*, Dad, will you listen to yourself. You think this is *normal*? *Are you fucked in the head*?'

The flashback caught like magnesium ribbon behind her eyes. Eleven years old again, and screaming at her father as he tried to explain what he had done and why she had to choose. It burned out as fast, after-image inked onto her retina and the returning dimness of the room. She looked up quickly, caught the expression on Erik's face, and knew he was remembering too.

'Dad, I'm sorry,' she whispered.

Too late.

He didn't say it, but he didn't need to. Silence was settling around them in little black shreds, like scorched down from a pillow shot through at close range.

'Dad—'

She had thought for a moment he might yell back, but he didn't. He only moved slightly, the way she sometimes saw Chris move when some piece of driving-induced injury caught him awkwardly. He moved and nodded to himself, as if her scream had been a swallow of rough but interesting whisky. She saw the way he was composing himself, and knew what was coming.

'Normal?' He said the word with careful pedantry that almost hid the returning gruffness in his voice. 'Well I think, in the context of the slaughter we've just seen committed by the man you share your bed with—'

'Dad, please—'

His voice trampled hers down. 'I'd call it normal, yes. In fact I'd call it comparatively healthy. Burnt furniture you can always replace. Burnt flesh is a little harder.'

She breathed deliberately, loosening the tightness in her chest. 'Listen, Dad, I'm not going to—'

'Of course, there is always the double standard to consider. As Mazeau would have put it, crime is a matter of degrees and the degree that really matters in society's eyes is the extent to which the criminal has asserted himself beyond his designated social class and status—'

'Oh, *bullshit*, Dad!'

But the anger had deserted her, and all she could feel now was the edge of tears. She held onto her drink with clumsy, eleven-year-old hands, and watched as her father retreated, swathing himself in the gauze bandage of political rhetoric to hide the hurt.

'The sons and daughters of the powerful buy and sell drugs amongst themselves with impunity, because all they have done is overstep slightly the licence their class entitles them to, misunderstood the lip service to legality that must be paid if the common herd are to continue grazing quietly. But let one child from the Brundtland enter their fairy kingdom and do the same, and watch the full bloody weight of the law fall on

108

him, because he has *presumed* to behave as he is not entitled, presumed to *not know* his place. And that we *cannot* allow.'

'Dad,' she tried one more time, voice pitched low and urgent. 'Please, Dad, look down there again. Never mind whose fault it is. Never mind the politics of it. Do you think anyone down there gives a flying fuck what you write? Do you think they give a fuck about *anything* any more?'

'And my son-in-law does?' He did not turn to the window, but his eyes were bright with the reflected fireglow. 'Chris gives a flying fuck for the bodies he left on the motorway today? Or the bodies that they'll be stacking in the streets of Phnom Penh a year from now? You know what I wish, Carla? I wish you'd married one of those edge dealers down there instead of that suited piece of shit you sleep with. The dealer, at least, I could make excuses for.'

'That's great, Dad.' Finally, with the insult to Chris, she had the anger back. The strength to hurt. Her voice came out flat and cold. 'You finally had the guts to say it to my face. The man who paid your rent and bought you a new kitchen last Christmas is a piece of shit. And I guess it's clear what that makes me.'

She set down the drink on the coffee table and made for the door. She saw how he lifted one arm involuntarily towards her as she passed him, but she shut it out.

'Where are you going?'

'I'm going to pack my bag, Dad. And then, if I don't get mugged and raped on the way out by one of your oppressed proletarians, I'm going home.'

'I thought you didn't want to be on your own in the house.'

He said it sulkily, but there was an undertone of fear and regret in his voice now. Dismayed, she realised that it was exactly what she wanted to hear. She could feel the relish bubbling up on hearing it.

'I didn't,' she said. 'But I'd rather be alone, somewhere safe and sane, than with you in this shithole.'

She didn't turn to see his face as she said it.

She didn't need to.

Some damage, Chris had once told her, *you don't need to see. You know what you've done on impact. You can feel it. All you have to do after that is disengage.*

She went to pack.

109

FILE#2:
ACCOUNT ADJUSTMENT

FIFTEEN

It finally hit Chris while he was waiting at the counter in *Louie Louie's* for a double-spike cappuccino.

He'd sat up late the previous evening, going over the possibilities, and by the time he finally came to bed, Carla was already asleep. More and more, that was becoming the pattern. Work on the Cambodia contract was keeping him later and later at Shorn. He was forced to relegate his self-defence classes and gun practice to lunch-time, which stretched the day even longer. Carla was getting home anything from two to five hours ahead of him during the week and they had given up any pretence of dining together. He ate the remains of what she had cooked for herself earlier and talked desultorily to her about his day. Loading the dishwasher was usually the only shared activity of the evening; after that, one of them would retire upstairs to read, leaving the other marooned down in the living room with the entertainment deck.

There was an air of detached politeness to their lives now. They had sex at increasingly irregular intervals and argued less than they ever had before, because they rarely had the time or energy to talk about anything of significance. They kept meaning to take a long weekend together somewhere like New York or Madrid and use the time to recharge, but somehow it never came together. Either Carla forgot to book the Saturday off with Mel, or Chris was suddenly needed for a weekend meeting with the Cambodia team. Summer came on, pleasantly mellow, but the layer of superficiality continued to thicken over their day-to-day life and Chris found himself enjoying the new weather only in moments of isolation that he was later curiously unwilling to share with Carla.

He lay awake beside her, turning the game over in his mind until he finally fell asleep.

On the drive in that morning he'd tried again, but he'd been too sleepy from the night before. In the last few weeks his habitual driver's caution had grown lax to a point that under other circumstances might have been called recklessness. As it was, the attitude made perfect sense. Following the Nakamura challenge, word had got out about the dangerous new player at the Shorn table and no one among the young no-name challengers was keen to go up against Chris Faulkner's clearly identifiable Saab Custom. The vehicle's spaced armouring and Mitsue Jones's demise at its owner's hands were equally thoroughly mythologised among the driving fraternity – detail upon invented detail until it was impossible even for Chris to separate the true facts from the thicket of embellishments that had sprung up around them. In the end, he gave up trying and started to live with the legend. In this, he was probably the last person on board. Amidst all the hype, one thing had been universally accepted in the City of London weeks ago – there had to be easier ways to carve a name for yourself than go up against Chris Faulkner.

'Double cap for Chris,' yelled the girl at the counter.

He was on first name terms with the staff of *Louie Louie's* these days – they'd torn out the front cover of GQ that month and pinned it up behind the counter. Reluctantly, he'd autographed it, and now, every time he went in, his carefully groomed features grinned back at him from beneath the imprisoning gloss and black ink scrawl. It made him slightly uneasy. Fame had dripped like sap all over him and now it was hardening into amber and he was trapped inside for all to see. Fansites were starting to give him serious coverage for the first time since the death of Edward Quain. East European working girls with unlikely stage names and credit-card hotlines were in his mail, plying him with suggestions of varying subtlety.

And you're pinned down, overdeployed, no way to—

The solution boiled out at him like the milk froth from the steamer, bubbling up on itself as it unfolded. It might have been the cross-hatched patterning of the yellow and black tiles behind the counter, or maybe just the results of dissociative thinking, a technique he'd picked up from a psych seminar the week before. Whatever it was, he fielded the insight and took it back up in the Shorn elevator with his coffee.

'Cambodia Resourcing continues to lead the rising stock trend,' the elevator informed him as they powered upward. 'With end-of-day trading at—'

He tuned it out. He already knew.

Mike Bryant was talking to the machine. Chris could hear him through the door, dictating in jagged pieces to the datadown. It was a chewed-over version of a document to the Cambodian rebels that they'd been working on most of yesterday. The East Asia Trade and Investment Commission was leaning on them for Charter compliance with an uncharacteristic fervour. Industrial espionage reports suggested Nakamura bribes were going in at high level.

'We have no interest in the so-called, no, scratch that, no interest in the areas you have designated resettlement zones, nor are we concerned with what goes on within those zones. The administration of the camps

114

is, of course, not within our jurisdiction provided no overt human rights abuse, uh-uh, provided no human rights abuse, mhmmm, no, back up again, not within our jurisdiction, uhhh, provided, given that, oh fuck it—'

Chris grinned and knocked at the door.

'What?' Bryant bellowed.

'Having trouble?'

'Chris!' Bryant stood poised in the middle of his office space, arms slung on a polished wood baseball bat that he'd braced at the nape of his neck. It gave him the posture of a man crucified, and the tiredness in his face did nothing to alter the impression. 'Would you believe I've been on this motherfucker since eight this morning. It has to go to the uplink at noon, and I'm still splitting fucking hairs on the covering letter. Listen to this.' He walked to the desk and read aloud from a piece of hardcopy that curled from the datadown printer. ' "The administration of the camps is, of course, not within our jurisdiction, provided no human rights abuse occurs." Sary's going to go through the roof if we send him that – he'll say we're implying the Friday statement's a lie.'

'It is, isn't it?'

'Please.' Bryant rolled his neck against the wood of the bat. 'I'm trying to do politics here. We can't imply he's lying.'

'I thought we were going to go with "given that no human rights abuse is occurring".'

Bryant shook his head. 'Won't wash with the UN. There's an Amnesty report doing the rounds in Norway and no one's prepared to deny it at ministerial level. We've got to stay "vague but firm". That's a direct quote from Hewitt.'

'Vague but firm.' Chris pulled a face. 'Nice.'

'Fucking Amnesty.'

'Yeah, well. Shit happens.' Chris came and stood at Bryant's shoulder, reading the hardcopy. 'What about . . .'

He tore the sheet from the printer and scanned it. Bryant unslung the baseball bat from his shoulder and parked it in a corner.

'. . . Confident. That's it, look. Admin of the camps blah blah blah not within our jurisdiction *and* we are confident that no human rights abuse, no, that *none* of the alleged human rights abuse has occurred.' He handed back the sheet. 'How about that?'

Bryant snatched it.

'You bastard. Forty-five fucking minutes I've been staring at this.'

'Caffeine.' Chris held up his take-out from *Louie Louie's*. 'Want some?'

'I'm all caffeined out. I was in at six with Makin, and this landed on my desk an hour ago from upstairs. Notley and the policy board.

Response required. As if I didn't have enough else to do. Let's see . . . "that none of the alleged human rights abuse has occurred". Right. Now what about this? "However we cannot permit your forces to obstruct the passage of fuel and supplies".'

'Try "forces operating in the area". Takes the sting out of it and makes him feel like a big man. Like you're asking him to police the zone generally, not just get a grip on his own troops.'

Bryant muttered and scribbled on the hardcopy as he read it back. ' "However we cannot permit forces *operating in the area* to obstruct the passage of fuel and" blah blah blah blah. That's it. Brilliant.'

Chris shrugged. 'Ready-wrapped. I used the same scam on the Panthers of Justice a couple of weeks back, and they lapped it up. Stopped the banditry dead. All most of these rebels really want is some kind of recognition. Paternal acknowledgement from some kind of patriarchal authority. According to Lopez, it had them swaggering around, posting police directives in every village.'

Mike barked a laugh. 'Lopez? That Joaquin Lopez?'

'Yeah.'

'So you put Harris up to tender after all.'

'Well, like you said. It was our investment he was fucking with. And Lopez works flat out for a half per cent less of total. Really took Harris apart in the bullring too, apparently.'

'Yeah, he's still young enough to have the drive. Harris burnt out years ago, it's just no one ever called him on it. You did the whole industry a service putting him out.'

'It was your idea. If anything, I owe you one for the advice. So anyway, what's this six a.m. shit with Makin? Anything I should know about?'

'Nah, shouldn't think—' Bryant stopped. 'Actually, maybe I should bounce it off you. You worked the NAME, didn't you? North Andean Monitored Economy? Back when you were at HM?'

Chris nodded. 'Yeah, we were into the ME in a big way. Anybody with a decent emerging markets portfolio had to be. Why, what's going on down there now?'

'Ah, it's fucking Echevarria again. You remember that first day we met in the gents, I told you I was off to see some greasy dictator for a budget review?'

'That was Hernan Echevarria? I thought he was dying.'

'No such luck. The old bastard's pushing eighty, he's had major surgery twice in the last decade, and he's still hanging on. He's grooming his eldest son, in true corrupt land-owning motherfucker fashion, to take over the whole show when he's gone. And, as you'd expect with these hacienda families, the son's a complete fucking waste of space.

116

Spends all his time in Miami doing the casinos, powdering his nose and fucking the local *gringas*.'

Chris offered another shrug. 'Sounds okay. Easy enough to control, anyway.'

'Not on present showing.' Bryant punched a couple of points on the datadown screen and the display shifted. 'See, Echevarria junior's making a lot of friends in Miami. Investor friends.'

'Oh.'

'Yes, oh. Fresh money, most of it homegrown, but some from Tokyo and Beijing via US management funds. Have a look at this little snap.' Bryant turned the datadown screen to face Chris. 'Taken aboard Haithem Al-Ratrout's private yacht last week. You'll recognise some faces.'

It was a standard paparazzi shot. Hurried and unflattering angles on people who usually only appeared in the public eye coated in a high media gloss. Chris spotted two Hollywood pin-ups of the moment displaying the cleavage for which they were famous, the US Secretary of State caught picking the olive out of his martini and—

'Over on the left you've got Echevarria junior. The one in the Ingram suit and the stupid hat. And that next to him is Conrad Rimshaw, executive head of Conflict Investment for Lloyd Paul New York. On the other side and towards the back you've got Martin Meldreck from Calders Rapid Capital Deployment division. The vultures are gathering.'

'But the father's still ours so far, right?'

'So far.' Bryant nodded and touched another part of the screen. The photo minimised and gave way to a spreadsheet. 'But it's an uphill struggle. These are from the budget review I mentioned. The stuff in red is contested. He wants more, we can't let him have it.'

There was a lot of red.

'The Echevarrias have been with Shorn's Madrid office ever since Hernan pulled the coup back in '27. Good solid clients. Our Emerging Markets division backed them all through the civil war and the crackdown afterwards.' Bryant bent back fingers one at a time as he enumerated. 'Fuel and ammunition, medical supplies, helicopter gunships, counter-subversion trainers, interrogation technology. All at knockdown prices, and for over twenty years it's all paid off big time. Quiescent population, low wage economy, export-oriented. Standard neoliberal dream.'

'But not any more.'

'But not any more. We've got another generation of guerrillas in the mountains screaming for land reform, another generation of disaffected student youth in the cities, and we're all back to square one. Emerging

Markets got scared and dropped the whole thing like a hot brick –
straight into Conflict Investment's lap. Hewitt gave it to Makin.'

'Nice of her.'

'Yeah, well this was just after Guatemala, so Makin's rep was riding
pretty high. Top commission analyst for the year and all that. I guess
Hewitt thought he'd swing it in his sleep. But things didn't work out, so
they brought me in to assist. Now Makin's having to share Echevarria
with me and I've got to say,' Bryant walked across to the door and
pressed it completely closed. His voice lowered. 'I've got to say he's not
handling it all that well.'

Chris leaned against the edge of Bryant's desk, feeling the friendly
warmth of trust and a shared conspiracy coming off the other man.

'So what's the problem?'

Bryant sighed. 'Problem is, Makin doesn't know how to handle
Echevarria. See, he's used to these penny ante revolutionaries holed up
in the jungle with their peasant education programmes and he thinks
Echevarria's just the same animal made good.'

'Oops.'

'Yeah, I've told him. The Echevarrias are as close as you get to
nobility in that part of the world. That's how come the link with
Europe. Old Hernan traces his ancestors right back to Pizarro's original
conquistadors. As he never fucking tires of telling us. 'course, all that
means is he's descended from some dirt-poor younger son mercenary
glory-roader who grabbed a seat on the boat over from Spain, but it
isn't cool to mention that in budget meetings.'

'Makin said that?'

Bryant laughed. 'No, I'm exaggerating. Makin's too damn good a
negotiator for that. But it smokes off him every time Echevarria starts in
on that nobility rap. You can almost see his lip curl. Echevarria sees it
too, and that fucking Hispanic pride stokes up, and Makin's lip curls
some more, and there we are, deadlocked. We're trying to lock him into
something long-term, so that when he finally croaks the NAME'll be
stable and, more importantly, ours, but he gets more hostile every time
we talk to him. Now he wants double-figure percentage increases in the
military budget to put down the rebels, and there's no way we can afford
to give that to him and keep the fund managers happy. The problem is,
he's taking the whole thing personally.'

'So he won't sign?'

'He might eventually,' Bryant picked up the baseball bat again,
twirled it through the air and shipped it across one shoulder. 'If I can
talk him round. But eventually might be too late. He's not a well man. If
he dies or his condition deteriorates too much, junior takes over and
then we're fucked. Junior hasn't got his old man's illusions about the

European connection, and he's pissed off with Makin for his attitude – he'll bring in Lloyd Paul or Calders RapCap just to snub us. And they'd just love to buy us out.'

Chris sipped at his coffee and thought about it while Bryant paced towards the window, playing imaginary curveballs off the bat. When the other man turned back to face him, he set the styrofoam canister down on the desk with studied calm.

'What about the rebels?' he asked.

'The rebels?' Bryant spread his hands in supplication. 'Come on, who the fuck are they? This is a twenty-year client we're talking about. You can't write that off against some bearded campesino hiding out in the hills. There's probably half a hundred different factions and fronts, all squabbling about their revolutionary lineage. We don't know them, we don't have the time to *get* to know them and anyway—'

'I know them.'

'What?'

'I said I know them. HM Emerging Markets did an in-depth survey of the ME's radical factions last year.' Chris gestured, open-handed. 'We flew out there, Mike. I've got the files at home somewhere.'

Bryant gaped. 'You're bullshitting me.'

'Do you a profile by Thursday.'

'Jesus. What did you do, just come up here to make my day?'

'Oh.' Chris picked up his coffee and crossed to the low table where Mike kept the chess board. He hooked up a knight between index and second finger and relocated it. 'Almost forgot. Check.'

Bryant grinned and feinted at him with the bat. Chris caught it with his other hand.

'Mother*fucker*.'

'Yeah.' Chris looked at the board. 'And mate in seven, I reckon.'

SIXTEEN

The HM files were in the garage, stacked on an upper shelf next to a box of worn gear bearings that Carla had hung onto for some unfathomable reason. Chris went up on a stepladder to retrieve the disc he wanted and nearly turned an ankle jumping down afterwards.

'Fuck.'

Had Carla been there to see it, he thought, she would have laughed. She would have laughed out loud, and he would have joined in, pretending that his ego was not pricked through, and after a few moments the fleeting anger at being mocked would have leached out for real.

But Carla was at an evening course with two other mechanics from Mel's Autofix, learning about developments in virtual design technology, and the house echoed with her absence.

He went through to the study and fed the disc into the datadown. A search protocol swam up onto the screen.

'North Andean Monitored Economy,' he told the machine. 'Hernan Echevarria, political opponents.'

The search protocol dissolved and in its place a series of thumbprint photos began to spring up like multicoloured blisters. Chris stood and watched for a moment as the programme resized the rapidly multiplying images, trying vainly to fit them all onto a single screen page. Then he went out to the lounge, to fetch the whisky.

He'd built this file in a no-star hotel room overlooking the luminous night-time surf of the Caribbean. Hammett McColl sent two teams out to the NAME – one highly publicised visit, booked into the Bogota Hilton, whose function was largely cosmetic, and one stealth audit crew, flown in undercover of a shoestring movie company's location scouting. It had been a stupid kind of fun at first, until the policing data started to flow in.

Chris remembered velvet black nights, street life and lanterns strung in the street outside. Sweat rolling off his body and brow, pricked out in almost equal quantities by the humidity and the details from the detention records. His fingers leaving damp prints on the keys of the laptop. He drank cane rum and smoked atrocious local cigarettes and somehow kept it all in perspective most of the time. Just sometimes he paused and lifted his fingers from the keyboard as if he had heard something,

120

because even the rum could not keep out the animal-instinctive knowledge that the things the reports described were going on right now in
police stations across the city.

He never heard screams, he told himself, then and later. It was the
reports talking, working at his imagination like a feeble dentist at an
infected tooth. That was all. He heard nothing.

The telephone rang.

He jerked round, one hand on the neck of the whisky bottle and
looked out towards the lounge. It was the home phone, the unscreened
line. He left the office and stood in the connecting doorway, staring
across at the little blue screen. The call bell symbol pulsed on and off in
green, in time with the soft chiming.

Who—

Can't be Carla. He checked his watch. The seminar still had half an
hour to run, and anyway he'd had the thought before he knew what time
it was. As their separate work schedules chewed off more and more of
the time they used to spend together, they'd fallen out of the habit of
checking in with each other for anything other than pure necessity.

The telephone rang.

He watched it stupidly, holding the whisky, thoughts locked up.

Work would have used the datadown. From habit and from the
manual. There was a Shorn directive against talking shop on unscreened lines.

The phone rang.

Erik, ringing to back down from the ludicrous sulk Carla had
described when Chris got back from the north. Chris grimaced. That
particular Viking? Not likely.

Just answer the fucking thing, for Christ's sake.

He crossed to the terminal and thumbed the accept. The blue background blipped out and a picture sank into place.

For a curious moment, Chris wasn't sure what he was looking at. He
made out dark glossy hair and a profile, seemingly pillowed on twin
cushions that . . .

Moaning gusted through the air from the speaker.

The profile turned, mouth open.

A hand appeared, enamel red-tipped.

Adrenalin bubbled abruptly through Chris's head as the picture made
sense. He was watching a slice of holoporn, downloaded direct to the
phone link. A heavily made-up woman with long black tresses was
crouched over an equally painted blonde partner, sucking and nibbling
at a pair of breasts so large and so perfectly rounded it was hard to
believe they were physically attached to either participant.

Chris sank onto the arm of the sofa, watching.

The shot dilated a little and background detail emerged. The two women were sprawled on what appeared to be some kind of exercise bench and wore nothing beyond a few studded leather accessories that served only to lift and separate curved areas of flesh. The blonde half of the duo was on her back and upside down, hair trailing to the floor. The other woman had somehow contrived to straddle her partner but leave her own backside raised high in the air like the top of a child-drawn heart. The twin mounds of buttocks mirrored the silicone-enhanced globes of the woman below so that a bizarre kind of vertical symmetry was created. You could almost believe you were looking at a single hourglass-shaped creature with the incidental appendages of limbs and faces added after the event.

Chris felt the blood stirring through his stomach and puddling into his prick as the two woman faked their way towards a mutual climax. The dark-haired performer was evidently cast in the role of dominatrix and she worked the other woman's flesh with much snarling and flashing of purple-painted eyes, while the blonde beneath her moaned and rubbed semi-convincingly at her own improbable breasts.

The dominatrix—

The thought skated almost casually across the rink of his mind, replacing something else he'd been going to think.

—was Liz Linshaw.

He leaned forward uncomfortably over his erection. Confirmed, the recognition sent a small shiver up his spine. Liz Linshaw had aged a few years since the footage was shot, but behind the purple eyeshadow and the dyed black hair, the face was unmistakable. It was the same line of cheekbone and nose, the same long, mobile mouth. The same slightly crooked teeth.

Chris's eyes flickered from the face to the exposed flesh below it. Six weeks ago, at the Tebbit Centre studio, he'd seen the steep curve of her cleavage loaded into just-glimpsed lingerie under an open-necked blouse. He'd fallen asleep that night thinking about it and – he only admitted it to himself now – he'd looked for it on the morning Prom and App bulletins since.

Now, here it was laid out for his perusal at leisure, and it was, he noticed, the same steep curve. Liz Linshaw's breasts were not of the same epic proportions as those of her performing partner, but they were still cosmetic-standard enough to defy gravity without external support. The nipples, now being forced mock-sadistically into the blonde woman's mouth, were large and dark and blunt. If there were scars where the implants had gone in, they were lost in the all-over tan.

Chris was rock hard.

He watched as the blonde woman's mouth dragged and smeared down the length of Liz Linshaw's body to the juncture of her thighs.

The panting and moaning grew mutual as the two women got into the inevitable top-to-tail clinch and filled their brightly taloned hands with bronzed flesh. Chris's hand moved unwillingly across the buckle of his belt. Semi-convincing or not—

White lights splashed across the window and drenched the curtains. The Landrover crunched up the drive.

Chris leapt up and snapped the phone off. The liquid sounds of orgasm evaporated into stillness. For a moment he stood over the unit, glaring at it. The message option pulsed, download message, dump message, replay message, download, dump, replay, download, dump replay, download—

He stabbed the screen and the copying bar filled from left to right like a tiny, unrolling carpet in mauve.

The Landrover's engine stilled. A door clunked, open and closed.

He stabbed the eject button and snatched the minidisc as it emerged. It fell from his fingers, hit the floor and rolled.

Footsteps on gravel.

He cast about, tiny triphammers in his temples. The disc glinted silver from under an armchair.

Carla's recognition tag scraped on the lock.

He bent and grabbed the disc, buried it in his pocket on the way out of the lounge. He heard the front door open as he reached the study. He made it to his seat.

'Chris? I'm home.'

'Just a minute.'

The erection, he was relieved to find, had melted in the panic. His jeans felt almost loose. He swivelled on the chair as Carla came in and kissed him on the cheek.

'Work?' There was just a hint of weary resignation in the single word as she glanced past him at the screen.

'That's right.' He returned the kiss, feeling as if he fitted badly into his own skin. The words were jumbled and overlarge on his tongue. 'It's some stuff I'm digging out for Michael.'

'You eaten?'

'Yeah, the rest of the curry. You?'

'On the way.' She grimaced. 'Kebab.'

'Yeah, I can smell it.'

'Yeah. Sorry.' She stopped abruptly and leaned back a little, holding his head between her palms. 'You okay? You look a bit pale.'

'I'm.' He gusted a sigh, pushing out some of the tension. Jerked his head at the screen so she had to let go. 'It's just some of this stuff. We're looking at the North Andean Monitored Economy. I'd forgotten the shit they get up to in police cells out there.'

123

She moved away. 'No worse than what's going on in Cambodia, from what I hear.'

'We're leaning on them to stop that,' he told her.

'Yeah?' There was a dull disinterest in her voice as she walked out of the room, a coat of detachment they had both started to evolve as an alternative to the rows there was no longer time or energy for.

He went after her. Back into the lounge, where the phone terminal stood in the corner. He remembered with a jolt through the stomach that he had not erased the original message.

'Carla.'

'What?'

He moved up close to her and put one arm on the juncture of neck and shoulder. The gesture felt clumsy, unaccustomed. It was weeks since they'd fucked. She looked at him out of suspicious eyes.

'What, Chris?'

He ran his fingers up into the hair behind her ear and tugged through until his hand was clasping the back of her head. It was a caress that invariably set her cooking, but it still felt awkward. He closed the final gap between them, relieved to find that his erection had returned in force. She felt it pressed between them and a thin little smile appeared on her lips.

'So what's got into you?'

He kissed her. After a couple of moments she warmed to it.

'I've missed you,' he said when their mouths split apart.

'I've missed you too.'

'Come upstairs with me.'

She had started to rub at the crotch of his jeans with one hand. The other worked at the buckle on his belt. 'What's wrong with right here?'

He hesitated. The passion in the moment guttered down. She looked up from what her hands were doing, terrifyingly attuned to the confusion fogging his head.

'Chris?'

'I don't want you getting carpet burns,' he said, and hauled her off her feet. The classic wedding threshold lift. One hand went to her breast, cupping and

the blonde gobbles down Liz Linshaw's nipple, smearing crimson lipstick

She laughed.

'Well, well. Romance.'

Staggering a little, he got her upstairs. They crashed onto the bed and shed their clothes. Carla turned towards him, naked, and he felt a tiny crystal of warmth drip and slide somewhere deep inside him. He had forgotten how beautiful her body was, the broad-shouldered, long-boned pale expanse of it, the flat width of stomach and the full breasts

124

above, breasts that would have been large on a smaller-framed woman but here

the swollen hemispheres, flesh taut to breaking point, kneaded by red taloned hands

He blinked and forced the image aside. Focused on the woman he was with, slotting into the old, comfortable sequence of postures and pressures, the places she liked to be touched, the eventual coupling

Liz Linshaw's mouth, burrowing

He could not lose it. Even when Carla got on her hands and knees ahead of him the way they both liked to finish, he fantasised the other two women into existence on the bed with them. He imagined them vampire-like, clutching and sucking at Carla's flesh and his own, and he came with that last image printed indelibly across his eyes.

They left then, dragging his post-coital warmth away with them like the fur of a newly slaughtered animal. And afterwards, when Carla shifted and murmured and tightened her arms around him, all he could feel was trapped inside something that wasn't his.

'This is fucking great stuff.'

Mike Bryant paced about the office space, leafing through the sheaf of hardcopy. Chris sat in a corner armchair and watched him. He hadn't slept well, and there was a spreading ache behind his left eye. He was having a hard time getting up to the same level of enthusiasm as Bryant.

'I mean, Jesus, these guys have got some grievances. Just look at it. Better than a dozen different insurgent leaders and every single one has got family tortured to death or disappeared. Fantastic. Primary Emotional Motivation, PE fucking M, right out of Reed and Mason. Textbook diehard revolutionaries. They'll never quit. Listen, we only need to hold about a third, no, less than a third, of this stuff over Echevarria's head, and he should cave right in.'

'And if he doesn't?'

'Of course he will. What's wrong with you? We'd only need to persuade about three of these groups to team up, give them some second-hand Kalashnikovs out of stock – and Christ knows we've got enough of those – they'd piss all over Echevarria's regular army.'

Chris's temple throbbed. 'Yeah, but what if he doesn't scare.'

'Chris, come on.' Mike looked at him reproachfully. 'You're ruining my day here.'

'What if, Mike. Fucking think about it.'

'Jesus, you got out of bed the wrong side today. Alright.' Bryant threw himself into another armchair opposite, dumped his feet on the coffee table between. 'Let's be grown up about it. What if. Contingency planning. Like I said, we wave about a third of these guys in his face.

And we *tell* him there are double as many more where those came from, right?'

'Right.'

'Then, if he doesn't see sense, we'll use someone out of the other two-thirds. That way, whatever reprisals he takes, he'll be hitting the wrong people. Meanwhile, we talk to the front runner, and if necessary set him up with what he needs. That'd be, let's see.' Bryant flipped through the hardcopy again. 'This guy Arbenz maybe, the People's Liberation Front for whatever it was. Or Barranco's Revolutionary Brigade. Or Diaz. They're all strong contenders. You were there. Who do you make for the best bet?'

'Well, not Arbenz. He got shot up in a gunship raid a couple of weeks ago. Didn't you catch the bulletin?'

'Fucked if I remember.' Bryant snapped his fingers. 'Wait a minute, that business with the villages in the south. Echevarria's been strafing them again, fucking shithead. You know he made me a direct promise those BAe helicopters wouldn't be used against civilians this year. Lucky we didn't issue a press statement on that one.'

'Yeah, well, your BAe gunships shattered Arbenz's legs from the hips down, and apparently they were running that bioware ammunition, the stuff we saw at Farnborough back in January, slugs coated with immune-system inhibitors. Very nasty. They've got him in a field hospital in the mountains, but the last I heard from Lopez, it's touch and go if he'll make it.' Chris rubbed at his eye and wondered about painkillers. 'And even if he does, he'll be in no condition to conduct a campaign any time soon.'

'Okay, so that's Arbenz out. What about Barranco?'

'Yeah, I'd leave Barranco alone too, unless you absolutely have to use him. I met him once. He's committed, and he's short on ego – tough to win over.'

Bryant pulled a face. 'You met Diaz too, right?'

'Couple of times, yeah. He's a better bet. Very pragmatic, strong sense of his place in history. He wants his name on a statue somewhere before he dies. Oh, and he's a real Shakespeare nut.'

'You're winding me up.'

'No, seriously. He can quote the fucking stuff. Got a scholarship on some bullshit liberal arts exchange programme in the States when he was a student. He gave me *Hamlet*, *Macbeth*, whatsit, *King Lear*, you name it. All word-perfect.' Chris shrugged. 'Well, sounded like it was word-perfect anyway. What do I know? Anyway, he told me, get this; he always wanted to visit Britain and *see the mother of parliaments*.'

'What?' Bryant barked laughter. 'You *are* winding me up.'

'I swear. Mother of parliaments. That's what he said.'

126

'The mother of parliaments. Man, I love it. I almost hope Echevarria doesn't cave in, just so we can have this guy across.'

Makin, perhaps predictably, was less amused by it all. He went through the stapled paperwork, one snatched-aside sheet at a time, without saying a word, then tossed the whole thing onto his polished desk-top so it slid away from him. He looked across the desk to where Chris and Mike sat in steel frame chairs, bracketing him. He focused on Bryant.

'I seiously don't think this is the way to go, Mike.'

Bryant wasn't up for it. He said nothing, just rolled his head in Chris's direction.

'Listen, Nick,' Chris leaned forward. 'I've worked the NAME before and I'm telling you—'

'Youah telling me nothing. I've been working Latin American CI longer than you've been here. I took top commission in the Americas market last yeah—'

Bryant cleared his throat. 'Year before last.'

'I'm in it for this year as well, Mike.' Makin's voice stayed even, but behind the steel glasses his face looked betrayed. 'When the unwesol-veds come in.'

'Ah, come on Nick,' Chris felt a tight, feral jag of pleasure as he swung the comeback. 'That was last season. First thing you ever said to me, man. *Can't live off stuff like that indefinitely. It's a whole new quarter. Time for fresh meat. Another new appoach.* Remember that?'

Makin looked away. 'I don't remember saying that, no.'

'Well, you did, Nick.' Bryant got up and brushed something off the shoulder of his suit. 'I was there. Now, this is no longer under dis-cussion. We are going to do it Chris's way, because, to be honest, your Echevarria game plan is making me tired.'

'Mike, *I know how these fucking spics work*. This is the wrong move.'

Bryant looked down at him. He seemed more disappointed with the other man than anything else. 'This isn't Guatemala, Nick. Chris is the resident NAME expert, you like it or not. Now you talk to him and get this stuff into a usable form by Monday. I meant what I said. I am tired of dicking about with that old fuck. We go uplincon with Echevarria and his cabinet next week, and I want the axe over his head by then. You coming for a coffee, Chris?'

'Uh. Sure.' Chris got to his feet. 'Nick. You'll call me, right?'

Makin made a noise in his throat.

At the door, Bryant turned and looked back across the office.

'Hey, Nick. No hard feelings, huh? It's just, we've let this slide too far. It's getting out of hand. Time to bring in the riot squad, you know. I

127

don't want Notley looking in on us like we're a bunch of kids just set fire to the kitchen. That's not good for anyone.'

They left Makin with it.

'You threatening him?' asked Chris, in the lift.

Bryant grinned. 'Bit.'

The doors opened at ground level and they walked out into the arching, light filled space of the tower's lobby area. Fountain splash and an ambient subsonic vibe filled the air. Chris felt his mouth flex into a grin of his own.

'You pissed off with him, then?'

'Nick? Nah. Just he's too fucking impressed with himself, is all. Ever since that Guatemala thing. He just needs to know where the orders are coming from, then he jumps. Jesus, look at that.'

Hanging in the air above one of the fountains, a huge Shorn Associates holo ran back-and-forth flicker-cut footage of the Cambodian conflict. Cross-hair graphics sprang up and tracked selected hardware as it appeared on screen – helicopters, assault rifles, medical gear, camera zeroing in, logistical data scrolling down alongside each sniper-caught item. Make, specs, cost. Shorn contribution and involvement.

'This the BBC footage?' asked Bryant. He'd handed publicity to Chris a couple of weeks ago.

'At base, yeah. We bought it right out of the can in Phnom Penh, in case there was something inappropriate in there. You never can tell with that guy Syal, he's a real fucking crusader. Won a Pilger Award last year. Anyway, the woman at Imagicians said they'd generate some of the closer detail themselves, like for the medical hardware. They can shoot some real state-of-the-art life-support stuff in the studio, then mix and match on the palette, so it looks like it was really there.' Chris nodded up at the holo. 'Looks good, huh?'

'Yeah, not too shabby. So did Syal cut up rough when they took his footage off him?'

Chris shrugged. 'Don't think he got any say. We made sure there was a programme producer out there for the handover. Standard sponsorship terms. And what we handed them back had enough battle sequences to come across as gritty realism. You know, corpses on fire, that sort of stuff.'

'No women or children, right.'

'No. Ran it myself on the uplink. It's clean.'

In the holo, a Cambodian guerrilla commander appeared, face weary. He rattled away in Khmer. Subtitling sprang up in red letters. *It is a hard fight but with the help of our corporate partners, our victory is as certain as*

'He really saying that?' asked Bryant curiously.

'Think so.' Chris was tracking a well-endowed blonde woman across the floorspace. 'Think they give them cue cards or something. You know, sometimes I think I could just come down here and stand under the subsonics for half an hour, save myself buying the coffee.'

Bryant spotted where Chris was looking. 'That's not subsonics.'

'Ah, come on Mike.'

'Yeah, that reminds me. Want to go to a party tomorrow night?'

'Party in the zones?' Chris and Mike had been back across the cordons a few times since the *Falkland* incident, though never back to that particular pub and never quite as wrecked as they had been that night. At first, Chris was nervous on these visits, but Mike Bryant's easy familiarity with the cordoned zones and their nightlife slowly won him over. He came to see that there was a trick to handling things there, and that Bryant knew it. You didn't flaunt your elite status, but nor did you try to play it down. You acted like who you were, you didn't try to be liked, and in most cases you were accorded a wary respect. In time the respect might develop into something else, but you didn't expect that. And you didn't need it to have a good time.

'Why should it be in the zones?' asked Bryant innocently.

'Oh, I don't know.' They stepped through the armoured-glass doors and into the street. The sun fell warm on their faces. 'Because the last three were?'

'Bullshit. What about Julie Pinion's bash.'

'Okay, the last two, then. And Julie's wasn't far off, come to that.'

'I'm sure she'd be thrilled to hear that, price she paid for that duplex. That's an up-and-coming regenerated area, Chris.'

'So it is. I'd forgotten.'

They pushed into *Louie Louie's* and nodded at familiar faces in the queue. Chris's fame had eroded sufficiently that all he got from his Shorn colleagues these days were grunts and the odd grin.

'So tell me about this party.'

Mike leaned back on the tiled wall. 'Remember Troy?'

'From the *Falkland*. Sure.' They'd run into the Jamaican a couple more times in clubs on the other side of the wire, but in Chris's mind he was irrevocably linked with the events of that night.

'Well. Turns out his eldest son just got a scholarship to the Thatcher Institute. Fast-track international finance and economics programme, guaranteed placement with a major consulting firm at the end of it. So he's throwing a party at his place. You are cordially invited.'

'So it is in the fucking zones.'

'What? Nah, Troy doesn't live in the zones. He moved out years ago, got a place on the edge of Dulwich.'

'Which edge?'

'Look, it's a better area than Julie Pinion picked, alright. You don't want to come, I'll tell him you're working late. On a Friday.'

'He invited me?'

'Yeah, like I said. Cordially. Bring Faulkner, he said.'

'Nice of him.'

'Yeah, you got to come. Troy's parties are fucking cool. Lots of powders and potions, big sound systems. Really good mix of people too. Suits, media, DJs, dealers.' Bryant's face fell abruptly. 'Shit, you know what. I bet fucking Liz'll be there.'

SEVENTEEN

'Look, I really don't think it's going to be your kind of thing.'

'Why not?' Carla folded her arms and leaned back against the door of the freezer. 'Too high-class for me? Am I going to show you up?'

'That isn't fair. I've asked you to come to every Shorn function we've had this year.'

'Yes. Very dutiful of you.'

'And that's *really* not fucking fair. I wanted you there, every time. Including all the times you said no, I wanted you to be there with me.' Chris lowered his voice. 'I was proud of you. I wanted to show people that.'

'You mean you wanted to show off.'

'Ah,' Chris made a helpless gesture. 'Fuck you, Carla. I put myself on the line for you every single—'

'If you're going to talk to me like that . . .' She was already moving, across the kitchen and away from him. 'I'm going to bed. Goodnight.'

'Fine. Fuck off, then.'

He stood, fists knotted, surrounded by the twinned debris of another evening's separate dining, while she walked out on him. Again. Her voice drifted back down the stairs.

'I've got better things to do tomorrow night, anyway.'

'Fine, then *fuck off*.' He bawled the last two words after her, dismayed at the sudden detonation of fury in his guts.

She didn't answer.

For a while, he crashed plates and cutlery about, loading the dishwasher with a lack of care or interest that he knew could sometimes drag her back into the kitchen to take over. He was kidding himself, and he knew it. This was a new level of hostility they'd reached.

He selected a clean tumbler and went to look for the whisky. Poured the glass half full while he stared into the dead blue glare of the TV. The end titles of whatever mindless terrorists-threaten-civilisation flick they had just spun was already gone, already wiped off the screen as cleanly as the details of plot and action from his mind. Rage evaporating into remorse and a creeping sense of desolation.

A vicious clarity caught up with him, just before he knocked back the drink.

He was glad of the row, he knew abruptly. Glad of the out it had given him.

He was relieved she wouldn't be coming with him.

Relieved, because—

He took the knowledge by the throat and drowned it.

Troy Morris's home might not have been in the cordoned zones, but Chris could see a zone checkpoint just down the street from his front door, and the quality of housefronts plunged rapidly on the way there. The street was restored Victorian, Troy's place and the surrounding facades carefully painted, windows clean. After that it started to get rough – at the checkpoint end, paint was a flecked rumour on most frontages and window glass had become strictly optional. Plastic coverings flapped in a couple of places.

The last three houses on both sides of the street had been demolished to provide open ground on either side of the checkpoint. The rubble had been cleared, and defoliant kept the weeds down. A hundred metres beyond the barriers, the closest structures on the other side were riot-fire blackened and crumbling. A shabby concrete block rose ten storeys high behind the shells, dirty grey facades stained darker with leakage from substandard guttering. Chris spotted someone watching him from a window near the top.

It was a perfect summer evening, still fully light after eight o'clock and the day's heat was leaching slowly out of the air without the rain that had been threatening all afternoon. Junk salsa thumped out of Troy's opened sash windows and when Bryant rang the doorbell, the door seemed to blow open on a gust of bassline.

'Mike! Good to see you, man.' Troy was kitted out in a Jamaica Test '47 shirt with Moses McKenzie's grinning victorious face poking out behind a holoshot fast-bowled cricket ball that seemed to come right off the fabric at them. In contrast, Troy's face seemed unusually sombre. 'Hey, Faulkner. You came. That's good.'

Chris murmured something, but Troy had already gone back to Bryant.

'Mike, listen. Need to talk to you later, man.'

'Sure. What's the deal?'

Troy shook his head. 'Later's better.'

'Whatever you need.' Bryant craned his neck to look down the hall. 'Any chance of a spliff?'

'Yeah, somewhere I guess. That blonde TV face you like, she's here, she's rolling.'

'Right.'

They went down the hall, into the heart of the party.

Chris had never been much of a fiesta machine. Growing up smart and strangely accented in a zone school had ensured he was routinely bullied nearly every day of his life and didn't get invited to many parties. Later, he learned to fight. Later still he grew into looks that a lot of the cooler female kids liked. Life got easier, but the damage was already done. He remained withdrawn and watchful around other people, found it hard to relax and harder to have fun if he was surrounded. A reputation for moody cool, approved and codified by male peers and female fans alike, nailed the doors shut on him. By the time he hacked his way into the corporate world, he had exactly the demeanour required for long-term survival. The edgy, peer-thrown parties and corporate functions, rancid with rivalry and display politics, were a comfortable fit. He turned up because he had to, faked his way through the necessary rituals with polished skill, never let his guard down and hated every minute. Just like the parties of his youth.

Accordingly, he was mildly shocked to discover, a couple of hours later, the extent to which he was enjoying himself at Troy Morris's gathering.

He'd ended up, as he often did at house parties, in the kitchen, mildly buzzed on a couple of tequila slammers and a single line of very good cocaine, arguing South American politics with Troy's son James and a glossy Spanish fashion model called Patricia, who they'd discovered – *wow, you're* kidding *me* – had appeared in the same issue of GQ as Chris, though wearing a lot fewer clothes. Not, Chris couldn't help noticing, that she was wearing a lot of clothes at the moment either. There were about a dozen of these exotic creatures sprinkled around the party like sex-interest models at a motorshow. They drifted elegantly from room to room, drawn occasionally into the orbits of the expensively dressed men they appeared to have come with, spoke English in a variety of alluring non-English accents and, without exception danced superlatively well to the junk salsa blasting out of the speakers in the lounge. To judge by Patricia and her end of the South America conversation, they had all been required to check their brains in at the door. Or had maybe just pawned them for the wisps of designer clothing they were fractionally wrapped in.

'For me, all these bad things they say about Hernan Echevarria, I think they exaggerate. You know, I have met his son in Miami and he is a really quite nice guy. He really loves his father.'

James, perhaps thinking of his imminent entry into the Thatcher Institute and the possible eavesdroppers on this conversation, said nothing. But he was young and unschooled as yet, and his face said it all.

'It isn't really a question of his son,' said Chris, making an effort. 'The point is that excessive use of force by a regime, *any* regime, can make investors nervous. If they think the government is stepping up repressive measures too much, they start to wonder how secure the regime is, and what'll happen to their money if it comes tumbling down. It's like scaffolding around an apartment block – it's not the sort of thing that makes you keen to buy in that block, is it?'

Patricia blinked. 'Oh, I would never buy a flat in a block,' she assured him. 'No garden, and you would have to share the swimming pool. I couldn't stand that.'

Chris blinked as well. There was a short silence.

'Actually, the right kind of repression is usually a pretty good booster for investor confidence. I mean, look at Guatemala.'

It was the dealer of the high-quality powdered goods. He'd been leaning into the conversation on and off for the last hour, each time making remarkably astute observations about the political and economic salients of Latin America. Chris couldn't make up his mind if this was a result of close association on the dealer's part with some of his corporate clients or just exemplary background knowledge of his supply chain. He thought it'd be unwise to ask.

'Guatemala's a different game,' he said.

'How so?' asked the dealer. 'From what I hear their indices are pretty close to Echevarria's, pro rata. About the same balance of payments. Same military budget. Same structural adjustment.'

'But not the same governance durability. The last twenty-five years, you've had over a dozen different regimes, a dozen regime shifts, most of them with violence. The US military has been in and out of there like it was a urinal. Violent change is the norm. The investors expect it there. That's why they get such a huge return. And, sure, violent repression is part of the picture, but it's *successful* violent repression. You're right. Which does inspire investment.'

James cleared his throat. 'But not in the North Andean Monitored?'

'No, Echevarria's been in power a long time. Tight grip on the military, he's one of them himself. Investors expect stability, because that's what he's given them for decades. That's why shooting protesters on the steps of major universities isn't smart.'

'Oh, but they were *marquistas*,' broke in Patricia. 'He had to do that to protect the public.'

'Thirty-eight dead, over a hundred injured,' said Chris. 'Almost all of them students, and more than half from middle-class families. Even a couple of visiting scholars from Japan. That's very bad for business.'

'So are you handling the NAME account for Shorn these days?'

It was Liz Linshaw, suddenly propped against the worktop opposite, a spliff cocked in one upheld hand beside her face, spare arm folded across her body to support the other elbow. He looked across at her and felt her presence turn on a tiny tap in his guts.

He'd seen her a couple of times already, once in passing on the stairs up to the bathroom, once across the cleared space and dancers in the lounge where she was weaving back and forth alone to the junk salsa-beat. She was decked out in classic designer oil-stained Mao jeans, a deep red T-shirt and a black silk jacket. Her riotous blonde hair was gathered up and pinned at one side with an artful lack of care, left elsewhere to tumble down past her shoulder and partly mask that side of her face. There was a tigerish vitality in it all, he saw now, an animation that took the constructed charms of Patricia's kind and made them plastic and spray.

Now she tilted the hair away from her eyes and grinned at him.

He found himself grinning back. 'You know I can't answer that, Liz.'

'Just you sounded so informed.'

'I'm informed about a lot of things. Let's talk about Mars.'

It was that season's Dex and Seth ultra-cool quote, immortalised in a series of sketches featuring Seth's fawning, craven TV interviewer and Dex's high-powered American corporate shark. Whenever the interview steered into politically iffy waters, Dex started to make angry American noises that didn't actually contain any words and Seth's interviewer invariably reacted by cringing and suggesting *let's talk about Mars*.

With that line, you knew that across Europe, hundreds of thousands of watchers were reeling away from their illegally tuned screens, clutching their sides and weeping with laughter. Apart from being as far removed as you could humanly get from current affairs on Earth, news from Mars was famously dull. After nearly two decades of manned missions and exploration, the rotating teams of scientists were doing nothing anyone cared remotely about. Sure, people might be able to live out there in a century. Big fucking deal. Meanwhile, here are some more red rocks. *More Red Rocks* was another big Dex and Seth number, the two comedians done up in pressure suits and geeky masks, bouncing in faked low g and singing the lyrics to tunes ripped off from junk-salsa giants like Javi Reyes and Inez Zequina.

'Let's *not* talk about Mars,' said Liz Linshaw firmly, and everyone in the kitchen broke up with laughter. Amidst it, she leaned across the narrow space between them, and offered the spliff to Chris.

Her eyes, he suddenly noticed, were grey-green.

The dealer sniffed the air with professional interest. 'That the new Moroccan stuff?' he wanted to know. 'Hammersmith Hammer?'

Liz spared him a glance. 'No. Thai direct.'

'Anyone I know?'

'I seriously doubt it.'

Chris drew it down, coughed a little. Let it up again almost immediately. He wasn't a big fan of the stuff. Aside from a couple of parties at Mel's place with Carla, he hadn't smoked in years.

Liz Linshaw was watching him.

'Very nice,' he wheezed, and tried to hand the spliff back. She pushed it away, and used the motion to lean in close. Close enough that tendrils of her hair brushed his face.

'I'd really like to talk to you somewhere,' she said.

'Fair enough.' He found a stupid grin crawling onto his mouth and twitched it away. 'Garden?'

'I'll meet you out there.' She withdrew, nodded casually at James and the powder man, and wandered out of the kitchen, leaving Chris holding the spliff. Patricia watched her go with enough venom in her gaze to poison a city water supply.

'Who is that woman?' she asked.

'Friend,' said Chris, and drifted off in Liz Linshaw's wake.

Either Troy's garden was larger than he'd expected or the Thai grass was already beginning to kick in. It was full dark by now, but Troy had thoughtfully provided half a dozen garden torches, driven at intervals into the long tongue of well-kept lawn. The garden was bordered by a mix of trees and shrubs, amidst which the dwarf palms seemed to be doing the best, and at the far end a gnarled oak tree raised crooked limbs at the sky. From one lower branch someone had strung a simple wooden swing on blue plastic ropes that picked up the flickering light of the nearest torches and glowed. Liz Linshaw was seated there, one long leg drawn up to wedge her body back against one of the ropes, the other on the ground, idly stirring the swing in tiny arcs. There was a fresh spliff burning in her hand.

Chris hung from the moment, and felt something happen to him. It wasn't just the fact that he knew she was waiting for him. There was something in the air, something that caught in the luminous blue twistings of the swing ropes, in the casual elegance of the way she had folded her body like an origami sketch of sexual appeal. The lawn was a carpet laid out under his feet, and the other people in the garden – he only registered them now – seemed to turn in unison and approve his passage towards the tree.

He grimaced and threw away the spliff. Made his way warily to her.

'Well,' she said.

'You wanted to talk to me.' It came out rougher than he'd intended.

'Yes.' She smiled up at him. 'I've wanted to talk with you since the Tebbit Centre. Since the first time we met, in fact.'

It felt as if the ground beneath his feet had gone suddenly soggy and unsupportive.

'Why is that?'

She lifted a hand. 'Why do you think?'

'Uh, Liz, to be honest, I thought you and Mike—'

'Oh.' The crooked smile was back. She smoked some more and he struggled with his doped senses. 'He told you about that. Well, Chris, how can I put this? Mike Bryant and I are not some kind of exclusive event.'

The ground was, apparently, gone now.

'In fact,' she said very softly, 'there's no reason why I can't ask you for what Mike's been giving me. Is there?'

He stared at her. 'Sorry?'

'Interviews,' she said, and laughed. 'Your life so far, Chris. My publishers are promising me a half-million advance, if I can come up with another book like *The New Asphalt Warriors*. It's a guaranteed bestseller. And with the Nakamura thing, Cambodia and the rest of it, you're the man of the moment. Ideal focus.'

The ground came up and hit him in the heels, so hard he almost stumbled.

'Oh.' He looked away from the level grey-green gaze. 'Right.'

She was still grinning. He could hear it in her voice. 'Why, what did you think I was talking about?'

'No, I. Yeah. Fine, that, that's good.'

She pushed with her foot and cranked the swing back a little, then let go. The edge of the wooden seat hit him across the front of the thighs. Her weight swung with it, pressed against him.

'Was there something else you wanted, Chris?'

Sprawled, airbrushed bodies on the exercise bench, liquid moans

Carla, the house, the stagnant anger through empty rooms

You're a good guy, Chris. *Bryant, lolling semi-conscious on the hotel bed*

That's you. You're a. Fucking good guy.

It fell through his head like an avalanche, images crushing each other.

Liz Linshaw's cleavage loaded into an open-necked blouse

Carla, soaping him in the shower, hands still gritty with the work on the Saab

Mitsue Jones, trapped in the wreck of her Mitsubishi, struggling

what we value here at Shorn is resolution

you're a fucking good guy

was there something else you wanted

'Chris!'

It was Bryant. Chris took a sudden step back from Liz Linshaw and the swing. He saw her face, and the way it changed. Then he was facing Mike as he strode up the garden towards them.

'Been looking for you everywhere, man. Hi, Liz.' The conjunction

137

appeared to strike him for the first time. His eyes narrowed. 'What are you guys doing out here?'

'Talking,' said Liz, unruffled.

Chris scrambled for cover. 'Book deal.' He made a gesture at Liz that felt like a warding off. 'She says.'

'Yeah?' Bryant gave Liz an unfriendly look. 'Well, my advice is don't tell her anything too realistic. You wouldn't want to get labelled an animal.'

Liz, smiling to herself, turning away, unfolding herself from the swing. Chris shut it out and focused on Bryant.

'So what's happening?

'Ah, no big deal. Troy needs a favour. Liz, you want to give us a little privacy?'

'Already leaving, boys. Already leaving.'

They both watched her walk back down the garden and into the house. Mike turned and mimed a pistol at Chris's face. He wasn't smiling.

'Hope you know what you're doing here, Chris.'

'Oh, for fuck's sake, Mike. I'm married. She just wants another half-million advance from her publishers.'

'I wouldn't count on that being the whole story.'

'Mike, I am *married*.'

'Yeah, me too.' Bryant rubbed at his face. 'Not like you, though, huh?'

'You said that, not me.'

'Yeah.' Bryant smiled sadly and slung an arm across the other man's shoulders. 'You're a good guy, Chris. You're a good fucking guy.'

Chris stowed the unease slithering through him.

'So. What's the deal with Troy?'

It was all in the zones.

Mike said he'd drive, though Chris wasn't convinced he was in any way the more sober or straight of the two of them. They went out to the car together with Troy, who for the first time since Chris had known him seemed angry and uncomfortable.

'I'd come with you, Mike . . .'

'I know you would, man. But you can't.' Mike held up his corporate plastic. 'We're the only ones can do this for you. You know that.'

The Jamaican shook his head. 'I owe you for this. Big time.'

'You don't owe me shit, Troy. Remember Camberwell?'

'Yeah.'

'Right, well as far as I'm concerned, I'm still paying off the interest. 'kay? Now give Chris the camera.'

Troy Morris swallowed and handed over the shoulder set. His features were knotted up with rage and frustration. Chris remembered him at the *Falkland*, the sawn-off shotgun propped against his shoulder as he left laughing, the sense of street competence that radiated off the man. It was a brutal transition to the Troy he saw before him now. Chris felt a jagged pang of sympathy. He knew the feeling of sudden impotence from his own youth, knew how it could cook your brains in your head, chew up your insides until you couldn't sleep.

He got in the car. Stowed the shoulder set in the back seat.

'Be back before you know it,' said Mike as he swung himself in the driver's side. The engine rumbled awake. Gears engaged and the BMW swept out into the street.

'What was that about Camberwell?' Chris asked, as they came up on the checkpoint lights.

'Yeah, first time I met Troy. About ten years ago, back before he had this place. I was out in the zones, hitting the whiff pretty hard, went home with the wrong woman.'

'For a change,' said Chris sourly.

Mike chuckled. 'Yeah, guess you never can get all the spots off the tiger, huh?'

'Leopard.'

'What?' They pulled in beside the checkpoint. A nervous-looking kid in guard uniform came out of the cabin and glanced into the car. He seemed unsure of himself. Mike leaned out and handed over his plastic.

'Leopard,' said Chris, while they were waiting. 'Tigers used to have stripes, not spots. Leopards were the spotted ones.'

'You sure?'

'Yeah, saw it on some nature digest a while back. They used to be able to climb trees, just like a real cat.'

'What, tigers?'

'Leopards.'

The young guard finally got his hipswipe unit to work and Mike's card chimed through. The barrier rose and they were waved across.

'I swear these guys get younger every time we do the zones,' said Chris. 'I mean, is it *really* a good idea to give automatic weapons to teenagers like that?'

'Why not? They do it in the army.'

They hit their first pothole. Mike took a left. Around them, the housing grew increasingly haggard.

'So yeah, Camberwell. This was before I met Suki. I was pretty wild back then. Pretty stupid. Used to get through a can and a half of Durex a month, easily. And the drugs, ah, you know how it is when you've got money. Anyway, this tart wasn't really a tart, or maybe she was a tart and she changed her mind, I don't know. End result, there were these three guys waiting outside her apartment. They threw me down a flight of stairs and started dancing on my head. Troy was living in the apartment downstairs, he heard the noise, came out and chased them off.'

'All three of them?'

'Yeah, that's right. He's pretty fucking hard, Troy is. Or could be he faced them down. Don't know, I was out by then, semi-conscious. But, yeah, maybe he just talked them out of it. See, they were black, I was white, Troy was black. That maybe had something to do with it. Or maybe not. Anyway, the guy saved me getting hospitalised for certain, maybe saved me from a wheelchair. I owe him forever, and then some.'

They drove in silence the rest of the way, parked outside a nondescript little row of three-storey houses and sat for a moment. Mike hauled the camera out of the back seat and dumped it in Chris's lap.

'Okay, now just follow my lead. Back me up.'

They got out of the car, went through an ungated garden gateway and up a short, decaying concrete path. The door was cheap beige impact plastic, scarred and ugly. A Sony securicam lens and speaker grille gleamed incongruously from the chest-high panel in which it had been set. The installation looked professional. Mike touched the edge of the panel with one finger.

'See. Going up in the world. Just like the man said.'

Chris shook his head and whispered. 'I can't believe—'

'Believe it.' Mike hit the doorbell. 'Now turn that thing on.'

Chris found the on/off in the camera's grip. A cone of hard light leapt out of the front end and splashed on the scarred plastic of the front door. He wondered if this was going to play. Most state-of-the-art shoulder sets these days would shoot the whole range from infra-red to ultraviolet with no external lighting at all.

Movement behind the door. He shouldered the set and tried to look like a cameraman.

'You know what fucking time it is?' said a female voice from the speaker grille. 'This had better be fucking important.'

Mike pitched his voice media bouncy. 'Ah, Mrs Dixon? This is Gavin Wallace from *Powerful People*. Is your husband home?'

A silence. Chris imagined her peering into the securicam screen at the two expensively-dressed men on her doorstep. The voice came, tinged with suspicion.

'You from TV?'

'Yes, Mrs Dixon, that's what I said. Your husband has been selected from—'

A second voice, male and further from the speaker pick-up. The woman's voice faded as she turned away from the door.

'Griff, it's the TV. *Powerful People*.'

Another pause, laced with muffled voices. Someone had a hand over the pick-up. Mike looked at Chris, shrugged and put on the media voice again.

'Mr Dixon, if you're there. We don't have a lot of time. The helicopter has already left Blackfriars, and we need to get through the preliminaries before it arrives. We're on a very tight schedule.'

It was the right chord. Half the draw of *Powerful People* derived from the breakneck pace the programme sustained from the moment the names came out of the studio computer. There was much aerial footage, cityscapes tilting away beneath the swift-flying pick-up copters, locator teams sprinting through the zones in search of the night's contestants—

The door cracked open the width of a heavy-duty security chain. A lean, pale face appeared in the gap, blinking in the light from the shoulder set. There was a thin pink streak of artiflesh smeared over a cut on one temple.

'Mr Dixon. Good.' Mike leaned in, beaming. 'Gavin Wallace. *Powerful People*. Pleased to. Oh. That looks nasty, that cut. Make-up'll need to see that. In fact, I hate to say this but in all conscience—'

It was a stroke of genius. *Powerful People*'s selection teams had been known to pass over a candidate for as little as recent dental surgery. The door hinged in, the chain came off. Griff Dixon stood before them in all his midnight glory.

'It's just a scratch,' he said. 'Honest. I'll be fine. I'm fighting fit.'

It was an appropriate expression, Chris thought. Dixon was stripped to the waist, taut-muscled torso rising from a pair of jeans with real stains on them. His hair was a razored single centimetre all over, there were heavy black boots on his feet and in his hand was a crumpled-up white T-shirt that Chris somehow knew he had just tugged off.

'Well,' said Mike richly. 'If you're quite sure you—'

'I'm fine, I'm fine. Look, you want to come in, right.'

'Well, alright.' Mike made a show of wiping his shoes on the doorstep and walked into the threadbare hall, smiling a big TV smile. 'Hello, Mrs Dixon.'

A thin, worn-looking woman about Carla's age stood behind Dixon's sculpted musculature, one thin-boned hand resting on his shoulder. She squinted into the camera light and brushed vaguely at her shoulder-length brown hair.

'This is my colleague Christopher Mitchell. I'm sorry. Could we maybe film this in the living room?'

'Yeah, yeah. Sure.' Dixon's eagerness was almost pitiful. 'Jazz, make some tea, will you. Or would you like coffee?'

Bryant glanced round. 'Christopher?'

'Uhh, yeah.' Chris fumbled the question. 'Coffee. White, no sugar.'

'And black for me,' said Mike. 'One sugar, please. Thank you.'

The woman disappeared up the hall, while Dixon let them pass and closed the door behind them. In his excitement, he forgot the chain. They went left into a small living room dominated by a huge Audi entertainment deck set against one wall. The system didn't look any older than the securicam in the door.

'Ah, that corner, I think,' said Mike, nodding at Chris. 'I'll sit here and Griff, do you mind if I call you Griff, if you could sit here.'

Dixon lowered himself onto the edge of the armchair. There was something painfully vulnerable in the expression on his face as he looked at Bryant.

'You'll need to get dressed,' said Mike gently.

'Huh?'

'The T-shirt?'

'Oh. Oh, no, it's. Filthy.' He compressed the already crumpled piece of clothing in his hands. 'Been working on my bike. I'll go up and get another one.'

'Well.' Bryant lifted a forestalling hand. 'Perhaps in a moment. But we really need to get these questions sorted out. Uhm. You have a child, don't you?'

'Yeah.' Dixon grinned happily. 'Joe. He's three.'

'And he's,' Mike gestured at the ceiling. 'Upstairs asleep, I suppose.'

'Well, yeah.'

'Good, good. Alright, now the official questions,' Bryant reached into his jacket. 'Where are we, ah. Yes.'

The Nemex.

Even for Chris, the transition was an almost electrical jolt. Mike transformed in a single motion from beaming, chocolate-voiced media host to a man with a levelled gun.

For Dixon, it was clearly beyond the realms of comprehension.

'What's,' he shook his head, grin still licking around his lips. 'What's, what're you doing?'

'Chris.' Mike didn't look round. 'Close the door.'

Dixon still hadn't got it. 'Is this part of—'

'Show us the T-shirt.'

'Wha—'

'*Show me the motherfucking T-shirt, you piece of shit!*'

'Mike?'

'Just relax, Chris. Everything's under control. When Jazz comes back, you just keep her out of the way. We're not here for her.'

Dixon stirred. 'Listen—'

'No, *you* listen.' Bryant took a step forward and drew a fresh downward bead on Dixon's face. 'Throw the T-shirt on the floor. Now.'

'No.'

'I'm not going to ask you again. Show me the fucking T-shirt.'

'No.' It was like talking to a cornered child.

Bryant moved faster than Chris had ever seen another human being move. From standing, he was suddenly at Dixon's chair. The Nemex whipped out sideways and Dixon was reeling back, clutching at his head with both hands. The T-shirt fell to the threadbare carpet and Bryant scooped it up left-handed. Blood splintered bright through Dixon's fingers.

'You're not on TV, Griff.' Mike's tone had gone back to conversational. He crouched to Dixon's level. 'There's no need to be shy.'

He shook the T-shirt out and laid it on the floor, face up. It was clean and freshly ironed, black lettering on soft white cotton.

WHITE ARYAN RESISTANCE.

The words were printed horizontally, one under the other, the first letter of each limned in red in case someone didn't get the message.

The door swung open and Jazz backed into the room, still crouching from the contortion necessary to depress the handle without putting down the tray in her hands.

'I brought some—'

Turning, she saw Griff cringing and bleeding in the chair, saw the gun in Mike Bryant's hand. She dropped the tray and shrieked. The coffee leapt sideways, broad swipes of liquid on its way to the floor. Cheap crockery scattered and broke amidst something else. Biscuits, Chris saw. She'd brought biscuits.

'Be quiet,' snapped Bryant. 'You're going to wake Joe up.'

Naming the child seemed to do something to Griff Dixon. He dropped his hands from his face. The gouge that the forward sight of the Nemex had opened in his scalp showed clearly through his razored hair, and blood was running down his face into one eye.

'You fucking listen to me. Whoever you are, I know people. You touch any of us, I'll—'

'You'll do *nothing*, Griff. You'll sit there and fucking bleed, and you'll listen to me, and you'll do *nothing*. Jazz, will you *shut up*. Chris, for Christ's sake make her sit down or something.'

Chris got hold of the woman and forced her onto the sofa. She was trembling and making a high keening sound that might have had the words *my baby* in it somewhere.

143

'I know people who—'

'You know *political* people, Griff.' The scary thing about Mike's voice, Chris realised, was the energy of it. He sounded like an enthusiastic coach pushing a fighter who wasn't punching his weight. 'Political scum. Look at this gun, Griff. Recognise it?'

It was only then that Chris saw the fear appear on Dixon's face. For the first time since they'd entered the house, Griff Dixon was afraid.

'That's right.' Bryant had seen it too. He grinned. 'Nemesis Ten. Now you know the only people got access to these babies, don't you Griff. You're well enough connected for that. This is a corporate gun. And where it comes from, politicians mean less than a bucket of runny shit.'

Jazz's keening changed pitch.

'First question for you, Griff.' A tremor ran down Mike Bryant's face. It was the single indication of the fury he was working through. 'What possible reason does a member of the white master race have to stick his dick in a black woman?'

Dixon flinched as if struck. His wife's keening broke abruptly into something between a sob and a howl.

'Didn't you understand the question? Would you like to phone a friend? I asked you, *what possible reason does a member of the white master race have to stick his dick in a black woman*? Especially, Griff, if that black woman is screaming and fighting and begging you not to do it?'

The room settled down to quiet and the sound of Dixon's wife weeping. Bryant crouched again. He pressed his lips together hard. Pushed out a breath.

'Alright, Griff. Here's what we're going to do. I'm not going to hurt your wife or your son, because in the end it isn't their fault you're a piece of shit. But I'm going to shoot you in both kneecaps and the balls.'

Jazz erupted in shrieks. She tried to get up from the sofa and reach her husband. Chris held her back. Bryant got up.

'And then I'm going to blind you in one eye. There's no way around any of this. I want you to understand that. You and your friends picked on the wrong black girl.'

Dixon came out of the chair, screaming. For a brief second he reached Mike with his fists. Then the hollow boom of the Nemex shook the room and Dixon was convulsed on the floor, blood soaking the crotch of his jeans. The new sound that came out of him didn't sound human.

Mike Bryant got back to his feet, bleeding from the mouth. He got his breath back, then very carefully sighted on Dixon's left knee and pulled the trigger. The white supremacist must have passed out because the noise stopped. Bryant wiped his mouth and lined up on the other leg. By now Jazz had given up fighting Chris and was holding onto him as if he could rescue her from drowning. Her tears burnt on his neck. He covered her ears with his hands as Mike pulled the trigger for the third time.

In the cordite-reeking quiet, he watched as Bryant stowed the Nemex, took out a steel-cased pen, bent to Dixon's head, peeled back the eyelid and jabbed hard into the eye beneath. It all seemed to happen very slowly and without sound and somehow he found that his gaze had slipped away by the end and focused on the sleek lines of the entertainment deck.

'Chris.' Bryant was leaning over him.

'What? Yeah, yeah.'

It took both of them to unfasten Jazz's grip on Chris. When they had finally tugged her away, Bryant crouched in front of her and gripped her lower jaw in one hand. In the other, he held up a folded wad of notes.

'Alright, now listen to me. This money is for you. Here. Here, take it. Take it, for Christ's sake.' Finally, he had to open her hand and fold her fingers around the notes himself. 'If you want him to live, you'd better get help for him soon. I don't much care if he lives or dies, but if he lives you tell him. He, or anyone else around here, touches another person with the surname Morris or Kidd, I'll come back for the other eye, and I'll kill your son.'

Her whole body jerked. Bryant took her hand and squeezed the money into it again.

'Now you tell him that, and you make sure he understands I mean it. I don't want to come back here, Jazz. I don't want to do it. But I will if your fuckwit racist husband and his friends make me.'

In the car, Bryant put his hands on centre of the steering wheel in front of him and pressed his body back into the padded seat. He emptied his lungs in a long, hard single breath. Then, he just stared at the windscreen. He seemed to be waiting for something. There were lights on in some of the houses, but either no one had heard the gunshots or no one had any interest in finding out what they signified.

'Did you mean it?' Chris asked.

'The eye?' Bryant nodded to himself. His voice was barely above a murmur. 'Oh, yes. People like that, they've got to have something to lose. Otherwise, you've got no leverage on them.'

'No, his son. Did you mean it about his son?'

Mike looked across at him, outraged. 'Jesus Christ, of course not. Fuck, Chris, what kind of man do you think I am?'

He was silent for a while. Very faintly, the sound of a siren came wailing to them out of the night. Bryant looked at his watch. He grunted.

'Fast. She must have called a pricey one.'

He started the engine. The BMW's lights carved up the gloom in the poorly lit street.

'Let's get out of here, huh? We've got a lot to do.'

It took them the rest of the night to find the other two men. Both were young, neither had a family and it was Friday night in the zones. Troy Morris's information gave starting points, but from there on in, it was hard work. Mike drove, Chris checked streets, house numbers, the names on dismal little neon signs. They worked their way through mistaken addresses, dimly-lit pipe houses, underground clubs with promising names like *Cross of Iron* and *Endangered Race*, brothels, fast-food stands and even a local paycop garrison near the river. Everywhere they went, Mike Bryant brandished the Nemex or thick wads of cash to almost interchangeable effect. The money worked more often than the gun. It unzipped the right lips, opened the right doors.

They found the first man at a hot-dog stand, drunk and swaying. He didn't know they were looking for him. No one had bothered to warn him. The white supremacists weren't big on solidarity, and besides, functioning phones weren't all that common in the zones. The landlines got fucked up by technosmart vandal gangs and mobile cover was a bad joke, fatally compromised by rolling waves of government jamming aimed at satellite programming like Dex and Seth. Wheeled transport was all but non-existent. People didn't get about much, messages even less.

Bryant leaned on the stand, bought the man a burger and watched him eat it. Then he told him why he was there. The man took off, trying to sprint. They went after him. Halfway down a side alley they found him vomiting up Mike's burger and the rest of the night's intake. Mike shot him four times in the groin and stomach with the Nemex, then bent to peer at the damage in the dim light. When he was sure the man was bleeding to death, they left him alone.

They had to drag the second supremacist out of a bed that wasn't his own in a fifteenth-floor apartment that reeked of damp and rat poison. The woman next to him didn't even wake up. When they got him into the living room he was mumbling, incoherent with ingested chemicals and sleep. They took an arm each and ran him head first against the balcony window until it smashed through. Outside, on the glass-strewn balcony, dawn was turning the night air slowly grey and there were birds singing in the trees below. Neither of them were sure if the man was dead or not. They stopped over the body, careful to avoid getting

146

glass in their hands, picked him up and threw him over the rail. The birdsong stopped abruptly with the impact on the concrete below.

In the kitchen, Mike left money for the broken window.

EIGHTEEN

The sun caught them leaving the zones somewhere south of London Bridge. The streets were already full of pedestrians on their way to work and Mike had to hoot repeatedly to get them out of the road as they approached the checkpoint. Queues backed up hundreds long, snaking randomly away from the various turnstile entrypoints. There was even a queue at the road barrier, three rusting buses that looked almost pre-millennial, one of them belching oily fumes from its exhaust. Beyond the checkpoint, glimpsed through the low rise of preferential South Bank housing, gold light impacted and dripped on glass skyscraper panels across the river.

'Jesus, look at this,' said Bryant disgustedly. 'Emissions monitoring, my fucking arse. Look at the shit coming out of that bus.'

'Yeah, and it's packed. We're going to be here for a while.'

It was true. Armed guards were ordering the passengers out of the first bus, lining them up. The first line had already assumed the position – right hand on the back of the head, passcard held up in the left. A single guard moved down the line, scrutinising the cards one at a time and swiping them through his hip unit. Every second card needed repeated swipes.

'Don't know why they bother,' Chris yawned with a force that made his jaw creak. 'It's not like there's been anything resembling terrorism in London for the last couple of years.'

'Yeah, and you're looking at the reason why. Don't knock it, man.' Bryant drummed his fingers on the wheel. 'Still, this is going to take forever. You want to get breakfast?'

He jerked a thumb over his shoulder. Chris twisted about in his seat. A handful of frontages down the street they had just driven up, a grimed sign said *Cafe*. People flowed in and out with paper packets and garishly coloured cans.

'In there?'

'Sure. Cheap and nasty, plenty of grease. Just what you need.'

'Speak for yourself.' Chris still felt slightly queasy when he thought about what Mike had done to Griff Dixon's eye. 'Think I'll stick to coffee.'

'Suit yourself.' Bryant plugged the BMW into reverse and punted it back along the street. The engine whined high with unnecessary revs. Pedestrians scrambled to get out of the way. Level with the cafe, Bryant slewed into the curb and jolted to a halt at a rakish angle. He grinned.

'Man, I love the parking in this part of town.'

They climbed out to hostile stares. Bryant smiled bleakly and alarmed the car with the remote held high and visible. Someone behind Chris rasped something unintelligible and hawked up spit. Twitchy with the events of the night, Chris pivoted about. The phlegm glistened yellow and fresh near his feet. Not what he needed.

He scanned the bystanders' faces. Mostly they shuffled and looked away, but one young black man stood his ground and stared back.

'You got something to say to me?' Chris asked him.

The man stayed silent but he didn't look away. His white companion laid a hand on his arm. Bryant came round the car, yawning and stretching.

'Problem?'

'No problem,' said the white one, pulling his friend away.

'Good, you'd better get cracking then.' Bryant jerked a thumb up the street. 'That's a hell of a queue up there. You coming, Chris?'

He shoved back the door of the cafe and they worked their way past the line of people waiting at the take-out counter to the seating area at the back. There were no customers apart from a black-clad old man who sat alone, staring into a mug of tea.

'This'll do.' Mike slid into a booth and beat a drum riff on the tabletop with the flat of both hands. 'I'm starving.'

There was a menu scrawled in luminous purple marker across the quickwipe surface of the table. Chris glanced across it and looked away again, nervous of the standing queue at his back. He knew the food. He'd eaten in places like this most of his teens, and occasionally, after a mechanic's night out with Carla and the others from Mel's Autofix, he still did. Like prime-time satellite programming, it would be a loudly flavoured blend of low-grade bulking agents seasoned with garishly advertised vitamin and mineral additives. The sausages would average about thirty per cent meat, the bacon came swollen with injected water. He was glad he had no appetite.

A waitress appeared at the booth.

'Getya?'

'Coffee,' said Chris. 'White. Glass of water.'

'I'll have the big breakfast,' said Mike expansively. 'You get eggs with that?'

'They're Qweggs,' said the waitress sullenly.

'Right. Better give me, uh, six of those then. And plenty of toast. Coffee for me too. Black.'

The waitress turned her back and strode off. Mike watched her go.

'Friendly here.'

Chris shrugged. 'They know who we are.'

'Yeah, which means a massive tip if they can just secrete a little common courtesy. Pretty fucking short-sighted attitude, if you ask me.'

'Mike.' Chris leaned across the table. 'What do you expect? The clothes you're wearing cost more than that girl makes in a year. She probably lives in an apartment smaller than my office, damp walls, leaking drains, no security, and about two-thirds her weekly wage just to cover the rent.'

'Oh, and that's *my* fucking fault?'

'It isn't about—'

'Look, I'm not her fucking mother. I didn't pop her out in the zones, just so I could claim breeding benefit. And if she doesn't like it here, she can make her own sweet way out, just like anybody else.'

Chris looked at his friend with sudden dislike. 'Yeah, right.'

'That's right. Listen, Troy was born and bred in the zones, he made it out. James is off to the Scratcher in six weeks, he could end up making more money than both of us. So don't tell me it can't be done.'

'And what about Troy's cousin? The one got raped two nights ago by Dixon and his pals. How come she hasn't made it out?'

'How the fuck should I know?' Bryant's anger collapsed as rapidly as it had sprouted. He slumped back in his seat. 'Look, all I'm saying, Chris, is some of us have what it takes. Others don't. I mean, this isn't some cut-rate little African horrorshow of a nation. You don't have to live in the zones because of your *tribe* or something. No one cares what colour you are here, what religion or race. All you've got to do is make the money.'

'They seem to care what colour you are in Dixon's neighbourhood.'

'Yeah, that's fucking *politics*, Chris. Some maggots' nest of little local government thugs looking for a way to build a powerbase. It's got nothing to do with the way the real world works.'

'That's not the impression I get from Nick Makin.'

'Makin?'

'Yeah, you heard him in that meeting. He's a fucking racist, that's why he can't handle Echevarria.'

'Yeah, well.' Mike brooded. 'Might have to do something about Makin.'

The coffee came. It wasn't as bad as Chris had expected. Bryant drained his and asked for another cup.

'There going to be an investigation?' wondered Chris.

'Nah, shouldn't think so.'

'They got you for those jackers at the *Falkland*.'

'Yeah, that's a whole different story. Civil rights activists, off the back of grieving family members, my little Jason was a good boy, he only stole cars because social deprivation blah, blah, boo, hoo. That kind of crap. This thing with Dixon is different. There's an agenda. Dixon's political friends are on the anti-globalism wing. Britain for the British, immigrants out, fuck multiculturalism and tear down the international corporate power conspiracy. Right now, the last thing they need is for that to come out into the open. They'll sit on this.'

'But the zone police—'

'They'll buy them off. They'll get some paycop outfit to dig the slugs out of Dixon's floor and the street under that other piece of shit we wasted, and they'll make them as Nemex load.' Bryant grinned. 'That should send a message.'

Chris frowned. 'Isn't that going to be a whole stack of political capital for them? The big bad corporations, off the leash. They'll milk it 'til it bleeds.'

'Oh, yeah, on a local level, of course they will. They'll turn Dixon into a fucking martyr, no doubt. If he lives, they can have him in a wheelchair at the local Young Nazi fundraisers, and if he dies they can have his weeping widow do the same thing. But they aren't about to take on Shorn in the public arena. They know what we'd do to them.'

'And Dixon?'

Mike grinned again. 'Well, I'd say Dixon's got his hands full for the next six months just learning to walk again. And if he ever does, well he's got a family and another eye to worry about before he does anything stupid. Plus, you know what? Somehow, I don't think the civil rights crowd are going to be there for him. Just not the right profile.'

Mike's breakfast arrived on a tray and the waitress set about laying it out. While she worked, Bryant grabbed a Qwegg off the plate with finger and thumb, and popped it in his mouth. He chewed vigorously.

'You going to work today?' he asked through the mouthful.

Chris thought about the house, cold with Carla's absence or, even worse, with her unspeaking presence. He nodded.

'Good.' Mike swallowed the Qwegg, nodded thanks at the departing waitress and picked up his knife and fork. 'Listen, I want you to call Joaquin Lopez. Tell him to catch a flight down to the NAME and start sounding out the names on that list. Today, if possible. We'll pick up the expenses.'

Chris felt a small surge go through his guts, not unlike the feeling he'd had talking to Liz Linshaw the night before. He nursed his coffee and watched Mike eat for a while.

'You think we're going to have to do it?' he asked finally.

'Do what?'

'Blow Echevarria out of the water.'

'Well,' Bryant chased another Qwegg around his plate and after some effort managed to puncture it with his fork. 'Believe me, I'd love to. But in this case, you know how it goes. Regime change is our worst-case scenario. We'll only go that way if we absolutely have to.'

He gestured at Chris with his fork.

'You just get Lopez on the case. Get the names to Makin, make sure there's a clear strategy locked down for the uplincon next week.'

'You want me in on that?'

Bryant shook his head, chewing. He swallowed.

'Nah, you stay out of it. I want a clean break between current negotiations and whatever we need you to do. Echevarria doesn't know about you, he doesn't know about your contacts. There's no line for him to follow. Better that way.'

'Right.'

Bryant grinned. 'Don't look so disappointed, man. I'm doing you a favour. I tell you, every time I have to shake hands with that piece of shit, I feel like I need to disinfect. Murderous old fuck.'

They gave it another half hour to let the queues subside, then paid and left. Despite his grouching, Bryant left a tip almost as much as the cost of the whole meal. Outside, he yawned and stretched and pivoted about, face turned up to the sun. He seemed in no hurry to get in the car.

'We going to work?' asked Chris.

'Yeah, in a minute.' Mike yawned again. 'Don't feel much like it, tell you the truth. Day like this, I should be home playing with Ariana. Playing with Suki, come to that. Christ, you know, we haven't fucked in nearly two weeks.'

'Tell me about it.'

Bryant cocked his head. 'Carla giving you grief about that?'

'Only all the time.' Chris considered the reflexive lie. 'Well, recently not so much. We're both tired, you know. Don't see a lot of each other.'

'Yeah. Got to watch that shit. Come the end of quarter, you ought to take some time out. Maybe get out to the island for a week.'

'You see Hewitt signing off on that?'

'She'll have to, Chris, the profile you've got on Cambodia. It's turning into the year's premium contract. Shorn owe us all some serious downtime before the end of this year. Hey, who knows, maybe me and Suki'll get out there the same time as you guys. That'd be cool, huh?'

'Yeah. Cool.'

'Well, don't sound so fucking enthusiastic about it.'

Chris laughed. 'Sorry. I'm wasted.'

'Yeah, let's kick this in gear.' Bryant disarmed the BMW's alarm and cracked the driver's side door. 'Sooner we get out of here, sooner we can get home and act like we have a life.'

They cleared the checkpoint without incident, threaded onto the approach road to the bridge and accelerated up across the river. Sunlight turned the water to hammered bronze on either side of them. Chris fought down a wave of tiredness and promised himself a take-out from *Louie Louie's* as soon as they hit the Shorn tower.

'Be good to get some real coffee,' he muttered.

'That coffee wasn't bad.'

'Ah, come *on*. It was about as real as the eggs. I'm talking about something with a *pedigree* here. Not fucking Malsanto's Miracle beans. Something with a hit you can feel.'

'Fucking speedfreak.'

They both laughed, as if on cue. The BMW filled up with the sound as they left the river behind and cruised into the gold-mirrored canyons beyond. To Chris, groggy with no sleep and the events and chemicals of the night before, it felt good at a level deeper than he could find words to explain.

NINETEEN

Mike dropped him outside *Louie Louie's* and drove off into the car decks with a wave. Chris shot himself full of espresso at the counter, then ordered take-out and another coffee to carry up to his office. Shorn was unusually quiet for a Saturday, and he barely saw anyone on his way in. Even the security shift was made up of men and women he barely knew well enough to nod at.

It was the pattern for the day. Outside of the datadown, there was no one to talk to. Makin had not shown, which was going to make for a tight squeeze when they tried to put together the NAME package on Monday. Irritated, Chris rang Joaquin Lopez anyway and told him what he wanted. Lopez, at least, was keen, but it was still the early hours of the morning in the Americas and Chris had got him out of bed. His conversation wasn't sparkling. He grunted back understanding, possible flight times and hung up.

Chris rang Carla at Mel's and discovered she'd taken the day off. He checked his mobile, but there was no message. He phoned home, and heard her voice telling anyone who rang she was flying up to Tromsö to see her mother. She would probably stay the week. It sounded, to Chris's tutored ear, as if she had been crying. He threw the mobile across the office in a jag of caffeine-induced rage. He rang Mike, who was on the other line. He retrieved the mobile, got a grip on himself and went back to talking to the datadown.

By five o'clock, he'd had enough. The work was a seamless plane, extending to the horizon in all directions. Cambodia, Assam, Tarim Pendi, the Kurdish Homeland, Georgia, the NAME, Parana, Nigeria, the Victoria Lake States, Sri Lanka, Timor – in every single place, men were getting ready to kill each other for some cause or other, or were already about it. There was paperwork backed up weeks. You had to run just to stand still.

The desk phone rang. He snapped the 'open' command.

'Faulkner.'

'You still here?'

Chris snorted. 'And where are you? Calling from the island?'

'Give me time. Listen, rook to bishop nine. Check it out. Think I've got you, you bastard.'

Chris glanced over at the chess table.

'Hang on.'

'Yep.' He could hear the grin in Bryant's voice.

It was a good move. Chris studied the board for a moment, moved the piece and felt a tiny fragment of something detach itself from his heart and drop into his guts. He went back to the desk.

'Pretty good,' he admitted. 'But I don't think it's locked up yet. I'll call you back.'

'Do that. Hey, listen, you and Carla want to drop round tonight? I rang Suki and she's just bought a screening of that new Isabela Tribu movie. The one that won all the awards, about that female marine in Guatemala.'

'Carla's away at the moment.' He tried to make it sound casual, but it still hurt coming out. 'Gone to see family in Norway.'

'Oh. You didn't mention—'

'No, it was a spur-of-the-moment thing. I mean, we'd talked about it.' Chris stopped lying abruptly, not sure why he suddenly needed to justify himself to Bryant. 'Anyway, she's gone.'

'Right.' There was a pause. 'Well, look Chris. Why don't you come across anyway. If I've got to watch this fucking tearjerker, I'd sooner not do it alone, you know.'

The thought of escaping the silence waiting for him at home for the warmth and noise of Mike's family was like seeing the distant lights of a village through a blizzard. It felt like cheating Carla out of something. It felt like rescue. On the other hand, given the fury of the last knock-down drag-out bare-knuckle bout with his own wife, he wasn't sure he could face Suki Bryant's saccharine Miss Hostess 2049 perfection.

'Uh, thanks. Let me think about it.'

'Got to be better than going home to an empty house, pal.'

'Yeah, I—' The phone queeped. 'Hang on, I've got an incoming. Might be Lopez from the airport.'

'Call me back.' Mike was gone.

'This is Chris Faulkner.'

'Well, *this* is Liz Linshaw.' There was a dancing mockery in the way she said it, a light amusement that reminded him of something he couldn't quite touch. He groped after words.

'Liz. What, uhm, what can I do for you?'

'Good question. What *can* you do for me?'

The last twenty-four hours fell on him. Suddenly, he was close to angry. 'Liz, I'm about to call it a day here, and I'm not really in the mood for games. So if you want to talk to me—'

'That's perfect. Why don't I buy you dinner this evening.'

155

About half a dozen reasons why not suggested themselves. He swept them to the edges of perception.

'You want to buy me dinner?'

'Seems the least I can do, if we're going to cooperate on a book. Look, why don't you meet me uptown in about an hour. You know a place called *Regime Change?*'

'Yes.' He'd never been inside. No one who worked Conflict Investment would ever have considered it. Just too tacky.

'I'll be in there from about six-thirty. The Bolivia bar, upstairs. Bring an appetite.'

She hung up.

He called Mike back and made some excuses. It was tougher work than he'd expected – he could hear the disappointment in the other man's voice, and the offer of the night with the Bryants now carried added overtones of comfortable safety compared to—

'Look, to be honest with you, Mike, I need some time on my own.'

A brief silence down the line. 'You in trouble, Chris?'

'It's.' He closed his eyes and pressed hard on the lids with finger and thumb. 'Carla and I aren't getting on too well right now.'

'Ohhh, shit.'

'No, it's. I don't think it's that serious, Mike. It's just, I wasn't expecting her to take off like that. I need to think.'

'Well, if you need to talk . . .'

'Yeah. Thanks. I'll keep it in mind.'

'Just take it easy, huh.'

'Yeah. Yeah, I will. I'll talk to you Monday.'

He wandered aimlessly about the office for a while, picking things up and putting them down. He studied Mike's move, tried out a couple of half-hearted responses. He leaned on the window glass and stared down at the lights of *Louie Louie's* in the street fifty floors below. He tried not to think about Carla. Tried, with less success, not to think about Liz Linshaw.

In the end, he killed the office lights and went down to sit in his car. The enclosed space, recessed instruments, the stark simplicity of wheel and gearshift, were all more bearable than life outside. As the Saab's security locks murmured and clunked into place, he felt himself relaxing measurably. He sank back into the seat, dropped his hand onto the gearstick and rolled his head side to side in the neck support web.

'Now then,' he told himself.

The car deck was almost deserted. Mike's BMW was gone, the other man no doubt well on his way home to Suki and Ariana. There was a thin scattering of other BMWs across the luminous yellow-marked

156

parking ranks, and Hewitt's Audi stood off in the partners' corner. It dawned on Chris how little he'd seen of the executive partner since Cambodia took off. There'd been the usual brushes at quarterly functions, a few team briefings and a couple of congratulatory mails, copies to himself, Bryant and Makin. For the rest, Hewitt had ignored him as completely as was possible given the work they both had to do.

For a moment he entertained the fantasy of waiting behind the wheel until she came down to the car deck. He thought about ramming the vehicle into drive and smashing the life out of her. Smearing her across the deck surfacing, the way Edward Quain—

He shook it off.

Time to go. He fired up the engine, rolled the Saab up the ramp and out into the street. He let the vehicle idle westward. There was no traffic to speak of, *Regime Change* was five minutes away, and with the corporate ID holoflashed into the windscreen glass he could park anywhere.

He left the Saab on a cross street filled with the offices of image consultants and data brokerage agencies. As he alarmed the car and walked away from it, he felt a slow adrenal flush rising in his blood. The buzz of a London Saturday evening drifted to him on the warm air, streets filling slowly with people, talk and laughter punctuated with the occasional hoot from a cab trying to get through the tangle of pedestrians. He slipped into it, and quickened his pace.

Regime Change was the end building on a thoroughfare that folded back on itself like a partially-opened jackknife. Music and noise spilled out onto the streets on either side from open-slanted floor-length glass panels in the ground floor and wide open sash windows above. There were a couple of queues at the door, but the doorman cast an experienced eye over Chris's clothes and nodded him straight in. Chorus of complaint, dying away swiftly as Chris turned to look. He dropped the doorman a tenner and went inside.

The ground floor bar was packed with propped and seated humanity, all yelling at each other over the pulse of a Zequina remix. A cocktail waitress surfed past in the noise, dressed in some fevered pornographer's vision of a CI exec's suit. Chris put a hand on her arm and tried to make himself heard.

'Bolivia Bar?'

'Second floor,' she shouted back. 'Through the Iraq Room and left.'

'Thanks.'

Screwed-up face. 'What?'

'*Thanks.*'

That got a strange look. He took the stairs at a lope, found the Iraq Room – wailing DJ-votional rhythms, big screens showing zooming

157

aerial views of flaming oil wells like black and crimson desert flowers, hookah pipes on the tables – and picked his way through it. A huge holoprint of Che Guevara loomed to his left. He snorted and ducked underneath. A relative quiet descended, pegged out with melancholy Andean pipes and Spanish guitar. People sat about on big leather beanbags and sofas with their stuffing coming out. There were candles, and some suggestion of tent canvas on the walls.

Liz Linshaw was seated at a low table in one corner, apparently reading a thin, blue-bound sheaf of paperwork. She wore a variant on her TV uniform – black slacks and a black and grey striped silk shirt buttoned closed at a single point on her chest. The collar of the shirt was turned up, but the lower hem floated a solid five centimetres above the belt of her slacks. Tanned, toned TV flesh filled up the gap and made long triangles above and below the single closed button.

Either she didn't see him approaching, or she let him get close deliberately. He stopped himself clearing his throat with an effort of will, and dropped into the beanbag opposite her.

'Hullo, Liz.'

'Chris.' She glanced up, apparently surprised. 'You're earlier than I thought you'd be. Thanks for coming.'

She laid aside what she'd been reading and extended one slim arm across the table. Her grip was dry and confident.

'It's.' Chris looked around. 'A pleasure. You come here often?'

She laughed. It was distressingly attractive, warm and deep-throated and once again Chris had the disturbing impression of recall he'd had on the phone.

'I come here when I don't want to run into anyone from the Conflict Investment sector, Chris. It's safe. None of you guys would be seen dead in here.'

Chris pulled a face. 'True enough.'

'Don't be superior. It's not such a bad place. Have you seen the waitresses?'

'Yeah, met one downstairs.'

'Decorative, aren't they.'

'Very.' Chris looked around reflexively. There was a long bar bent into one corner of the room. A woman stood mixing drinks behind it.

'What would you like?' Liz Linshaw asked him.

'I'll get it.'

'No, I insist. After all, you're making yourself available to me, Chris. It's the least I can do, and it's tax-deductible.' She grinned. 'You know. Research costs. Hospitality.'

'Sounds like a nice way to live.'

'Whisky, wasn't it? Laphroaig?'

158

He nodded, flattered that she remembered. 'If they've got it.'

Liz Linshaw pressed a palm on the table top and the menu glowed into life beneath her hand. She scrolled about a bit, then shook her head regretfully.

'No Laphroaig. Lot of bourbons, and, ah, what about Port Ellen? That's an Islay malt, isn't it?'

'Yeah, it's one of the new ones.' The sense of flattery crumbled slightly. Had she being doing research on him, he wondered. 'Reopened back in the thirties. It's good stuff.'

'Okay, I'll try it.'

She pressed on the selection and swept a hand across the send patch. At the bar, the woman looked down, face stained red by the flashing table alert on her worksurface. She glanced across at them and nodded.

'So, Chris.' Liz Linshaw sat back and smiled at him. 'Where did you develop your taste for expensive whisky?'

'Is this part of the interview?'

'No, just warming you up. But, I'm curious. You grew up in the zones, didn't you. East End, riverside estates. Not much Islay malt around there.'

'No. There isn't.'

'Is it painful to talk about this, Chris?'

'You're a zone girl yourself, Liz. What do you think?'

The drinks came, hers with ice. Liz Linshaw waited until the waitress had gone, then she picked up her tumbler and looked pensively into it. She swirled the drink and the ice cubes clicked about.

'My zone origins are mostly, shall we say, artistic licence. Exaggerated for exotic effect. The truth is, I grew up on the fringes of Islington, at a time when the lines weren't as heavily drawn as they are now. My parents were, still are, moderately successful teachers and I went to university. There's nothing that hurts in my past.'

Chris raised his glass. 'Lucky you.'

'Yes, that's a fair description. You weren't so lucky.'

'No.'

'Yet age nineteen you were driving for Ross Mobile Arbitrage. You were their top paid haulage operative, until you moved sideways into LS Euro Ventures. Two years after that Hammett McColl, headhunted. No qualifications, not even driver's school. For someone with zone origins that's more than remarkable, it's nigh on impossible.'

Chris gestured. 'If you want out badly enough.'

'No, Chris. The zones are full of people who want out badly enough, and then some. It gets them nowhere. The dice are loaded against that kind of mobility, and you know it.'

'I know other people who've made it out.' It felt strange to suddenly be on the other end of the argument he'd had with Mike Bryant that morning. 'Look at Troy Morris.'

'Do you know Troy well?'

'Uhh, not really. He's Mike's friend more than mine.'

'I see.' Liz Linshaw lifted her drink in his direction. 'Well, anyway. Cheers. Here's to Conflict Investment. Small wars.'

'Small wars.' But there was something vaguely disquieting in hearing it from her lips. He didn't like the way it sounded.

She set down her tumbler. Beside it a microcorder. 'So. How does it feel to be the rising star at Shorn CI?'

The interview went down as smoothly as the Port Ellen. Liz Linshaw had a loose, inviting manner at odds with her screen persona, and he found himself talking as if to an old friend he hadn't seen in many years. Such areas of resistance as he had, she picked up on and either backed smoothly away from the topic or found another way in that somehow he didn't mind as much. They laughed a lot, and once or twice he caught himself on the verge of giving up data that he had no business discussing with anyone outside Shorn.

By nine o'clock they were working up to Edward Quain, and he had drunk far too much to be able to drive the Saab safely.

'You didn't like him, did you.' There was no question in her voice.

'Quain? What makes you think that?'

'Your form.'

He laughed, slurring slightly. 'What am I, a fucking racehorse?'

She smiled along. 'If you like. Look, you've made a total of eleven kills, including Mitsue Jones and her wingmate, plus the Acropolitic driver on the same run. Eight before that. Three at LS Euro, two tenders and one Prom and App duel. Then the move to HM, and out of nowhere you take Quain down.'

'It was the easiest way to get up the ladder.'

'It was off the wall, Chris. Quain was the top end of your permissible challenge envelope. As senior as it gets without exempted partner status. At that level in some companies he *would* have been an exempted partner.'

'Yeah, or out on his ear.' Chris drained his current whisky. 'You want to know the truth, Liz? Quain was a burnt-out old fuck. He wasn't bringing in the business, he drank way too much, did too much expensive coke, he fucked his way through every high-price whore in Camden Town, and he paid for it all with bonuses taken out of money junior analysts on a tenth his income were generating. He was an embarrassment to everyone at Hammett McColl, and he needed taking out.'

'Very public-spirited of you. But there must have been easier targets on the way up the HM ladder.'

Chris shrugged. 'If you're going to kill a man, it might as well be a patriarch.'

'And what I find curious is the duels after Quain. Four more kills, none of them even close to as brutal as Quain's and—'

'Murcheson burnt to death,' Chris pointed out. The screams, he did not add, still came back to him in his nightmares.

'Yes, Murcheson was trapped in wreckage. It was nothing to do with you.'

'Hardly nothing. I created the wreckage.'

'Chris, you ran over Quain five times. I've seen that footage—'

'What are you, Liz? An X fan?'

The crooked smile again. 'If I was, I'd have been pretty unhappy with your performance for the next eight years. Like I said, four more kills, all clean bar Murcheson, who was an accidental burn. And alongside that, another seven inconclusives, including one you actually rescued from wreckage and drove to hospital. That's not going to get you an honourable mention on any of the Xtreme sites, is it.'

'Sorry to disappoint you.'

'Relax, Chris. I didn't say I was an Xer. But when you're trying to build a profile, this stuff matters. I want to know what you're made of.'

He met her eyes, and the look lasted. Went on far longer than it should have. He cleared his throat.

'I'm going to go home now.'

She raised an eyebrow. 'You're going to drive?'

'I.' He stood up, too fast. 'No, maybe not. I'll get a cab.'

'That's going to cost you a fortune, Chris.'

'So. I earn a fortune. 's not like the fucking army, you know. I get well paid for murdering people.'

She got up and placed a hand on his arm.

'I've got a better idea.'

'Yeah?' Suddenly he was aware of his pulse. 'What's that, then?'

'I live in Highgate. That's a *cheap* cab ride, and there's a spare futon there with your name on it.'

'Look, Liz—'

She grinned suddenly. 'Don't flatter yourself, Faulkner. I'm not about to tear your clothes off and stuff your dick down my throat, if that's what you're worried about. I like the men I fuck to be sober.'

Unwillingly, he laughed. 'Hey, give it to me straight, Liz. Don't let me down gently.'

'So.' She was laughing too. 'Do we get this cab?'

They ordered the taxi from the same table menu as the drinks. This

161

early in the evening, it wasn't hard to get one. Liz cleared the tab, and they left. There was frenetic dancing in the Iraq Room, harsh, mindless beats drawn from early millennium thrash bands like *Noble Cause* and *Bushin'*. They ducked through the press of bodies, got the stairs and made it out into the street, still laughing.

The taxi was there, gleaming black in the late evening light like a toy that belonged to them. Chris fetched up short, laughter drying in his throat. He glanced sideways at Liz Linshaw and saw the hilarity had drained out of her the same way. He could not read the expression that had replaced it on her face. For a moment they both stood there, staring at the cab like idiots, and like a Nemex shell the realisation hit Chris in the back of the head. The sardonic amusement on the phone, the maddeningly familiar note in her deep-throated laugh. The sense of recall about this woman came crashing down on him.

She reminded him of Carla.

Carla when they first met. Carla, three or four years back. Carla before the creeping distance took its toll.

Suddenly, he was sweating.

What the fu—

It was the fear sweat, chasing a rolling shudder across his body. A feeling he'd left behind a decade ago in his early duels. Pure, existential terror, distilled down so clear it could not be pinned on any single identifiable thing. Fear of death, fear of life, fear of everything in between and what it would do to you in time. The terror of inevitably losing your grip.

'Oy, are you getting in or what?'

The driver was leaning out, thumb jerked back to where the door of the black cab had hinged open of its own accord. There was a tiny light on inside, seats of cool green plush.

Liz Linshaw stood watching him, face still unreadable.

The sweat cooled.

He got in.

TWENTY

Westward, there were mountains spearing up grimly under gathered blue cloud. Weak ladders of late afternoon sun fell through at infrequent intervals, splashing scant warmth where they hit. Carla shivered slightly at the sight. There was no darkness yet – this far north, daylight held the sky as it would for another full month, but the Lofoten skyline still looked like the watchtowers of a troll city.

'Cold?' Kirsti Nyquist glanced sideways from the jeep's driving seat. Her ability to pick up on her daughter's moods and feelings sometimes verged on the witchy. 'We can close the hood, if you want.'

Carla shook her head. 'I'm fine. Just thinking.'

'Not happy thoughts, then.'

The road unwound ahead of them, freshly carved from the bleak terrain and laid down in asphalt so new it looked like liquorice. There were none of the luminous yellow markings as yet, and they kept passing raw white rock walls that still had defined grooves where the blasting holes had been sunk. A sign said *Gjerlow Oceanic Monitoring – 15 kilometres*. Carla sighed and shifted in her seat. Kirsti drove the big Volvo All-Terrain with a care that, to Carla's London-forged road instincts, seemed faintly ridiculous. They'd seen five other vehicles in the last hour, and three of those had been parked outside a fuelling post.

'Tunnel,' called her mother cheerily. 'Mittens.'

Carla reached for her gloves. This was the second tunnel of the trip. The first time, she'd ignored her mother's warning. They were less than two hundred kilometres inside the Arctic circle, and the weather had been pleasant since she got off the plane at Tromsö two days ago, but tunnels were another matter. Deep in the mountain rock, an Arctic chill hit you in the lungs and the fingers before you'd gone a hundred metres.

Kirsti flipped on the headlamps and they barrelled down into the sodium yellow gloom. Their breath frosted and whipped away over their shoulders.

'Now you're cold, hey?'

'A bit. Mum, did we really have to come all this way?'

'Yes. I told you. It's the only chance we'll get to see him.'

'You couldn't invite him up to Tromsö?'

Kirsti made a wry face. 'Not any more.'

Carla tried primly not to laugh. Kirsti Nyquist was well into her fifties now, but she was still a strikingly handsome woman and she changed her lovers with brutal regularity. *They just don't grow with me*, she once complained to her daughter. *Perhaps that's because they're all young enough to be your children*, Carla had retorted, a little unfairly. Her mother's choices often were younger men, but not usually by more than a decade or so, and Carla herself had to admit most of the options in the fifty-plus male range weren't much to look at.

The tunnel was six kilometres long. They made the other side with teeth chattering and Kirsti whooped as she drove into the fractured sunlight outside. The temperature upgrade soaked into Carla's body like tropical heat. The chill seemed to have gone bone-deep. She tried to shrug it off.

Get a fucking grip, Carla.

She was already missing Chris, a lack for which she berated herself because it felt so pathetic alongside her mother's cheerful self sufficiency. The anger at him that had driven her out of the house was already evaporating by the time her plane took off, and all she had by the time she arrived in Tromsö was maudlin drinking talk of distance and loss.

Now, out of the mess she had laid out for her mother the night she arrived, Kirsti had snatched the possibility of meaningful action. Carla wondered vaguely what you had to do to attain operational pitch like that – have a child, write a book, lose a relationship? What did it take?

'There it is.' Kirsti gestured ahead, and Carla saw the road was dropping down to meet one side of a small, stubby fjord. On the other side, institutional buildings were gathered in a huddle, lit up shiny in a wandering shaft of sunlight. It looked as if the road ran all the way up to the end of the inlet and then back round to the monitoring station.

'So this is all new as well?'

'Relocated. They were based in the Faroes until last year.'

'Why did?' Carla remembered. 'Oh, right. The BNR thing.'

'Yes, your beloved British and their nuclear reprocessing. Gjerlow reckons it's contaminated local waters for the next sixty years minimum. Pointless taking overview readings. None of the tests they do will stand the radiation.'

Not for the first time, Carla felt a wave of defensiveness rising in her at the mention of her adoptive home.

'I heard it was just heat exchanger fluids – not enough to do much damage.'

'My dear, you've been living in London too long if you believe what the British media tell you. There is no *just* where nuclear contaminants are concerned. It's been a monumental disaster and anyone with access to independent broadcasting knows it.'

Carla flushed. 'We've got independent channels.'

'Does Chris buy off the jamming?' Her mother looked interested. 'I didn't think you could do that effectively.'

'No, he's exempted. Under licence. For his job.'

'Oh, I see.' There was a studied politeness in Kirsti's voice that didn't quite shroud her distaste. Carla flushed again, deeper this time. She said nothing more until the wheels of the Volvo crunched across the gravel parking lot beside the monitoring station. Then, sitting still in the passenger seat as Kirsti killed the engine, she muttered, 'I'm not sure this is such a good idea.'

'It was a good idea when we had it on Friday night,' said her mother emphatically. 'It's still a good idea now. One of my best. Now, come on.'

Kirsti's Tromsö University ID got them in the front door, and a quick search of the building's locational database at reception told them Truls Vasvik was up on the top floor. They took the stairs, Kirsti leading by a couple of steps on every flight. *Good for the buttocks*, she flung over her shoulder in response to her daughter's puffed protests to slow down. *Only five levels. Come* on.

They found Vasvik in the staff cafe. He was, Carla thought, a classic Kirsti type – gaunt and long-limbed, radiating self-sufficiency like the effects of some drug recently injected. He wore a crew-neck sweater, canvas work trousers, walking boots and an uncared-for heavy black coat that he somehow hadn't got around to removing. The clothes hung off him, incidental drapings on his lean frame, and his silver-threaded black hair was long and untidy. He looked to be in his early forties. As they approached, he got up and offered a bony hand.

'Hello Kirsti.'

'Hello Truls. This is my daughter, Carla. Carla, Truls Vasvik. It's good to see you again.'

Vasvik grunted.

'Have you seen Gjerlow yet?'

'About an hour ago.'

'Oh, sorry. I didn't realise—'

'Shall we all sit down. There's machine coffee over there, if you want it.'

'Can I get you one?'

Vasvik indicated the cup in front of him and shook his head. Kirsti went off to the bank of self-service machines across the cafe and left Carla stranded. She offered Vasvik an awkward smile and seated herself at the table.

'So, you've known my mother for a while.'

He stared back at her. 'Long enough.'

'I, uh, I appreciate you taking the time to see us.'

'I had to be here anyway. It wasn't a problem.'

'Yes, uh. How's it going? I mean, can you talk about it?'

A shrug. 'It isn't, strictly speaking, confidential, at this end anyway. I need some data to back up a case we're putting together. Gjerlow has it, he says.'

'Is it a British thing?'

'This time around, no. French.' A marginal curiosity surfaced on his face. 'You live there, then?'

'Where, Britain? Yes. Yes, I do.'

'Doesn't it bother you?'

She bit her lip. Kirsti arrived with coffee cups and saved them both from the rapidly foundering conversation.

'So,' she said brightly. 'Where are we up to?'

'We haven't started yet,' said Vasvik.

Kirsti frowned. 'Are you okay, Truls?'

'Not really.' He met her gaze. 'Jannicke died.'

'Jannicke Onarheim? Oh, shit. I'm sorry, Truls.' Kirsti reached out and put her hand on Vasvik's arm. 'What happened?'

He smiled bleakly. 'How do ombudsmen die, Kirsti? She was murdered. I only got the call this morning.'

'Was she working?'

Vasvik nodded, staring into the plastic-topped table. 'Some American shoe manufactury up near Hanoi. The usual stuff, reported human rights abuse, no local police cooperation.' He drew a deep breath. 'They found her car run off the road an hour out of town, nowhere near where she should have been. Looks like someone took her for a ride. Raped. Shot. Single cap, back of the head.'

He glanced up at Carla, who had flinched on the word *raped*.

'Yeah. It's probably good you hear this. Jannicke is the third this year. The Canadians have lost twice that number. UN ombudsmen earn their money, and often enough we don't get to spend it. From what Kirsti says, your man might not suit the work.'

The implied slight to Chris, as always, fired her up.

'Well, I doubt you'd last long in Conflict Investment.'

The other two looked at her with chilly Norwegian disapproval.

'Perhaps not,' said Vasvik finally. 'It was not my intention to insult you or your man. But you should know what you are trying to get him into. Less than fifty years ago, this was still a comfortable, localised, office-based little profession. That's changed. Now, at this level, it can get you killed. There is no recognition of the work we do – at best we are seen as fussy bureaucrats, at worst as the enemies of capitalism and the bedfellows of terrorists. Our UN mandate is a bad joke. Only a handful of governments will act on our findings. The rest cave in to corporate pressure. Some, like the United States and so, of course, Britain, simply refuse point blank to support the process. They are not even signatories to the agreement. They block us at every turn. They query our budgets, they demand a transparency that exposes our field agents, they offer legal and financial asylum to those offenders we do manage to indict. We shelve two out of every three cases for lack of viability and,' he jerked his chin, perhaps out to wherever Jannicke Onarheim's body now lay, 'we bury our dead to the jeers of the popular media.'

More silence. Across the cafe, someone worked the coffee machine.

'Do you hate your job?' asked Carla quietly.

A thin smile. 'Not as much as I hate the people I chase.'

'Chris, my husband, hates his job. So much that it's killing him.'

'Then why doesn't he just quit?' There was scant sympathy in the ombudsman's voice.

'That's so fucking easy for you to say.'

Kirsti shot her a warning glance. 'Truls, Chris was born and brought up in the London cordoned zones. You've seen that, you know what it's like. And you know what happens to the ones who manage to claw their way out. First-generation syndrome. If quitting means going back to the zones, he probably would rather die. He'd certainly rather kill. And in the end, we know how closely those two can be intertwined.'

Another smile, somewhat less thin. 'Yes. First-generation syndrome. I remember that particular lecture quite well, for some reason.'

Kirsti joined him in the smile. She flexed her body beneath her sweater in a fashion that made her daughter blush.

'Thanks,' she said. 'I hadn't realised it was that memorable.'

It was as if something heavy had dropped from Vasvik's shoulders. He sat up a little in the moulded plastic chair, turned back to Carla.

'Alright,' he said. 'I don't deny it. Someone like your husband could be useful to us. The information he has alone would probably be enough to build a couple of dozen cases. And, yes, a background in Conflict Investment would go a long way to making a good ombudsman. But I can't promise you, him, a job. For one thing, we'd need an extraction team to get him away from Shorn. But, yes, if he really wants out, I can ask around. I can set some wheels in motion.'

It was what she wanted to hear, but somehow it didn't fill her with the feeling she'd expected. Something about Vasvik's clamped anger, the news of sudden death or maybe the bleak landscape outside, something was not right.

And later, when they got up to go and Kirsti and Truls embraced with genuine affection, she turned away so that she would not have to watch.

TWENTY-ONE

Monday was soft summer rain and a nagging pain behind the eyes. He drove in with a vague sense of exposure all the way, and when he parked and alarmed the car, tiny twitches of the same discomfort sent him scanning the corners of the car deck for watchers.

This early, there was nobody about.

There were phone messages on the datadown – Liz Linshaw, drawling, ironic and inviting, Joaquin Lopez from the NAME. He shelved Liz and told the datadown to dial up Lopez's mobile. The Americas agent had called four times in the last two hours and he sounded close to panic. He grabbed the phone at the third ring, voice tight and shaky.

'*Si, digame.*'

'It's Faulkner. Jesus, Joaquin, what the fuck's the matter with you?'

'*Escuchame.*' There was the sound of movement. Chris got the impression Lopez was in a hotel room, getting up from the bed, moving. The agent's voice firmed up as he crossed into English. 'Listen, Chris, I think I'm in trouble. I got down here last night, been making some enquiries about Diaz and now I got a clutch of Echevarria's political police all over me like *putas* on payday. They're in the bar across the street, downstairs in the lounge. I think a couple of them have taken a room on this floor, I don't—'

'Joaquin, calm down. I understand the situation.'

'No, you don't fucking understand my situation, man. This is the NAME. These guys will cut my fucking *cojones* off if they get the chance. They bundle me into a car, and that's it, I'm fucking history, man—'

'*Joaquin, will you just shut up and listen!*' Chris went direct from the command snap to enabled conciliatory without allowing the other man a response. Textbook stuff. 'I know you're scared. I understand why. Now, let's do something about it. What do these guys look like?'

'Look like?' A panicky snort. 'They look like fucking political police, what do you want me to say? Ray Bans, bellies and fucking moustaches. Get the picture?'

Chris did get the picture. He'd seen these cut-rate bad guys in operation on his own trip to the Monitored Economy with Hammett

McColl. He knew the gut-sliding sense of menace they could generate simply by appearing on the scene.

'No, Joaquin, I meant. Did you get pictures? Have you got your shades set down there?'

'Yeah, I brought them.' A pause. 'I didn't use them yet.'

'Right.'

'I freaked. I'm sorry, Chris, I fucked up. I didn't think.'

'Well, think *now*, Joaquin. Get a grip. You can fuck up on your own time, right now you're on the Shorn clock. I'm not paying you to get your arse killed.' Chris glanced at his watch. 'What time is it there? One a.m.?'

'A little after.'

'Right. How many of these moustaches are there?'

'I don't know, two down in the lobby.' The panic started to seep back into Lopez's voice. 'Maybe another two or three more across the road.'

'Can you get me pictures?'

'I'm not fucking going outside, man.'

'Alright, alright.' Chris paced, thinking. Trying to put himself in the hotel room with Lopez. The Nikon sunglasses and the data transmission gear had been an end-of-quarter gift from Shorn – they were very high spec. 'Look, can you see the ones in the bar from your window? Go and check.'

More movement. Lopez came back calmer.

'Yeah, I can see their table. I think I can get a decent shot from here.'

'Alright, that's good. Do that.' Chris cranked his voice down, as soothing as possible. 'Then I want you to go down to the lobby and get full frontals of the other two. They shouldn't try anything there. Are you armed?'

'Are you kidding? I came through US security at the airport, just like everybody else.'

'Fine, doesn't matter. Just get the pictures and mail them through to me as quickly as you can. I'll be waiting. And, Joaquin. Remember what I said. You don't get killed on the Shorn clock. We'll pull you out of there. Got it?'

'Got it.' A brief pause in which he could hear Lopez breathing down the line.

'Chris. Thanks, man.'

'*De nada*. Stay cool.'

Chris waited until he heard the disconnect. Then he slammed a foot against the desk leg, knotted a fist.

'Fuck.' Another kick. '*Fuck*.'

Back to the datadown. He estimated Lopez's performance time, placed forward calls. Then he went to the window and stared out at the London skyline until the phone chimed.

The images came through, two clear face-and-trunk shots that must have been taken from less than five metres. Lopez had got close. The two parapoliticals were grinning unpleasantly into the Nikon's hidden lens. Their teeth showed, spotted brown with decay. The cafe snap was less to rejoice about, but there was a pavement table centred in the shot, three clear figures around it, faces turned in the camera's direction.

The first of the forward calls went through. Even with the fore-warning, the other end took a while to pick up, and the first sound to come through was a noisy yawn. Chris smiled for the first time that day.

'Burgess Imaging.' The screen caught up, filled with a dark unshaven face in its late teens. 'Oh, hello, Chris. What can I? Uh, those satellite blow-ups okay?'

'Yeah, fine, it's not that. Listen, can you do me step-ups of a street shot, right now? Faces good enough for machine ID?'

Jamie Burgess yawned again and scratched at something in the corner of one eye.

'Cost ya.'

'I guessed. Look, I'm wiring it through on inset. Just take a look.'

Burgess waited, blinked at the screen a couple of times and nodded.

'Nikon shot, yeah?'

'Yeah.'

'Give me two minutes. Leave the line open.'

'Thanks, Jamie.'

Another yawn. 'Pleasure.'

Burgess was as good as his word. The datadown spat back perfect head-and-shoulder shots ninety seconds later. Chris punched them up next to the two he already had from the lobby and nodded.

'Okay, motherfuckers. Let's hope you've been to church recently.'

The second forward call picked up on the first ring. A grizzled virtual head above crisp army khaki fatigues. The accent was American, the real-life version of Mike Bryant's Simeon Sands burlesque.

'Langley Contracting.'

'This is Chris Faulkner, Shorn Associates, London. Do you have operational units in the Medellín area?'

There was a pause, presumably while Chris's scrambler code and authorisation cleared at the other end. Then the virtual customer service agent nodded.

'Yes, we can work in that area.'

'Good, I need five extreme prejudice deletions with immediate effect. Exact locational data and visual ID attached.'

'Very good. Please indicate the level of precision required.'

171

'Uh.' This was a new refinement. 'Sorry?'

'Please indicate level of precision required from the following five options; surgical, accurate, scattershot, blanket, atrocity.'

'Jesus, uh.' Chris gestured helplessly. 'Surgical.'

'Please note the surgical option may incur a substantial time delay. Char—'

'*No.* That's no good. This is with immediate effect.'

'Do you wish to supersede precision levels with an urgency marker?'

'Yes. I want this done now.'

'Charge card or account?'

'Account.'

'Your contract is enabled. Thank you for choosing Langley Contracting. Have a nice day.'

Chris looked once more at the five faces floating on his screen. He nodded again and pressed a thumb down on each one to make it go away.

'Adios, muchachos.'

When the last face had wiped, he wired the datadown line to his mobile and went out to get coffee from *Louie Louie's*.

Lopez called him about an hour later. Voice rampant down the line, whooping shrill with delight. Sirens in the backdrop.

'Chris, you're beautiful man!!!! You did it. *Hijos de puta*, they're all over the street, man! They're all over the *fucking* street!'

'What?' said Chris faintly.

'Drive-by, man. Fucking exemplary. They must have used one of those shoulder-launchers. Whole fucking cafe's on fire. I'm telling you, there's nothing left but pieces.'

Chris sat down heavily behind the desk. He saw it, lit in tones of night and flame. Pastiche newsreel footage, memories of a hundred such scenes. Bodies and bits thereof, streak-scorched black and red. Screams and blundering panic from the sidelines.

'The hotel.' It was almost a whisper, like words he couldn't be bothered to push out of his mouth. 'The people in the hotel.'

'Yeah, they got them too. I heard the shots. Spray guns.' Lopez made a stuttering machine gun noise. He was drunk on his own narrow escape. 'Just been down to check, right now. See, I was still looking out the window at the fire when—'

'No, Joaquin. Stop. The *other* people in the hotel. You know, staff. Other customers. Did they hit anybody else?'

'Oh.' Lopez stopped. 'I don't think so, I didn't see any other bodies. Man, who'd you call?'

'Never mind.' It was like tasting ashes. He could smell the blast, smell the scorched flesh on the scented night air. Over the phone, the sirens sobbed out and he heard screaming in the space it left. 'You best get out of there. Better yet, get back to Panama City. You're blown down there for now. You'll have to work through someone else.'

'Yeah. What I thought.' Lopez's voice shifted. 'Listen, Chris. I lost it for a while back there, but I know my work. I didn't make one wrong move in the last twenty-four hours. Those *hijos de puta*, they knew I was coming.'

Chris nodded drearily, for all it was an audio link.

'Right, Joaquin.'

'Give me another two days. We can still make this run. I know the right people. You don't have to worry.'

He squeezed his eyes shut. 'Right.'

'Count on it, man. I'll hook you up, I swear.'

Behind Lopez, someone started using an ampbox to yell down the noise of the crowd. Chris reached out and cut the link.

Bryant and Makin got in about the same time. Chris went down to the car deck to meet them. Mike grinned when he saw him.

'Hey, Chris! Jesus, what time did you get in?'

He ignored the greeting and went straight for Makin. Right fist in under the rib cage with the full force of the last stride behind it. Makin doubled up and vomited a spray of breakfast. Chris stepped back and hooked into his face from the side. The glasses flew. Makin hit the deck and rolled, retching. Chris got a single kick in, and then Mike had him pinioned from behind and was dragging him out of range.

'That's it, Chris. Time out.'

'Fucking piece of *shit*. Sell out my agents, you *fuck*.'

'I don't,' Makin got to one knee, holding his face. 'Know. What the fuck. Youah talking about.'

Chris renewed his efforts to break Mike's hold. Makin straightened, wiped his mouth and looked up. He raised his free arm.

'I'll see you on the fucking woad for that, Faulkner.'

'*Hey!*' Mike loosened his hold on Chris's shoulders. 'That's enough of that shit, Nick. Nobody sees anybody on the road in this team. No*body*. You save that shit for the tenders. Chris, I'm going to let you go now, okay. Now you behave. No brawling on the car decks, it's undignified. This isn't the zones.'

He let go of Chris and stepped away, carefully poised between the two men, arms spread slightly upward from the waist, ready. Makin prowled sideways and spat. Chris felt the reaction twitch through him from the fist back to the shoulder. Mike Bryant drew a deep breath.

'Okay, guys. What the fuck is going on?'

'This piece of shit,' Chris was still adrenalin fired, thrumming with the need to do violence. 'Wired through our detail on Diaz to Echevarria.'

'Yeah, *so?*'

Bryant blinked. 'You did that, Nick?'

'Jesus, *yes*. You said to light a fiah under Echevaia's arse.'

Chris felt the fury drop out of him to make room for disbelief. He saw the same in Bryant's stare. The big man shook his head.

'But—'

'Christ, Mike. *I want the axe over his head by Monday*, that's what you said. What was I supposed to do?'

Chris flared. 'That's fucking bullshit. You weren't in here at the weekend.'

'How the fuck do you know wheah I was? What are you, my fucking mother?'

'I didn't see you Saturday,' said Bryant quietly.

'I took the stuff home, Mike. Look, Echevaia was holding rallies for the faithful all weekend. It seemed like a good time to shake him. The uplincon is tomorrow, what was I going to do? Wait and then twy and paste it all together today? I've got Cambodian logistics to think about, a palace wevolution in Yemen. The Kashmiah thing. Guatemala's coming apart again. I don't have *time* for this shit.'

Chris surged forward a step. Fetched up with Mike Bryant's arm across his chest.

'I sent Joaquin Lopez down to the ME, *fuckhead*, asking after Diaz. He nearly fucking *died* today.'

'That's supposed to be *my* fault?'

Bryant sighed. 'Diaz was off-limits, Nick. He was our holdout if old scumbag didn't fold.'

'*You knew that!*'

'Oh, what am I? A fucking telepath? No one told me not to use Diaz, and he's the stongest theat we've got.'

'Alright.' Mike rubbed at his face. 'Maybe we didn't make it clear enough. But you should have checked with Chris first. Same goes for you, Chris. You should have run it by Nick before you sent Lopez down there.'

'But.' Chris couldn't identify the sudden feeling in his chest. 'You *told* me to send him.'

'Well, yeah, but not without consultation.' Bryant looked back and forth between the two men. 'Come *on*, people. A little communication. A little *cooperation*, for Christ's sake. Is that too much to ask?'

Neither of the other men even glanced at him. Chris and Makin were either end of a hardwired stare.

'People *died*, Mike, because of this fucking clown.'

Makin snorted.

Bryant frowned. 'I thought you said *nearly*.'

'Not Lopez. Other people. I had to call in Langley to get the goons off his back, and they blew up a whole fucking cafe.'

Makin traded in his snort for a sneer. Bryant made a noise only slightly less dismissive.

'Well, what'd you expect? Come on, Chris. *Langley?* These guys used to be the CIA, for fuck's sake. Even *before* deregulation, they were a bunch of cack-fisted incompetent fucking clowns.' He looked across at Makin, grinned and made an imploring gesture with one hand. 'I mean, *Langley*, for Christ's sake.'

Chris felt himself losing his temper with his friend. 'There was no fucking option, Mike,' he snapped. 'No one else in the ME has the response time. You know that.'

'Yeah, well, that's one for the Monopolies Commission.' Mike pressed thumb and forefinger to the bridge of his nose. 'Look. It's a shame about the cafe, but it could have been worse. I mean, with Langley you're lucky they didn't kill Lopez for you as well.' Makin laughed out loud. Bryant joined in. 'Fuck, the kind of punk *sicarios* they're contracting out to these days, you're lucky they didn't take out the whole block.'

'It isn't funny, Mike.'

'Oh, come on, it is a bit.' Bryant shelved his grin. Sobered. 'Alright. A fuck-up, is what it is. But we can cover the damage. We'll ride out any waves Echevarria makes tomorrow, keep it in the team, and we'll bury the Langley account. Pay it off, I don't know, through one of the Cambodia slush funds or something. No one else has to know. Clean hands all round, come the quarterly. Alright?' He looked round at his team. 'Agreed?'

Makin nodded. Chris, finally, too. Bryant's grin came back.

'Good. But remember, gentlemen. A little more attention to detail next time, *please*.'

TWENTY-TWO

Hernan Echevarria, predictably, did not take it so well.

'You sit this out,' said Mike, rather grimly, as they stood in the covert viewing chamber, waiting for the uplink to go through. 'We'll do the lying.'

As usual when faced with politics, he had slung his baseball bat across his shoulders cruciform, and now he prowled about, rolling his neck back against the polished wood. On the other side of a one-way glass wall, Nick Makin busied himself with bottled water and screen control mice along one edge of the conference table. The rest of the slate grey expanse was bare, but for the shallow slope of recessed display screens near the centre.

'You think this is the break point?' Chris asked.

Mike pulled a face. 'If yesterday's performance is anything to go by, it's pretty fucking close. It's only the fact he *is* actually yelling at us that makes me think we might still have a chance. If he was planning to walk, I don't think we'd even be talking. Well, shouting.'

The call had come in a couple of hours before lunch, barely past dawn back in the NAME. Echevarria must have spent all night talking to his forensic experts in Medellín. Mike took it. Chris never heard the detail, but understood it had gone something like *what the fuck did you gringo sons of whores think you were doing on my turf, who the fuck do you think you are, talking to this Marquista traitor Diaz behind my back, if you were men of honour and not grey suited scum I would etcetera etcetera, blah, blah,* apoplexy.

'Okay, not quite,' Mike admitted. 'Figure of speech. He hasn't dropped dead, fortunately. Otherwise we really would be in trouble. I don't rate our chances of negotiating with Echevarria junior at all. So, at the meeting, let's try and keep temperatures low. Conciliatory approach.'

Later that day, they heard the news. The gunships had flown, the highlands west of Medellín were in flames and the Monitored Economy's pet press were proclaiming Diaz either dead or fleeing for the Panamanian border where he would be cornered and caged like the cowardly Marquista dog he was. In the cities, the arrests ran into triple figures.

'He'll be riding high, we've got that going for us.' Mike, trying for upbeat as the three-minute countdown for the uplink commenced. 'Taste of blood in his teeth, with a bit of luck he'll think he's invincible. With the right amount of cringing apology, I think we can talk him round.'

Chris hauled up a chair and leaned on the back. 'You sure you don't want me in there instead of Makin?'

Bryant just looked at him.

'What?'

'You going to let this go?'

'Mike, it isn't even my fucking account. In the end, I don't *give* a shit. But you're not going to tell me this wasn't deliberate.'

'Oh, give me a fucking break with the conspiracy theories, Chris. Why can't you just accept it was a communications fuck-up? Is basic incompetence so hard to believe in?'

In the conference room, Makin stood facing them and rapped on the glass.

'Two minutes, Mike.'

Bryant leaned down to one of the mikes and pressed *trans*. 'Be right there, Nick. Fasten your seatbelts, ladies and gentlemen.'

He slipped the baseball bat off his shoulders and leaned it in a corner. Chris put a hand on his arm.

'Mike, you *saw* his face when we ran it by him on Thursday. You were there. He resented the change of tack, and he made damned sure it blew up in our faces. He handed up Diaz so we'd have nothing else to work with, and you know it.'

'And nearly blew out his own account? Cost himself maybe thousands in lost bonuses, come quarterly. Chris, come *on*. It makes him look bad. Why would he do that? What's in it for him?'

Chris shook his head. 'I don't know, but—'

'Exactly.' Mike gripped his shoulders. 'You don't know. I don't know either. There is nothing to know. Now let it go.'

'Mike, I've got no axe to grind here. I came—'

Another sharp rap on the glass. 'Youah cutting it fine, Michael.'

'I only came on board to help you, and I'm—'

The shoulders, squeezed tighter. Mike met his eye. 'Chris, I know that. And I'm grateful. And I'm not blaming you for what happened. But you've got to let it go now. Get back to Cambodia. Start worrying about your own quarterly review.'

'Mike—'

'I'm out of time, Chris.' He squeezed once more, then darted for the door. Chris watched through the glass as he zipped into the seat next to Makin and settled, instants before the uplink chimed.

One thing that every Conflict Investment client Chris had ever dealt with had in common was their love of developed world technotoys. It was basic CI wisdom, handed down from partners to analysts everywhere in the trade. *Don't stint on toys*. At the top of every hardware gift list, you placed your state-of-the-art global communications gadgetry. That, and personalised airliners. Then the military stuff. Always that order, it never failed. Echevarria's uplink holocast was razor-sharp in resolution, and came with about a dozen attached display screens.

Chris knew his face, of course, from the HM files and occasional newscasts from the ME. Still, it had been a while since he'd seen Echevarria for real. He leaned in close to the glass wall and focused on the sagging, leathery face; the pouched eyes and clamped mouth, the scrawny neck, held ramrod straight, disappearing into the neck of a dress uniform laden with medals and awards. The peripheral display screens fanned out behind him unignited, like a black halo. The hands resting on the holocast table top looked bloated.

'Ah, General,' said Bryant, with plastic charm. 'There you are. Welcome.'

Echevarria raised one hand to his lips and looked to his left. The uplink chime sounded again and about a metre down the table, a second holocast image blipped and fizzled into existence.

'My son will be joining us for these proceedings.' The dictator smiled, showing brilliant white teeth, clearly not his own. 'If you *gentlemen* don't object.'

The irony was heavy, but worse lay behind it. Francisco Echevarria was currently in Miami, Chris knew. And the speed with which the holocast had come in past Shorn's databreaks, uninvited, suggested a level of intrusion equipment beyond that usually on offer to guests at the Miami Hilton.

He's with the fucking Americans. Rimshaw or Meldreck, got to be. Chris scrabbled for a hold. *Most likely Rimshaw. Lloyd fucking Paul. Calders aren't usually this flamboyant.*

The new holocast settled down. Francisco Echevarria emerged, darkly handsome in one of his habitual Susana Ingram suits. His face was already flushed with anger looking for discharge.

Mike Bryant took it and ran with it.

'Of course. We are delighted to have Señor Echevarria with us as well. In fact, the more varied the input at a time—'

'*Hijo de puta*,' spat Echevarria junior without preamble. 'The only fuckin' input I have to tell you is that if my father was not so sentimental about old attachments, you would be drivin' for tender tomorrow. I am sick of your Eurotrash duplici—'

'Paco! Please.' There was a light amusement in the father's voice. His English, Chris noticed, had a mannered southern-states drawl to it, at odds with the Miaspanic rhythms of his son's speech. 'These gentlemen have an apology to make. It would be rude not to hear them out.'

So.

Chris saw how Makin tautened. He wasn't sure if the father and son noticed.

'Certainly,' said Mike Bryant smoothly. 'There has been a serious misunderstanding, and I do feel that the responsibility is ours. When my colleague brought our files on the rebels to your attention, he perhaps did not stress enough that we were concerned—'

Echevarria junior rasped something indistinct in Spanish. His father looked in his direction and he shut up. Bryant nodded grateful acknowledgment to the father, and picked up the threads again.

'Were concerned that perceived instability was going to draw new and less scrupulous investors than ourselves.'

Hernan Echevarria smiled bleakly from around the globe.

'This instability you speak of has been dealt with. And you're right, Señor Bryant. That was not how your colleague presented the matter.' One of the peripheral screens woke into static prior to transmission. 'Would you like to see the message?'

Bryant raised a hand. 'We've all seen the message, Colonel. I don't propose to take up any more of your valuable time here than absolutely necessary. As I said, it was a case of poor communication, for which we take full responsibility.'

He looked pointedly at Makin.

'General Echevaia.' It sounded as if the words were being ripped out of Makin with pliers. 'I apologise. Unconditionally. For any. Misunderstanding I have caused. It was never my intention to. Suggest that we would be intested in dealing with your political enemies—'

'The enemies of my *country*, señor. The enemies of our national honour, of all Colombian patriots. Condemned, you will recall, by the Catholic church and every other symbol of decency in the Americas.'

'Yes,' said Makin stiffly. 'As you say.'

'I have something here.' Bryant came to his rescue. 'Which you may be interested in.'

One of the recessed screens flickered to life, and Chris knew that on the other side of the world the Echevarrias were watching the image emerge from somewhere over Mike Bryant's shoulder.

'This is some of the primary documentation you received from us in its original format,' said Bryant, steering the control mouse with one casual hand. 'As you'll see from the blow-up, it is not a document originating from Shorn. In fact, *this*, as I'm sure you'll recognise, is the logo of Hammett McColl.'

It could have been computer-generated fakery, and everyone in the room knew it. But Echevarria had invited HM out to the NAME himself the year before, and he knew it fitted.

'Where did you get this?' he asked.

'From a source.'

Echevarria junior erupted again in mother-related Spanish insults. Bryant waited him out. The father silenced the son again, this time with an irritated gesture.

'What source?'

'At this stage,' said Bryant carefully, 'I am not prepared to reveal that information. A source is only useful so long as it remains secure, and this link-up is not. *However*,' He caught the son's bristling and moved to beat it. 'In a genuine face-to-face situation, I would be happy to discuss all and any details pertaining to this matter. I feel that we owe you a certain candour after the weekend's confusion.'

'You are suggesting I fly to London?'

Bryant spread his hands. 'In your own time, naturally. I am aware that you have a number of pressing engagements at home.'

'Yes.' Echevarria smiled again, with about as much warmth as before. 'Notably clearing up the mess created by one of your agents.'

Mike sighed. 'General, I have done what I can to demonstrate our good faith. I give you my word—'

A repressed snarl from Echevarria junior.

'—that whatever this man was doing in Medellín, it was not at our request. He may have been operating at the behest of Hammett McColl, or someone else. I do not deny that our source in HM could very well have sold the same data to anyone else willing to pay corporate prices. I understand this person, let us say, has good contacts in both New York and Tokyo and—'

'Alright, Señor Bryant. I believe I have heard this excuse. You have offered a face-to-face meeting. To what end?'

'Well.' Mike went back to the mouse. The HM document faded and was replaced by one of the hardware lists he'd shown Chris the week before. 'There is an outstanding question over the matter of military equipment. In view of these new developments, and the disturbances they are bound to cause, I had it in mind to review the budget.'

Chris caught the reaction. He wondered how Mike managed not to grin.

'You are saying?'

'Next month, London hosts the North Memorial arms fair. I am suggesting that you kill two birds with one stone and that we visit the

180

fair together with an eye to your immediate requirements. While you are here, we can discuss the matter of Hammett McColl's information and its US implications.'

Echevarria's eyes narrowed. '*US* implications?'

'I'm sorry, I meant international implications.' Mike did a good imitation of embarrassment. 'I tend to leap to conclusions that cannot always be justified, but. Well. We can discuss this further when you are in London.'

After that, it was just noise. Bryant layered on the apologies, with a couple of wheeled-in words from Makin. Echevarria junior growled and snapped at intervals, always brought to heel by his father who just looked thoughtful throughout. Goodbyes were said cordially enough. Mike came storming back into the viewing chambers and slammed the door behind him.

'Get on to Lopez. I want contact with the rebels by the end of the week. This motherfucker is going to turn on us.'

Chris blinked. 'I thought you'd hooked him.'

'Yeah, for the moment. The military stuff ought to hold him for a while, and that smear about US involvement will stave off junior's Miami connections. But in the end, it's a slum block waiting to come down. Old Hernan doesn't really buy anything we said in there, he's just biding his time to see what he can get out of us. And he's not going to stay bribed with a handful of cheap cluster bombs, which is about all we can afford right now, the state things are in. No, the Americans are going to get him, sooner or later, and I want a player of our own in position before that happens.'

'Yeah, but who?' Chris gestured out through the glass to where Makin still sat at the table, staring into the middle distance. 'Fuckhead there's managed to trash Diaz. Who does that leave us?'

'We'll have to go with Barranco.'

'*Barranco?*'

'Chris, he's what we've got. You said yourself, Arbenz isn't going to be in any position to lead an armed insurrection this year.'

'Yeah, but *Barranco*. He's committed, Mike.'

'Ah, come on. They all start out that way.'

'No, he's a real fucking Guevara, Mike. I don't think we're going to be able to control him.'

Bryant grinned. 'Yeah, we will. You will.' He glanced back through at Makin. The other executive hadn't moved. 'I'm going to take this shit to Hewitt and get Nick reassigned. It's high fucking time. Meanwhile, you get Barranco to sit down. I don't care what it takes. Fly out there yourself if you have to, but get him to a table.'

There was a brief rush off the words, an image from the Hammett

McColl visit, a Caribbean night sky shingled with stars, the warm darkness beneath and the noises of the night time street.

'You want me to go out to Panama?'

'If that's what it takes.'

'Hewitt isn't going to like this. She gave the account to Makin in the first place. It isn't going to look good if he's written off as the wrong choice. And that's without her feelings about me. She's hardly a fan.'

'Chris, you're fucking paranoid. I told you before. Hewitt's a fan of money, and right now you're making plenty of it. Bottom line, that's what counts.' Mike grinned again. 'And anyway, she gives me any static, I'll go talk to Notley. You are in, my friend, like it or not. Welcome to the NAME account.'

Out in the conference room, Makin stirred in his chair and turned to look towards them. It was as if he'd heard the conversation. He looked beaten and betrayed. Chris stared back at him, trying to chase out a faint disquiet that would not go away.

'Thanks.'

'Hey, you earned it. Run with it.' Bryant slung an arm around his shoulders. 'Besides, we're a fucking team. Now let's kick Hernan Echevarria into touch and make some fucking money.'

TWENTY-THREE

Someone had tied up a damaged speedboat beside the jetty and then left it to drown. The boat's prow was raised, roped tightly to a mooring iron, but behind the fly-specked windscreen, the water was up over the pale leather upholstered interior almost to the dashboard. Chris saw a fish hanging suspended below the surface like a tiny zeppelin, nibbling at something on the lower arc of the submerged steering wheel. Twigs and decaying leaf matter floated around the sunken stern, shifting sloppily back and forth as the wake of a passing water taxi rolled up to the jetty. Wavelets slapped at the wooden supports. Out across the lagoon, low cloud adhered like grey candyfloss to trees on the islands, and drifted across the seaward view, trailing rain. The sun was a vague blot on the lighter grey overhead. The air was warm and clammy.

Chris turned away. It wasn't the Caribbean as he remembered it. He went back to where Joaquin Lopez sat with his back to the wooden shack that justified the jetty's existence.

'You sure he's coming?'

Lopez shrugged. He was a tall, tightly-muscled man, mostly Afro-Caribbean, and he radiated a calm at odds with the panic he'd shown over the phone from Medellín. 'He has every reason to. I wouldn't have brought you for nothing, man. Smoke?'

Chris shook his head. Lopez lit a cigarette for himself and plumed smoke out across the water. He scratched absently at a scar on his forehead.

'It will not have been easy for him. There's a lot of heat along this part of the coast. The turtle patrols have authority to stop and search anyone they think is poaching. And you sometimes got US drug enforcement boats up from the Darien. They don't have any authority, but . . .'

He shrugged again. Chris nodded.

'When did that ever stop them, right?'

'Right.' Lopez looked away and grinned.

'What?'

'Nothing. You don't talk like a gringo.'

Chris yawned. He hadn't slept much in the last couple of days. 'I'll take that as a compliment.'

'Keep it up. It may help with Barranco.'

It was piling up behind his eyes now. London, Madrid, San Jose Costa Rica. A blur of airports, executive lounges in muted pastel shades, the grey whisper of air-conditioned flight. Chasing down the sun, gaining a day. Helicoptered out of San Jose at dawn and across the border into Panama. Touchdown on a sun-drenched airfield outside David, where Lopez had sneaked out of Panama City and west to meet him. Another short hop north to Bocas del Toro, a series of shacks and people Lopez knew, a gun on loan, a water taxi out *here*, wherever exactly it was, and waiting, waiting for Barranco.

'You ever meet him?'

Lopez shook his head. 'Spoke to him on the videophone a couple of days ago. He's looking tired, not like the pinups they did of him back in '41. He needs this, Chris. This is his last throw.'

The year echoed in his head. In '41, Edward Quain had died in smeared fragments on the cold asphalt of the M20. At the time, it had seemed like some kind of ending. But Chris had woken the next day to find the world intact and nothing he'd begun at Hammett McColl even close to tidy, let alone finished. It had dawned on him only then that he'd have to go on living, and that he'd have to find some new reason to do it.

A soft snarling, out across the water.

'Boat coming,' said Lopez.

The vessel came into view around a forested headland, raising a bow wave to match the noise of its engines. It was a big, navy-grey vessel, built for speed and, judging by the twinned machine guns mounted behind an impact-glass cupola on the foredeck, for assault. A flag flapped at the stern, white design on a green background. Lopez breathed a sigh of relief when he saw it.

'Turtle patrol,' he said.

The powerboat slowed and settled in the water as the motors cut to an idle. It nosed into the jetty and someone dressed in khakis came up on the foredeck. Yells in Spanish. Lopez responded. The deckhand gathered up a line and jumped blithely to the jetty with it. He landed with a practised flex in the legs. A woman, similarly attired, came and leaned on the machine-gun cupola, staring at them. Chris felt caution creep through him.

'You're armed too, right?' he muttered to Lopez.

'Sure. But these are turtle guys, they aren't—'

The next man off the boat wore the same army fatigues and had a Kalashnikov assault rifle slung over his shoulder. He passed Chris without a glance, ambled up to Lopez and rapped out something in Spanish. When he got the answer, he disappeared into the shack behind

184

them. Chris looked at the water on the other side of the jetty and wondered how deep it was. He'd want a good half metre over his head to be sure of not getting shot. The Smith and Wesson Lopez had lent him was apparently guaranteed to fire wet, but against assault rifles—

Let's face it, Chris, you wouldn't last five minutes. This isn't a Tony Carpenter flick.

'Señor Faulkner?'

He jerked back to the boat. Another khaki-clad figure had joined the woman on the foredeck. As the man vaulted to the jetty, Chris caught up with the voice. It was Barranco.

It was the same weathered set of features Chris remembered from the HM meeting just over a year ago – a face darkened by sun and altitude, broad across the cheekbones, chipped with the blue of eyes tossed into the gene pool by some European colonist decades or centuries absorbed. The same close-cropped greying hair, the same height and length of limb as Barranco moved to greet him. The same calloused grip, the same search in the eyes when you got up close. It was a gaze that belonged on the bridge of some warship from the last century, or maybe the last of the pirate trawlers, scanning the grey horizon for signs.

'Señor Faulkner. I remember you now, from the Hammett McColl mission. The man with the laptop. You were very quiet then.'

'I came to listen.' Chris reached into his jacket. 'This time I—'

'Very easy, please.' Barranco raised his own hands. 'My companions are a little nervous this far from home, and it wouldn't do to let them think you're planning to use that badly concealed gun in your belt.'

He gestured in turn at the woman by the cupola and the first deck-hand ashore, who now straightened from the mooring iron with a pistol gripped in one fist. Chris heard the snap of a weapon being cocked, looked back at the shack and saw the man with the assault rifle emerge from the building again, weapon cradled at his hip.

'So,' said Barranco. 'Welcome again to Latin America.'

The interior of the shack was equipped with basic facilities – a toilet behind a wall of plastic partitioning, a tiny stove in a corner and an ancient wooden table two metres long, scarred with decades of use and carved with what looked like whole generations of grafitti. A half dozen tired-looking plastic moulded chairs were gathered around the table – Chris's choice from among the untidy pile they'd found behind the shack when they arrived. Hardly Shorn conference standard. The windows were small and liberally grimed, but bulbs from an aqualight system hung suspended at intervals in the roof space and the long uptake taper was still intact, dangling down through a crudely bored hole in the floorboards and into the water below the pilings. Chris had tested the system earlier and the taper was well soaked. Now he flipped the wall switch and gentle light sprang up in three out of the five bulbs.

Barranco glanced around the shack and nodded.

'Well, it's not the Panama Hilton,' he said. 'But then, I suppose I am not Luis Montoya.'

It seemed to require a reaction. Chris tried a chuckle and gestured towards the table. 'Please sit down, Señor Barranco. I'm afraid our concern so far has been security rather than comfort. Outside of one or two deluded drug enforcement diehards, Luis Montoya has no real enemies in the Americas. You, unfortunately, have many.'

'A problem you are offering to solve for me, no?' Barranco did not sit down. Instead, he nodded at his own security, two of whom had follow-ed him in. Without a word, they moved to positions at the windows and took up an at-ease stance that fooled no one. Neither of them spared Chris more than a glance, and that filled with easy contempt.

Chris walked to the table and pulled out the chair for Barranco.

'I'm sure that, given time and a little luck, a man such as yourself is probably capable of solving the problem without any help from men like me. Given time and luck. Please. Have a seat.'

Barranco didn't move. 'I am not susceptible to flattery.'

Chris shrugged and took the seat for himself. 'I didn't think you were. I was making a statement of fact. I believe, which is to say we, my colleagues at Shorn and I, believe you are capable of resolving a number of the issues facing Colombia at present. That is why I am here. This visit is a demonstration of our faith in you.'

It brought Barranco to the table, slowly.

'You call it Colombia,' he said. 'Is that how your colleagues refer to it in London?'

'No, of course not.' Chris brushed at the table top and held up his hands, seeking the gaze of Barranco's security before he reached slowly into his jacket and brought out the folded laptop. He thought he made it look pretty cool, considering. 'We call it the North Andean Mon-itored Economy, as I'm sure you're aware. As I'm also sure you're aware, we are hardly alone in this.'

'No.' There was a flat bitterness in the words. Barranco's hands had fallen on the back of the chair opposite Chris. 'You are not. The whole world calls us that way. Only that son of a whore in Bogotá uses the name Colombia, as if we were still a nation.'

'Hernan Echevarria,' said Chris softly, 'milks the patriotism of his countrymen to shore up a regime that rewards the top five per cent of the country with riches and keeps the remainder with their faces in the dirt. You do not need me to tell you this. But I think you need me to help you do something about it.'

'How quickly we move.' There was a look on Barranco's face, as if he could smell something bad seeping through the plastic partition from the toilet. 'How quickly, from flattery to bribery. Did you not say that a man such as myself could resolve—'

'*Given*. Time.' Chris locked gazes, made sure he'd stopped the other man, then set placidly about unfolding the laptop. 'I said, given time. And given luck. And I said "probably".'

'I see.' Chris wasn't looking at him, but Barranco sounded as if he was smiling. *How quickly we move. From a sneer to a smile.* But he didn't look up yet. The laptop was heavily creased in a couple of places and it was taking a while to warm up. He busied himself with flattening out the screen. He heard the chair opposite him scrape out. Heard it take Barranco's weight.

The screen lit with a map of the Monitored Economy.

Chris looked up and smiled.

Later, with the numbers wrung out to dry, they walked out along the jetty and stood at the end, watching the weather. To the east, the sky was clearing in patches.

'Smoke?' Barranco asked him.

'Yeah, thanks.' Chris took the proffered packet and shook out a crumpled cylinder. Barranco lit it for him from a battered silver petrol lighter that bore engraving in Cyrillic around a skull and cross bones and the date 2007. Chris drew deep and promptly coughed himself to tears on the smoke.

'Whoh.' He took the cigarette out of his mouth and blinked at it. 'Where'd you get these?'

'A shop you haven't been to.' Barranco pointed what looked like southwest. 'Seven hundred kilometres from here, up in the mountains. It's run by an old woman who remembers the day Echevarria took power. She won't sell American brands. It's black tobacco.'

'Yeah, I noticed.' Chris took another, more cautious draw on the cigarette and felt it bite in his lungs. He gestured. 'And the lighter? Military issue, right?'

'Wrong.' Barranco held up the lighter again, rubbing a finger back and forth across the Cyrillic characters. 'Advertising. It says *Death Cigarettes – too bad you're going to die*. But it's a, what do you call it in English, a knock-out? An illegal copy?'

'Knock-off.'

'Yes, a knock-off. Some crazy English guy back in the last century, he actually made cigarettes with that name.'

'Doesn't sound too smart.'

Barranco turned and breathed smoke at him. 'At least he was honest.'

Chris let that one sit for a while. Barranco wandered the width of the jetty, smoking, waiting him out.

'I think you should come to London, Señor Barranco. You need—'

'Are your parents alive, Señor Faulkner?'

It stabbed him through, punctured the slowly inflating sense of a deal done that was filling him up.

'No.'

'Do you remember them?'

He shot a glance across at the face of the man beside him, and knew this was not negotiable. This was required.

'My father died when I was young,' he said, surprised at how easy it had become to say it. 'I don't remember him well. My mother died later, when I was in my teens. Of thorn fever.'

Barranco's eyes narrowed. 'What is that? Thorn fever.'

Chris smoked for a moment, checking his memories for leakage before he answered. He thought he had it locked down.

'It's a TB variant. One of the antibiotic-resistant strains. We lived in the zones, what you'd call the favelas, and there's a lot of it there. She couldn't afford the smart drugs, no one there can, so she just took basic ABs until she collapsed. No one's sure what killed her in the end, the thorn fever or something else her immune system was too wasted to cope with. It took—'

He didn't have it locked down. He looked away.

'I am sorry,' said Barranco.

'It,' Chris swallowed. 'Thanks, it's okay. It was a long time ago.'

He drew on the cigarette again, grimaced suddenly and flung it away from him into the water. He pressed the back of his index finger against his eyes, one by one, and looked at the scant streaks of moisture they left.

'My mother was taken away,' said Barranco from behind him. 'In the night, by soldiers. It was common at the time. I too was in my teens. My father had long ago left us, and I was out, at a political meeting. Perhaps it was me they came for. But they took her instead.'

Chris knew. He'd read the file.

'They raped her. Echevarria's men. They tortured her for days, with electricity and with a broken bottle. And then they shot her in the face and left her to die on a rubbish tip at the edge of town. A doctor from La Amnestia told me they think it took her about two hours.'

Chris would have said sorry, but the word seemed broken, drained of useful content.

'Do you understand why I am fighting, Señor Faulkner? Why I have been fighting for the last twenty years?'

Chris shook his head, wordless. He turned to face Barranco, and saw

188

that the other man had no more emotion on his face than he'd shown when they were discussing cigarettes.

'You don't understand, Señor Faulkner?' Barranco shrugged. 'Well, I cannot blame you. Sometimes, neither do I. Some days, it makes more sense to take my Kalashnikov, walk into any police station or barracks bar and kill everything that wears a uniform. But I know that behind those men are others who wear no uniform, so I change this plan, and I begin to think that I should do the same thing with a government building. But then I remember that these people in turn are only the front for an entire class of landowning families and financiers who call themselves my compatriots. My head spins with new targets.' Barranco gestured. 'Banks. Ranches. Gated suburbs. The numbers for slaughter rise like a lottery total. And then I remember that Hernan Echevarria would not have lasted a year in power, not a single year, if he had not had support from Washington and New York.' He raised a finger and pointed at Chris. 'And London. Are you sure, Señor Faulkner, that you want me in your capital city?'

Chris, still busy hauling back in the emotional canvas, mustered a shrug of his own. His voice rasped a little in his throat.

'I'll take the chance.'

'Brave man.' Barranco finished his own cigarette and pinched it out between finger and thumb. 'I suppose. A brave man, or a gambler. Which should I call you?'

'Call me a judge of character. I think you're smart enough to be trusted.'

'I'm flattered. And your colleagues?'

'My colleagues will listen to me. This is what I get paid for.'

'Yes. I suppose it is.'

Chris caught the drip of it in Barranco's voice, the same thing he'd seen in the other marquistas' eyes in the shack.

fuck

He'd overplayed it, too much macho boardroom acceleration coming off the emotional bend. He was leaning in for damage limitation, but what he wanted to say twisted loose on its way out. Aghast, he heard himself telling the truth, raw.

'What have you got to lose? You're in shit-poor shape, Vicente. We both know that. Backed up in the mountains, outgunned, living on rhetoric. If Echevarria comes for you now, the way he did for Diaz, you're history. Like Marcos, like Guevara. A beautiful legend and a fucking T-shirt. Is that what you want? All those people in the NAME, going through what your mother went through, what good are you to them like that?'

For a moment that froze as the last word left his mouth, he imagined

189

the world caving in around him with the deal. Barranco's eyes hardened, his stance tightened. Telegraphed so clear it sent the security guard on the patrol boat's deck smoothly to her feet. An assault rifle hefted. Chris's breath stopped.

'I mean—'

'I know what you mean.' Barranco's posture relaxed first. He turned to the woman on the boat and made a sign. She sank back to her seat. When he turned back, something had changed in his face. 'I know what you mean, because this is the first time you've come out and said it. You can't imagine how much of a relief that is, Chris Faulkner. You can't imagine how little all your numbers have meant to me without some sign that you have a soul.'

Chris breathed again. 'You should have asked.'

'Asked if you had a soul?' There wasn't much humour in Barranco's parched laugh. 'Is that a question that can be asked in London? When I am seated around the table with your colleagues, discussing what slices of my country's GDP I must offer up to gain their support. What crops my people must grow while their own children starve, what essential medical services they must learn to live without. Will I ask them where they keep their souls then, Señor Faulkner?'

'I wouldn't advise it, no.'

'No. Then what would you advise?'

Chris weighed it up—

fuck it, it's worked so far

—and told the unbandaged truth again.

'I'd advise you to get what you can from them with as little commitment on your side as possible. Because that's what they'll be doing to you. Leave yourself escape clauses, remember, nothing's ever written in stone. Everything can be renegotiated, if you can make it worth their while.'

A pause. Barranco laughed again, warmth leaking into the sound this time. He offered the cigarettes again, lit them both with the Russian knock-off.

'Good advice, my friend,' he said through the smoke. 'Good advice. I think I would hire you as an adviser, if I could afford you.'

'You can. I'm part of the package.'

'No.' The trawlerman's gaze settled on him. 'I know a little about you now, Chris Faulkner, and you are not part of any package in London. There is something in you that resists incorporation. Something.' Barranco shrugged. 'Honourable.'

It flickered across Chris's memory before he could stop it. Liz Linshaw's body in the white silk gown that untied and opened like a gift. The curves and shadowed places within. The sound of her laugh.

'I think you are mistaken about me,' he said quietly.

Barranco shook his head. 'You will see. I am not a bad judge of character myself, when it counts. You may get paid by these people, but you are not one of them. You do not belong.'

Lopez got him back to Bocas by nightfall, and they sat in a waterfront cafe waiting for the late flight to David. Across the water, the sequin twinkle of restaurant lights on another island seemed threaded directly onto the darkness. Local-owned pangas puttered about in the channel between, cruising for taxi custom. Voices drifted out over the water like smoke, Spanish shot through with an occasional English loan word. Kitchen noise clattered in the back of the cafe behind them.

The whole meeting with Barranco already seemed like a dream.

'So it went well,' Lopez asked.

Chris stirred at his cocktail. 'Seems that way. He's going to come to London, anyway.' His mind cut loose the replays of Liz Linshaw and went wearily to work. 'I want you to set that up as soon as possible, but safe. Above all, safe. Quick as you can without endangering his life or his strategic position. I'll move things around at my end to fit in with whatever that means.'

'Billing?'

'Through the covert account. I don't want this to show up until . . . No, better yet you pay for it yourself. Cash. I'll have the money dumped to you in Zurich soon as I get back. Mail me an advance estimate at the hotel tomorrow morning. Oh yeah, you got anything that'll help me sleep?'

'Not on me.' Lopez dug out his phone. 'You're at the Sheraton, right?'

'Yeah. 1101. Jenkins.'

The phone screen showed a cosy green glow. Lopez punched his way down a list and held up the instrument to face him. After a couple of rings, a voice answered in Spanish.

'*En inglés, guei,*' said Lopez impatiently.

Whoever he was looking at grumbled something filthy and then switched. 'You here in town, man?'

'No, but a friend of mine will be shortly. And he needs a little something to help him sleep.'

'Is he a *fizi*?'

Lopez looked up from the phone at Chris. 'You do a lot of this sort of stuff?'

'Christ, no.'

The Americas agent dropped his gaze to the phone screen again. 'Definitely not. Something gentle.'

'Got it. Address.'

'Sheraton, room 1101. Mr Jenkins.'

'Charge card or account.'

'Very fucking funny. *Hasta luego.*'

'*Hasta la cuenta, amigo.*'

He folded up the phone. 'Stuff'll be waiting for you at the desk. You go in, just ask if you got any messages. There'll be an envelope.'

'You can vouch for this guy, right.'

'Yeah, he's a plastic surgeon.'

Chris couldn't see why that was supposed to reassure him, but he was getting past caring. The thought of crushing his jetlag beneath the soft black weight of seven or eight hours of chemically guaranteed sleep was like a finishing line ahead. Liz Linshaw, Mike Bryant and Shorn, Carla, Barranco and the skipper's scrutiny; he let them all go like a pack he'd been carrying. Sleep was coming. He'd worry about everything else tomorrow.

But behind the aching relief, Barranco's words floated like the voices out on the water.

You do not belong.

TWENTY-FOUR

He woke in the standard issue luxury of the Sheraton, to the softly insistent pulse of an incoming signal from his laptop. He flopped over in the bed and glared blearily around the room. Located the fucking thing, there on the carpeted floor amidst the trail of his dropped clothes. *Bleeee, bleeee,* fucking *bleeee.* He groaned and groped, half out of bed, one hand holding his body rigidly horizontal off the floor. He snagged the machine, dragged it onto the bed and sat up to unfold it in his lap. Mike Bryant's recorded face grinned out at him.

'Morning. If I timed this right, I figure you've got about three hours before your flight, so here's something to think about while you're waiting. You are under attack. And this time, you are going down!'

Groggy from the plastic surgeon's special delivery, Chris felt a sluggish spasm of alarm rip through him. Then the other man's face blinked out and a stylised chessboard took its place. Mike had launched an unlooked-for rook-and-knight assault on him while he slept. It looked bad.

'Motherfucker.'

He got up and shambled about, packing. Still not flushed clean of the sleeping fix, he reacted unwisely to Mike's gambit over breakfast and lost a bishop. Bryant, it seemed, was playing in real time. He went to the airport smarting from the loss and picked up the pieces in the exec lounge. It was Saturday and Mike, if he'd known what was good for him, should have let the game ride for the weekend. He could have thought it out over the next couple of days and taken Chris apart at leisure, but Chris knew him better. Bryant was lit up with the taste of his victory and he'd stay in real-time play now. View, absorb, react, all night if he had to. Chris had lent him Rakhimov's *Speed Chess and the Attack Momentum* a couple of months ago, and the big man had swallowed it whole. He was in for the kill.

Somewhere over the Caribbean, Chris beat off the attack. It cost him his only remaining knight and his carefully constructed castled defence was in ruins, but Mike's attack momentum was down. The flurry of moves slowed. Chris played doggedly across the Atlantic and by the time they touched down in Madrid, he had Bryant nailed to a lucky stalemate. Mike sent him a Tony Carpenter clip attachment in response

– the post-fight stand-off from *The Deceiver*. Carpenter's trademark lack of acting talent, lines creaking with the burden of cliché. *We are well matched, you and I. We should fight on the same side.* It was so bad it was almost camp.

Chris grinned and folded the laptop.

He got off the flight with a bounce in his step, grabbed a sauna and a shower in the exec lounge while he waited and slept naturally on the shuttle back to London. He dreamed of Liz Linshaw.

At Heathrow, leaning on the barrier at arrivals, made up and dressed in clothes that hugged at her figure, Carla was waiting.

'No, it's just. You didn't need to. You know, I'm running on the Shorn clock. They'd pick up the tab for a taxi all the way home.'

'I wanted to see you.'

So why the fuck'd you go to Tromsö? He bit it back, and watched the curving perspectives of the road ahead. Saturday morning traffic on the orbital was sparse, and Carla, with the easy confidence of the professional mechanic, had the Saab up to a hundred and fifty in the middle lane.

'How was your mum?'

'She's good. Busy. They want to bring out an interactional version of the new book, so she's been rewriting, slotting in the GoTo sections with some datarat from the university.'

'Is she shagging him?' It didn't quite come out right. Too harsh, too much silence around it. There was a time Chris could get away with these riffs on Kirsti's sex life, and Carla used to laugh in mock outrage. Now she just looked across at him and went back to watching the road, tight lipped. The chill filled the car almost palpably.

'Sorry, I—'

'That was nasty.'

'It wasn't meant to be.' Helplessly.

What the fuck is happening to us, Carla. What the fuck are we doing here? Is it just me? Is *it*?

He saw Liz Linshaw again, the easy smile in the spare room, face and hair dappled with street lighting through the tree outside, the glass of water in her hand. She had navigated the moment with the same ease that Carla drove the Saab. Stepping closer than necessary to hand him the water, the warm tang of whisky on her breath. A soft, surprised *oh*, in ladylike tones her newscasts had never seen, as he pulled at the raw silk belt and the gown fell open. Broken street light across the curves within. The feel of her breast, as he laid one hand on it, was burnt into his palm. The soft sound of the laugh in her throat.

Highgate.

Involuntarily, he opened the hand at the memory. Looked at it, as if for some sign of branding.

I, uh, I can't do this, Liz, he'd lied, *I'm sorry*, and he'd turned away to stare out of the window, pretty sure this was the only way to stop the landslide. Trembling with the force of it.

Fair enough, she told him and in the window he watched her bend to leave the glass on the table by the futon. She stood for a moment at the door before she left, looking at his back, but she said nothing. She had not retied the gown. The gap between its edges was black in the reflected image, empty of detail that his own mind was feverishly happy to fill.

In the morning, he woke to find the gown draped across the quilt he had slept under. At some point during the night she had come in, taken it off and stood naked, watching him sleep. Even through the layers of mild hangover, it was an intensely erotic image and he felt himself hardening at the thought.

The house was silent around him. Birdsong from the tree outside the window, a solitary car engine somewhere distant. He lay propped up on one elbow in the bed, vague with last night's drinking. Without conscious thought, he reached for the gown, dragged it up the bed and held it to his face. It smelled intimately of woman, the only woman's scent outside of Carla's that he had breathed in nearly a decade. The shock was visceral, dissolving the hangover and dumping him out into reality like an exasperated bouncer. He threw off the gown and the quilt in a single motion, threw on clothes. Watch and wallet, off the bedside table in a sweep, stamping into shoes. He slid out of the spare room and paused.

There was no one home. It was a feeling he knew well, and the house echoed with it. A handwritten note lay on the kitchen table, detailing where breakfast things could be found, the number of a good cab company and how to set the alarms before leaving. It was signed *stay in touch*.

He got out.

No appetite for breakfast, no confidence that he wouldn't do something really stupid like go through her things or, worse still, wait around for her to come back. He triggered the alarm set-up and the door closed him out on a rising whine as the house defences charged.

He found himself on a tree-lined hill street that swept up behind him and down then up again in front. A couple of prestige cars and a four track were parked at intervals along the kerbs, and down near the base of the parabola the street described, someone was walking a German Shepherd. There was no one else about. It looked like a nice neighbourhood.

He didn't know Highgate, had been in the area only a couple of times before in his life, to drink- and drug-blurred parties at the homes of HM execs. But the air was mild and the sky looked clear of rain in all directions.

He chose the downslope at random, and started walking.

The Saab jolted on a badly mended pothole. Dumped him back into reality. The memory of Highgate dropped away, receding in the rearview.

'Carla.' He reached across the space between them. He touched her cheek with the back of his fingers. 'Look, I'm sorry. I didn't mean anything about your mother. It was a joke, alright.'

'Ha fucking ha.'

He held down the quick flare of anger. 'Carla, we've got to stop this. We've only been in each other's company half an hour, and we're fighting already. This is killing us.'

'You're the one who.' She stopped, and he wondered what she was biting back the way he'd bitten back words a few moments earlier.

Is this it, he wondered dismally, *is this the only way to survive a-long term relationship? Hide your thoughts, bite back your feelings, build a neutral silence that won't hurt. Is that what it's all about? Neutrality for the sake of a warm bed?*

Is that what I turned Liz down for?

Liz, waiting, wrapped in the white silk that carried her scent.

'Carla, pull over.'

'What?'

'Pull over. Stop. There, on the hard shoulder. Please.'

She shot him a look, and must have seen something in his face. The Saab bled speed and drifted across the lanes. Carla dropped a gear and brought the car under a hundred kilometres an hour. Onto the hard shoulder and they crunched to a halt. Carla turned in her seat to face him.

'Alright.'

'Carla, listen.' He put his hands on her shoulders, feeling his way towards what he needed to say. 'Please don't run off like that again. Like you did. I missed you. I really did. I need you, and when you're not here I really. I miss you so much. I. I do stupid things.'

Her eyes widened.

'Things like what?'

And he could not fucking tell her. He couldn't.

He thought he was going to, he even started to, started with Troy Morris's party, even got as far as talking about Liz and her book proposal, but he couldn't do it, and when she knew there was more behind it and pushed for it, he veered off into the zones and what he and Mike Bryant had done to Griff Dixon and his friends.

She whitened as he told it.

'That can't be,' she whispered. 'You, they can't,' scaling almost to a shout. 'People can't *do* things like that. It's not *legal*.'

'Tell that to Mike. Ah, Christ, tell it to the whole fucking Shorn corporation, while you're at it.' And then it all had to come tumbling out, the morning after, the NAME contract, the fuck-up with Lopez and Langley, the dead in Medellín and the quick-fix burial of the facts, Panama and Barranco and his quiet insistence. *You do not belong.* Chris found he was trembling by the time he got to the end and there was what felt like a laugh building in his throat, but when it finally came out his eyes were wet. He unfastened his belt and leaned across the space between the seats. He pulled himself across and against her, teeth gritted on the fraying shreds of his control.

They clung together.

'Chris.' There was something in Carla's voice that might have been a laugh as well, and what she was saying made no kind of sense, but the way she held him that didn't seem to matter much. 'Chris, listen to me. It's okay. There's a way out of this.'

She started to lay it out for him. Less than a minute in, he was shouting her down.

'You can't be fucking serious, Carla. That's not a way out.'

'Chris, *please* listen to me.'

'A fucking *ombudsman*. What do you think I am, a *socialist*? A fucking loser? Those people are—'

He gestured at the enormity of it, groping for words. Carla folded her arms and looked at him.

'Are what? Dangerous? Do you want to tell me again how you murdered three unarmed men in the zones last weekend?'

'They were scum, Carla. Armed or not.'

'And the car-jackers, back in January. Were they scum too?'

'That—'

'And the people in that cafe in Medellín?' Her voice was rising again. 'The people you killed in the Cambodia playoff. Isaac Murcheson, who you dreamed about every night for a year after you killed him. And now, you have the insane fucking nerve to tell me the ombudsmen are *dangerous*?'

He raised his hands. 'I didn't say that.'

'You were going to.'

'You don't know what I was going to say,' he lied. 'I was going to say those people are, they're losers Carla, they're standing against the whole tide of globalisation, of *progress*, for fuck's sake.'

'Is it progress?' she asked, suddenly quiet. 'Balkanisation and slaughter abroad and the free market feeding off the bones, a poverty-line economy and gladiatorial contests on the roads at home. Is that supposed to be progress?'

'That's your father talking.'

'No, *fuck* you Chris, this is me talking. You think I don't have opinions of my own. You think I can't look around and see for myself what's happening? You think I'm not living out the consequences?'

'You don't—'

'You know, in Norway when I tell people where I live, where I *choose* to live, they look at me like I'm some kind of moral retard. When I tell them what my husband does for a living, they—'

'Oh, here we go.' He turned away from her in the narrow confines of the car. Outside his window, the wind whipped along the embankment, flattening the long grass. 'Here we fucking go again.'

'Chris, listen to me.' A hand on his shoulder. He shrugged it off angrily.

'You've got to stand outside it for a moment. That's what I did while I was in Tromsö. You've got to see it from the outside to understand. You're a paid killer, Chris. A paid killer, a dictator in all but name.'

'Oh, for—'

'Echevarria, right? You told me about Echevarria.'

'What about him?'

'You talk as if you hated him. As if he was a monster.'

'He pretty much is, Carla.'

'And what's the difference between the two of you? Every atrocity he commits, you underwrite. You told me about the torture, the people in those police cells and the bodies on the rubbish dumps. You put those people there, Chris. You may as well have been there with the electrodes.'

'That's not fair. Echevarria isn't mine.'

'Isn't *yours?*'

'It isn't my account, Carla. I don't get to make the decisions on that one. In fact—'

'Oh, and Cambodia's different? You get to make the decisions on that one, because you *told* me you do, and I read the reports while I was away, Chris. The independent press for a change. They say this Khieu Sary is going to be as bad as the original Khmer Rouge.'

'That's bullshit. Khieu's a pragmatist. He's a good bet, and even if he gets out of hand we can—'

'Out of *hand?* What does that mean, out of hand? You mean if the body count gets into the tens of thousands? If they run out of places to bury them secretly? Chris, for fuck's sake listen to yourself.'

He turned back. 'I didn't make the world the way it is, Carla. I'm just trying to live in it.'

'We don't have to live in it this way.'

'No? You want to live in the fucking zones, do you?' He reached across and grabbed at the leather jacket she was wearing. 'You think they wear this kind of stuff in the zones? You think you get to jet off to Scandinavia when you fucking feel like it if you live in the zones?'

'I'm not—'

'You want to be an old woman at *forty?*' She flinched at the lash in his voice. He was losing control now, tears stinging in his eyes. 'Is that what you want, Carla? Obese from the shit they stuff the food with, diabetic from the fucking sugar content, allergies from the additives, no money for decent medical treatment. Is that what you want? You want to die poor, die *because* you're poor? *Is that what you fucking want, Carla, because—*'

The slap turned his head. Jarred loose the tears from his eyelids. He blinked and tasted blood.

'Now you listen to me,' she said evenly. 'You shut up and hear what I have to say, or this is over. I mean it, Chris.'

'You have no idea,' he muttered.

'Don't try to pull rank on me, Chris. My father lives in the zones—'

'Your *father?*' Derisively. Voice rising again. 'Your father doesn't—'

'I'm warning you, Chris.'

He looked away. Cranked down the anger. 'Your father,' he said quietly, 'is a tourist. He has no children. No dependents. Nothing that ties him where he is, nothing to *force* him. He isn't like the people he surrounds himself with, and he never will be. He could be gone tomorrow if he chose to, and that's what makes the difference.'

'He thinks he can make a difference.'

'And can he?'

Silence. Finally, he looked back at her.

'Can he, Carla?' He reached out and took her hand. 'Yesterday I was on the other side of the world, talking to a man who might be able to kick Echevarria out of the ME. If I get my way, it'll happen. Isn't that worth something? Isn't that something better than the articles your father hammers out for readers who'll shake their heads and act shocked and never lift a fucking finger to change anything?'

'If it matters to you so much to change things all of a sudden, why can't you—'

The heavy throb of rotors overhead. The car rocked on its suspension. The radio crackled to life.

'Driver Control. This is Driver Control.'

The rotor noise grew, even through the Saab's soundproofing. The helicopter's belly dropped into view, black and luminous green, showing landing skids, underslung cameras and gatlings. It skittered back a few metres, as if nervous of the stopped car. The voice splashed out of the radio again.

'Owner of Saab Custom registration s810576, please identify yourself.'

What the fuck for, dickhead? The thought was a random jag of anger. *Match me from the footage you've just shot through my windscreen, why don't you? Instead of wasting my motherfucking time.*

'This is a security requirement,' admonished the voice.

'This is Chris Faulkner,' he said heavily. 'Driver clearance 260B354R. I work for Shorn Associates. Now fuck off, will you. My wife's not feeling well, and you're not helping.'

There was a brief silence while the numbers ran. The voice came back, diffident.

'Sorry to trouble you, sir. It's just, stopping like that on the carriageway. If your wife needs hospitalisation, we can—'

'I said, fuck off.'

The helicopter dithered for a moment longer then spun about and lifted out of view. They sat for a while, listening to its departing chunter.

'Nice to know they're watching,' said Carla bitterly.

'Yeah.' He closed his eyes.

She touched his arm. 'Chris.'

'Alright.' He nodded. Opened his eyes. 'Alright. I'll talk to them.'

FILE#3:
FOREIGN AID

TWENTY-FIVE

Two weeks.

For Chris, marooned on the fringes of the preparations, it passed like a waking dream. He lived a distorted copy of his real life, tinged in equal portions by nightmarish tension and an odd, unlooked-for romantic nostalgia.

Work was as he'd expected. He acted normal and watched his back. Troop movements in Assam, hostage-taking in Parana, and in Cambodia a handful of executions no one had foreseen. He handled it all with eerie calm.

At home, he dared not talk openly to Carla so they took up a bizarre dual existence, life in the house as if nothing had changed, set against hushed exchanges snatched in the secure confines of the Saab. Carla, somehow, had persuaded Erik and Kirsti to act together as the link with the ombudsmen, and she went regularly to the Brundtland to gather details from her father. Some kind of code was in use over Erik's netlink, a fake reconciliation underway between the parents to serve as cover for the information Chris and Carla agreed in their hasty conferences in the car.

And here came the nostalgia, the bittersweet taste of something almost used up. The moments grabbed in the Saab had the tang of illicit sexual encounters, and once or twice even ended that way. And the rest of the time, acting out normality for any possible listeners, they treated each other with an abnormal tenderness and consideration. In both aspects of their new existence, they were getting on better than they had in months.

It was weird.

Two weeks, and the ombudsman came.

He disliked Truls Vasvik on sight.

Partly, it was the Norwegian thing – the same irritating aura of easy outdoor competence that he'd noticed in most of Carla's friends on the few occasions they'd been up to Tromsö together. But more than that, it was the clothes. Here was a trained professional who, Carla claimed, earned at least the same as he did, and Chris could have bought the man's entire outfit for less than he usually spent on a haircut. The grey wool of the jersey was stretched and pilled, the nondescript trousers were bagged in the knees and the walking boots had shaped themselves to Vasvik's feet with constant use. The coat looked as if he'd slept in it. It only needed the carelessly-tied-back greying hair to complete the image of a teen antiglobalist who'd never grown up.

Which is exactly what he is.

'Thanks for coming,' he said guardedly.

Vasvik shrugged. 'I should thank you. You are taking a far greater risk than I.'

'Really?' Chris tried to ignore the jolt Vasvik's comment delivered to his stomach. The set-up had left him jangled and twitchy. A shrill part of him wondered if the ombudsman was trying to psych him out. 'I would have thought we'd both be arrested pretty fucking rapidly.'

'Yes, we would. But your government would be forced to release me intact. That much power we still have. The police might work me over a little while they have me, but it's unlikely to be worse than some other close encounters I've had.'

'Hard man, huh?'

Another shrug. Vasvik looked around the workshop and spotted an ancient steel bar stool shoved against one wall. He went to fetch it. Chris mastered his irritation and waited for the Norwegian to come back. Again, he couldn't be sure if Vasvik was doing it deliberately or not. The ombudsman's detached calm was impenetrable.

Out in the rest of Mel's AutoFix, tools whined and screeched. The noise raked along his nerves. It hadn't been easy, finding a safe place to meet, and even now he wondered how far he could trust Carla's boss.

'Well.' Vasvik dragged the stool under the jacked-up Audi Mel had left on the lifter, and seated himself. 'Shall we talk about extraction?'

'In a minute.' Chris prowled the space beneath the Audi. *Extraction.* The way the word hung there was another jolt in itself, like walking up to Louise Hewitt at the quarterly and asking her out loud if she wanted to fuck. 'I'm still getting used to this. Maybe I still need to be convinced.'

'Then we're wasting each other's time. I'm not here to talk you into something, Faulkner. We can live without you at UNECT.'

Chris stared at him. 'Carla said—'

'Carla Nyquist cares about you. I do not. Personally, Faulkner, I don't give a shit what happens to you. I think you're scum. The ethical commerce guys would like to hear what you have, that's why I'm here, but I'm not a salesman. I don't have to reel you in to get my name up on some commission board somewhere, and frankly, I have a lot of better things to do with my time. You come in or you don't. Your choice. But don't waste my time.'

Chris flushed.

'I'm told,' he said evenly, 'that UNECT recruit people, *scum*, like me for the ombudsmen. That's important, because I need a job. Now. Have I been misinformed?'

'No. That's correct.'

'So we could end up colleagues.'

Vasvik looked at him coldly. 'It takes all sorts.'

'Must be hard,' Chris taunted. 'Working alongside people that disgust you. Putting up with such a low grade of humanity.'

'It's good preparation for undercover work. Living with the stink.'

The workshop Mel had lent them had been swept for bugs an hour ago, and there was too much metalwork going on in the other shops for exterior scanning to be possible. Still, there seemed to be an audience waiting as the pause smoked off Vasvik's words. Chris felt his fists curling.

'Do you have any idea,' he said, 'who the fuck you're talking to?'

The other man's grin was a baring of teeth, a challenge. 'Why don't you enlighten me.'

'I have treated you with respect—'

'You've got no fucking choice, Faulkner. I'm your escape hatch. You want out so bad I can smell it on you. Your shrivelled little soul has finally got tired of what you do for a living, and now you're looking for redemption with no drop in salary. I'm your only hope.'

'I doubt you earn what I'm used to.'

'Doubt away.'

'Oh yeah? Blow it all on clothes, do you?' Chris stabbed a finger at the Norwegian. 'I know your sort, Vasvik. You grew up in your cosy little Scandinavian nanny state, and when you found out the rest of the world couldn't afford the same propped-up artificial playgroup economic standards, you never got over it. Now you're out there sulking and throwing moral tantrums because the world won't behave the way you want it to—'

Vasvik examined the palm of one hand. 'Yeah, but on the other hand I didn't watch my mother die of a curable illness and—'

'*Hey*—'

'And then go to work for the people who made it happen.'

It was like a lightning strike. The slow burning anger sheeted to split second fury, and Chris was in motion. Attack raged at the edges of his control. A Shotokan punch to the temple that would have killed Vasvik, had it landed. Somehow, the ombudsman was not there. The stool staggered in the air, tumbled sideways. Vasvik was a whirl of black coat and reaching hands, off to one side. Chris felt his wrist brushed, turned in some subtle way, and then he was hurled across the workshop on the wings of his own momentum.

He crashed into the bench, hands trying to brace. A sound behind him and something hooked his legs out from under him at the ankles. His face smashed the bench surface among scattering drill bits and bolts. Something sharp gouged his cheek in passing. He felt Vasvik's weight on him and tried to kick. The Norwegian locked his arm up to the nape of his neck, grabbed his head by the hair and rammed it back down on the bench sideways.

'*Mistake*,' he gritted in Chris's ear. 'Now, you going to behave, or am I going to break your fucking arm?'

Chris heaved up once against the weight, but it was useless. He slumped. Vasvik let go suddenly and was gone. Somewhere behind him, Chris heard the ombudsman picking up the stool. When he got himself upright and turned, Vasvik was seated again. There was a faint beading of sweat across the pale forehead, but otherwise the fight might never have happened.

'My mistake,' he said quietly, not looking at Chris. 'I shouldn't have let you get to me like that. In a Cambodian enterprise zone, that kind of giveaway'd get me a bullet in the back of the head.'

Chris stood there, blinking tears. Vasvik sighed heavily. His voice was dull and weary.

'As an operational ombudsman, you'll earn approximately a hundred and eighty thousand euros a year, adjusted. That includes a hazardous-duties bonus, which you can reckon on getting for about sixty per cent of the work you do. Undercover assignments, swoop raids, witness protection. The rest of the time they keep you on backroom stuff. Admin and forward planning. That's so you don't burn out.' Another deep breath. 'Housing and schools for your kids are free, accommodation and expenses while on assignment, you claim. I'm sorry for that crack about your mother. You didn't deserve that.'

Chris coughed a laugh. '*Told* you I made more than you.'

'Yeah, well fuck you then.' Vasvik's voice never lifted from the tired monotone. His gaze never shifted from the corner of the workshop.

'Do you like it?' Chris asked him finally.

The ombudsman looked at him. 'It matters,' he said, pausing on each word as if English were suddenly difficult for him. 'You're doing something that matters. I don't expect you to understand that. It sounds like a bad joke, just saying it. But it means something.'

· They faced each other for a while. Then Chris reached into his jacket and pulled out a plastic sheathed disc.

'This is a breakdown of the accounts I service for Shorn. There's nothing here you can use, but anyone who knows the ground will be able to work out what I know. Take it back and ask them if I'm worth extracting. I want the package you just talked about, plus a million-dollar or -euro equivalent payout on extraction.'

He saw the look on Vasvik's face. He heard his own voice harden.

'It's not negotiable. I'm losing heavily if I pull out now. I'm plugged in here. Comfortable. Stock options, executive benefits. The house. Industry rep, client connections. All of that's worth something to me. You want me, you've got to make it worth my while.'

He tossed the disc across. Vasvik caught it and examined it curiously. He looked back up at Chris.

'And if we don't want you that badly?'

Chris shrugged. 'Then I'll stay here.'

'Yeah? You sure you've still got the stomach for that?'

'I'm not like you, Vasvik.' Chris wiped at the gouge in his cheek and his fingers came away specked with blood. 'I've got the stomach for whatever they can feed me.'

Vasvik left in the back of a covered truck, supplied by Mel and on its way to Paris for Renault parts. Jess drove, no shotgun rider along. UNECT operatives would vanish the ombudsman at the other end. No questions. Carla had sold the whole thing to Mel as wrangling over preferential supply contracts, a new covert bid from Volvo coming in to upset the BMW status quo at Shorn. Both Mel and Jess hated BMWs with a deep and abiding passion, and as far as they were concerned anything that might reduce the number of them on the streets of London just had to be a good thing, dear, just *had* to be.

Carla came in a couple of minutes later, a welding mask still pushed up on her head. Chris was trying to assess the damage to his face in a propped-up fragment of mirror he'd found on the floor.

'What did you say to him?' she asked angrily.

Chris pressed at his cheek, peering at the gouge in the mirror shard. 'I told him our terms. And I gave him the disc. Went like swimming.'

'You had a fight, didn't you.'

'We had a minor disagreement.' He gave up on the mirror and turned to face her. 'I said some things I shouldn't have. Then he said something he *really* shouldn't have. Took a while to straighten out.'

'He's trying to *help* you, Chris.'

'No.' He couldn't keep the snap out of his voice. 'He's looking for benefits, Carla. Just like every other fucker in this world. Quid pro fucking quo.'

She stared at him, wordless for a moment, then turned away and walked out of the workshop.

He let her go.

TWENTY-SIX

It rained hard most of the next week, and the roads turned treacherous. As usual, patchwork repairs hadn't stood up to the summer weather, and the various service providers were still squabbling about whose responsibility it was to put it right. Chris drove the Saab at careful velocities, getting in to Shorn later than usual and doing a lot of his phone work from the car. The datadown ran remote scrambling and patched through flagged callers on automatic.

Back to work. Back to the pretence.

It was easier now he was committed. Two weeks of jittering uncertainty, of not knowing if they'd get away with it, knowing even less what would come of the meeting – now it all gave way to solid data. He knew they wanted him now, knew at a level he could trust more than Carla's wishful thinking assurances and his own mixed feelings. Now it was just a matter of waiting to see if they could afford him. A no-lose situation. They could afford him, he went. They couldn't afford him, he stayed. Either way, he had work, he had guarantees. He had *income*.

A small part of him knew that he would lose Carla if he stayed, but somehow he couldn't make that matter as much as he knew it should.

Back to work.

Wednesday morning, turning onto the Elsenham ramp, he heard from Lopez. Confirmation of Vicente Barranco's arrival date.

'It's good,' said the Americas agent through the crackle of the scrambler and a bad satellite link. 'The way I figure it, you've got North Memorial on. You could show him round, maybe buy him a few assault rifles.'

'Yeah, that's. *Fuck.*' His foot came off the accelerator as the realisation hit. He nearly braked.

'Chris?' Lopez sounded concerned. 'You still there?'

He sighed. The car picked up speed again, down the ramp. 'Yeah, I'm still here. I don't suppose there's any way you can set that date back about a week?'

'A *week*? Jesus, Chris, you said as soon as possible. You said you'd move things around to—'

'Yeah, I know.' The rain intensified as he came off the ramp. Chris turned up the wipers. 'Look, forget it, send him anyway. My problem, I'll deal with it here.'

'Is this something I need to worry about?'

'No. You did the right thing, it's fine. I'll be in touch.' He cut the connection and redialled.

'Yeah, this is Bryant.'

'Mike, it's Chris. We've got—'

'Just the man. You in yet?'

'On the way. Listen, Mike—'

'How about lending me some of that old Emerging Markets background you don't like to talk about these days, huh? You wouldn't fucking believe what happened in Harbin this morning.'

'Mike—'

'You remember that thing we were putting together with the guys in EM? The transport net sell-off?'

Chris gave up and searched his memory. The north-eastern end of the former People's Republic of China wasn't his sphere of interest. Outside the tendencies of ethnic Chinese where Tarim Pendi was concerned, he didn't pay the area much attention. And his dealings with Shorn's Emerging Markets division had been minimal so far. They were a hard enough bunch, but still pretty urbane by CI standards.

Still, listening to Mike's tale of woe might help take the sting out of the minor fuck-up he had to report.

So think.

He recalled a late night wine bar bitching session a week back. Mike and some elegant Chinese woman from Shorn EM. Crossover with an old CI account, guerrilla figures from the last decade, now snugly installed as political leaders. Privatisation schematics and character assassination of the major players. Who could be trusted further than they could be thrown. Macho stuff. The wine had been crap.

'Chris?'

'Yeah, yeah.' He groped after a name. 'The Tseng thing, right?'

'Right.' It was hard to tell if Bryant was angry or amused. 'Had it all lined up and ready to roll. Now some shithead civil servant has taken out, get this, a fucking *injunction* to prevent the sell-off. They're claiming it's unlawful under the '37 Constitution.'

'Well, is it?'

'How the fuck would I know? I'm not EM, am I. Irene Lan's team handle the legal stuff.'

'Well, can't you, I don't know, pass a law or something? Change the current law? It's not like this is Conflict as such. You *are* the government out there.'

Mike sighed audibly. 'Yeah, I know. Fucking politics. Give me a Kalashnikov and a dickhead to fire it any day. So. What's up?'

'What?'

'You sounded worried.'

'Ah, yeah. Just a glitch. Barranco's down to arrive in London on the eighteenth—'

'The eigh*teenth*. Ah, fuck, Chris. That's two days after Echevarria.'

'I know.'

'Couldn't you have—'

'Yeah, my fault, I know. I gave Lopez carte blanche to get him here asap. No other parameters.'

'Carte Blanche?' He could hear Mike grinning. 'Who's she? Yeah, alright, I don't suppose it matters much. We'd better just make sure they don't bang into each other in a corridor.'

'Or at the North Memorial. I was thinking—'

Impact!

The meaty crunch of metal on metal. The Saab jolted hard left and started to skid from the back. His foot slipped on the accelerator and he felt the treacherous slither as the wheels spun in water.

'*Fuck!*'

'Now what?' Bryant, through a yawn.

He fought the skid, shedding speed as fast as he dared. Eyes ripping across the mirrors, searching for the other car. Teeth gritted.

'Where are you, motherfucker?'

'Chris? You okay?'

Another crunch from the rear. He wasn't yet fully out of the skid and it sent him slithering again. He hauled on the wheel.

'Mother*fucker!*'

'Chris?' By now, Mike had got it. His voice came through urgent. 'What's happening out there?'

'I'm—'

Impact, again. He thought the Saab might spin clear round this time. Fighting it, he caught a glimpse of the other vehicle as it pulled clear. Primer-grey, looked like an old Mitsubishi from what he could see of the lines, but with the amount of custom-built armouring, it was hard to tell.

No-namer?

It was coming back, and the skid—

He made the decision too fast for it to register until afterwards. As the other car leapt forward, he jerked the wheel back the way he'd hauled it and opened the skid up. His guts sloshed. The no-namer struck, but Chris had read the manoeuvre correctly. With the spin on the Saab, his attacker's impact was a barely felt jab, in a direction he was already sliding.

211

The Saab spun about.

For a heartbeat they were parallel, facing each other. He saw a pale face, staring through the windscreen of the other car. Then it was gone, past him southward as he braked the Saab to a wagging halt, pointed north.

Rain drummed down on the roof. He felt his pulse catch up.

'*Chris?*'

'I'm fine.' He slammed the car into gear and cut a sharp U-turn, peering through the sluicing water across his windscreen. Up ahead, he spotted brake lights. 'Some. Motherfucker. Is about to have his chassis squeezed.'

'You're fighting a challenge?'

'Looks like it.' He took the Saab up through the gears, pushing each one as hard as he dared in the rain. The brake lights ahead of him went out and he had to work to spot the outlines of the other car. 'Guy just landed on me, Mike. No-namer, and no warning.'

He frowned. *And no proximity alarm.*

'Chris, call Driver Control.' Bryant sounded worried. 'You don't have to drive this, if he hasn't filed. He's in breach of—'

'Yeah, yeah. Be with you in a minute.' The car was swelling in his forward view, moving but throttled back, waiting for him. 'Come on, you *fucker*. Let's see what you've got.'

The grey car braked suddenly, trying to get behind him. He matched the manoeuvre and slewed into the vehicle's side. Metal screeched and tore. His wing mirror went, ripped free and bouncing away in their wake like a grenade. He looked across and made eye contact through windows streaming with rain. He saw the other driver flinch.

The side-to-side clinch came apart. The no-namer picked up escape speed. Chris grinned savagely.

Rattled.

He went after him.

His own shock was ebbing now, pulse coming down, brain working. *Time to kill this piece of shit.* Bryant seemed to have rung off, and the only sound was the roar of the engine and the hammering rain. The other car held him off. Neither driver could afford to go flat to the floor in a rain duel, and the no-namer was cool enough to know it. Chris stopped trying to close the gap, and thought about the road ahead.

'This is Driver Control.'

He glanced down at the radio in surprise.

'Yeah?'

'Driver clearance 260B354R, Faulkner, C. You are engaged in an unauthorised duel—'

'Hardly my choice, Driver Control.'

'You are required to disengage immediately.'

'No fucking way. This piece of shit is going down.'

A pause. Chris could swear he heard a throat being cleared.

'I repeat, you are required to disengage and—'

'Have you tried telling that to our little primer-painted friend?'

Another pause. The gap was less than ten metres. Chris upped his velocity, higher than he could afford on the rain-slick road. He felt a tiny bubble of fear rising in his chest with the knowledge.

'Your opponent does not respond to radio address.'

'Yeah, well, I'll just go talk to him.'

'You are required, *immediately*, to—'

He flattened the accelerator, momentarily, and clouted the no-namer across the driver-side rear wing. Driver Control wittered from the speaker as the Saab slipped and he dropped speed, fighting the urge to brake hard. The no-namer was trying to slow down. He drifted across and blocked the move. Another clank as they jammed together, nose to tail. The other car flailed spray off the road as it tried to pull away and lost purchase in the wet. Chris felt his upper lip peel back from his teeth. He pulled fractionally left, shivery with the lack of firm control he had over the Saab, and accelerated again.

'*Good* night, motherfucker.'

He hit at an angle and the skid kicked off in both cars. He felt the Saab start to skate from the front, saw the other car doing the same from the rear, in graceful mirror image. Fragments of control left to him, like sand through his fingers. He made a noise behind his teeth and fed all he had to the engine. Hard and fast and raking uncontrolled across the no-namer's sideways-skating rear fender. Enough to push the whole thing beyond any hope of redemption for either of them. The nose-to-tail clinch came apart like a stick broken across a knee.

It was like cutting a cable.

Loss of control, seeming weightlessness, something approaching calm as the Saab spun out. For a timeless moment, it was almost quiet. Even the snarl of the frustrated engine seemed to fade. Then, he felt a sideswiping impact as the two cars glanced off each other in drunken ballet. The Saab lurched. Time unlocked again. He was on the brakes. His hands were a blur on the wheel, hopelessly late behind the uncontrolled motion of the vehicle. The rain took over. In the wind-screen, it seemed to curtain back momentarily, to show him the embankment, coming up fast.

Deep breath.

The Saab hit.

The force of impact lifted the car up on two wheels. It hung there for a moment – he had time to see the grass on the bank flattened against the passenger side window – then fell back to the asphalt, hard. The landing snapped his teeth together and clipped a chunk out of his tongue.

For what seemed a very long time, he sat in the stilled car, arms on the wheel, head down, tasting the blood in his mouth.

The steady drumming of rain on the roof.

He lifted his head and peered out across the carriageway. Fifty metres off in the slashing grey, he spotted the other car jammed against the crash barrier. There was steam pouring out of the crumpled hood.

He grunted, and sucked at the damage to his tongue. One hand crept out more or less automatically, knocked on the hazard lights, killed the Saab's engine, which – *I fucking* love *you, Carla* – had not cut out. He opened the glove compartment and found the Nemex. Checked the load and snapped the slide.

Right.

He cracked the door and climbed out into the rain.

It drenched him before he'd gone half the distance to the other car, plastered his shirt to transparency on his body, turned his trousers sodden and filled his Argentine leather shoes. He had to blink the stuff out of his eyes, rake his hair back from his face to peer into the wrecked car. It looked as if the other driver was trapped in his seat, struggling to free himself. Oddly, the expected victory surge didn't come. Maybe it was the rain that dampened the savagery, maybe a rapidly assimilating picture of angles that didn't fit.

No proximity alarm.

No filed challenge.

He stared at the side of the primer-painted vehicle. There was no driver number anywhere on the body.

No point.

He circled the wreck warily, Nemex held low in both hands, as Mike had shown him. He blinked rain out of his eyes.

The other driver had the door open, but it looked as if the whole engine compartment had shifted backwards with the impact and the steering column had him pinned back in the seat. He was young. Not out of his teens, by the look of it. The unhealthy pallor of his skin suggested the zones. Chris stared at him, Nemex down.

'What the fuck did you think you were doing back there?'

The kid's face twisted. 'Hey, *fuck* you.'

'Yeah?' The anger came gushing up, the memory of the attack suddenly there. He sniffed the air and caught the scent of petrol under the rain. 'You got a cracked fuel feed there, son. You want me to *fucking light you, you little shit?*'

The bravado crumpled. Fear smeared the kid's eyes wide. He felt a sudden flush of shame. This was some car-jacker barely out of nappies, some joy-rider who

just happened to jack an unnumbered crash wagon? Some joy-rider who just happened to be cruising a motorway ramp an hour out of town? Who decided to take on an obvious corporate custom job whose proximity alarm just happened to fail? Yeah, right.

Chris wiped rain from his face, and tried to think through the adrenalin comedown and the drenching he was getting.

'Who sent you?'

The kid set his mouth in a sullen line. Chris lost his temper again. He took a step closer and ground the muzzle of the Nemex into the boy's temple.

'I'm not fucking about here,' he yelled. 'You tell me who you're a sicario for, I might call the cutters for you. Otherwise, I'm going to splash your fucking head all over the upholstery.' He jabbed hard with the gun, and the kid yelped. 'Now, *who sent you?*'

'They told me—'

'Never mind what they told you.' Another muzzle jab. It drew blood. 'I need a name, son, or you're going to die. Right here, right now.'

The kid broke. A long shudder and suddenly leaking tears. Chris eased the pressure on the gun.

'A name. I'm listening.'

'They call him Fucktional, but—'

'Fucktional? He a zoner? A gangwit?' He jabbed the gun again, more gently. 'Come on.'

The kid started to cry out loud. 'He run the whole estate man, he's going to—'

'Which estate?'

'Mandela. The crags.'

Southside. It was a start.

'Okay, now you're going to tell me—'

'STAND AWAY FROM THE VEHICLE.' The sky filled with the metal voice. 'YOU ARE NOT AUTHORISED ON THIS STRETCH. STAND AWAY.'

The Driver Control helicopter swung down from the embankment where the Saab had wound up and danced crabwise across the air to the central reservation, ten metres up. Chris sighed and lifted his hands, Nemex held ostentatiously by the barrel.

'STAND ASIDE AND PLACE YOUR WEAPON ON THE GROUND.'

The kid was looking confused, not sure if he was off the hook yet. He couldn't move enough to wipe the tears off his face, but there was an ugly confidence already surfacing in his eyes.

Well, whoever said a good driver had to be smart as well.

'I'll be talking to you later,' Chris snapped, wondering how the hell he was going to ensure it happened. Estate ganglords had a nasty habit of disappearing their sicarios when they became a liability, and he didn't have much faith in the regular police's ability to keep undervalued zone criminals alive in custody. He'd have to call a contractor, get private security onto the cutting crew and trace the kid to whatever charity clean-up shop they dumped him at. Then talk to Troy Morris about the southside gangs.

He backed off a half-dozen steps, bent and placed the Nemex on the ground, then straightened up and spread his arms at the helicopter.

'RETURN TO YOUR VEHICLE AND AWAIT INSTRUC-TIONS.'

He went, arms still raised, just in case.

He was about halfway back when the gatlings cut loose.

The sound of whining, whirling steel and the shattering roar of the multiple barrels unloading. He hit the asphalt, face down, a pair of seconds before the realisation hit him, that they were not firing at him, could not be because he was still alive. He lifted his head a cautious fraction, craned it to look back.

The helicopter had sunk almost to asphalt level, and swung around, nose to nose with the wrecked car. Later, he guessed the manoeuvre was intended to keep him out of the field of fire. The zone kid must have got it head-on, the full fury of the gatling hail as it tore through the windscreen and everything behind it.

The tank went up with a dull crump. Chris clamped his hands over his head, face to the road. An insanely calm part of him knew there wouldn't be much shrapnel off a vehicle that armoured, but you always had glass. He heard some of it hiss past.

The gatlings shut off. In their place, there was a greedy crackling as the fire took hold in the wreck. The departing throb of the helicopter. He lifted his head again, just in time to see it disappear over the embankment the way it had come. Flames curled from the strafed car, bright and cheery through the rain. Thinking about getting up, he heard a sudden ripple of explosions and flattened himself to the asphalt again. Slugs in the abandoned Nemex, he guessed, cooked to ignition point by the backwash of heat from the fire. He stayed down. The fucking Nemex. He found himself grinning.

Louise will be pleased.

Finally, he judged it safe and picked himself up. He lifted his arms wide and stared down at himself. His shirt was sodden and grimed from contact with the road, but there was no blood that he could find. No pain but the faint sting of abrasions on his palms and a couple of numb spots on hip and knee. He couldn't tell if he'd done any serious damage to the suit trousers, but he guessed they were as soiled as the shirt.

In the wreck, the rain was already beating out the flames.

TWENTY-SEVEN

The inquest was held, in stark corporate style, around a huge oval table in Notley's penthouse conference chamber. Shorn had given the public sector three days – *overly generous in my opinion*, was Hewitt's comment – and now it was smackdown time.

The conference chamber was an apt arena. The walls were full of violent commissioned art from the new brutalist school, solid blocks of primary colour dumped amidst vague scattered scrawls that might have been writing or crowds of tiny people. Obvious videoscan units gleamed beadily from the ceiling, but there was a standard forty-second delay on the recording system, and two Shorn lawyers sat in, to make sure anything potentially awkward got stopped before it was halfway said. In the run-up, Chris and Mike both got repeated briefings from the legal team until they were coached almost to a line. Louise Hewitt and Philip Hamilton joined Notley to form an operational quorum, though everybody on the corporate side of the table knew no serious decisions would be taken at this particular meeting. This was noise-making. Shorn was coiled up like a rattlesnake, signalling loud offence. Any genuine strike would come later, when no one was around to take notes.

Across the table from Chris sat the crew of the helicopter and the Driver Control duty officer from the day of the duel. They were recognisable by their suits – you could have bought any three of the outfits they wore for the price of Jack Notley's shoes.

Between Notley and the duty officer sat the Assistant Commissioner of Traffic Enforcement and the District Police Superintendent for London South Nine. Holographically present at the opposite end of the table, the current Minister for Transport floated like an apologetic ghost.

'What remains most disturbing about this matter,' said Notley, as the recriminations began to run down. 'Is not the *type* of response elicited from Driver Control, but the rapidity of that response. Or should I say the *lack* of rapidity.'

The duty officer flinched, but stoically. He'd already had a pretty rough ride and he was learning not to react. Any attempt at defence from the public sector players around the table had led to a shredding at the hands of the Shorn partners. Hewitt led, wet razor-swift and slicing,

Hamilton provided soft-spoken, insolent counterpoint and Notley came in behind, picking up the points and swinging the mace of Shorn's corporate clout. There wasn't a person in the room, the Minister included, whose job was secure if Notley decided the time had come to slop the coffee cup hard enough.

The Assistant Commissioner, nobly, essayed a rescue. She'd been working salvage throughout the meeting. 'I think we're agreed that the response team would have been scrambled earlier if Mr Bryant's original emergency call had been supported by Mr Faulkner's responses to radio communication. The recording shows—'

'The recording shows an angry executive, acting unwisely,' said Louise Hewitt, with a thin smile in Chris's direction. 'I think we can all understand how Chris Faulkner felt, but that does not mean he reacted correctly. He was, shall we say, overwrought. As duty officer, with the advantage of a detached view, it was your job to realise that and react accordingly.'

The duty officer met her gaze bravely. 'Yes, I appreciate that. I should not have allowed an executive to override my professional instincts. I shall not let it happen again.'

'Good.' Hewitt nodded and scribbled on her display pad. 'That's noted, and appreciated. Superintendent Lahiri, can we go back to the matter of the criminal who, according to Chris Faulkner's testimony, was responsible for hiring the sicario.'

The superintendent nodded. He was a wiry, tough-looking man in his fifties, an obvious hangover from the autonomous days. He had kept quiet for most of the proceedings and watched the interplay with shrewd attention. When he spoke, it was with the precision of a man who measured and cut his sentences before uttering them.

'Khalid Iarescu, yes. He has been arrested.'

'Has he confessed?'

Lahiri frowned. 'He is a career criminal, Ms Hewitt. Simply arresting him has caused serious injury to three of my men. We are unlikely to extract a confession.'

'Can't we put pressure on his family?'

'Not without further large-scale incursions into the southside, and that I would not recommend. The populace is already stirred up more than we'd like. And Iarescu has unchallenged control of the Mandela estate, as well as agreements with the ganglords in neighbouring areas. His immediate family are doubtless already well hidden and protected. And his lawyers are now attempting to have him released under the Citizen's Charter.' Lahiri spread his hands. 'I can have him charged with resisting arrest, maybe with one or two outstanding drug offences, but beyond that, I am not hopeful. Even *within* that framework I am not hopeful that we can secure a conviction. Khalid Iarescu is a well-connected man.'

Bryant snorted. 'He's a fucking gangwit, is what he is.'

Notley cut him a sharp look. 'The name, Superintendent. It's what, Hungarian?'

'Romanian. That is, his father was a Romanian immigrant. His mother is Moroccan.'

'Can we threaten him with expulsion?' Notley had shifted focus. The question was addressed to the Minister.

The holo shook its head regretfully.

'No, I've examined the files. Both parents were naturalised. He is, in technical terms, as English as you or I.'

Notley rolled his eyes.

Hamilton made a sleepy gesture. 'Just a thought. The boy who actually stole the car. He had family?'

'Yes.' Lahiri looked down at his notes, did not look up again while he spoke. 'The Goodwins. Mother and father, two brothers and a sister. They've been evicted. As per policy.'

'Yes, good.' Hamilton reached for his glass of water and sipped at it. 'I don't suppose there's any chance that this Iarescu will be seen to associate with them. Offer them succour, so to speak. Solidarity from the estate patriarch. The, uh, *big man* ethos.'

Lahiri shook his head. 'It doesn't work like that, sir, outside of the movies. Iarescu is a *successful* criminal. He knows the ropes both within and without the zones. If anything, he will distance himself from the whole affair. In fact,' – a hesitant look at Chris – 'I'm afraid there really is nothing substantial to make the connection in the first place.'

Chris held down his temper. They'd been round this block before. 'I told you what I heard, Superintendent. I didn't imagine it. The boy named the estate, and Iarescu.'

'Yes, I understand that, sir. But you must see that this in itself is not evidence. No, please.' He raised a hand. 'Hear me out. In gang culture, status is accorded by association. The boy may have believed that by naming a major player as his sponsor, he could protect himself.'

'Fascinating,' murmured Hamilton. 'Almost talismanic, isn't it. Almost tribal.'

Lahiri's lip almost curled. 'Moreover, the tag *Fuktional* is close to generic. In the southside zones alone, you have gang leaders styling themselves *Fuktion Red, Sataz Fuktion, Fuktyal, Fuktyal Bass.* The list goes on. Gang culture is mimetic, imaginative only within very limited given parameters. To my ears, what you heard has the ring of stock response.'

Chris shook his head.

'Do you have something fresh to add, Chris?' asked Louise Hewitt sweetly.

Silence. Some shuffling from the duty officer. The Minister's holo checked its watch, surreptitiously. Jack Notley uncapped an antique fountain pen with a loud snap.

'Well, then,' he said briskly. 'If we can proceed to recommendations.'

'Motherfucking whitewash *bullshit.*' Chris wasn't sure if Mike's place was secure or not; pre-Vasvik, he'd never even have given it consideration. Now he just didn't care. The long squeeze of keeping to the Shorn script had festered in him for too long. 'Fucking lies and shit-mouthed expediency from end to motherfucking end.'

'You think so?'

Mike leaned across the kitchen table with the rioja and topped up his glass. Behind the gesture, he raised his brows at Suki, who shrugged and went on sculpting roses into the carrot sections on her chopping board.

Chris missed it. 'Of course it was. Stock response, my fucking arse. That kid was hired by Iarescu to grease me, and someone hired Iarescu to get it done. Someone with money.'

Mike was silent. Chris gestured with his wine glass.

'You heard what Lahiri said. Iarescu's connected, in the zones and out. This is corporate, Mike. This came down from on high.'

'Chris, you realise how paranoid you sound?'

'I was there, Mike. They blew that kid away to stop him talking.'

Bryant frowned and leaned back in his chair. 'The report says he went for a weapon.'

'Oh, Mike. *He was pinned in the fucking wreckage.*' Chris caught Suki's glance at the ceiling. She'd only put Ariana to bed an hour ago. He lowered his voice. 'Sorry, Suki. I'm just. Upset.'

'We're all upset, Chris.' Mike got up and prowled the kitchen. 'Obviously. I mean, yeah, we can't have just anybody on the roads, raging without authorisation. The whole damn system'll collapse.'

'That's what I'm telling you, Mike. This *wasn't* just anybody. This was allowed to happen. They didn't scramble the heli until they knew I'd driven that little shit off the road. They did what they were told, and they *let it happen.* I mean, why'd you think no one got sacked? The heli crew, the duty officer—'

'Come on. They all got reprimands. It'll go—'

'*Reprimands?*'

'—on their file. Christ, the duty officer got three months' suspension without pay.'

'Yeah, and did you see how happy he was with that? He'll be taken care of, Mike.'

'I think,' said Bryant sombrely, 'that he was happy because he still has a job to go back to. Notley could easily have kicked him into touch.'

'Exactly. So why didn't he? Someone's got dual control here, Mike, and you know it. Someone's cranking Notley's cable.'

This time Mike Bryant laughed out loud. Suki frowned at him.

'Michael, that's not very nice. Chris is upset.'

'Okay, I'm sorry. It's just the thought of someone cranking the cables on Jack Notley. I mean come on, Chris. You know the man. Suki, you've met him. He's not exactly malleable.'

They both looked at Chris. He sighed.

'Alright, maybe not Notley. Maybe not that high up. Maybe Hewitt, she's never liked me. Or, listen, maybe it's as simple as Nick Makin looking for payback on that punch I landed.' This time he caught the exchange of glances between husband and wife. 'Alright, alright, I know. But I'm not paranoid, Mike. Someone tampered with my proximity alarm.'

'The report said it was the rain, Chris. You saw that crack.' Bryant turned to include Suki. 'The mechanics at Driver Control found a leak in the access panelling on Chris's security masterboard. It shorted out the whole alarm system.'

'Oh *bullshit*, Mike. Carla checks those panels every—' He gestured, suddenly unnerved by his lack of certainty. 'I don't know, every week, at least. She would have spotted it.'

He didn't tell them that he'd had a screaming row with Carla when the preliminary results of the Shorn investigation came in. That he'd jumped automatically towards blame and belief in what Mike obviously still believed, that Carla had missed the leak.

It had taken her over an hour to talk him down.

I know what I'm fucking doing, she told him grimly, when the row had burnt itself out. *If there was a crack in that panelling, someone fucking put it there, and not that long ago.*

'Carla knows what she's doing,' he said, staring into his wine glass.

Nobody answered him. The silence started to creak under its own weight. Chris stared at the table top, trying to think of something to say that wouldn't sound deranged.

'You really believe this, don't you, Chris,' said Suki. It didn't come out as supportive as she was obviously trying to be.

Chris shook his head. 'I don't know what I believe. Look, Mike, is it possible this is something to do with the NAME contracts? Somebody outside Shorn, I mean. Maybe I was tagged getting in and out of Panama.'

Bryant gestured. 'You said you were careful.'

'I was. But something is going down, Mike. I can feel it.'

222

Sure, something's going down. You're about to sell out your colleagues for a public sector sinecure with the bleeding-heart UN leech gang. That's what's going down, Chris.

And maybe someone knows that.

The paranoia made icy tracks down his spine.

'Okay.' Mike sat down again. He steepled his fingers on the table. 'Tell you what. We'll look into it. Unofficially, I mean. I'll talk to Troy, get him to ask around. He's got friends in the southside zones. We'll see what he turns up. Meantime, we've got other stuff to worry about. Echevarria—'

Chris groaned. 'Don't remind me.'

'—flies in *Tuesday*, Chris. And we've got Barranco arriving right behind him. Not even two full days between.'

'The week from hell.'

Mike grinned. 'That's right. So tonight, let's just forget about the whole fucking thing and get wrecked. What time you reckon Carla'll be here?'

'She said before eight.' Chris glanced at his watch. 'Maybe she got held up at the checkpoints.'

'Want to call her?'

'No, it's.' He realised how it looked. 'Yeah, maybe I should.'

Carla was running an hour late, for no reason she felt like offering. Chris bit back his annoyance.

'Well, when—' he began thinly.

'Oh, Chris, just start without me. I'm sure you're already having fun.'

He looked round at Mike and Suki, glad he'd used the mobile and not the videophone. Bryant was leaning against his wife and nuzzling at her ear through the immaculate auburn mane. She laughed, flinched away, then reached round to grab the ends of his loosed tie and pull him close. The little scene radiated groomed marital content, a synthetic blend of sex and wealth and domesticity straight out of a screen ad. He thought suddenly of a kitchen in Highgate, and an unforgiveable wish surged up in him.

'Well, get here as soon as you can,' he said, and hung up.

Mike looked up. 'She okay?'

'Yeah, be here in about an hour. Some kind of crisis with a lubricant system.' He smiled weakly. 'Suppose I should be glad she's that obsessive.'

'Shit, yeah. If Suki was my mechanic, I'd never let her out of the fucking garage. Ow!'

'Bastard.'

He tried to join in with the laughter, but his heart wasn't in it.

'Chris, you know the horse joke?' Bryant poured more wine. 'Guy

223

goes into a bar and sees a horse standing there. So he goes up to him and says *So. Why the long face?*'

More laughter, filling up the beautiful kitchen like the smell of cooking he wasn't invited to share. He wished Liz would hurry up and

Carla!

He wished *Carla* would hurry up and

And what? Come on, Chris. Finish that thought.

It must have shown on his face. Mike came across and clapped him on the shoulder. 'Ah, Chris. Come on, man. Honestly. I really don't think you should be worrying. I mean, in the end, you trashed the little fucker. He's smoked meat. And let's face it, with the rep you've got, no one smarter than a fuckwit gang sprog is going to want to drive against you.' He raised his glass. 'You got *nothing* to worry about, man.'

TWENTY-EIGHT

Midweek, *Regime Change* was quiet. Cheap cocktails and genteel pole dancing brought in a scattering of suits from the local offices and recently-paid zone workers who knew they'd never get in on a Friday or Saturday night. By eight-thirty or nine they were mostly leaving, the zone types headed home with their shallow finances drained, the suits going on to less genteel clubs where you could get your hands on the dancers.

'I would have suggested somewhere else.' Chris gestured at the centre of the Iraq Room, where a veiled woman, naked from the neck down, flexed around a newly installed silver pole to the unwinding cadences of Cairo Scene. The spectators sat at pipe tables or stood about in small knots, staring. 'I didn't realise.'

Liz Linshaw laughed and sipped at the pipe between them. She plumed whisky scented smoke in the dancer's direction.

'You don't approve?'

'Uh.' He spread his hands helplessly. 'Well, it's just not what I had in mind when I. You know, called you.'

'Chris.' She leaned closer to beat the music, grinning. 'You really don't have to work so hard at not looking at her. I already know you're an honourable man. Way past honourable, in fact.'

The dancer bellied up to the pole, slid it up and down between her breasts. Chris took a deep interest in the low hammered copper table the pipe stood on. Liz Linshaw laughed again.

'Look.' She leaned across to place one hand gently against his cheek and pushed his head back towards the performance. He fought down a jagged impulse to grab the hand and twist it away. 'I mean, *look*, really look at her. Let's get this over with. She's sexy, isn't she. Young. No, don't look away. It's a great body. Worked out. And worked *on*, obviously, unless someone invented anti-gravity fields recently. Yeah, if I were a man, she'd do it for me. She'd make me, *Chris*, hey, Chris, you're *blushing*.'

'No, I'm—'

'You *are*. I can feel it. Your face is hot.' She laughed again, delightedly. 'Chris, you really are in trouble. You're a grown man, you've got a dozen kills under your belt, and you can't look at soft porn without flushing like a teenager. I mean, what do you and Carla Nyquist *do* in the bedroom?'

She must have seen the change in his face. Before he could move, she reached out and touched his arm.

'Sorry. Chris, I'm sorry. That was bitchy.'

This time he did take hold of her hand. He pushed it back across the table and sat looking at her in silence.

'Chris, I said I'm sorry.'

They were saved by the pipe waitress. She sauntered across, lifted the cage and cast a practised eye over the glowing embers of tobacco in the pan. She glanced at Chris.

'Bring you another?'

He hadn't smoked much of the first, it was just the price of sitting there while he waited for Liz Linshaw. He shrugged.

'No, I think we're pretty much done here.'

The waitress left. He met Liz Linshaw's gaze and held it.

'Chris—'

'Reason I asked you here, Liz. You've got friends in Driver Control, right?'

She looked away, then back. 'Yes. Yes, I have.'

'Inside sources? People who can get information for you?'

'Is this really why you called me, Chris?'

'Yes. You have sources, right?'

A shrug. 'I'm a journalist.'

'There's something I need to know. I need to find out if—'

'Whoa, Chris.' She gave him a hard little smile. 'Slow down. Now I may have just gone over the line a little with that bitchy crack about your wife. But that doesn't mean you own a part of me. Why the fuck would I put pressure on one of my hard-won sources for you? What's in it for me?'

'You're writing another book, right?'

She nodded.

'So this is a whole chapter if you're lucky.' He hesitated at the edge, looking for something to fill the gap that had suddenly opened up between them. 'You heard I was up against a no-namer last week?'

'Yes. Inconclusive, I heard. Driver Control had to come in and mediate.' She smiled, a little more warmly this time. 'I'm sorry, Chris. I like you but I don't shadow you through the net on a day-to-day basis. There was something about a software failure, the challenge didn't register in the system or something?'

'Yeah, that's the official line.'

One eyebrow arched. He thought there was a little mockery in it. 'And the *un*official line?'

'The no-namer was never registered in the first place. Some zone kid jacked a battlewagon and tried to take me down in the rain. No challenge issued. And Driver Control didn't mediate, they turned up with an enforcement copter after I drove the kid off the road and they fed him a couple of cans of gatling shells for breakfast.'

He saw, with some satisfaction, the way the shock went through her. How her carefully constructed cool fractured open. Her voice, when it came, was almost a whisper.

'They killed him?'

'Pretty conclusively, yeah.'

'But haven't they traced the car?'

Chris nodded. 'To an unemployed datasystems consultant. He reported it stolen from outside his house in Harlesden about an hour after the duel.'

'He must have known before that!'

'Not necessarily. He hadn't driven it for a while, apparently. Couldn't afford to renew the licence this quarter.'

'Do you believe that?' Journalistic interest kindling.

'From the look of him in the interview tape, he'd be hard-pushed to afford a full tank of fuel, let alone a licence to use it, so yes, I do. But in the end it doesn't matter. Whoever set this up is a long way up the chain from either him or the kid who nicked the car. And whoever set this up also has their claws into Driver Control.'

'Alright, I'll buy that. What else do you have?'

'That's the lot.' He wasn't about to get into the Mandela estate connection. Troy Morris was already running down rumours across the southside, asking softly after Robbie Goodwin's displaced family, trying to find a safe approach to Khalid Iarescu's underworld machine. The last thing he'd need was a high-profile journalist crashing the zones and stirring things up. Liz Linshaw was most use where she already was – highly placed in the world of competition driving, reeking of cachet and connection.

She smiled, as if she could read his thoughts.

'No, there's more. You just don't feel like telling me right now.' She shrugged. ''sokay, I can live with that. Sure, I'll talk to some people I know. Shouldn't take much leverage to see if something's being covered up. I can take it from there.' She picked up the pipe and drew on it. Inside the cage, the last of the embers flared. 'You understand, this doesn't come for free. I do it, and you'll owe me, Chris. Big time.'

'Like I said, it'll make a chapter of—'

'No.' She shook her head, and her hair fell across her face. It made him want to clear it away with one hand. 'That's not what I mean.'

'So what do you mean?'

The corner of her mouth quirked and she looked away. 'You know what I mean, Chris.'

That sat between them for a while, smouldering out like the pipe.

'Listen,' he said.

'I know, Chris. I know. In fact, I've seen it all before. You've got some stuff you've got to work through. Don't worry about it and. Don't flatter yourself. I'm not short of male company, believe me.'

'You seeing Mike again?' It was out before he could stop himself.

She raked fingers into her own hair and grinned up at the corner of the room. 'That *really* is none of your business, Chris.'

'I'm not like him, Liz.'

'No, you're not.'

'I don't see the women around me as. Product.' The images from the porn segment glowed in his head. Studded leather parting buttocks, encircling breasts impossibly full. Fully clothed, the Liz Linshaw sitting opposite him shrugged.

'Mike Bryant knows what he wants, and he takes it and then he looks after it as best he can. I don't think his morality stretches much further than that, but he does at least know what he wants.'

Her eyes flickered up to meet his. She was still smiling.

'Listen, Liz. That night, I.' He swallowed. 'I'm having some problems with my marriage, but that doesn't mean I—'

'Chris.' He'd never in his life been interrupted so gently. 'I don't care. I want to fuck you, not replace your wife. But I'll tell you something for nothing. You came home with me that night, and you grabbed hold of the merchandise when it was on display. Whatever's going on in your relationship with Carla, you might as well have fucked me then. You've got the same guilt, and the same hard-on for me. The fact you didn't do it is a technicality.'

'You—'

She waved it off. Getting up, shouldering her way into her jacket.

'I'll get back to you about Driver Control. But the next time you get a bed for the night at my place, you'll work your passage.'

In the end, the pipe waitress came and told him he'd have to order something else if he wanted to sit there any longer.

TWENTY-NINE

Lopez routed Barranco's flight plan through Atlanta and Montreal before a dawn arrival at Reagan International, New York, where a Shorn jet would pick the two of them up under paperwork that identified them as economic advisers for the Parana Emergency Council. Lopez spoke Brazilian Portuguese almost as well as his native Spanish, and Barranco, like most political figures in Latin America these days, had enough to get by. Lopez was betting security at Reagan International would neither know the difference nor care.

Apparently, his assessment was on the nail. The Shorn jet lifted without incident and touched down in London just after lunch. Chris rode the courtesy copter out to meet it.

'Señor Barranco.' He had to shout above the racket of the rotors and the unseasonally cold wind that came buffeting across the asphalt of the private carriers' terminal. His grin felt sandblasted onto his face. Armed security stood around in suits, jackets whipping up constantly to reveal their shoulder holsters. 'Welcome to England. How was your flight?'

Barranco grimaced. He looked good in the smart-casual mobile consultant wardrobe Lopez had disguised him with, but above the knitted wool jacket his face was smeared with jet lag.

'Which flight do you mean? I seem to have been in transit for a week. And now a helicopter?'

'Believe me, Señor Barranco, you wouldn't want to drive through this part of London. Is Joaquin Lopez with you?'

Barranco jerked a thumb back at the Shorn jet. 'He's coming.'

Lopez appeared in the hatch and clambered down, followed by two more men with baggage. He grinned and waved at Chris. No sign of the weariness you could see on Barranco. Beneath his mobcon clothing, there was a prowling energy that Chris guessed was chemical. In the absence of any other escort, he'd been Barranco's only security since leaving Panama City.

Chris ushered everybody aboard the copter and into seats. The door cranked itself closed and shut out the wind with an airtight clunk. The pilot turned to look at Chris.

'Yeah, that's it. Take us home.'

The copter drifted into the sky. They bent away over the city.

Barranco leaned across to the window and peered down at the sprawl below.

'This doesn't seem so terrible,' he remarked.

'No,' Chris agreed. 'From up here, it's not.'

The tanned face turned to look at him. 'I would not be safe walking in those streets?'

'Depends on the exact neighbourhood. But as a general rule, no, you wouldn't. You might be attacked and robbed, maybe just have stones thrown at you. At a minimum you'd be recognised as an outsider and followed. After that,' Chris shrugged. 'Depends on the kind of crowd you draw.'

'I am not dressed like you.'

'Wouldn't matter. They don't care about politics in the zones. It's tribal. Localised gangs, territorial violence.'

'I see.' Barranco's gaze went back to the city sliding past beneath them. 'They have forgotten who did this to them.'

'That's one way of looking at it.'

The rest of the flight passed in silence. They crossed the westward cordons and picked up the beacon for the West End cluster. Machines took the controls, read the flight data and drew the helicopter along a preprogrammed path. Hyde Park opened up under them. The hotels beckoned at its edge, like moored cruise liners from an earlier age.

Mike had Hernan Echevarria buried in the heart of Mayfair, well away from the modern hotels. They were playing to the dictator's old-world pretensions. A Royal Suite at Brown's, the whiff of two centuries' tradition and the dropped names of European royalty along the historical guest list. An armoured Shorn limo collected Echevarria daily at the Albemarle Street frontage and ferried him about on a carefully balanced programme of meetings with senior banking officials, A-listed arms dealers and one or two house-trained political figures. Evenings were given over to opera and dinners with more tame dignitaries.

'I'll keep him busy,' Bryant promised. 'And I'll keep him away from the Park end. You stash Barranco in the Hilton or something. Get a tower suite. I'll cross-reference with you on programme, we'll make sure these two guys never come within a couple of klicks of each other.'

The Hilton it was. They touched down on the tower helipad and were met by liveried attendants who busied themselves with the baggage and led Barranco and Lopez off in the direction of the access elevators. Chris went with them, mainly to take care of tips.

'You won't have to do that,' he said, as the last attendant slipped out and closed the door with trained noiselessness. 'Just sign gratuities on any room service you ask for, and we'll cover it. I'd recommend about

230

ten per cent. Expectations are a lot less than that, but it never hurts to be generous. So anyway, uh. I hope you'll be comfortable.'

'Comfortable?'

Barranco stood in the midst of the suite's opulence, looking like a hunter whose large and dangerous quarry has suddenly disappeared into the surrounding undergrowth.

Chris cleared his throat. 'Yes, uh. Joaquin Lopez will be staying on the floor below. Room 4148. I've put two armed security guards into 4146 as well. The hotel has pretty good security of its own, but you can't be too careful, even up here.' He produced a small matt black mobile and held it out. 'This is a dedicated phone. A scrambled line direct to me. wherever I am. Any problem, night or day, call me. Just press the dial key.'

'Thank you.' Barranco's tone was distant, but if there was irony in it, Chris couldn't hear it.

'I thought you'd probably want to rest now.'

'Yes, that would be good.'

'I'd like to introduce you to a colleague of mine later on, and also to my wife. I thought perhaps we could have dinner together. There's a good Peruvian restaurant in the hotel mezzanine. We could eat late, say about nine-thirty. Or if you'd prefer to stay here and leave it for another night, that's entirely up to you.'

'No, no. I would.' He drew a deep, jet-lagged breath. 'Like to meet your wife, Señor Faulkner. And your colleague, of course. Nine-thirty will be fine.'

'Good, that's great. I'll call here just after nine, then.'

'Yes. Now I think I would like to rest.'

'Of course.'

He let himself out and went down to talk to the security detachment. They were pretty much what he'd expected – two hard-faced men past their physical prime in shirt sleeves and shoulder holsters. They answered the door and then his questions with impassive calm. The surveillance equipment he'd ordered wired into Barranco's suite stood unobtrusively on a low table to one side. Standby lights winked below the row of small liquid crystal screens. On one of them, Barranco had already collapsed onto a bed, fully clothed. Chris bent and peered.

'He asleep?'

'Out like a light.'

'You sure he isn't going to be able to find any of these cameras?'

'Yes, sir. Unless he's a surveillance specialist. And he hasn't shown any signs of looking for them yet.'

'Well, let me know if he does start looking.'

'Yes, sir.'

'And if he moves from the suite, I want to know before it happens. You've got my direct line?'

They exchanged weary glances. One of them nodded.

'Yes, sir. It's under control.'

He took the hint and left to check on Lopez. The Americas agent had been waiting for him. Chemical impatience made his movements about the room erratic and irritating. Chris tried to project calm.

'No transit problems then?'

'No, man. Onward tickets.' Lopez grinned speedily. 'They don't give a fuck who you are, so long as you're going someplace else.'

'And Barranco? Did he talk to you at all?'

'Yeah, he told me I was a running dog for the global capitalist tyranny, and I ought to be ashamed of myself.'

'No change there, then.' Chris wandered across to the window and stared out over the park.

'Yeah, you want to watch him, Chris. He's out of his depth with all this corporate stuff, he's going to be defensive. Most likely, he'll cling to what he knows. My guess is you're going to hear a shitload of out-of-date dogma this week.'

'Well, he's entitled to his point of view.'

That cracked Lopez up.

'Yeah, 's a free country,' he chortled. 'Right? Everyone's entitled to their point of view, right? 's a *free* country! That's right!'

'Joaquin, you need to take some downers.'

'No. Less time around these Marquista hero types is what I fucking need, man.'

The sudden, bright vehemence brought Chris around from his contemplation of the view. Lopez was standing glittery-eyed in the centre of the room, fists knotted, surprised by his own sudden rage.

'Joaquin?'

'Ah, *fuck* it.' The anger fled as rapidly as it had come. Lopez looked abruptly drained. 'Sorry. It's just my kid brother hands me the same fucking line all the time. Running-dog capitalista, running-dog capitalista. Ever since I got my PT&I licence. Like a fucking skip-burned disc.'

'I didn't know you had a brother.'

'Yeah.' The Americas agent waved a hand. 'I don't advertise the fact. Little squirt's a union organiser in the banana belt, up around Bocas, where we were. Not the kind of thing you put on a Trade and Investment CV if you can avoid it.'

'I guess not.'

Lopez's eyes went hooded. 'I try to keep the worst of the shit from raining on him. I made contacts that are good for that much.

232

And when the strike-breakers do come round, I pay his hospital bills, I feed his kids. Gets back on his feet and he drops by to insult me again.'

Chris thought feelingly of Erik Nyquist. 'Family, huh?'

'Yeah, family.' The agent lost his drugged introspection. Shot Chris a sideways look. 'We're just talking here, right, boss? You're not going to go telling tales on me to the partners?'

'Joaquin, I don't give a shit what your brother does for a living, and nor would any of Shorn's partners. They've got altogether bigger game to shoot. Everyone's got an Ollie North or two hanging in the classified record. So long as it doesn't interfere with business, so what?'

Lopez shook his head. 'Maybe that's a London attitude, Chris, but it wouldn't wash that way with Panama T & I. I don't want to wake up one morning and find myself served with a Plaza de Toros summons like you did to old man Harris.'

'Hey, Harris was a fuck-up.'

'Yeah, not much of a knife fighter either, even for a gringo.' Lopez skinned an unpleasant grin, but something desperate leaked from the edges, around the eyes. 'Time I reach that age, I want to be out of this fucking game. I do good work for you, Chris. Right?'

'Yeah. Sure.' Chris frowned. Candour wasn't something he'd looked for here, weakness still less. The naked anxiety in the agent's tone was touching him in places he'd thought long sealed away.

And we're still not into the brutal honesty shitstorm with Barranco yet. Jesus fucking Christ

'I mean, I called it right everywhere you asked me, right? I set up what you need, soon as you needed, right?'

'You know you have.' He didn't know which direction to roll this. Maybe—

'I know I lost it back there in the NAME, I still owe you for that, but—'

'Joaquin, you've got to drop that shit.' Chris made for the mini-bar. Shipped bottles and ice up from the chiller unit onto a table, talking as he worked. 'Look, it was a problem at this end. I told you that, and I told you we look after our own. Just think about it. Christ, if you don't trust me, think about the logistics of the thing. Would I have hauled your arse out of there, with all the expense we incurred, just so I could can you six weeks down the line?'

'I don't know, Chris. Would you?'

'Joaquin, I'm serious. You *really* need to take something.'

'You know Mike Bryant, right?'

Chris stopped, a glass in each hand. 'Yeah. He's a colleague, so watch what you say next, alright.'

'You know he's working a Cono Sur portfolio at the moment? Running contacts through Carlos Caffarini out of Buenos Aires?'

'Yeah, I heard. Didn't know it was Caffarini, but—'

'It isn't any more,' said Lopez abruptly. 'Last week Bryant canned Caffarini because there were call-centre strikes in Santiago, and he didn't see it coming. Or maybe he didn't think it was important enough to chase. Now he's on a ventilator in intensive care until his health cover runs out, and some fucking seventeen-year-old is running the portfolio at a quarter the old retainer. They were only *strikes*, Chris. Management abuse of female workers, localised action, *no* political demands. I checked.'

Chris put down the glasses and sighed. Lopez watched him.

Fuck, Mike, why can't you just

'Look, Joaquin. Strikes can get out of hand, whatever the original rationale. Reed and Mason, it's chapter one stuff. You know that.'

'Yeah.' The Americas agent had the manic splinter back in his tone. 'So tell me this, Chris. What's going to happen to me if a banana strike gets out of hand on a certain plantation up near Bocas?'

Chris looked at him.

'Nothing.' He kept Lopez's eyes while it sank in. 'Alright? Got it? *Nothing* is going to happen to you.'

'You can't give me—'

'*I am not Mike Bryant.*'

The snap in his voice came out of nowhere, jolting them both. He clamped down on it. Made his hands work on the drinks. He dumped ice into two glasses, decanted rum over the cubes and swirled the mix. Spoke quietly again.

'Look. I'm happy with what you've done for us and I don't give a shit about what happened in Medellín. Forget about Caffarini and whatever's going on in Buenos Aires and Santiago. I give you my word, you're secure with us. Now let's drink to that, Joaquin, because if you don't crank down soon, you're going to pop. Come on, this is expense account overproof rum. Get it down you.'

He offered the glass. After a couple of seconds, Lopez took it. He stared into the drink for a long moment, then his face came up.

'I will not forget this, Chris,' he said quietly.

'Nor will I. I look after my people.'

The glasses chimed in the room. The liquor burned down. Outside the windows, something happened to the light as afternoon shifted smoothly towards evening.

THIRTY

'I still don't see why you want me there.' Carla checked her make-up again in the drop-down roof mirror as Chris rolled the Saab down into the Hilton's parking deck. 'It's not like I know anything about the NAME.'

'That's exactly the point.' Chris scanned the crowded deck, found nothing to his liking and steered down the ramp to the next level. 'You can get him to tell you about it. I don't want this guy to feel he's surrounded by suited experts. I want him to relax. To feel in control for a while. It's textbook client handling.'

He felt her eyes on him.

'What?'

'Nothing.'

The lower level was all but empty. Chris parked a good half dozen spaces away from the nearest vehicle. Since the proximity alarm had failed on him, he'd taken to parking out in the open where the security cameras could see him. It was irrational, he knew – no one short of a full covert ops squad was going to breach the perimeter defences of the Hilton or the Shorn block in the first place, let alone have time and skill to get through the Saab's security locks before they were noticed. But the proximity alarm *had* failed. How exactly was still up for grabs, but in the meantime he didn't intend it to happen again.

'I'll go up and get him,' he said, killing the engine. 'The restaurant's on the mezzanine level. *El Meson Andino*. Mike said he'd meet us there.'

'You don't want me to come up with you?'

'There's really no need.'

He didn't tell her that he wanted to check in on the security squad on the way, and that in some undefined way he felt ashamed of the two blunt middle-aged men and their assemblage of little screens and mikes.

'Suit yourself.' She dug out a cigarette and put it to her lips. She seemed to draw into herself as she lit it.

'I'll see you there, then.'

'Yes.'

The security men had nothing to report. On the screen, Barranco prowled back and forth like a prisoner in a cell. He had dressed in a black dinner suit a decade out of fashion. Chris went up to collect him.

'I don't know much about Peruvian food,' he said as they rode down in the lift together.

'Nor do I,' said Barranco shortly. 'I'm from Colombia.'

The food turned out to be excellent, though how Peruvian it was became a matter for dispute a few glasses of wine into the meal. It broke the ice with a resounding crack. Barranco argued that a couple of dishes were pure Colombian, and Chris, casting his mind back to his time in the NAME, had to agree with him. Mike, on good social form, reasoned with great persuasiveness and almost no evidence, that the cuisine of the different regions must have *interpenetrated* over time. Carla suggested rather acidly that this probably had more to do with marketing than regional mobility. Peruvian was a consumer label here, not a national identity. Barranco nodded sober approval. He was obviously quite taken with Carla, whether because of her blonde good looks or her unorthodox political attitudes, Chris didn't know or much care. He stowed an unexpected twist of jealousy and resisted the temptation to shift his chair closer to his wife's. Relief at the way the evening was going closed it out.

Business leaked into the conversation in low-intensity bursts, mostly from Barranco's side and nurtured by the warmth of Carla's genuine interest. Chris and Mike let it run, sonar-tuned for the dangers of political reefs and set to steer rapidly away where necessary.

'Of course, solar farms are a beautiful idea, but it is the old instability argument. The infrastructure is too costly and too easy to sabotage.'

'Doesn't that go for nuclear power too? I thought the regime was going to build two of those new Pollok reactors.'

'Yes.' Barranco smiled grimly. 'Francisco Echevarria is a close personal friend of Donald Cordell, who is CEO of the Horton Power Group. And the stations will be built a long way from Bogotá.'

Carla flushed. 'That's disgusting.'

'Yes.'

Mike shot Chris a warning glance and picked up the bottle.

'Señor Barranco. More wine?'

'I had a question about Bogotá,' said Chris, feigning memory failure. 'Oh, yeah. Last time I was there, I saw this really beautiful church in the centre of town. I was wondering . . .'

And so on. If Barranco resented the steerage, it didn't show. He let the tides of the conversation carry him, and stayed polite throughout. Chris knew from the look on Carla's face that she saw what was going on, but she said nothing.

Only once, when Mike Bryant retired to the toilets for the second time, did the veneer crack. Barranco nodded after him.

'That kind of thing's not a problem where you work?'

'What kind of thing?'

Carla sniffed delicately. Chris looked in the direction of the toilets. He'd honestly not thought anything of it.

'Well,' said Barranco. 'I wouldn't say your colleague has a problem. But nor is he particularly subtle about it. In the Bogotá Hilton, in a restaurant full of people, things would be a little different. Even our ruling families have to watch their drug stance in public these days.'

'Must be why Francisco Echevarria spends so much time in Miami.' It hit Chris, just too late, that he'd drunk a little too much.

Barranco's eyes narrowed. 'Yes, I imagine it is. Meanwhile, his father uses the helicopter gunships you buy him to firebomb coca farmers into oblivion. Ironic, isn't it.'

The silence opened up. Carla made a small noise into it, a mixture of amusement and disgust that told Chris he'd get no help from that quarter.

'I, uh, that isn't,' he stumbled. 'Shorn policy as such doesn't outlaw coca production. In fact, we've done feasibility studies on bringing the crop into the legitimate commodities market. Shorn's Financial Instruments division actually commissioned work along that line.'

Barranco shrugged. 'You expect me to be impressed? Legitimisation will only send coca the way of coffee. Rich men in New York and London will grow richer, and the farmers will starve. Is that part of the package you plan to sell me here, Chris Faulkner?'

That stung. More so, with the fierce satisfaction he saw rising on Carla's face. Mike had not reappeared. Feeling suddenly very alone, he scrambled to salvage the evaporating good humour around the table.

'You do me an injustice, Señor Barranco. I merely mention the study to demonstrate that at Shorn we are not blinded by moralistic prejudice.'

'Yes. I find that easy to believe.'

A small, colourless smile from Carla. Chris plunged on doggedly.

'In fact, I was going to say, the study found legitimisation on the commodities market would be too problematic to consider seriously. For one thing, there's a very real fear that it would drain immediate finance out of practically every other investment sector. And clearly we can't have that.'

It was meant to be funny, but no one laughed. Barranco leaned across the table towards him. His blue eyes were bright and marbled wet with anger.

'I give you fair warning, Chris Faulkner. I have little compassion to spare for the spoilt stupid children of the western world and their expensive drug problems. I look through the lens that your free marketeers have sold us, and I see a profitable trade. So.' A short, hard gesture, one upward-jutting calloused palm, halfway between a karate blow and an offer to shake hands. 'Sell us your weapons, and we will sell you our cocaine. This will not change when the Popular Revolutionary Brigade takes power in Colombia, because I *will not* sacrifice the wealth it can bring my people. If your governments are so concerned about the flow of product, let them buy up the supply on the open market like anybody else. Then they can burn it or put it up their noses as they see fit.'

'Hear, hear!' Mike Bryant was back, clapping slow applause as he circled the table back to his seat. His eyes burned bright enough to match Barranco's pale blue glare. 'Hear, *hear!* Outstanding analysis, really. You were right, Chris. This is the man for us. No doubt about it.'

He seated himself with a grin.

'Of course, it'll never happen. Our governments don't really care enough to take that rather obvious step. They operate a containment policy in the cordoned zones, so crack and edge addiction there costs them almost nothing. And the rich, well, you can always rely on the rich to take care of their own misdemeanours without recourse to public process.'

Barranco looked at him with open dislike. 'Strange, then, Señor Bryant, that there should have been so much loudly publicised military activity devoted to destroying the coca trade over the last seventy years.'

Mike shrugged and helped himself to more wine. 'Well, of course, things weren't quite as clearly defined a few decades back. There was a lot of playing to the gallery back then.' He smiled again. 'Something we don't have to worry about these days.'

'And yet the frigates sit at anchor in Barranquilla harbour still, flying foreign flags. Our coastal waters are smart-mined in contravention of UN law and our people are showered with napalm for trying to make a living.'

Another shrug. 'Matters of control, Señor Barranco. I'm sure you're familiar with the dynamic. It's distasteful, I agree, but it *is* the stance the Echevarria government and its creditors have settled for. That, in a very real sense, is one of the reasons why we're all here right now. If we can reach a realistic agreement with you, Señor Barranco, you could be the man to change that stance.'

Barranco's lip curled. Bryant, seeming to miss it, sniffed and rubbed with a knuckle at both sides of his nose.

'In the meantime, you have my word as a representative of the Shorn Conflict Investment division that until the time comes to implement those changes, you'll be given access to the same covert export routes Hernan Echevarria currently turns a blind eye to.'

'You're going to take me to the table with Langley?' Barranco's gaze shuttled back and forth between Chris and Bryant. His tone had scaled towards disbelieving.

'Of course.' Mike looked surprised. 'Who did you think I was talking about? They're the premier distributors of illicit narcotics in the Americas. We don't believe in doing things by halves at Shorn. I mean, we'll hook you up with some other European and Asian distributors as well, naturally, but to be honest none of them are in the same class as Langley. Plus you'll probably shift the bulk of your product in Langley's back yard anyway, and they can do pretty good onward sales to most of the western Pacific Rim if you're interested. More wine? Anybody?'

Carla drove them home, focused wholly on the road ahead. In the dashboard-lit warmth of the car, the silence came off her in waves. Chris, still smarting from the way she'd lined up with Barranco, turned away and stared out of the passenger-side window at the passing lights of the city.

'Well, that was fucking great,' he said finally.

Carla picked up the motorway feeder lane. She said nothing. If Chris had looked at her, he would have seen how close to the edge they were.

'Mike in the bathroom powdering his fucking nose, Barranco on a political rant and you backing him up every fucking—'

'Don't start with me, Chris.' The Saab never wavered from its accelerating trajectory up the feeder ramp, but there was a ragged edge in Carla's voice that did finally make him look across at her face.

'Well, didn't you?'

'You should be overjoyed I did. Wasn't that my job tonight? Make your client feel good. *Relax* him. Isn't that what you said?'

'Yeh, that didn't mean hang me out to dry in front of him.'

'Well perhaps you should have made yourself clearer. I'm your wife, remember, not some grinning whore out of the escort pages. I don't do this shit for a living.'

'*You fucking enjoyed watching Barranco lay into me!*'

It drew a sideways look from her. For a full two seconds she stared at him in silence, then her eyes went back to the road.

'You going to shout like that at Mike Bryant tomorrow?' she asked quietly. 'For his bathroom manners?'

'Don't avoid the fucking question, Carla!'

'I wasn't aware you'd asked me one.'

'You enjoyed watching Barranco lay into me, *didn't you*?'

'You sound pretty convinced already.'

'*Just fucking*—' He clenched a fist, clamped his mouth. Locked down the fury. Forced out the words close to normal volume. 'Just answer me the question, Carla.'

'You answer mine first. You ever shout at Mike like this?'

'Mike Bryant is on my *side*. Whatever else he might do, whatever problems he might have, I know that much. I don't need to yell at him.'

'Don't need? Or don't dare?'

'Fuck you, Carla.' It was almost a murmur. The sheeting fury had guttered out inside him. It wasn't gone, but abruptly it was cold, and that frightened him more. Frightened him because in the chill he thought he could feel something slowly dying.

'No, fuck *you*, Chris.' Her voice was barely louder than his had been, but it hissed at him. 'You want an answer to your question? Yes. I enjoyed it tonight. You know what I enjoyed? I enjoyed seeing a man who's fighting for something more than his fucking quarterly bonus get the upper hand for once. I enjoyed hearing someone who cares what happens to other people telling the truth about the way your sick-making little world works.'

'A man who *cares*.' Chris bounced the loosely curled edge of his hand off the window in the weary ghost of a punch. 'Oh, sure. A man who wants to sell crack cocaine and edge to children in the zones. Yeah, he's a real fucking hero, Barranco is. You heard what he said.'

'Yes, and I heard Mike Bryant promise to hook him up with Langley, who supply eighty per cent of North America's inner cities. Langley, who you work with on a day-to-day basis. And this weekend, the two of you are taking Echevarria and Barranco *both* to the North Memorial to sell them the weapons they need to fight each other. And now you're taking some kind of *moral* stance here? Jesus Christ, you could give lessons in hypocrisy to Simeon fucking Sands. What choice have we left these people, Chris? What favours have we done them? Why *shouldn't* they swamp us all in crack?'

'I didn't say they shouldn't.'

'No, because the truth is you don't care about that either. You don't care about anything, in fact, except making your end of the deal stick so you can stay at the top table with the other big players. That's what this is about, isn't it Chris?' She laughed, something that was almost a sob. 'Chris Faulkner, global mover and shaker. Observe the cut of his suits, the cool command he brings with him to the table. Princes and presidents shake his hand, and when he speaks, they listen. Oil flows, where and when he says it will, men with guns rise up and fight at his command—'

'Why don't you just shut the *fuck* up, Carla.' The anger was suddenly warming again, heating his guts, looking for the way to do damage. 'You got such a thing for Barranco and his moral crusade, maybe you should have just gone up to his fucking room with him instead of coming home with me. Maybe a man of conscience'll light you up a little better than I do.'

240

Sudden pressure across the chest, almost pain. The belt gripped him into his seat. He heard the brief shriek of tyres as the Saab slammed to a halt.

'You fucking bastard, Chris. You fucking *piece of shit*.'

She sat with her fists clenched on the wheel, head down. The car stood slewed fractionally off centre beneath the sodium glare of the motorway lamps. The engine rumbled to itself. As he watched, she shook her head slowly and lifted her face. There was an unsteady adrenalin-shock smile pinned to her mouth. She shook her head again, whispered it like a discovery.

'You piece of shit.'

It was her end-of-the-line insult, the one she'd never used on him except in play. In the whole seven years of their relationship, he'd only heard her label perhaps a half dozen acquaintances with it. Men, and on one single occasion a woman, that she wanted to wipe out of her life, and in most cases had. For Carla, it meant total shutdown. Beneath contempt.

He sat and felt it dripping off him like a physical thing.

'You'd better mean that,' he said.

She would not look at him.

'This is a new level, Carla.' He looked at his hands in the stained orange radiance coming down through the windscreen. There was a fierce exhilaration pumping through him that he dared not examine closely. 'We haven't been getting on, but. This is new. This is.'

He lifted a hand to gesture. Gave it up half-formed.

It must have caught her peripheral vision. She stole a glance at him. Behind her eyes he saw fear, not of him.

'I ought to make you get out of this fucking car.' Her voice was shaking, and he knew she was going through the same pounding near-the-edge rush. 'I ought to make you fucking walk home.'

'It's my car,' he said gently.

'Yeah, and every centimetre I built for you, and rebuilt and rebuilt again, you ever, Chris, you *ever* speak to me like that again, you—'

'I'm sorry.' It was out of his mouth before he realised he'd said it.

And then they were groping for each other across the space between, tears spilling down her cheeks, stopped up unshed in his throat, both of them held back by the idiot grip of the belts on their bodies. The solid ground of the relationship was suddenly back under their feet, the edge was gone, shoved back from convulsively, the thundering pulse of the drop receding in his ears, the familiar warm sticky slide of remorse and regret, the

safety

of it all again, bearing them up and binding them together.

241

They fought loose of the belts and held each other without speaking. Long enough for the hot, wet tear ribbons on her cheeks to cool and dry against his face. Long enough for the swollen obstruction in his own throat to ease, and the locked-up trembling to stop.

'We have to get out of this,' she said at last, muffled, into his neck.

'I know.'

'It's going to kill us, Chris. One way or the other, on the road or not, it's going to kill us both.'

'I know.'

'You've got to stop.'

'I *know*.'

'Vasvik will come back to you. I know he will. *Please*, Chris, don't fuck it up when he does.'

'Alright.' There was no resistance left in him. He felt drained. It occurred to him, for the first time in the whirl of the last three days: 'Have you heard anything more?'

She shook her head, still pressed against him.

He found a single tear welling up in one eye. He blinked it away. 'They're taking their sweet fucking time.'

'Chris, it's a lot of money. A big risk for them. But we haven't heard and that means, Dad says that means they're going to do it. He says otherwise we'd have heard by now. They're raising the finance, justifying it at budget level, that's what he thinks.'

Chris stroked her hair. Even the irritation at Carla's constant undying faith in her father's superhuman bloody wisdom was gone, temporarily dynamited in the shock of how close they'd come to the break.

'Okay, Carla.' There was a mirthless smile creeping out across his face now. 'But whatever they're doing, they need to hurry it up. Someone out there's trying to kill me. Someone connected. And if they can't take me down on the road, then they'll find some other way.'

She raised her head to look at him.

'Do you think they know? About Vasvik?'

'I don't know. But I do know that if Vasvik and his pals don't get a move on, they're going to be too late to do anything except clean up the blood. Just like Nigeria and the Kurdish homeland and every other fucking gig the UN have ever played.'

He found, oddly, his smile was gaining strength. He couldn't pick apart the knot of feeling behind it. Carla drew back from him as if he wore a stranger's face. He looked away from her and along the night-time perspectives of the road.

'Doesn't give you much hope, does it.'

THIRTY-ONE

They got a good day for the North Memorial. The unseasonal gales drove out the cloud over the rest of the week and by Sunday the Norfolk sky was scraped almost clear. They spotted a big jet banking lazily against the blue while they were still a dozen kilometres off.

'Surveillance mother,' was Mike's opinion. 'Probably the new Lockheed. I hear they finally ironed the bugs out of the drone retrieval. They'll be showing off. Ah, here we go. Junction seventeen.'

He swung the BMW into the off-lane. Behind him, someone hit a horn with what sounded like both feet. Chris turned across the back seat and saw a streamlined red Ford jockeying to get past them. Beneath the tinted glass of the windscreen, he made out an angry young face.

'Should have indicated, Mike.'

'Yeah, yeah.' Mike squinted up at the mirror. 'Fucking asshole. If this strip wasn't triple-monitored for the fair, I'd fucking have you, my son.'

'What is it?' Barranco had been catnapping in the front passenger seat.

'Nothing,' said Bryant. 'Just someone looking to die young.'

Barranco craned round to look. Chris shook his head not to worry and grinned. The traffic had been heavy all the way up from London. They must have seen close to a hundred cars since they left, and as they drew closer to the Lakenheath turn-off, the density went steadily up. Bryant wasn't used to driving in these conditions. No one was.

The red car edged up beside them as they hit the ramp. Bryant grinned and accelerated up the slope.

'Maybe we should have flown,' said Barranco nervously.

'On a day like this?' Mike was still grinning. 'Come on!'

The Ford came level, on the right. Chris cast an eye over the vehicle's lines and reckoned cheap, look-good armouring. Probably a junior analyst or a recruitment sprog. No contest. He braced himself without thinking and a second later Bryant feinted sideways. The other driver spooked, braked and slewed aside. Mike carved up the space he'd left and straightened out in the middle of the lane. He started to brake a couple of dozen metres off the summit, and came to a smooth halt at the roundabout junction. He waited, eyes on the mirror. After a couple of moments, the Ford crept up and queued respectfully behind them.

'Thank *you*,' said Mike, and turned sedately onto the curve.

Barranco looked back at Chris for guidance. 'Did this mean something?'

'Not a thing,' said Bryant breezily. 'No challenges permissible on this stretch today. Just teaching the guy a little something about respect.'

Chris winked.

Ten minutes later they cleared the main gate at the airbase and a uniformed attendant waved them through into the parking segment. The place was packed with corporate battlewagons and hired limos. Here and there, one or two khaki-drab armed forces utility vehicles had been left out, mainly, Chris suspected, to enhance the genuine feel of the fair. On occasion, new developing world clients remained resolutely unimpressed by the suited godparents they had come to depend on. It helped to accentuate the military aspect, gave dictators and revolutionaries something to relate to.

As they climbed out, a trio of venomous-looking fighter planes came screaming across the airfield at rooftop height, then trailed the gut-crunching roar of lit afterburners back up into the azure sky. Out of the corner of his eye, Chris saw Barranco flinch.

'Fucking clowns,' he said. 'Don't know why they got to do that.'

'Those are Harpies,' Barranco told him quietly. 'Demonstrating a strafe run. They are made in Britain. Last year you sold fifteen of them to the Echevarria regime.'

'Actually,' said Mike, alarming the BMW, 'they're made under licence to BAe in Turkey. Have been for a couple of years now. This way, I think.'

He set off in the direction of the hangars, where a loosely knotted crowd could be seen drifting about. Chris and Barranco followed him at a distance.

'You did not need to bring me here,' muttered Barranco.

Chris shook his head. 'I think you'll be glad we did. The North Memorial pulls in state-of-the-art weaponry from every leading manufacturer in the world. Not just the big stuff, you've got assault rifles, grenades, shoulder launchers, area denial systems. New propellants, new ammunition, new explosives. Vicente, even if you don't buy much of this stuff, you need to know what Echevarria might be deploying against you.'

Barranco fixed him with a hard look. 'Why don't you just tell me what Echevarria's got, and save us both some time.'

'Uh . . .'

'You know, don't you. You supply him, you pay for it all.'

'Not me.' He stamped down the coil of guilt inside him, shook his

244

head again. 'That's not my account, Vicente. I'm really sorry. I've got no more access to it than you do.'

'No, but you could get access.'

Chris coughed. Bent it up into a laugh. 'Vicente, that's not how it works. I can't just walk into another executive's office and go through his client files. Quite apart from the security systems, it's a question of ethics. No, seriously. I mean it. I could lose my job over something like that.'

Barranco turned away. 'Okay, never mind. Forget I asked. I realise you have a lot to lose.'

It didn't *seem* to be meant ironically, and Chris thought he was beginning to get the measure of Vicente Barranco enough to spot these things. Over the past two days, he reckoned he'd built some pretty solid scaffolding for his relationship with the Colombian. He'd had the man out to dinner at his home and actively encouraged Carla to reprise her solidarity of the night at the Hilton. He'd gone drinking with him in some semi-risky clubs at the edges of the cordon. And on the Saturday morning after, at Barranco's insistence, he'd even taken him on a short tour of the eastern zones in the Saab. This last, the Colombian sat through in almost total silence until he asked the single question. *Is this where you grew up, Chris?*

It was the first time he had used Chris's first name on its own. A watershed. Chris considered a moment, then he spun the wheel of the Saab and made a U turn in the empty street. He headed southward through a maze of deserted one-way systems and roads he thought he would have forgotten by now, but had not. He found the abandoned, half-built multi-storey car park that overlooked the riverside estates to the west and drove up the spiral pipe to the roof. He parked at the edge and nodded forward through the windscreen.

'Down there,' he said simply.

Barranco got out of the car and wandered to the edge of the deck. After a while, Chris got out and joined him.

Riverside.

The name was like a taste in his mouth. Metallic bitter. He stared down at the low-stacked housing, the shaggy green of miniature park spaces allowed to run wild in between, the oil-scummed expanses of water the estates backed onto on three sides. It wasn't the Brundtland, he told himself, it wasn't the labyrinthine concrete expanse of homes never designed for any but the dregs. That wasn't it. Something altogether different had gone wrong here.

'In my country,' said Barranco, echoing his thoughts with uncanny accuracy, 'you would not be considered poor if you lived here.'

'It wasn't built for poor people.'

The Colombian glanced back at him. 'But poor people moved in.'

245

'Well, no one else would, you see. After the domino recessions. No facilities. No local shops, no transport unless you could afford taxis or fuel and a licence. Which, increasingly, no one could. You want to get anywhere?' Chris turned and pointed north. 'The nearest bus stop is two kilometres that way. There used to be a rail link, but the investors got scared and pulled out. When I was growing up, a few of the ones who had jobs used to cycle, but the kid gangs started throwing stones at them. They knocked one woman right off a dock into the river. Kept dropping stones on her 'til she went under for good.' He shrugged. 'Having a job, a real job, marked you out.'

Barranco said nothing. He stared down at the estate as if he could push the whole place back in time and spot the woman floundering in the oiled water.

'A couple of the kids I used to play with died that way too,' said Chris, remembering clearly for the first time in a long while. 'Drowned, I mean. No security fence along the wharf, see. They just fell in. My mother was always telling me not to—'

He fell silent. Barranco turned to him again.

'I am sorry, Chris. I should not have asked you to come here.'

Chris tried on a smile. 'You didn't ask me, exactly.'

'No, and you brought me nonetheless.'

The obvious question hung there in the air between them, but Barranco never asked it. Chris was glad, because he didn't have an answer.

They got back into the car.

'Do you guys want to see this stuff, or what?'

It had dawned on Mike Bryant that Chris and Barranco were lagging behind and he'd come back for them.

Barranco exchanged glances with Chris and shrugged.

'Sure. Even if I don't buy much, I'll need to see what Echevarria might be deploying against me. Right?'

'Exactly!' Mike clapped his hands and snapped out a pointed pistol finger. 'That's the spirit.'

Inside the hangars, big air conditioning units blasted warm, spice-scented air down from the ceiling. The exhibits sat in pools of soft light, interspersed with crisp repeating holos showing them in sanitised use. Brand names hung in illuminated capitals. Logos badged the walls.

Bryant made for the assault rifles. An elegant saleswoman glided forward to meet him. They seemed to know each other far better than Mike's visit yesterday with Echevarria would explain.

'Chris. Señor Barranco. I'd like you to meet Sally Hunting. She reps for Vickers, but she's a freelance small-arms consultant in her spare time. Isn't that right, Sal? No strings.'

246

Sally Hunting shot him a reproachful look. Beneath her Lily Chen suit and auburn tumbling spike haircut, she was very beautiful in a pale, understated fashion.

'*Spare* time, Mike? What is that, exactly?'

'Sally, behave. This is Señor Vicente Barranco, a valued client. And my colleague, Chris Faulkner.'

'Of course, Chris Faulkner. I recognise you from the photos. The Nakamura thing. Well, this is a great pleasure. So what can I do you gentlemen for?'

'Señor Barranco is fighting a highland jungle war against an oppressive regime and well-supplied government forces,' said Bryant. 'It's our feeling he's under-equipped.'

'I see. That must be very difficult.' Sally Hunting was all mannered sympathy. 'Are you relying on Kalashnikovs? Mmm? Yes, I thought so. Marvellous weapons, I have clients who won't look at anything else. But you may want to consider switching to the new Heckler and Koch. Now, it's a little more complicated to operate than your basic AK, but—'

Barranco shook his head. 'Señorita, my soldiers are often as young as fourteen years old. They come from bombed-out villages where most of the adults have been killed or disappeared. We are short of teachers, even shorter of time to train our recruits. Simplicity of operation is vital.'

The saleswoman shrugged. 'The Kalashnikov, then. I won't bore you with details, they've been making essentially the same gun for almost a hundred years. But you might like to have a look at some of the modified ammunition we have here. You know, shredding rounds, toxic jacket coatings, armour piercing. All compatible with the standard AK load.'

She gestured across at a display terminal.

'Shall we?'

Barranco left the North Memorial armed – on paper – to the teeth. Seven hundred brand new Kalashnikovs, eight dozen Aerospatiale shoulder-launched autoseek plane-killers, two thousand lightweight King antipersonnel grenades and two hundred thousand rounds of state-of-the-art ammunition for the assault rifles. They were unable, despite Sally Hunting's best efforts, to sell him landmines or a complex automated area-denial sentry system.

'No big deal,' she told them while Barranco was with one of the clinical experts, having immune-inhibitor toxins explained to him. 'I'll get standard commission on the AKs. Not as much as the Heckler and Koch, obviously, they're still trying to break the lock Kalashnikov have on the insurgency market, and they're being *very* generous this year. Still, with what I'll make off the Aerospatiale stuff and the grenades, I'm not complaining.'

'I'm glad to hear that,' growled Mike, 'because my impression was I just handed you a crippled rabbit on a four-lane drag. You owe me big time for this, Sally.'

She twinkled at him. 'Collect any time, Mike. I'm a busy girl, but I can always fit you in, you know.'

'Behave.'

On the drive back, Barranco was quiet. If his new acquisitions pleased him, he gave no sign. For the whole journey he held a single jacketed rifle slug in his hand, rolling it back and forth between his fingers like a cigar. His face invited neither conversation nor comment. He looked, Chris thought in one particularly morbid moment, like a man who has just been told he has a disease for which there is no known cure.

THIRTY-TWO

They dropped Barranco at the Hilton, and were about to pull away again when the security entry alarms went off in violently coloured LEDs and nasal braying. Still buried in his brooding, the Colombian had tried to walk through the scanner with the AK round in his hand. Chris nipped up the steps to the entrance and unwrinkled things, clapped Barranco on the shoulder and told him to get some rest. He'd see him at nine the next morning to go over contractual stuff. Then he piled back in the BMW and they drifted out into the sparse traffic. Mike hooked around Marble Arch and picked up Oxford Street heading east. Still plenty of light in the sky.

'Want to get something to eat?' Mike asked him.

'Sure, why not.'

'Noodles?'

'Sounds good to me.' Chris jerked a thumb back the way they'd come. 'You think he's okay?'

'Barranco? Yeah. Just shellshocked. Probably never seen so much hardware in a single day.'

'I don't know. He didn't look happy.'

Mike snorted. 'Well he bloody *should* be happy. That's the biggest single credit-card payment I've ever made.'

'You didn't buy any toys for Echevarria yesterday?'

'On account.' Mike grinned at him. 'Sixty-day cancellation clause.'

'You route that stuff through Sally Hunting as well?'

'No *way*. Total account separation, remember. Anyway, Sally doesn't get her commission unless the money clears. Wouldn't want—'

The BMW's phone lit up with a priority call. Mike made a *quiet* gesture at Chris, and answered.

'Yeah, Bryant.'

'Mike. It's Troy. That stuff about Faulkner you ran past me? Something came up.'

'Right, he's here with me, Troy. Tell us what you got.'

There was a brief pause. 'It's better we meet. I don't want to talk on this line. Can you come out to my place?'

Mike glanced across at him. Chris nodded.

'We're on our way.'

Troy's house seemed strangely quiet in the early evening light. It took Chris a moment or two to understand that he was comparing it with memories of the last time he'd been here, when the party was in full swing. He got a determined lock on his creeping paranoia, and followed Mike up to the front door.

The worry must have shown on his face. Mike grinned encouragingly at him.

'Be alright,' he said.

Troy Morris answered the bell by securicam before he opened up, ushered them in as if there was a storm coming, and then threw every bolt and security device the door had before he spoke again. The anti-tamper unit whined rapidly up to full charge. Mike looked at Chris and raised an eyebrow.

'Little jumpy, aren't we?'

'You'd better come through,' said Troy. 'Someone I want you to meet.'

In the lounge, a thin black man in his early twenties sat twitching restlessly in one of Troy's armchairs. There was a scar across his lower jaw and his clothes said zone gangwit. He surveyed the new arrivals without enthusiasm.

'This is Marauder.' Troy told them. 'Marauder, this is Mike Bryant. Chris Faulkner. Friends of mine.'

'Yeah, yeah. Whatever.'

'Mike, Chris, you want to sit down? Get you a drink?'

Mike Bryant nodded, most of his attention fixed on Marauder. 'Some of that Polish vodka you keep in the freezer. Small one.'

'Chris? Single malt, right?'

'Yeah, if you've got it. Thanks.'

'Aberlour or Lagavulin? Or I've got Irish.'

'Lagavulin's good. No ice.'

'Marauder?'

The gangwit rolled his head once back and forth, slowly. He said nothing. Troy shrugged and went out to the kitchen. They sat and waited.

The silence stretched.

'Who you run with?' asked Mike suddenly.

Marauder lifted his jaw. 'Fuck's it got to do with you?'

Chris tensed. Neither he nor Mike were carrying, and Marauder looked street enough to be a problem in a straight fight. He checked Mike out of the corner of his eye, but saw no signs of impending violence.

'Just curious,' said Mike lazily. 'Just wondered what kind of fuckwit outfit lets its soldiers get strung out on the merchandise.'

Marauder sat up. 'Hey birdshit, you want to fuck with me?'

'You don't understand.' Mike Bryant's voice was patient. 'I'm a suit. I represent the establishment. I wanted to fuck with you, you'd be in a penal hospital donating a kidney to society and your momma'd be out on the street, evicted and giving blowjobs to pay your post-op. *Sit down.*'

The gangwit was up out of his chair. On the way there, he'd magicked a blade out between the knuckles of his right hand. He brandished it.

'Hey, *fuck* you, birdshit.'

'I'd put that away as well, if I were you. Touch me, and I'll have your fucking house bulldozed. That's a promise.'

Marauder dithered, rage etched into his stance. If Mike had got up to meet him, Chris reckoned the gangwit would already have slashed at him.

'Ernie, put that fucking thing away before I take it off you myself.' It was Troy, back with a tray of bottles and glasses and an exasperated look on his face. 'What do you think this is, the Carlton Arms lounge bar? This is my fucking home.'

'Ernie?' A huge grin lit up Bryant's face. '*Ernie?*'

'You behave as well, Mike. You should know better.' Troy nodded at the gangwit, who looked away and snicked the blade back out of sight. He lowered himself onto the front edge of the armchair. Chris felt the tension leaking slowly out of him, and breathed again. Mike examined the nails of his right hand. Troy Morris hadn't even put down the drinks tray.

'That's better.'

'Call yourself a black man,' muttered Marauder weakly. 'Fucking line up with them every time, you're nearly birdshit yourself.'

'Ah, belt up.' Troy wasn't even looking at him any more. He handed drinks round and parked the tray on a coffee table. Settled into the remaining armchair with a whisky of his own, and gestured. 'This fine example of urban youth has a story to tell. I told him you'd pay him.'

'Well.' Mike looked up at the ceiling. 'That seems fair. Let's hear it. *Ernie.*'

There was a sullen, hate-filled pause. Everyone looked at Marauder.

'Going to cost you,' he said finally, looking at Chris.

'Two hundred.' Chris told him. 'That's a promise. Maybe more, if I like it.'

'You ain't going to *like* it at all,' the gangwit sneered. He seemed to be

251

getting back his poise. 'You're Faulkner. Knew that 'cause I seen you on the TV. Big popular driver, right. Well, turns out you ain't so fucking popular after all. Turns out someone thinks you're a fucking sellout.'

Chris felt his guts chill. 'Go on.'

Marauder nodded. 'Yeah, that's it. Crags Posse got the word. Jack a wagon, put a sicario behind the wheel. Someone paid out fifty grand to have you bunnied.'

'That's not so much.'

'It is around the crags, Mike,' Troy said sombrely. 'You can get a sicario hit on Iarescu's patch for a grand, grand and a half. Maybe five, if they have to go into town.'

'Well, expenses.' Mike gestured. 'Jacking the car.'

Marauder sneered again. 'Wasn't no fucking jack, birdshit. That guy, he knew they were coming. Iarescu sent a sparkman and datarat up to Kilburn to wire that wagon two days before it was jacked. Fucking suit *knew*, man, they *paid* him for it.'

'How do you know all this?' Chris asked him.

'Defector. I run with the Gold Hawks—'

Mike Bryant threw up his hands. 'Well, why was it such a big fucking secret before, you're telling us now like it was nothing? Fucking—'

'Mike, *shut up*.' Chris looked back at the gangwit. 'Yeah, the Gold Hawks. And?'

Marauder shrugged. 'Like I said, defector. The sparkman, he came over. He's black, the Crags are a birdshit gang, they only ever tolerated him for the wirework. He's got a new girl in Acton now, suits him to get out from under Iarescu. He told me this shit couple of nights ago. I heard Troy was asking, so. Like that.'

Troy leaned forward. 'Now tell them what the sparkman was doing to the wagon.'

'Yeah. Said they put in a frequency jammer.'

Chris and Mike looked at each other.

'A *what?*'

'Sparkman didn't know much about it.' Marauder seemed to be settling into his role as storyteller. 'The datarat did most of the work. Seems like he told him it was a system to trick out some kind of alarm. Very expensive, he said. Iarescu got it given to him specially.'

Chris nodded to himself. 'Uh uh. Mike? Believe me now?'

'Shit.' Mike threw himself to his feet. Marauder twitched, but by then Bryant was at the window, staring out. '*Shit*.'

'You said someone thinks I'm a sellout.' Chris focused on the gang-wit. He had to ask. 'What does that mean? Who told you? The spark-man?'

'Sure. Iarescu was full of it, talking up how the suits were selling each other out. How this guy Faulkner wasn't a team player, he didn't belong and that's how come he was getting greased.'

'Chris, that *could* just be Iarescu reinforcing his own loyalty system. *Look how much better we are than these fucking suits. Fucking each other over at every opportunity. Not like us, we stand together, and I'm the best fucking boss you ever had.* Someone outside Shorn could have got hold of the prox frequencies on the Saab, if they were jacked in at the right level. Lloyd Paul. Nakamura, maybe. Any of them could have bought the information.'

'I don't think so.'

Outside the car, it was getting dark. The buildings of the financial district loomed around them as Mike threaded the BMW through deserted streets towards the Shorn block. Most of the lights in the towers were out, and there was a ghost town hush over the whole place. The emptiness of Sunday dying, like the last day of some cycle of civilisation now reaching its end. Chris felt the chill leaking into him again.

'Why would they do it that way, Mike? It doesn't make sense. Why trust some punk sicario more than one of their own drivers? Comes to another tender, they can field the best they've got against me.'

'Not if they wanted to use that trick with the jammer. Trade Standards authorities'd be all over them like a crack whore. They'd fine them into bankruptcy.'

'Exactly.' Chris shook his head. 'It doesn't pay a major corporation to break the rules for the sake of a single driver. Not when there's no money in it.'

'So maybe it was personal. Mitsue Jones's family or something.'

'Same applies, Mike. They lose the insurance, the pension, the bereavement pay. Fuck it, they go to *jail*. Nakamura would drop them like vomit, and with no corporate protection more than likely Shorn would have them greased just to make an example.'

'If they get caught. And revenge is a powerful—'

'You think I don't fucking know that. I—' Chris got a leash on himself, appalled at what he'd been about to tell the other man. 'You're reaching, Mike. How many families of men you crashed have come after you?'

'None, but—'

'That's right. None. This is the way things get done, Mike. Road-raging is here to stay. No one breaks the rules any more. They test, they probe, they hammer out new road precedent, but *nobody* does this. Nobody goes to the trouble unless there's a hard cash reason. And that means someone inside Shorn.'

'You're thinking Makin?'

'Or Hewitt.'

Bryant shook his head. The Shorn block appeared and he drew to a halt a few metres off the car deck security entry. He leaned his arms on the steering wheel. Stared up at the blank face of the tower.

'Alright.' He sighed. 'Let's assume you're right.'

'Yes, let's.'

'Let's assume the fix was in, like you said, from inside Shorn. That means you were right about Driver Control as well. You know Liz has got contacts with those guys. Maybe I'll give her a call, get her to do me a favour and ask some questions in the right places.'

'What?' Chris looked round, tried to squeeze the sudden pulse of alarm back out of his voice. 'Liz Linshaw? Ah, maybe that's not, I mean, is that a good idea? Involving her?'

'Relax. You could trust Liz with your life.'

'Yeah, but. I thought you and her were, you know. Over.'

Mike grinned. 'That woman? No way. It runs hot and cold, depends on what else is going on in our lives. But it's like gravity. No escape for either one of us. Longer we stay apart, hotter it is when we finally fuck. The last time, she left this bite on my shoulder you wouldn't believe.'

Chris stared hard at the dashboard. 'Yeah? What did Suki have to say about that?'

'Well.' Mike's grin turned conspiratorial. 'You're not going to believe this either, but you know what I did? Went back to the office, smashed myself in the nose with the end of that baseball bat I've got.'

'*What?*'

'Yeah. Fucking agony. Gave myself a serious nosebleed. Dripped it all over my practice gi. Told her I'd snagged a psycho in a sparring session.'

Chris remembered the bruised nose from a few weeks back.

'That's what you told me, too.'

'Well, yeah. Didn't want to force you to lie for me if it ever came up with Suki.' Mike Bryant's expression grew musing. 'You know, if it weren't that I already had Suki and Ariana, I really think Liz might have been the one.'

'You think so, do you?'

Mike nodded sagely. 'Yeah, I do. She's really something, Chris.'

On the Shorn car deck, the Saab stood isolated in the gloom. Anyone else clocking weekend time had gone home for dinner. Chris sat in the car for a long time before he started up. The quiet whined in his ears. Across the deck, a faulty roof light spattered on and off like an obscure distress signal. It felt as if he was waiting for someone.

When he finally powered the Saab up and got out into the streets, it was like driving in a dream. The city slid by on either side of him as if cranked past on rollers. The Saab's interior was a bubble of neurasthenic calm, a safe place he was scared he might not be able to leave easily. The dashboard and wheel, pedals and shift, gave him remote control and a distant, autopilot strength. Options murmured in his ear. Let's go *there*. No, *here*. No. Fuck *going* anywhere, let's just *leave*.

Leave it all behind.

He was almost into the streets of Highgate before the autopilot neurasthenia cut out and he realised this was not the way home.

FILE#4:
CAPITAL VOLATILITY

THIRTY-THREE

Carla was already asleep when he got in. He vaguely remembered she'd told him something about a crack-of-dawn start with Mel's recovery unit on the western periphery. Partnership trials in some structural adjustment consultancy. Chris had never heard of them, but these days that wasn't so unusual. He had a lot less to do with adjustment programmes now he was out of Emerging Markets, and new SAP consulting groups were always springing up, like mushrooms on a manure heap. It wasn't rocket science, after all. Slash public health and education spending, open to foreign capital flows, dynamite local blockages in the legal and labour sectors. Lie about the results, and get the local military to crush inconvenient protest. A trained ape could do it. You could get the paper qualifications by distance learning inside ten weeks. Then all it took was a suit and a driver's licence.

He stood in the bedroom, watching Carla sleep, and was overcome by a wave of almost unbearable tenderness. He pulled the quilt up a little higher around her shoulders and she muttered something without waking. He slipped out, closed the door gently behind him and went downstairs to the study. Behind another closed door, he ran the porn segment of Liz Linshaw and her plastically enhanced playmate.

He sat for an hour, head propped on one hand, trying to sort out what he felt.

He slept badly, twisted by brutal dreams that evaporated in vague traceries of impending menace when he finally woke. Carla was gone, her side of the bed was almost cold, and light was streaming in through half-open curtains. The bedside clock said ten past eight.

'*Fuck.*'

He got out from under the quilt, groped after shirt and trousers and got them on. In the bathroom mirror, he stared at the angry eyes and the stubble, picked up a razor then flung it into the basin and settled for sticking his head under the cold tap. Chilly water trickled around his neck and down his back. He raked it out of his hair, crushed a towel over his head without taking it off the rail and closed his shirt. Slung a tie around his neck. Shoes and cuffs. Wallet and watch. Into the jacket and out the d—

Keys, fuckwit.

He ran back upstairs, couldn't find them on the bedside table. Remembered his vigil in the study, darted in and grabbed them up off the desk. He kicked the Saab backwards out of the driveway, swerved untidily round in the road at the bottom and left rubber on the worn grey asphalt as he took off westward. He made the Elsenham ramp in record time.

Rolling in past junction ten, he checked his watch. Couple of minutes off quarter to nine. *Great. Fucking great.* He put through a call to Barranco at the Hilton. There was no answer from the room. Growing irritation sprouted suddenly into irrational fear. He cut the connection, redialled for the security detail. Someone answered on a yawn.

'Yeah?'

'Faulkner. What happened to Barranco?'

'What's the matter, he not turn up yet?'

Chris felt a spike of ice run him through the heart.

'Turn up where?'

The voice on the other end got suddenly deferential. 'At Shorn, sir. Weren't we supposed to let him go? He took the secure limo. Called Shorn for it to come and get him.'

Foot to the floor, now. Head still fogged. *Think.*

'Who authorised the fucking limo?' he grated.

'I, uh, I can check.'

'You do that. Do it now. And stay on the line.' He summoned a map of the day from memory and tried to place Hernan Echevarria on it. His head refused to cooperate. Breakfast with the partners, or was that Tuesday? Touring Mil-Tac's new smart-mine facility in Crawley? If that was it, he was already out of town, under Mike Bryant's watchful eye. He felt the tension ease a little.

Security came back on line from their room in the Hilton. 'Transit was authorised at partner level,' the voice said, smug with belated relief. 'Louise Hewitt. She said she was surprised you weren't around to cover it.'

'Ah, *shit.*'

'Was there anything else? Sir?'

Chris made a noise in his throat and killed the connection. The Saab barrelled down the approach road to the first underpass.

He was on the raised section that ran across the northern zones when he suddenly remembered where Mike Bryant and Hernan Echevarria were that morning.

He floored it again.

The damage was done.

He knew. Jolting the Saab into a space as close to the lifts as he could get, he knew and wondered why he was still bothering. Riding up alone with the chatty elevator voice for company, he knew and nearly screamed aloud at the waiting. Shouldering past a brace of startled admin assistants on the fifty-second floor, he knew beyond doubt. Staring at the coded entry door to the covert viewing chamber, the nightmarish confirmation of its carelessly ajar angle, he knew. Still, through all the knowing, as he threw the door all the way open and saw Barranco standing there, it hit him like sludge in his guts.

Beyond the glass, Nick Makin and Mike Bryant sat with Hernan Echevarria and another uniform, apparently discussing interrogation training. Their voices strained through into the chamber. A brittle burst of laughter rang so sharp it was almost static.

'Vicente . . .'

Barranco turned the face of a corpse towards him. He was pale beneath his tan, mouth drawn down tight. A vein beat at one temple.

'*Hijos de puta*,' he whispered. 'You—'

In the conference room, Echevarria was nodding sagely.

'Vicente, listen to me—'

He flinched back, went halfway to a karate guard as he saw Barranco's eyes. The Colombian was trembling. He wondered fleetingly what combat skills honed in genuine combat would look like up against his corporate Shotokan training. Barranco looked at him with sick wonder and then turned away. He stood staring down at the desk where someone had left a bound copy of the Echevarria schedule.

'I did not believe,' he said quietly. 'When the assistant told me. Asked me if I was with Hernan Echevarria. If I had got *lost*, and brought me here, smiling, fucking *smiling*. Let me in here to watch you—'

'Vicente, this isn't what it looks like—'

'*It is exactly what it looks like!*' The yell rang in the confines of the chamber. It seemed impossible those beyond the glass wall could not hear. Barranco lashed out with one foot. The desk skidded, spilled schedule, associated discs and papers. A chair fell, caught Mike's baseball bat and sent it rolling.

'Vicente.' In his own ears, Chris could hear the pleading in his voice. 'You must have known Echevarria was still at the table. But he's out now. You're in. Can't you see that?'

The Colombian turned back to face him, crook-handed.

'In,' he hissed. 'Out. What is this, a fucking game to you? What do you have in your veins, Chris Faulkner? What the fuck kind of human being are you?'

Chris licked his lips. 'I'm on your side, Vicente—'

'Side? On my *side*?' Barranco spat on the floor. His voice scaled up

261

again. 'You grinning, fucking whore, don't talk to me about sides. There are no sides for men like you. A friend to murderers,' he gestured at the glass, eyes glistening. 'To torturers, if it pays. You are a fucking *waste*, a soulless gringo *puto*, a *stench*.'

Something ripped open behind Chris's left eye. He felt himself flinch physically with the impact. Red-veined wings billowed upward in his head. The HM file opened for him like a brightly-coloured trap door. He saw helicopters hanging from a tattered-cloud rain-forest sky, whine and clatter of gatlings, whoosh-thump of rockets. Villages in flames, cremated trees, charred bundles scattered across the scorched earth. He heard discordant jail-cell screams spiking a tropical night. A visitation he hadn't had since the death of Edward Quain was there beside him, shouting hoarse in his inner ear.

The bat.

It was in his hand.

The door code. Five tiny queeping touches across the keypad. The glass door hinged back and he erupted into the conference.

'Faulkner, what the *fuck* are you doing?'

Makin, voice almost girlish in shock.

Mike, turning from a side table where he was building drinks.

Echevarria, eyes fixed past Chris on Barranco. His swollen, old man's face mottled and worked as he struggled to his feet. Voice reedy with outrage.

'*This is—*'

Chris hit him. Side on, both hands, full swing with the baseball bat and all he had behind it. Into the dictator's ribs. He heard the bones go, felt the brittle crunch through the bat. Echevarria made a noise like a man choking and slumped against the edge of the table. Backswing, in again. Same spot. The old man shrilled. Mike Bryant waded in. Chris stabbed him handily in the solar plexus with the bat end. Bryant staggered and sat down against the wall, whooping for breath. The other uniform bellowed and tried to get round the table to his boss. He tangled in his own chair and went over backwards. Chris swung again. Echevarria raised an arm. The bat broke it with an audible snap. The old man screamed. Back up, and swing again. He got the face this time. The dictator's nose broke, the bone over one eye caved in. Blood ripped out, spraying warm and wet on his own face and hands. Echevarria went down and lay on the floor, curled foetally and still screaming. Chris spread his stance low and wide, and chopped down as if he was splitting logs. Head and body, an indiscriminate frenzy of blows. He heard hoarse yelling, and it was his own. Blood everywhere, running off the bat, in his eyes. The white glint of exposed bone in the mess at his feet. Choking, bubbling sounds from Echevarria.

The other uniform came flailing round the table at last. Chris, down now to adrenalin-cold clarity, swung about and let him have the bat sideways across the throat with full swing. The man jerked back as if tugged on an invisible string. He hit the floor like an upturned beetle, strangling noisily.

Everything stopped. On the floor, Echevarria made a bubbling sigh and fell silent. A metre and a half off, Nick Makin had finally made it to his feet.

'Faulkner!'

Chris hefted the bat. His face twitched. His voice seemed to come from the bottom of a well, rasping tones unrecognisable in his own ears.

'Back off, Nick. I'll do you, too.'

He heard Mike crawling to his feet. He looked back to the door he'd come in, where Vicente Barranco stood staring at the carnage. Chris wiped some of the blood off his face and grinned dizzily at him. The trembling was starting to set in. He tossed the bat to the floor, next to Echevarria's crumpled form.

'Okay, Vicente,' he said shakily. 'You tell me. Whose fucking side am I on?'

'You know, that wasn't the smartest thing I've ever seen you do.'

Mike Bryant handed him the whisky glass and went back to sit behind his desk. Chris huddled on the sofa in the blanket the paramedics had lent him, still shivering. In front of him on the table, the chess board pieces faced off against each other in the silence. The onyx gleamed.

'Sorry I hit you.'

Mike rubbed at his chest. 'Yeah, with my own fucking bat. Could have done without that as well.'

Chris sipped at the whisky, both hands cupped around the glass as if it was hot coffee. The spirit went down, warming. He shook his head.

'I just lost it, Mike.'

'Yeah, no shit.' Bryant glared at him. 'Think I spotted that one too. Chris, what the fuck was Barranco doing at Shorn unsupervised? You knew we had Echevarria in for budget review today. Why didn't you take Vicente out for a drive or something? Or at least keep him in the Hilton until you could check with me.'

Chris shook his head again. The words limped out of his mouth. 'I was running late. He went out without me.'

'That doesn't explain how he got in here. Who cleared him for the tower?'

'That's what I tried to tell you earlier. Hewitt authorised a limo to bring him here.'

Mike's eyes narrowed. 'Hewitt?'

'Yeah. Louise fucking Hewitt. I'm telling you, she's been gunning for me since the day I walked in here. She wants—'

'Oh, *bullshit*!' Bryant came to his feet, hands braced on the desk. He shouted for the first time since the aftermath in the conference chamber. '*For Christ's sake*! Now is not the fucking time for your bullshit paranoia and hurt feelings. This is *serious*.'

The anger evaporated as fast as it had arrived. He sighed and sat down again. Swivelled the chair away and stared out of the window. One hand opened in Chris's direction. 'Well, I'm open to suggestions. What do *you* think we should tell Notley?'

'Does it matter what we tell him?'

'Fuck, yes.' Mike jerked back round to look at him. What's the matter, you *want* to lose your job or something?'

Chris blinked. 'What?'

'I *said*. Do you want to lose your job?'

'I. But.' Chris gestured helplessly and nearly dropped his whisky. 'Mike, the job's already lost. Isn't it? I mean, you can't just go round clubbing the clients to death, can you.'

'Oh, I'm glad you realise that *now*.'

'I'm. Mike, of course I don't want to lose this job. I like what I do.' Chris made the curious, prickling discovery that he was telling the truth. 'We're just getting somewhere important at last. I'm telling you, Barranco's the one. He can turn the whole NAME around, if we get behind him. He can make it work. He can make us the. What?'

Mike Bryant was watching him narrowly.

'Go on.'

'Mike, I'm good at this. The people stuff. You know that. And after this, I've got Barranco for keeps. We're close now. Really close. This one *matters*.'

'And Cambodia doesn't?'

'That's not what I mean. There's nothing new in Cambodia. They've been down this road at least four times before. Same old song, just a different decade. All we have to do is ride the wave, and make sure the enterprise zones don't catch any damage. The NAME's different. You're looking at a radical restructuring of a regime that's been in place almost since the beginning of the century. How often do you get to do work like that any more?'

Mike said nothing for a while. He seemed to be thinking. Then he nodded and got up from the desk.

'Alright, good. We'll go with that. Radical restructuring. Tone down the stuff about Cambodia, though. *All* our accounts are important, and whatever Sary eventually does or doesn't achieve, we stand to make a lot of money over there. Remember that.'

Raised voices from outside Mike's office. The unmistakable tones of Louise Hewitt arguing with security. Mike made a wry face.

'Here we go,' he said. 'Block and cover. Start talking. And get rid of that fucking blanket, you look like an evicted criminal.'

'What?'

'Something about the NAME, Chris. Relevant detail. Come on, *quick*. Try to sound intelligent.'

'Uh,' Chris groped. 'The, uh, the urban situation's no better. Sure you've got a pretty contented overclass but that's only—'

'The *blanket*.'

He shrugged it off. Got up and started to pace. Voice strengthening as he picked up the thread again. Improvising. 'The thing is, Mike, that business with the students was crucial. Some of those kids were *from* the overclass, okay not many, but with an extended family system like the one you've got in the NAME, pretty much everybody knows someone who—'

Louise Hewitt burst into the office.

'What the fuck have you done, Faulkner?'

He turned to look at her and what struck him like a physical blow was how drop dead gorgeous she looked angry.

He'd always been aware that Hewitt was attractive in a hard, dark fashion, but it wasn't the kind of look that drew him. Too severe, too buttoned up and in the end, *let's be honest here, Chris*, blonde was really what did it for him. Louise Hewitt was manifestly a dark-haired woman in utter control of her own destiny. It didn't help matters that he hated her guts.

Now, with colour burning in her cheeks, her hair in light disarray and her jacket settled with less than perfect attention on her shoulders, he suddenly saw through to the woman beneath. She stood with legs braced slightly apart, as if the fifty-second floor was the deck of a yacht in suddenly choppy waters, hands floating just off her hips like those of a movie gunfighter. The stance was unconsciously sensual, stretching the fabric of her narrow knee-length skirt and highlighting the lines of her hips.

One tiny part of Chris's mind stayed rational enough to register the bizarre perversity of his sexual programming. The rest of him was shit-scared of what was going to happen next.

'Louise,' said Mike Bryant cheerfully. 'There you are. I imagine you've heard, then.'

'Heard? *Heard?*' She advanced into the room, still half-focused on Chris. 'I've just come from the fucking sickbay, Mike. They've got Echevarria on a ventilator. What the *fuck* is going on?'

'Is he likely to die?'

Hewitt pointed her finger. 'I asked you a question, Mike. Spare me the executive deflection techniques.'

'Sorry.' Mike shrugged. 'Force of habit. The Echevarria end of things is played out. He was making the situation unmanageable.'

'*So you beat him to death?*'

'It's unfortunate, but—'

'Un*fortunate?* Are you—'

Chris cleared his throat. 'Louise, Barranco is—'

'You,' she swung on him like combat, 'shut the fuck up. You've done enough damage today.'

Mike Bryant came out from behind his desk, hands lifted, soothing. 'Louise, we had no choice. It was lose Echevarria or lose Barranco. And Barranco is the key to this. He can turn the whole NAME around, if we get behind him. He can make it work.'

Chris just stopped himself staring as he heard his own words coming out of Bryant's mouth. Hewitt looked from one man to the other. Her anger seemed to crank down a notch.

'That's not what Makin says.'

'Well.' Mike gestured. 'That doesn't surprise me. Nick is running scared from his own mistakes. Come on, Louise, you know he's fumbled this one since the outset. Why else did you call me in?'

'Not to do *this*, that's for sure.'

'Look, let's sit down for a moment.' Mike gestured at the sofas around the chess table. 'Come on. There's no point in yelling at each other. It's not an ideal situation, but it is manageable.'

'Is it?' Hewitt raised one immaculate eyebrow. Some of her customary cool seemed to be reasserting itself. 'This I've got to hear.'

They sat. Mike bundled up the paramedic blanket and dumped it casually over the side of the sofa.

'The thing is, Louise, Vicente Barranco's our only shot. Echevarria was on his way out the door to the Americans. He was playing with us. And Barranco's the only viable insurgency alternative. Chris'll tell you. There are no other available choices.'

Hewitt switched her gaze to Chris. 'Well?'

'Yeah.' Chris tried to snap out of his daze at the suddenly civilised turn events had taken. He'd expected by now to be either sitting in a holding cell or clearing out his desk. 'Yeah, it's true. Arbenz is dead or dying of a collapsed immune system. MCH bioware ammunition. And Diaz is either on the run or already caught and we just haven't heard yet, in which case Echevarria's secret police will have tortured him to death by now.'

'There you go.' Mike nodded along. 'Barranco's what we've got, and we nearly didn't have him an hour ago. All we had was Echevarria getting ready to grab the hardware we'd advanced him and then kiss us goodbye and head out for Lloyd Paul or Calders RapCap. And Barranco thinking we'd sold him out. Under the circumstances, I think Chris did the only thing that had any hope of salvaging the situation. Now, at least, we have a chance.'

Hewitt shook her head.

'This has got to go to Notley.'

'I agree. But it can go to Notley as a handled package, or it can go as a mess.'

'It *is* a mess, Mike. Barranco should never have been allowed anywhere near Echevarria in the first place.'

'We all make mistakes, Louise.'

Something in Bryant's tone brought Hewitt round. 'Meaning?'

'Well, you did authorise the limo for Barranco.' Mike was all innocence. 'I mean, sure, you probably assumed that Chris would be here to meet him. And then Chris was at the Hilton instead, so—'

'Chris was fucking late,' said Louise Hewitt delicately.

'Yeah. That was a mistake. The limo was a mistake. Shit, it was my mistake, or Nick's, leaving the viewing-chamber door open. Not to mention the idiot who told Barranco where to find us. You're right, Louise, we have made a mess of this. But there's no percentage for any of us in presenting it that way to Notley. We need to accentuate the positive.'

For a pair of seconds, Hewitt was silent. Chris could almost hear the whine of concentration as she played it through. Then she smiled sourly at both of them and nodded.

'Alright,' she said. 'Let's spin it, shall we.'

THIRTY-FOUR

Echevarria died just before noon, of repeated internal haemorrhaging. He never regained consciousness. Vicente Barranco was there to watch him die. Everybody else was too busy.

They'd been scrambling since Hewitt gave the green light.

'Get his phone records from Brown's,' she flung at them on her way out to find Notley. 'See if he posted any forward calls for this afternoon, and find out if he was checking in with anyone regularly. That way, we'll have some idea of how much time we've got to play with. And start coming up with a disposal plan.'

Chris spent the next hour digging through files on useful terrorists.

Mike Bryant's office became the command post. Chris commandeered the datadown while Mike paced about with his mobile, talking to people. They sent Makin after the phone records. All incoming business got routed down to the forty-ninth floor where junior analysts had orders to shelve it unless there was a NAME connection. In the cleared space it gave them, they built the contingency plan. A Langley shadow unit was hired out of Miami, sent to find and track Echevarria junior. The conference-chamber recordings were isolated from all external dataflow ports, and played back on a stand-alone projector to a grey-haired datafake expert on secondment from Imagicians. The expert tut-tutted like a disappointed schoolmistress, hit replay and started making notes. A stony-faced internal security squad with high-level clearance arrived, courtesy of Louise Hewitt, and Mike sent them to clean up the blood.

Makin called in from Brown's with the phone data. There were no forward calls placed on Echevarria's account.

'Prai*ii*se the Lord,' said Mike, doing Simeon Sands with remarkable good cheer, given the circumstances. He flourished with his free hand. 'There is a *God* because I am *saved*. Good work, Nick. They give you any static down there? Uh-uh. Good. No, but you never know. Bite the hair of the cliché that fed you and all that. What about regular stuff? Uh-uh. Uh-uh. Yeah, well, to be expected, I guess. Yeah, we've got the hounds out in Miami. Yeah, Langley, best we could do at short notice. They're on a tight leash. What? Ah, come on, Nick, this isn't the fucking time for recrimin— Yeah, well I'm sure he knows that too.' He

268

glanced at Chris and rolled his eyes. 'Look Nick, we haven't got the time for this. Pay them off, get copies of everything and get back here.'

He cut off the call, held the mobile away from him and massaged his ear.

'Like a dog with a fucking bone. Blame, blame, blame, like it's going to fucking help now. So what do you reckon, Elaine?'

The datafake expert froze the tape and raked a hand through her silvered hair. On the pastel shaded wall, Chris towered four metres tall, leaning into the swing, face blind with fury.

'Does it need to stand up in court?'

'No. Nothing like that.'

She shrugged. 'So we can fix it. Just tell me what you want.'

'Okay, good. Chris, how you doing?'

Chris nodded at the datadown. 'Got a few possibilities, yeah. But Mike, none of these guys have pulled off a successful bombing in London for years.'

'Yeah, well, they won't have to. All they need do is claim responsibility. There ought to be plenty of the little fuckers up for that. No effort, no risk, instant media coverage. What more could they want?' Mike flicked a finger at the screen. 'What about them? They look ugly enough.'

'No good.' Chris shook his head. 'Christian militants, anti-gay, anti-abortion. No axe to grind. Besides, they're too fucking inept for anyone to believe they could get something like this together.'

'Yeah, but—' Mike's phone queeped in his hand. 'Yeah, Bryant. Uh-uh. Alright, thanks. What about the other one? Uh-uh. Okay, well keep him that way then. No, I don't know how long. Alright. Yes. Goodbye.'

He weighed the phone in his hand and looked pensively at it.

'Echevarria's dead. Just now. Dead and cooling fast. And Nick reckoned he promised to call his son in Miami some time this evening. We're losing our window.'

In the end, they opted for a group of antique revolutionary socialists with a complicated acronym no one was likely to remember very well. The group had enjoyed a sudden resurgence in recent years, drawing disaffected zone youth in a number of European cities, staging the machine-gun assassination of low-level executives and causing big explosions in, or at least in the vicinity of, rather vaguely designated 'globalist strongholds'. They'd managed to kill nearly two dozen people in the last five years, often including their intended targets. They used a wide range of military-grade automatic weapons and explosive devices, acquired mainly through Russian black-market channels and very easy to get hold of. Their justificatory rhetoric was a dense mesh of outmoded Trotskyist sentiment and anti-corporate eco-babble, and it appeared they spent almost as much energy purging the ranks and backbiting as they did killing people. Shorn's infiltration ops wing had labelled them noisy but essentially harmless.

They were perfect.

Mike went to get fitted for a Weblar vest.

Chris was chasing up the hardware, when Jack Notley walked into the office unannounced and stood looking around with the non-chalance of someone on a guided tour. His Susana Ingram jacket was buttoned closed and he held his hands lightly clasped in front of him. He nodded pleasantly at the Imagicians consultant, who'd been back and forth from the imaging studio down the hall with variations on the requested footage and now, in Mike's absence, was packing up her stuff.

'Elaine. Glad to see we're keeping you busy.'

'Wouldn't be here otherwise, Jack.'

'No, I suppose not.' Notley's gaze switched to Chris and he lost his smile. His eyes were unreadable. 'And you. Are you busy as well?'

Chris fought down a tremor. 'I, uh, we're pretty much done here. But I need to check in with Vicente Barranco. He's been—'

'I've had Señor Barranco taken back to his hotel. Elaine, could you give us a few minutes?'

'Sure. I'm done here anyway. I'll come back for this stuff later.'

She slipped out. Chris watched her go with a pang of envy. Notley came round the desk to stand at his shoulder.

'What are you doing?' he asked flatly.

'Hardware profile.' Chris gestured at the screen, scrabbling after composure. He found, oddly, that he was more embarrassed than afraid. 'We've found a group to take the fall for Echevarria. I'm matching most-used weapons against our local inventory. We'll need to use our own people, of course, there's no time for anything else.'

'No. We are pressed for time, aren't we.'

'Yes, although to be honest it's probably better this way.' His throat was dry. 'It, uh, lowers our exposure, and it means we can control the situation.'

'Control, yes.' He felt Notley move behind him, out of his peripheral field of view. It took an effort of will not to twist round in the seat. Now the warm blush of embarrassment was shredding away into cold fear. The senior partner's voice was hypnotically tranquil at his back. It felt like hands laid on his shoulders. 'Remind me, Chris. Why are we in this situation, exactly?'

Chris swallowed. He drew a deep breath.

'Because I fucked up.'

'Yes.' Now Notley had moved back into peripheral view on the left. 'Putting it mildly, you have indeed. Fucked. Up.'

He came round the side of the desk and he had the Nemex levelled. This time, there was no fighting down the tremor. Chris flinched, violently. Notley stared at him. There was nothing in his face at all.

'Is there anything you want to say to me?'

Chris felt the pounding calm of a road duel descend on him. He measured angles, knew he was caught. His replacement Nemex was back in his own office, still not out of the factory wrapping. The desk pinned him. He couldn't rush Notley, and there was nothing on the desktop worth throwing. He was used to making these calculations at combat speed, measuring and acting in the time it took for the Saab to cover a handful of asphalt metres. The immobility and the limping time scale made it unreal, a floating fragment of a dream.

the supermarket swam before his eyes, the painful bang of the gun in his ears, the sudden warm rain of blood

He wondered if

'Well?'

'I think.' Suddenly it was easy. All he had to do was let go. 'I think you're making a big fucking mistake. Echevarria was a bag of pus waiting to burst. All I did was save you the trouble.'

Notley's eyes narrowed. Then, out of nowhere, he lowered the Nemex and tucked it away in his waistband. He shook his head.

'Nice image, that. A bag of pus, waiting to burst. Charming. You need to refine your act, Faulkner.'

He cast about and found a chair, pulled it up to the desk and sat down. Chris gaped at him, still swamped in chemicals by a nervous system expecting to be shot. Notley smiled.

'Tell you a story,' he said comfortably. 'Guy called Webb Ellis. Went to my old school about two hundred years before I did. What does that tell you, incidentally?'

Chris blinked. 'He was rich?'

'Very good. Not wholly accurate, but close enough. Webb Ellis was what, these days, we'd call jacked-in. He had connections. Father died when he was still young, but his mother bootstrapped him up on those connections and come sixteen he was still a student. Among other things, he played a pretty sharp game of football and cricket. And *apparently*, during one of those football games he broke the rules pretty severely, by picking up the ball and running with it. You know what happened to him?'

'Uh. Sent off?'

Notley shook his head. 'No. He got to be famous. They built a whole new game around running with the ball.'

'That's.' Chris frowned. 'Rugby.'

'That's right. In the end they named it after the school. You can see why. Webbellisball would have been a bit of a mouthful. But that's the legend of how rugby got started. There's even a plaque on the wall at the school, commemorating old Webb Ellis and the day he broke the rules. I used to walk past it every day.'

Quiet soaked into the room.

'Is that true?' Chris asked, finally.

Notley grinned. 'No. Probably not. It's just a useful piece of school mythology, graven in stone to resemble the truth. But it is representative, in all likelihood, of what a whole gang of different elite schoolkids were doing at around that time. Breaking the rules, and making up new ones. Later that century, you get a formalised game and creative back-marketing lays it at the door of one man, because that's what people relate to. But the interesting thing is this, Chris. The game was never new. It dates back to Roman times, at least. They'd been playing games just like it for centuries in the streets of villages and towns all over Britain. And you know what? Just around the time Webb Ellis and his friends were making sporting history, the common people were being told, by law and by big uniformed men with sticks and guns, that they weren't allowed to play this game any more. Because, and this is close to a quote, it disturbed the public order and was dangerous. Do you see, Chris, how these things work? How they've always worked?'

Chris said nothing. It wasn't five minutes since this man had held a gun on him. He didn't trust the ice enough to walk on yet.

'Okay.' Notley leaned back in the chair. 'Fast forward a couple of centuries. Here's something you should know. Who made the first competition road kill?'

'Uh, Roberto Sanchez, wasn't it? Calders Chicago partnership challenge, back in, no, wait a minute.' Chris sieved an unexpected chunk of information from the sea of TV junk he'd been letting wash over him in recent months. 'Now they're saying it wasn't Sanchez, it was this guy Rice, real thug from the Washington office. He beat Sanchez to it by about three months or something?'

Notley nodded. He seemed, for a moment, to be lost in thought. 'Yes, they say that. They also say it was Begoña Salas over at IberFondos. That's the feminist revisionist angle, but it holds some water. Salas was cutting edge around then, and she always drove like a fucking maniac. There's another school of thought that says Calders stole the idea from a strategic-thought unit in California. That people like Oco Holdings and the Sacramento Group were already trialing it secretly. You want to know what I remember?'

Once again, the distance behind Notley's look, the sense that most of him was suddenly elsewhere.

'Sure. What?'

Notley smiled gently. 'I remember it being me.'

Fleetingly, Chris recalled his first impression of the senior partner, the day he came to work at Shorn. Like a troll in the elf pastel shades of the interview room. He looked at Notley now, at the brutal crackle of power about the man, shoehorned into the Susana Ingram like too much upper body muscle, and an initial urge to match the partner smile for smile slid abruptly away. His pulse began to pick up slowly.

Notley seemed to shake himself.

'It was a different time, Chris. We're all used to it now, but back then you could smell the change in the air.' He breathed in, deep. 'Fresh, like spilt fuel. Reeking with potential. The domino recessions had come and gone, we'd been bracing ourselves for it all that time, for the worst we could imagine, and it came and went, and we were all still standing. Better than still standing. We'd barely missed a step. A few riots, a few banks out of business, that nuclear nonsense in the Punjab. We *surfed* it, Chris. We rode it out. It was *easy*.'

He paused. He seemed to be waiting for something to fill the gap. Chris hurried to oblige, mesmerised by the intensity coming across the desk at him.

'You still had to drive, though? Right?'

'Oh yes.' A casual gesture. 'The domino *gave* us competitive driving. Hard-edged solution for hard-edged times. But it was still pretty civilised back then, still pretty close to its roots. You know how road-raging started?'

Chris stumbled, wrongfooted. 'What? Uh, yeah, sure. Those formula cars, ones you see on the history channel, looked like little rockets, right? They started getting owned by the same people that made the money. And then, uh, with the roads empty and everything . . .'

He stopped. Notley was shaking his head.

'No?'

'Not really. Well. Yes, sure, you had that dynamic. That's part of it, I suppose. But it all goes back a lot further than that. Back to late last century, the pre-millenial stuff. Stuff my father told me about. Back then some of the harder-nosed firms were already experimenting with conflict incentives for their new recruits. It was an American thing. Eight trainees in a section, sectional office space, and only seven desks.' Notley made a QED motion with both hands. 'So. Get to work last, you had to work on a window ledge. Or beg space from someone with a better alarm clock. Let that happen to you more than a couple of times, you can see how the group dynamic starts to lean. The late guy's the weakest link. So the rest gang up on him. Chimp behaviour. Lend him your desk-space, and *you're* weak, by association. You're making the wrong alliances. So you don't do it. You can't afford to.'

Chris couldn't decide, but he thought he saw a faint distaste rising in Notley's eyes. Or maybe it was just the energy again.

'Now. You transfer that idea, not just for trainees but for everyone. Think about the times. The domino recessions are scratching at the door, you've got to *do* something. Most investment houses and major corporations are waterlogged with top-end personnel. Ex-politicians on sinecure non-executive directorships, useless executive directors shipped around on the old-boy network from golden handshake to golden handshake, headhunted bright young things staying the obligatory two years then shipping out for the next move up on rep vapour and nothing else, because I ask you what, in two years, have you really achieved in a corporate post? And that's just how we were fucking things up at the anglo end of the cultural scale. Elsewhere, you've got fuckwit younger sons and daughters being cut in on Daddy's pie straight out blatantly, because in those cultures who's going to tell Daddy otherwise? And all of this is teetering on the brink as the dominos start to fall. Something has to be done, at a minimum something has to be *seen* to be done. Something harsh.

'So what do you do? You go right back to that eight-trainee section with seven desks, and you extrapolate. Late to work, you don't lose your desk. You lose your job. At a time when you had a dozen identically qualified people for every real executive post, why not? It was as real as any other measure. You sure as hell couldn't depend on sales figures or productivity, not with a global economy in tailspin. And since no one could afford to lose a job at a time like that, you got some pretty fierce driving. Some genuine road rage. But back then,' Notley produced another of his smiles, wintry this time. 'Back then, it was still enough to just *get* there first. Have you got anything to drink in here?'

'Uh.' Chris gestured across at Mike Bryant's brushed steel, fitted drinks cabinet. 'I don't know, it's Mike's office. He'll have some stuff in there.'

'I imagine so.' Notley hulked to his feet and wandered over to the cabinet. 'You want anything?'

'I, uh, I've got to—' He nodded at the datadown. 'You know, finalise. The, uh—'

An impatient wave. 'So finalise it. I'll make you a drink in the meantime. What do you want?'

'Uh, whisky. Laphroaig, if it's there.' He knew Mike kept that around; he produced it with a flourish every time they ended up in the office late. Chess juice, he'd taken to calling it. 'Just a small one. No ice.'

Notley grunted. 'Think I'll join you. I'm a gin man, myself, but I'm buggered if I can see any in here.'

Chris bent to the datadown. Nailed the explosives along with the cheap Russian machine pistols he'd already selected and thumbed it all down to issuing, tagged with Mike's notification code. Notley placed a brimming tumbler at his elbow, swallowed some of his own drink and glanced over the on-screen detail.

'You done? Good. So put on a tolerant expression and listen to the old man's story.' He went back to the seat and hunched forward over his drink. 'Let's see, I was working at Calders UK, I would have been what, twenty-four, twenty-five, something like that. Younger than you, anyway. About as stupid, though.'

No smile with that. Notley took another chunk off his drink.

'I had this promotion playoff. Not the first I'd driven, not even one of the first, but it was the first time I'd thought I might be in trouble. Barnes, the other analyst, was my age, good rep, on the road and off, and he drove this flame-red Ferrari roadster. Very fast, but very light-weight. Nothing like the ones they make now. I was on Audis at the time, no choice back then, it was what I could afford. Good wagon, in its own way, but heavy, very heavy.'

'No change there, then.' For the first time in the conversation, Chris felt he was on familiar ground.

Notley shrugged carelessly. 'Armouring is what they do. Same with BMW. Maybe it's a German thing. Look, I knew if I could just get in front of Barnes, I could hold him off all the way there. Nothing that little roadster could do to my back end that wouldn't straighten out in the shop. Back then it was the rule, everybody knew. You didn't have to kill anyone, you just had to get to work first. So, that was it. Get ahead, stay ahead. Block and cover. And I had Barnes like that, every mile 'til the last. Then the little cunt slipped past me.'

He raised his eyebrows, maybe at his own sudden profanity.

'To this day, I still don't know how he did it. Maybe I was too confident. Maybe it was a gear change I left too loose, do that on a heavy wagon, you know how it is, suddenly you're underpowered.'

Chris nodded. 'Happened to me a couple of times, before I got the Saab.'

'Yeah, you've got that spaced armouring now, right?'

'Yeah.' He wasn't sure if it was the whisky, or just the slide after the hours of tension and the rollercoaster ride of facing Notley's gun, but Chris could feel himself starting to relax. 'Works like a dream. I hear BMW are trying to get past the patents and do their own version.'

'Quite possibly.' Notley stared into his glass. 'But we were talking about Barnes. Barnes, and that last bend on the overhead as you come into the Eleven off-ramp. It used to be a lot narrower then, barely even a double lane. We hit it with Barnes ahead, and I knew there was no way past him. And the way I remember it, there was no Roberto Sanchez making headlines then, no Harry Rice either. Could be it was just still under wraps, all denial and cover-up until Calders decided what needed to go into the shredder and what they could get away with. But I don't remember any precedent, I just remember fury. Fury that I was going to lose by a couple of fucking metres.'

He took another mouthful of whisky and held onto it. Swallowed, grimaced.

'So. I pushed him off. Down a gear, pedal flat, revs up to the red on that last bend. Into the back of that little roadster as if I was giving it one up the arse. It went through the crash barrier like a fist through tissue paper, right over and nose first into the Calders car park. Hit another car and one of the tanks blew, then the other one. By the time I got down there, it was all over. But they showed me security-camera footage later.'

Notley looked up and gave Chris a grin that slipped just a little.

'He tried to get out. *Was* almost out, when the tank went. There was this two-minute sequence of Roger Barnes lit up in flame, still tangled in the belt. He tore free, he was screaming, screaming all the way. It must have been the pain that got him out, finally. He ran about a dozen steps on fire, and then he just seemed to . . . melt. Collapsed and folded over himself there on the asphalt, and stopped screaming.

'And the next time I checked, I was a pin-up. Magazine covers, car ads, introduced to the CEO of Calders in Chicago. It was out in the open all of a sudden. It was precedent, Chris, it was *legal*, and Calders were the new field leaders. Pointing the way out of the domino trap. Turn up with blood on your wheels, or don't turn up at all. It was the new ethic, and we were the new breed. Jack Notley, Roberto Sanchez, transatlantic mirror images of the same new brutalist dynamic. Worth our body weight in platinum.'

Notley seemed to have coasted to a halt. He looked up at Chris again.

'Precedent, Chris. That's what counts. Remember Webb Ellis. In the elite, you don't get punished for breaking the rules. Not if it works. If it works, you get elevated and the rules get changed in your wake. Now. Tell me Barranco is going to work.'

Chris cleared his throat.

'It'll work. The NAME's a special place. We're talking about the radical restructuring of a regime that's been in place almost since the beginning of the century. It's time for that change. Echevarria was just a, a—'

'Yeah, yeah, a bag of pus waiting to be. I remember. Go on.'

276

'With Barranco, we can build a whole new monitored economy. He believes in things, he believes in change, and he can get other people to believe. That's a power we can harness. We can use it to build something out there that no one in this fucking business has ever seen before. Something that gives people—'

It was the whisky. He clamped shut.

Notley watched him, features shrewd and attentive. He nodded, set his whisky on the edge of the desk and got up. Abruptly the Nemex was in his hand again, but gripped flat in his upheld palm.

'Careful,' he said, enunciating the word as if to demonstrate its meaning. 'I like you, Chris. If I didn't, make no mistake about this, they'd be taking you out of here in plastic. I think you've got what not one Shorn exec in ten has got, what we can't ever get enough of round here, and that's the ability to *create*. To build new models in your head without even realising you're doing it. You're a changemaker. And we have to have the guts to let you be what you are, to take the risk that you *may* fuck up, and to trust that you won't. But you need to be clear on what we're about here, Chris.

'Shorn exists to make money. For our shareholders, for our investors and for ourselves. In that order. We're not some last-century, bleeding-heart NGO pissing funds into a hole in the ground. We're part of a global management system *that works*. Forty years ago, we dismantled OPEC. Now the Middle East does as we tell it. Twenty years ago we dismantled China, and East Asia got in line as well. We're down to micro-management and the market now, Chris. We let them fight their mindless little wars, we rewrite the deals and the debt, and it *works*. Conflict Investment is about making global stupidity work for the benefit of Western investors. That's it, that's the whole story. We're not going to lose our grip again like last time.'

'I didn't mean—'

'Yes, you did. And it's natural to feel that way sometimes, above all when you're rubbing up against someone like Barranco. You said it yourself, he can make other people believe. Do you think, just because you wear a suit and drive a car, that you're immune to that?' Notley shook his head. 'Hope is the human condition, Chris. Belief in a better day. For yourself, and if they really get to you, for the whole fucking world. Give Barranco time and he'll have you believing in that. A world where the resources get magically shared out like some global birthday tea for well-behaved kids. A world where everyone's beaming content with a life of hard work, modest rewards and simple pleasures. I mean, *think* about it Chris. Is that a likely outcome? A likely *human* outcome?'

Chris licked his lips, watching the gun. 'No, of course not. I just meant that Barranco is—'

But Notley wasn't listening. He was lit up with the whisky and something else that Chris couldn't get a fix on. Something that looked like desperation but wore an industrial-wattage grin.

'Do you *really think* we can afford to have the developing world *develop?* You think we could have survived the rise of a modern, articulated Chinese superpower twenty years ago? You think we could manage an Africa full of countries run by intelligent, uncorrupted democrats? Or a Latin America run by men like Barranco? Just imagine it for a moment. Whole populations getting educated, and healthy, and secure, and aspirational. Women's rights, for Christ's sake. We can't *afford* these things to happen, Chris. Who's going to soak up our subsidised food surplus for us? Who's going to make our shoes and shirts? Who's going to supply us with cheap labour and cheap raw materials? Who's going to store our nuclear waste, balance out our CO_2 misdemeanours? Who's going to buy our arms?'

He gestured angrily.

'An educated middle class doesn't want to spend eleven hours a day bent over a stitching machine. They aren't going to work the seaweed farms and the paddy fields 'til their feet rot. They aren't going to live next door to a fuel-rod dump and shut up about it. They're going to want prosperity, Chris. Just like they've seen it on TV for the last hundred years. City lives and domestic appliances and electronic game platforms for their kids. And cars. And holidays, and places to go to spend their holidays. And planes to get them there. That's *development*, Chris. Ring any bells? Remember what happened when we told *our* people they couldn't have their cars any more? When we told them they couldn't fly. Why do you think anybody else is going to react any differently out there?'

'I *don't.*' Chris spread his hands. He couldn't work out how things had got back up to this pitch. 'I know this stuff. I don't need convincing, Jack.'

Notley stopped abruptly. He drew a deep breath and let it out, hard. He seemed to become aware of the Nemex in his hand for the first time. He grimaced and put it away.

'My apologies. Shouldn't touch the hard stuff this early.' He picked up his glass from the edge of the desk and drained it. 'So. Getting back to practicalities. You've got the disposal handled.'

'Yeah. We pin the rap on the CE—, I mean CA—, uh—' Chris gave up and gestured at the screen. 'These guys. Mike's down sorting out the limo and the logistics, but basically we're all set.'

'Louise tells me there's another body. Echevarria had an adjutant? Is that correct?'

'Yes. That's right.'

'And I understand you battered him too, in the same rather impulsive fashion you took care of Echevarria.'

'Yes. He, uh, he got in the way.'

Notley raised an eyebrow. 'That was inconsiderate of him. So, is he dead?'

'No, not yet.' Chris hurried into explanation. 'But that's okay. Sickbay have got him on life support, sedated until we're ready. In fact, that's one of the strengths of the way we've set this up. If I can just show you the—'

'No, that won't be necessary. As I said before, this is about having the guts to let you run with the ball.' A faint smile. 'Just like our old friend Webb Ellis. Illustrious company you find yourself in, Chris Faulkner. Maybe they'll put up a plaque for you too, one day.'

THIRTY-FIVE

He caught it on the radio as he drove home. Some general news reporter from the scene, a woman but not—

Cut that out.

'—were shocked by this terrorist attack in the heart of London's West End. I'm standing outside the famous Brown's Hotel, only a few metres from the spot where less than an hour ago visiting head of state, General Hernan Echevarria and his aide, Lieutenant Colonel Rafael Carrasco, were fired upon by masked gunmen. Details aren't clear as yet, but it seems two men opened fire with machine pistols as General Echevarria was brought to his hotel in a Shorn Associates limousine. The general's aide and an unnamed Shorn executive were both hit by machine-gun fire as they exited the vehicle ahead of the general. The terrorists then threw some kind of anti-personnel grenade into the interior and made their escape on a motorcycle. All three men and the driver of the limousine have been rushed to intensive care at—'

He turned it off. He knew the rest. Michael Bryant, thrown miraculously clear of the explosion, recovers from gunshot wounds in hospital. The limo driver, protected by the armoured partition, gets off with burns, abrasions and shock. General Echevarria and his aide go home in body bags, scorched and shell- and shrapnel-riddled beyond useful autopsy. State funeral, full military honours. Rifles volley, women weep. Closed caskets. Everybody in black.

In the highlands, Barranco's insurgents stir to freshly-equipped life.

You're a changemaker, Chris.

He felt it rising in him, stirring like the hard-eyed men and women in the NAME jungle. He saw himself. Embodied purpose, rushing over asphalt in the darkness, carving a path with the Saab's high beams like some furious avatar of the forces he was setting in motion on the other side of the globe. Riding the quiet power of the engine across the night, face masked in the soft backwash of dashboard light. Bulletproof, careproof, unstoppable.

He called Barranco at the Hilton.

'You heard?'

'Yes, it's on the TV. I'm watching it now.' For the first time that

Chris could remember, Barranco's voice sounded unsure. 'You are okay?'

Chris grinned in the dark. 'Yeah, I'm okay.'

'I, would not have believed. Something like that. To do something like that. In front of your colleagues. In your situation. I did not expect—'

'Skip it, Vicente. The old fuck had it coming.'

Barranco was silent. 'Yes. That is true.'

And more silence across the connection, like snow drifting to the ground on the other side of the world. For a beat, Chris could feel the cold out there, like something alive. Like something looking for him.

'I saw him die,' said Barranco.

Chris shook himself. 'I, uh. Good. I hope that was worth something to you, Vicente. I hope you feel. Avenged.'

'Yes. It is good to know he is dead.'

When the Colombian showed no further sign of speaking, Chris cleared his throat.

'Listen, Vicente. Get some rest. With what's coming down in the next few weeks, you're going to need it. Plane's not 'til noon, so sleep in. Lopez'll get you up in plenty of time.'

Silence, sifting down.

'Chris?'

'Yeah. Still here.'

'They aren't going to punish you for this?'

'No one's going to punish me for anything, Vicente. Everything's under control, and you and I are going right to the top of this thing, together. I give it six months before you're in the streets of Bogotá. Now get some sleep. I'll see you tomorrow.'

He waited for a reply. When there was none, he shrugged, cut the connection and gave himself to the driving.

changemaker!

He got off at the Elsenham ramp, and picked up the road east, pushing the Saab faster than was smart. The car jolted in potholes and the engine grew shrill as he dropped gears late on the bends. Trees stood at the roadside, sudden and dusty-looking in the glare of the Saab's lights. When he got to Hawkspur Green, he shed some of his speed, but he was still rolling too fast. The car snarled angrily to itself as he took the turn into the driveway, and he had to lean on the brakes.

He killed the high beams and up ahead in the sudden dark, the house security lights flared to life. He frowned and glanced at the ID broadcast set. A tiny green active light glowed back at him, reassuring as far as it went. He felt tension go stealing along his nerves, wondering if Notley had, after all, gone conservative on him and sent night-callers with silenced guns. The Saab crunched up the winding drive. He reached across to the glove compartment and opened it. The Nemex fell out into his palm, still slightly greasy from the factory wrapping oils. He straightened up again and cleared the last bend.

Carla was waiting for him, wrapped tight in a towelling robe, hair wet and straggling. Backlit by the security system's lamps, she looked like the ghost of a drowned woman. When she bent to his window, face hard-boned from the wet and the lack of make-up, he almost jumped.

He stopped the Saab short and opened the window.

'What are you doing out here? You'll catch your death of cold.'

'Vasvik,' she said. 'He just called.'

The rest of the week snapped by like scenery.

He got Barranco out of the country, got final signatures on the regime term sheets on the way to the airport. Sandwiched between Lopez and Chris in the helicopter, Barranco signed it all like a man under sedation. Chris waved him goodbye from the asphalt.

He dropped in on Mike at the hospital. The other executive had nothing worse than severe bruising across the ribcage from the machine-gun fire, but it seemed politic to keep him in the intensive care unit for a few days at least. There were news crews queuing in the corridor outside, but Shorn security had them managed.

'So now you're a fucking celebrity?'

Mike grinned from a chair beside the bed. There were a couple of small cuts on his face, and his left hand was bandaged. He got up, wincing with the effort.

'You see Liz out there?' he asked.

'No. You expecting her?'

'Never know.' Mike poured himself a drink from a pitcher beside the bed. 'Nah, to be honest, she'd be the last thing I need right now. I'm in enough pain just breathing heavily. You want some of this?'

'What is it?'

'What does it look like? Juice.'

'Maybe later. What happened to your face?'

'Ah.' Mike waved dismissively. 'Did it myself with a broken bottle-neck, beforehand. Good for the media to see a real wound or two, I reckon.'

'And the hand?'

A scowl. 'Sprained my wrist going down on the pavement. Like a fucking idiot. I was trying to keep Carrasco upright for the machine gun, like this. And then dive out of the way, this way, when they tossed in the grenade. It was awkward.'

'Any witnesses?'

Bryant shook his head. 'Monday night, and it's a quiet street, anyway. A couple of people might have looked our way once the firing started maybe, but too late to notice anything odd. There'll be footage from the hotel security cameras, maybe that street scanner we couldn't mask out at the corner of Stafford Street. Elaine's already on it. No problem, she says. Barranco get off okay?'

Back at Shorn, Chris sat in the covert viewing chamber while Nick Makin and Louise Hewitt talked to Francisco Echevarria by uplink. The young man was pale and hollow-eyed, and it was clear he had been crying. From the way he kept looking off to the side, it was also clear he was not alone in the projection room at the other end. Hewitt conveyed smooth corporate sympathies, and encouraged him not to concern himself with contractual details at such a time. Shorn's own principal officer for the NAME account was, in any case, unable to leave hospital for the foreseeable future. There was no sense in rushing into anything. Shorn CI would be very happy to put the whole issue on ice until the family felt more able to deal with the negotiations.

by which time, Barranco will have your worthless nuts in the fucking vice, you and your whole stinking hacienda clan

The sudden violence of his own thoughts took Chris by surprise.

Francisco Echevarria flickered out. They adjourned to Hewitt's office to discuss a tentative calendar for Barranco's revolution.

He went down to the forty-ninth floor to thank the junior execs that had covered the other accounts for them while the crisis was in full swing. He took gifts – cask-strength Islay single malt, Galapagos bourbon ground coffee, single estate Andaluz olive oil – and got into mock sparring sessions with a couple of the known hardcases in the section. No full-force blows, he stayed just the right side of friendly, but he pushed hard and fast and got close-up body contact each time. It wasn't wise to show raw gratitude, untempered by signs of strength. It could get taken the wrong way.

He got back his caseload. Started mechanically through the detail, building back up to operational pitch where necessary.

He took a basket of Indonesian fruit and a crate of Turkish export beer up to the hospital, and found Liz Linshaw sitting on the corner of Mike's bed. Mike sat there grinning like a post-blow job idiot, Liz was a study in her usual off-screen rough-and-ready elegance. She showed Chris exactly the civilised blend of camaraderie and casual flirtation that he remembered from their earliest meetings. The downshift cut him to the quick.

'Listen, Chris,' Mike said finally, waving a hand at the bedside seat Liz wasn't using. 'We've been talking about your no-namer problem. Liz says she could ask around, no problem.'

'That's great.' He looked across at her. 'Thanks.'

'My pleasure.'

It was more than he could handle. He caught himself with a barbed comment about Suki rising to his lips, and called time. He made workload excuses and got out.

As he opened the door to go, Liz Linshaw called him back.

'Chris, I'll be in touch,' she said.

Back at Shorn, he went down to the gym and did an hour of full contact with the autobag.

He worked late.

He took the Nemex to the firing ranges, and emptied two dozen clips into the ghost-dance of holotargets there. The machine scored him high on accuracy and speed, abysmally low on selection. He'd killed too many innocent bystanders.

And then it was Saturday.

It was time.

THIRTY-SIX

There were police trucks gathered at the entrance to the Brundtland. Revolving blue lights slashed the poorly-lit walkways and stair-stacks with monotonous regularity, each touch fleeting and then gone, giving way again to the gloom. Torch beams and bulky armoured figures moved on the exterior walkways. An ampbox blattered across the night.

'Ah *fuck*.' Chris braked the Landrover to a halt.

Carla stared at out at the lights, wide eyed. 'Do you think . . .'

'I don't know. Stay here.'

He left the engine running and climbed down, digging in his pocket for corporate ID, hoping the Nemex didn't show under the jacket. A body-armoured police sergeant noticed the new arrival and detached himself from the knot of figures beside the trucks. He strode across the cracked concrete, torch and sidearm held high.

'You can't come in here.'

Chris held his ID out in the beam of the torch. 'I'm visiting someone. What's going on?'

'Oh.' The sergeant's tone shifted, abruptly conciliatory. He holstered his pistol. 'Sorry, sir. With what you're driving, you know, I didn't realise.'

'Don't worry about it.' Chris manufactured a grin of forbearance. 'Easy mistake to make. My wife's wheels. Sentimental value. So what's going on here?'

'It's drugs, sir. Bathroom edge. A couple of the local gangwits have been bad boys. Exporting their product across the line, dealing in the Kensington catchment. Hanging around the schools and such.' The sergeant grimaced in the torchlight and shook his head. 'Not the first time either, and the community leaders have been warned before, so it's the next step. We've been told to turn up the heat on cases like this. You know how it's done, sir. Break a few doors, break a few heads. Only thing gets through to these animals in the end.'

'Sure. Look, I need to get up to the fifth floor and see my father-in-law. It's quite urgent. Can you do something about that?'

Hesitation. Chris switched on the grin again. Reached carefully into his jacket pocket, well above the Nemex.

'I understand it's trouble you don't need right now, but it is important. I'd be very grateful.'

The torchlight gleamed off the edges of the racked plastic and the
Shorn Associates hololigo on the front card. At the back, the wallet was
stiff with a thick sheaf of cash. The sergeant was looking down at it like
someone afraid of falling.

'Fifth floor?' he said.

'That's right.'

'Just a moment, sir.' He dug out a phone and thumbed it to life.
'Gary? You there? Listen, are we working on five? No? So what's the
nearest? Okay. Thanks.'

He stowed the phone. Chris handed across a slice of currency.

'Should be safe enough to go up there, sir. I'll have a couple of my
men take you up, just to be sure.' He folded the notes into his palm with
an awkwardness that bespoke lack of practice, and looked back at the
Landrover. 'Your wife too?'

'Yeah. Tell the truth, she wants to be here a lot more than I do.'

Their escort took the form of two helmeted, body-armoured uniforms with pump action shotguns and hip-holstered pistols. They
bounded from the rear of the reserve truck like eager dogs when their
names were called. One was white, one black, and neither looked old
enough to be shaving yet. They covered angles in the stairwell with a
kind of self-conscious intensity that on older men might have looked
like professionalism, and once or twice they grinned at each other. The
white kid chewed gum mechanically throughout, and the black kid
appeared to be rapping under his breath. They both seemed to be
enjoying themselves. When the party reached the fifth floor, Chris
gave them a fifty apiece and they clattered back down the stairs with
what sounded like none of the drilled caution they'd exhibited on the
way up.

Carla knocked at the door of fifty-seven. Erik answered, looking
haggard.

'I tried to call. The police—'

'Just talked to them,' said Chris, luxuriating in the advantage. 'It's an
edge bust. Nothing to worry about.'

Erik Nyquist's mouth tightened.

'Yes, I forgot,' he said thinly. 'A different matter when you're a
member of the elite, isn't it. When—'

'Dad!'

'Maybe we could come in,' added Chris.

Nyquist gave him a venomous look, but he stood aside and they filed
through into the lounge. Behind him, Chris heard the door being
locked and bolted. Almost as loud through the cardboard-thin walls of

the lounge, he could hear raised voices from the flat next door, and what sounded like a baby crying. He glanced around the cramped living space, kept an expression of distaste off his face with an effort, and seated himself gingerly in one of the battered armchairs. He looked up as Nyquist followed Carla into the room.

'Getting on with the neighbours okay?' he asked brightly, nodding towards the noise next door. 'Sounds a little below your level of intellectual debate.'

interfering fucking cunt came leaking through the wall.

Erik looked at him stonily. 'He's a dealer. He's probably expecting to have his skull caved in by your stormtroopers out there.'

'No danger of that. Their commander told me they're not working this floor. Want me to go next door and tell him?'

'In those clothes?' Erik sneered. 'He'd probably stab you as soon as look at you.'

'He could try.'

'Oh yes, I forgot. I have a professional killer for a son-in-law.'

Chris rolled his eyes and was on his way to his feet when he caught a glare from Carla that stopped him.

'Dad, that's enough.'

Nyquist looked at his daughter and sighed.

'Alright,' he said. 'Let's get on with this.'

Chris clapped his hands together, pistol-shot loud. The voices next door stopped abruptly.

'Suits me. So where is Vasvik? Hiding in the toilet?'

Carla made an angry gesture at him. Erik moved to a table loaded with bottles and glasses. His voice was toneless with suppressed anger. He picked up a bottle and studied the label intently.

'Perhaps you'd like to act as if you were civilised for a change, Chris. I'm aware that the strain might be too much, but maybe you should try. This man is a guest in my house, and he, in fact everyone in this room, is taking chances for your benefit.'

'*Glem det*, Erik.' Truls Vasvik had appeared in the lounge doorway, scruffily dressed and running stubble. He looked tired. 'Faulkner's here to negotiate, just like me. The only favours he owes are to you for getting involved.'

Chris shook his head. 'You're wrong about that, Vasvik. I'm not here to negotiate. I've told you what I want and it's not negotiable. Simple yes or no will do.'

'Well then.' Vasvik dropped into the other armchair, eyes speculative on Chris's face. 'The answer is yes. UNECT will take you. But I'm afraid there's a catch. A sub-clause, I guess you'd call it.'

Chris looked up at Carla, whose face had gone from tension to

287

relieved delight to puzzlement in as many seconds. He felt a petty, jeering sense of vindication rising in him.

'What sub-clause?' he asked.

'You'll have to wait.' Vasvik was still watching him carefully. 'For the extraction, I mean. We will extract you, and you will be paid what you ask. But we need you in place for another three to six months. Until the Cambodia contract has matured.'

'What the—' Chris stopped himself with an effort of will and worked back to the easy confidence he'd come in with. 'What the fuck do you know about the Cambodia contract, Vasvik?'

'Probably more than you imagine.' The ombudsman made a dismissive gesture. 'But that isn't really the issue—'

'No,' snapped Chris. 'The issue is, you're fucking with me.'

Vasvik smiled faintly. 'I don't believe a time-frame was mentioned at any point. What did you think? I would come here and magic you out with one sweep of my UN wand? These things take time, Chris. You have to wait your turn. For a change.'

Pushing. The realisation seeped into Chris's consciousness, damping down the instinctive anger to an irritated curiosity. *Why's he pushing me?*

The previous meeting in the workshop at Mel's. Vasvik's face, hard with distaste.

Personally, Faulkner, I don't give a shit what happens to you. I think you're scum. The ethical commerce guys would like to hear what you have, that's why I'm here, but I'm not a salesman. I don't have to reel you in to get my name up on some commission board somewhere, and frankly, I have a lot of better things to—

But the ethical commerce guys have sent you back here, haven't they, Vasvik? Chris felt the answer light up in his head like an arcade game. *You warned them not to bite, but they overruled you and they sent you back for me, and now you've got to swallow that shit whole.*

Unless, that is, you can trip me into blowing out the offer of my own accord.

He felt a grin building. The manoeuvring room was immense. And at the back of it all he had Notley's avuncular indulgence spread like dark, protecting wings. He could run Vasvik ragged, grind his bony nose up against his own controllers' orders to acquire Chris Faulkner at asking price, and even if he pushed the ombudsman over the edge and blew it, he could walk away from the wreckage of the deal. *Fuck* 'em if they couldn't take a joke. He'd stay at Shorn.

'Alright.' He grinned. 'Let's talk about Cambodia then.'

The tension in the room eased. Carla seemed to sag slightly with it, and Chris saw how her hand fell on her father's shoulder. Erik reached up and clasped it without looking back from the drink he was building. Neither of them looked at Chris.

'Good,' said Vasvik. 'So. The way we see it at the moment, you've got Khieu Sary on the customary long-leash arrangement, nominally acting in line with the accords you all signed up to, but in actual fact pretty much doing what he feels like. Recruiting from the villages that'll listen to him, burning the ones that won't. Standard terror tactics. My question is, what are you going to do about the enterprise zones?'

Chris shrugged. 'We've got an understanding with him about that whole area. Gentleman's agreement, nothing on paper.'

'I see. Any reason why he should stick to that any more than he's stuck to the Geneva Convention stuff so far?'

'Yeah. If he doesn't, we pull the plug on his mobile cover. Ever tried coordinating a guerrilla war by landline?'

Erik Nyquist leaned over and handed Vasvik a tall glass. There was a conspicuous lack of a drink in his other hand as he turned to look at Chris, and a familiar anger rising on his face.

'Very neat,' said Vasvik thoughtfully.

'Yeah, because that kind of thing *matters*, doesn't it, Chris. Can't have some first-world sportswear manufacturer losing productivity, can we.'

Chris sighed.

'Erik, you still got any of that Ardbeg non-chill filtered I bought you for your birthday?'

'No.'

'Oh. Can I get some of that cheap blended stuff you like, then?'

Erik's right arm twitched at his side. Chris saw the fist knot up. Then Vasvik murmured something in Norwegian, and the older man stopped himself.

'Get your own fucking drink,' he said, and stalked across to the lounge window. The police lights outside pricked the blue in his eyes as he stared downward. Chris shrugged, pulled a face at Vasvik and rose to follow his father in law's advice. Carla turned away from him as he got there. She disappeared into the kitchen, arms wrapped around herself. Chris shrugged again. It was a view he was getting used to. He selected a clean glass and a bottle from the table, poured four inches of something apparently called Clan Scott.

'I don't see where you're going with this, Vasvik,' he said over his shoulder. 'It's standard CI operating procedure. Protect the foreign capital base at all costs. Sary understands that, like all the rest of these toy revolutionaries.'

'And presumably you have informed those with interests in the EZs that this is the state of play.'

'Yeah, sure. Most of them are buying their protection through our reinsurance arm anyway.' Chris sniffed dubiously at the Scotch and took it back to his armchair. 'Why?'

'Did you know that Nakamura are modelling for a military coup against the Cambodian government?'

'No.' Chris swallowed some of his drink and grimaced. Next door the shouting seemed to be starting up again. 'But it doesn't surprise me. With Acropolitic still holding the official advisory angle, it'd be their only chance of carving themselves a slice of the action. Our indesp guys should bring it in before they make any substantial moves.'

'Industrial espionage might give you backroom detail on the models, but it won't help you on the ground. What are you going to do if it looks like Nakamura can get the Cambodian army to do what they want?'

Chris shrugged. 'Call Langley, I suppose. Have the relevant uniforms capped at home.'

At the window, Erik Nyquist made a noise in his throat. Chris glanced across at him.

'Hey, I'm sorry if that upsets your sensibilities, Erik. But this is the way the world is run.'

'Yes. I know that.'

fucking bastard screamed the woman next door. The baby was crying again. Chris frowned into his drink.

'Well, Erik, maybe you'd prefer it if we left these generals with their skulls intact, and then they could roll their tanks out to play in the streets of Phnom Penh and slaughter a few thousand people.'

'The way Khieu Sary is going to, you mean?'

'That's not the way we've modelled it.'

'Oh, *good*.'

Again, Vasvik said something in Norwegian, and Erik looked back out at the night. He seemed to see something of interest down below.

'Your friends are leaving,' he said flatly. 'That's obviously enough law enforcement for this month. We must have used up our credit.'

'Hey, not *my* friends, Erik.' Chris grinned at the older man. 'I just paid them off, that's all. Just because I give someone money, doesn't mean I like them. You should know that.'

'The *point*,' said Vasvik sharply, 'is that we would like you to remain in position until the Nakamura move is completed one way or another. The Cambodian EZs are under investigation—'

Chris hissed through his teeth. 'Yeah, so what else is new. Don't tell me you're actually getting ready to take someone to that joke court of yours.'

Something smashed against the wall in the next flat. The male voice was back, competing for air time with the woman. The baby's crying scaled up a couple of notches, maybe in an attempt to be heard over all the yelling. Chris raised an eyebrow and drank some more Clan Scott.

'We need inside information from *after* any move by the Cambodian military.' For all the change in Vasvik's voice, the fight going on next door could have been on TV. 'I don't want to disclose details but if we don't have clear data then a number of the people we've got our eye on will be able to use the confusion of the coup to muddy the waters over their own actions. They'll get through the reasonable doubt loophole and they'll walk. We'll lose the whole case.'

'Don't you usually?'

cunt, cunt, cunt screamed the guy next door. *Fucking CUNT*

A blow, and someone falling. A broken shriek.

The baby, wailing.

Carla came out of the kitchen, as if fired from a gun.

'Dad, what the fuck is he doing to—'

'I know.' Erik came to take his daughter's hands. He looked suddenly very old. 'It's, he's. It happens a lot. There's nothing you can—'

Vasvik stared into the middle distance with no more emotion than a cat.

Another shriek. A meaty thump. Chris stared around and coughed out a laugh.

'You guys are fucking hysterical, you know that. Erik, with your fucking *writing*, and the fucking ombudsman here. All going to change the fucking world for the better.' Suddenly he was yelling himself. '*Look at yourselves*. You're fucking *paralysed*, all of you.'

Something hit the wall, big enough to be a body. Blows followed, regular, spaced. Chanting.

you cunt, like that? you cunt, like that? you fucking like that cunt?

He was in motion, and it was like the Saab ride home all over again. Embodied purpose, unstoppable. He went out, along the tiny entry hall, out the front door, left, along to the next door. He kicked it in. Cheap wood splintered in the frame, the door flew back. Slammed into the wall, rebounded. He kicked again and erupted into the space beyond, through the hall and into the lounge.

They'd heard him come in. The woman was sprawled across the carpet, dressed in a short, moth-eaten, grey towelling robe and moving weakly like an injured soldier trying to crawl to cover. She was bleeding from the mouth. Below the hem of the robe, her thighs were mottled with old bruises. The baby was in a plastic carry chair, marooned atop a cheap entertainment stack near the kitchen door, mouth open wide as if in surprise. The father was turning, garish purple shellsuit bottoms and a red sleeveless T-shirt tight across a boxer's physique. MEAT THE RICH was inked across his chest in white capitals stretched wide. His eyes were defocused with fury and his fists were clenched. Blood on the knuckles of the right hand.

'You're making too much noise,' said Chris.

'What?' The man blinked. The lack of uniform registered. Maybe the cut of Chris's clothes too. 'Fuck are you doing in my house, cunt? You looking for a fucking fight?'

'Yeah.'

Another blink. 'You fucking *what*?'

'Yeah. I'm looking for a fight.'

For some reason, the answer seemed to stall the other man. Chris, who'd been worried about the baby, used the moment to take two neat steps sideways and give himself a clear field of fire. The other man gaped as if the executive in front of him had just done a pirouette. Chris cleared the Nemex and pointed the weapon in a single fluid move that he reckoned Louise Hewitt would have been proud of. The man gaped some more.

'Never mind.'

Bang

Chris shot as low down the thigh as he trusted himself to hit. The target screamed and collapsed, clutching at his leg. Chris reversed his grip on the gun, stepped in close and clubbed the man hard, sideways across the head. He went down, eyes rolled up. The woman on the floor shrieked and scuttled backwards into a corner.

'It's okay,' Chris said absently. 'I won't hurt you.'

'*Chris!*'

Carla stood in the doorway, face ashen. Staring at him.

'It's okay, he's not dead.' Chris thought about it for a moment, then put the Nemex to the man's knee, just below the first wound, and pulled the trigger. The man jerked with the impact, but didn't come round. Carla and the other woman's screams seemed to blend in the wake of the shot. The baby started wailing again. He looked across at the woman, whose left eye was rapidly swelling closed. Thought some more. He placed the Nemex muzzle on the man's right elbow—

'Chris – *don't*.'

—and pulled the trigger again.

Carla jerked back as if it was her he'd shot.

He put the Nemex away and crossed to where the woman was crouched in the corner. He took out his wallet and gave her about half of the cash he was carrying.

'Listen,' he said, pressing it into her hand. 'Pay attention, listen. This is for you. Call him an ambulance if you like, but don't let them take him in. They'll try to. It's what they're paid to do, that's how they make the big money. Don't let them. They'll dress the wounds here if you ask them to. It's cheaper and it's all he needs. He's not in any danger. He won't die. Do you understand?'

She just stared at him.

He sighed and folded her hand around the money. She flinched as he touched her. He sighed again and got up. Looked at the baby. The mess around him. He shook his head and turned away.

They were all there now. Erik Nyquist, features tight with disgust. Carla, hugged in her father's arms, face buried in his chest. Vasvik silent and impassive.

'What?' he asked them. '*What?*'

THIRTY-SEVEN

The Landrover jolted over another pothole, hard and too fast. Coins and other dashboard detritus cascaded onto the floor. Chris swayed in the grip of his seatbelt. He glanced across at Carla.

'You want to slow down a bit?'

She looked back at him, then away. Said nothing. The Landrover bounced again. High beams splashed jerkily across the curve of the unlit street and a ravaged concrete structure that looked as if it might once have been the back end of an arena. Dead street lamps stood at intervals, most of them remarkably intact and upright.

'For Christ's sake, Carla, this is the zones. You really want to have to stop and change a flat tyre around here?'

She shrugged. 'You've got a gun. I'm sure you can cripple anyone who gives us a hard time.'

'Oh, for fuck's sake.'

They left the curving street and swung left past decayed low-rise housing and steel-shuttered frontages. The usual graffiti leered from the walls, incoherent tribal rage and abstract flashing that looked like stretched purple and white skulls. Carla stared ahead, tight-lipped. Chris felt his post-fight mellowness charring at the edges.

'Hey, perhaps you'd rather he'd beaten her to death while we all sat there and listened to it. Good training for my future in the ombudsmen. Observe, take notes and never, *never* fucking intervene in anything.'

No response.

'Your father lives next door to that every fucking day of his life, Carla. And he does *nothing*. Worse than nothing. He just shakes his fucking head and writes his agonised social commentary and he feeds it to people who'll never know the realities of the situations he describes, and *they* all shake their heads and do nothing. And next door, a thug goes on beating his wife to pulp.'

'My father's a man in his sixties. Did you see the size of that piece of shit?'

'Yeah. That's why I shot him.'

'*That's no solution!*'

'I don't know – it seemed to slow him down.'

'And what about when he recovers, Chris? When he's back on his feet and twice as angry as he ever was.'

'You're saying I should have killed him?'

'*This isn't fucking funny!*'

Chris twisted round to face her. 'No, you're right Carla, it isn't. It's sick. You're trying to get me, out of some twisted sense of moral outrage, to quit my job at Shorn and go work for men like Vasvik. And you saw how concerned *he* was back there. What a moral stand the fucking ombudsmen are prepared to take in the face of injustice.'

'He wasn't there for that, Chris.'

'Neither was I, Carla. But I *did* something about it. Just like I'm going to do something in the NAME. Jesus, you think you can go through this life with your pristine ideals, taking notes and trusting some fuckwit UN judge to make everyone play nice. You think—'

The Landrover leaned abruptly on its suspension. The road swung away in the high beams, replaced by the cross-hatching of an empty parking area. An abandoned supermarket loomed up ahead, facades smashed in and boarded up in about equal measures. There seemed to be a white tubular metal reindeer riveted to the roof, face turned blankly to greet the shoppers in their cars. Vague, tangled debris that had once presumably been a sleigh trailed from the animal's rear and spilled down the roof as far as the sagging gutters. For one bizarre moment, the image reversed for Chris and he saw an amorphous tentacled creature dragging the reindeer down to its death.

Carla braked them to a halt in the middle of the car park.

For a moment, they both sat staring out at the mall front. Then she turned to look at him.

'What's happened to you, Chris?' she whispered.

'Oh, *Christ*, Carla—'

'I.' She gestured convulsively. 'I don't. Recognise you any more. I don't know who you are any more. Who the fuck are you, Chris?'

'Don't be stupid.'

'No, I mean it. You're angry all the time, *furious* all the time, and now you carry that gun around with you. When you started at Shorn, you told me about the guns, and you laughed about it. Do you remember that? You made fun of it. You made fun of the whole place, just like you used to at HM. Now you barely laugh at anything. I don't know how to talk to you any more, I'm scared you're going to just snap and start yelling at me.'

'Keep on like this,' he said grimly, 'and guess what, I'll probably snap and start yelling at you. And no doubt it'll be *my fucking fault again.*'

She flinched.

'You want to know who I am, Carla?' He was leaning across the Landrover towards her, in her face. 'You *really* want to know? I'm your fucking meal ticket. Just like I always have been. Need new clothes? Need tickets to Norway? Need a handout for Daddy? Need to move out of the city and live somewhere nicer? Hey, that's okay. Chris has got a good job, he'll pay for it all. He doesn't ask much, just keep the car clean and the odd blow job. *It's a fucking bargain, girl!*'

The words seemed to do something coming out. He felt tearing, somewhere indefinable. He felt dizzy, suddenly weak in the numb quiet that swallowed up what he'd said. He propped himself back away from her and sat waiting, not sure what for.

The silence hummed.

'Get out,' she said.

She hadn't raised her voice. She didn't look at him. She hit the central locking console and his door cracked open.

'You'd better be sure about—'

'I warned you before, Chris. You called me a whore once. You don't get to do it twice. Get out.'

He looked out at the deserted parking area, the darkness beyond the Landrover's lights. He smiled thinly.

'Sure,' he said. 'Why not. Been coming to this for long enough.'

He shouldered the door fully open and jumped down. The night air was warm and comfortable, edged with a slight breeze. It was easy enough to forget where you were. He checked he still had the Nemex in its holster, his wallet in the jacket pocket, still thick with cash.

'See you then, Carla.'

Her head jerked round suddenly. He met her eyes, saw what was in them and ignored it.

'I'll be at the office. Call me if the bills need paying, huh?'

'Chris—'

He slammed the door on it.

He strode away without looking back, aiming only to get beyond easy hailing distance. Behind him, he heard the Landrover put in gear and moving. He wondered briefly if she'd come after him at kerb-crawl speed across the car park, and what, in that ridiculous scenario, he would do. Then the high beams washed once over him and fled left, away across the white boxed acreage of the parking area. The engine lifted through the gears as she picked up speed.

He felt a single stab of worry, that she might not be safe getting home on her own. He grimaced and slammed a door on that as well.

Then she was gone. He turned, finally, to look, and was in time to catch the tail lights of the Landrover disappearing amidst the low-rise huddle of housing on the other side of the car park. A few moments later the engine noise faded into the vehicle-free stillness of night in the zones.

He stood for a while, trying to get his bearings, geographical and emotional, but it was all utterly unfamiliar. There was nothing recognisable on the skyline in any direction. The supermarket faced him with its wrecked frontages, and he felt a sudden insane desire to lever loose some of the boarding, use the butt of the Nemex to do it, and slip inside, looking for—

He shivered. The dream marched through his head in neon-lit pulses.

sudden warm rain of blood
falling

He shook his head, hard. Turned his back on the facade. Then he picked an angle across the car park at random and started walking.

Up on the roof, the tube metal reindeer watched him go through eyes empty of anything except the cool evening wind.

Saturday night, Sunday morning. The cordoned zones.

He'd expected trouble, had even, with some of the same twisted joy that had driven his actions at the Brundtland, been looking forward to it. The Nemex was a grab away beneath his jacket. His hands were Shotokan-toughened and itchy with the desire to do damage. Worst-case scenario, his mobile would get him a police escort out, should he really need it.

Rather coldly, he knew he'd have to be literally fighting for his life before he'd make that call.

Anything less, he'd never live it down.

He'd expected trouble, but there was nothing worthy of the name.

He walked for a while through anonymous, poorly-lit estates, emerging once or twice onto main thoroughfares to take his bearings from scarred and vandalised road signs and then plunging back in, heading what he estimated was east. TV light flickered and glowed in windows, game-show noise escaped through the cheap glazing. Occasionally figures moved within. Outside, he saw children perched on walls in the gloom, sharing cigarettes, two-litre plastic bottles and crudely home-made solvent pipes. The first set he ran across spotted the clothes and came jeering towards him. He drew the Nemex and met their eyes, and they backed off, muttering. He kept the gun where it could be seen after that, and the other groups just watched him pass with bleak calculation. Whispered invective slithered in his wake.

Eventually, he came out onto a main road that looked as if it might run due east. Between the buildings on his left he thought he could make out the vaulted march of the M40 inrun converging from the north, which suggested he was somewhere near Ealing. Or Greenford, if he'd miscalculated how far out Carla had dumped him. Or Alperton. Or

Or you're lost, Chris.

Fuck it, you don't really know this part of town, so stop pretending you do. Just keep moving. Pretty soon the sun's got to come up, and then you'll damn well know if you're heading east or not.

Keep moving. It had to be better than thinking.

He started to see signs of nightlife. Clubs and arcades at intervals along the street, in various stages of turnout. Junk food carry-outs, most of them little more than white-neon-blasted alcoves in the brickwork. The low-intensity stink of cheap meat and stale alcohol, laced once or twice with acid spikes of vomit. Little knots of people in the street, eating and drinking, shouting at each other. Turning to stare at him as he passed.

It couldn't be helped. He lengthened his stride, kept the Nemex lowered but clearly in view. Kept to the centre of the street.

In theory, he could have tried to call a cab. He had landmarks now, identifiable club frontages and, if he was prepared to look hard enough in the gloom, street name plaques. In practice, it was probably a waste of time. The companies his mobile knew numbers for mostly wouldn't come more than a few hundred metres the wrong side of the cordons, especially at this time of night. And those few that would tended to follow an esoteric driver's mythology on exactly which streets were safe to pick up from. Get the wrong configuration in this tarot of zone codes, and you could wait all night. Hearing a location they didn't like – *better yet hearing some idiot raving about the corner of Old Something Smudged street, some nameless club and a pink neon rabbit with tits and a top hat* – individual drivers were going to chortle grimly, ignore the controller and shelve the fare. There just wasn't enough zone custom to push things the other way. You went to the zones, you drove. Or you walked home.

He caught eyes, made no attempt to look away. He remembered Mike's demeanour on their previous expeditions to the zones, and aped it.

Be who you are, and fuck 'em if they don't like it.

The gun helped.

No one wanted to push it any further than a curled lip. No one came close. No one said anything.

Outside one of the clubs, two crack whores broke his run of luck. They registered the clothes and stumbled across the road towards him like kids wading into cold water on a shingle beach. Their bare legs worked as if badly jointed, their feet were wrenched on ludicrous stiletto heels. They wore push-up bras and black mesh microskirts cinched savagely tight. Their make-up was sweat-streaked and caked, and their eyes looked bruised half shut. One was skinnier than the other, but otherwise the pre-dawn whore's makeover rendered them uniform, wiped difference away.

They were all of fourteen years old.

'You want to get sucked?' asked the skinny one.

'You got a place we can go?' The other was clearly the brains of the outfit, the forward thinker.

Chris shook his head. 'Go home.'

'Don't be harsh, baby. Just want to do you good.' The skinny girl amplified her sales pitch with a finger-licking display. She stuck the wet finger inside one cup of her barely necessary bra and rubbed it back and forth with a fixed little smile. Chris flinched.

'I said, go home.' He raised the Nemex where they couldn't miss it. 'You don't want anything to do with me.'

'Baby, that's a *big* gun you got,' said the skinny girl.

'You want to put it somewhere warm?'

Chris fled.

He came through the westward cordons at Holland Park, an hour before dawn. The checkpoint detail gave him some strange looks, but they said nothing and once his Shorn card swiped clear, they called him a cab. He stood outside the cabin while he waited for it to arrive, staring back across the barriers the way he'd come.

His mobile queeped. He looked at it, saw it was Carla and turned it off.

The cab arrived.

He had the driver take him to work.

THIRTY-EIGHT

This early on a Sunday, the Shorn block was in darkness above the mezzanine level and the shutdown locks were still in place. He buzzed security, and they let him in without comment or visible surprise. He supposed, rather bitterly, that it couldn't be entirely unheard of for a Shorn exec to come in before dawn at the weekend.

He thought briefly about grabbing a few hours sleep in the hospitality suites, then dismissed the idea out of hand. Outside, it was already getting light. He wouldn't sleep unaided now. Instead, he rode the lift all the way up to the fifty-third floor, made his way through the cosy dimness of corridors lit at standby wattage and let himself into his office.

On his desk, the phone was already flashing a message light.

He checked it, saw it was from Carla and wiped it. He stood afterwards with his finger on the stud for a while, reached once for the receiver but never made it. Reached for the lighting control on the datadown but changed his mind. The grey pre-dawn quiet the office was steeped in had an oddly comforting quality, like a childhood hiding place. Like a pillow under his cheek and a clock in front of his face showing a good solid hour before alarm time. Without the lights, he was in limbo, a comfortable state in which decisions did not have to be made, in which you didn't have to move forward any more. The sort of state that just couldn't last, but while it did—

He muted the phone's ring tone, went to the built-in cupboards by the door and took down a blanket. Crossing to the sofa-and-coffee-table island in the corner of the office, he shucked his jacket, shoulder holster and shoes and then lowered himself onto the sofa. Then he covered himself with the blanket and lay staring at the white textured ceiling, waiting for the slow creep of morning to soak across it.

Back down at reception, the younger of the two security guards made bladder excuses and left his colleague while he went up to the mezzanine. He pushed through the swing doors of the toilets, locked himself in a cubicle and took out his phone.

He hesitated for a moment, then grimaced and punched out a number.

The phone purred beside a wide, grey-sheeted bed in a space lit by hooded blue softs. A massive picture window in one wall was polarised to dark. On a table under the sill, a chess set of ornate figurines stood next to a screen that displayed the state of play in silver, black and blue. Grecian-effect sculpture stood around the room on plinths in the shadows. Beneath the sheets, the curves of two bodies moved against each other as the ringing tone penetrated layers of sleep. Louise Hewitt poked her head up, reached for the receiver and held it to her ear. She glared balefully at the time display beside the phone.

'This had better be fucking important.'

She listened to the hastily apologetic voice at the other end, and her eyes opened wide. She twisted, struggled free of the sheet and propped herself up on one elbow.

'No, you were right to call me. Yes, I did say that. Yes, it is unusual, I agree. Of course. No, I won't forget this. Thank you.'

She cradled the receiver and turned over onto her back. Her gaze was dreamy on the blue-tinged ceiling, her tone thoughtful.

'Chris just rolled into work on his own. In a cab. Four-thirty on a Sunday morning. Looks like he's been up all night.'

The slim form beside her stirred fully awake.

Chris was dreaming about the supermarket again, but this time he was watching the whole scene from outside, and the car park was insanely, impossibly full of cars. They were *everywhere*, every colour under the sun, like spilled sweets, and all in motion, cruising and parking and reversing out like some immense robotic ballet, and *he couldn't get through them*. Each time he took a step towards the supermarket and the people in its brilliantly-lit interior, a car rolled into his path and stopped with a short squeak of brakes. He had to go round, he had to go round, and his time was running out. The people inside didn't know. They were shopping in anaesthetised warmth and content and they had no way of knowing what was coming.

Up on the roof, tube metal groaned and clanked in protest as the reindeer shook its head.

And the cars, he suddenly saw, were all empty. There were no shoppers in them, no one driving, no one loading, no one anywhere. Everybody was inside. Shopping. *Fucking* shopping.

He made it to the doors and tried to open them but they were closed up with impact plastic boarding and metres of heavy steel chain. He tried banging on the windows, shouting, but no one heard him.

The shots, when they came, rippled the glass under his hands. And as always, they drilled into his ear like something physical.

301

He yelped and woke up, fists clenched under his chin.

For a moment, he cringed there, curled defensively at one end of the sofa. He'd twisted the blanket up in his sleep and now it barely covered half his body. He blinked hard a couple of times, breathed out and sat up. Dawn had come and gone while he slept, and the office was full of bright sunlight.

He got up from the sofa and found his shoes. Bending to put them on, he felt his head throbbing. He'd drowsed himself into a low-grade headache. He shambled to the desk and opened drawers with myopic clumsiness, looking for painkillers. The phone flashed at one corner of his vision. He fumbled a snarl and checked numbers on the piled up messages. Carla, Carla, Carla, fucking Carla—

And Liz Linshaw.

He stopped dead. The call had come in an hour ago. He grabbed a foil of speed delivery codeine tabs out of an open drawer and hit 'play'.

'Chris, I tried you at home but your wife didn't know where you were.' A wry curl to the voice – he could see the faint smile that went with it. 'She, uh, she wasn't too helpful but I got the impression you might be coming into work today. So listen, there's a breakfast bar in India Street called *Break Point*. I'm meeting someone there at eight-thirty. I think you might want to be there too.'

He checked his watch. Eight-twenty.

Jacket, Nemex. He chewed up the codeine tabs on his way down in the lift, swallowed the powder and went out hurriedly into the sun.

It took him a little longer than he expected to find India Street. He remembered the breakfast bar from a damage limitation strategy meeting he'd had there once when he still worked at Hammett McColl. But because he associated the place with the reinsurance brokers at the meeting, he misremembered the address and found himself in an alley off Fenchurch Street with the wrong name. He cast about for a couple of minutes, blurry with the onset of the codeine, before the mistake dawned on him. Working off the new memory, he plotted a vague eastward course and set out again through the tangle of deserted streets.

He was walking north up the glass-walled canyon curve of Crutched Friars, when someone yelled his name.

'*Faulkner!*'

The word echoed off the enclosing steel and glass walls, bounced away down the curve of the canyon. Chris jerked around, sludgily aware he was in trouble. About twenty metres away, blocking his way to the right turn into India Street, five figures stood spread out across the width of the road. All five wore black ski-masks, all five hefted weapons that to his untutored eye looked like shotguns. They were faced off against him in the ludicrous cliché stance of a Western gunfight, and despite it all, despite the abrupt knowledge of his own rapidly approaching death, Chris felt a smirk creep out across his face.

'You what?'

Maybe it was the codeine. He laughed out loud. Shouted it.

'You fucking *what*?'

The men facing him shifted, apparently discomforted. They glanced inward to the figure at the centre. The man took a step forward. Hands pumped the shotgun's action. The *clack-clack* echoed along the street.

'Go foah it, Faulkner.'

The knowledge hit Chris like cold water. He opened his mouth to yell the name, knew he would be shot before he could get it out.

'*Just* a minute.'

Everyone looked round at the new voice. Mike Bryant stood at the mouth of a side alley about ten metres behind Chris, panting slightly. He raised his left hand, right floating close to his belt. Gripped in the upraised fist was a thick wad of currency.

Makin faltered behind his mask. The shotgun lowered a couple of degrees.

'This has got nothing to do with you,' he called.

'Oh, but it does.' Mike ambled out of the alley and drifted up the street until he was lined up beside Chris. There was a thin beading of sweat across his brow, and Chris remembered he couldn't be more than a day out of the hospital. He still held the wad of cash before him like a weapon. 'You take down one Shorn exec in the street, where's it going to end? Eh, *Nick*? You're breaking the fucking rules, man.'

And out of the corner of his mouth, he muttered to Chris.

'You carrying?'

'Yeah, I'm carrying.'

'Loaded this time?'

Chris nodded tautly. A surge of adrenalin punched through the codeine vagueness, a savage pleasure at the comradeship in the man at his side and the will to do harm together.

'Good to know. Follow my lead, this is going to go fast.'

'We only want Faulkner,' shouted Makin.

Mike grinned and raised his voice again. 'That's too bad, Nick, because you got me too.' It was the bright, energetic tone Chris had last heard when Bryant crippled and blinded Griff Dixon in his own living room. 'And before we start, gentlemen, just look at tonight's wonderful prizes.'

He held up the fistful of bank notes again. His voice resonated in the steel canyon acoustics, loud and game-show fruity.

'For the winners! Twenty thousand euros, in cash! Lay down your weapons and walk away with it all! Tonight! Or, take the gamble, lose and die! Ladies and gentlemen, you decide!'

He hurled the money up and outward. It was bundled together with a thick metallic band that glinted as it turned end over end, high in the bright morning air.

'Now,' he snapped.

After that, it all seemed to be happening on freeze-frame advance.

Chris tugged out the Nemex. It felt appallingly heavy in his hand, appallingly slow to bring round and point.

Beside him, Mike Bryant was already firing.

Makin's contingent were still staring up at the money. Mike's first slug took the man on Makin's right under his back-tilted chin, tore through his neck and dropped him in a shower of arterial blood.

The remaining four scattered across the perspectives of the street.

Chris held the Nemex out, memories of a hundred shooting-gallery hours like iron tracery in his right arm. He squeezed the trigger, felt the kick. Squeezed again. One of the men ahead of him staggered. Hard to see blood against the dark canvas clothes. He squeezed again. The man folded forward and collapsed on his face in the street.

A shotgun boomed.

He pointed and fired at Makin. Missed. Out of peripheral vision, he saw Mike Bryant stalking forward, face fixed in a grin, Nemex extended, shooting in an arc. Another of Makin's men went down, clutching at his thigh.

Another shotgun blast. Chris felt a thin stinging of pellets across his ribs. He spotted Makin, pumping another shell in. He yelled and ran towards him, firing wildly. Makin saw him coming and took aim.

Another figure stumbled into Makin's path, shooting across the street at Mike. The two men tangled. Chris shot indiscriminately into them both.

Makin got clear, raised the shotgun again. There seemed to be something wrong with his arm.

Chris emptied the Nemex into him. The gun locked back, breech open on the last shot.

And it was over.

The echoes rolled away, like trucks moving off down the street. Chris stood over Nick Makin and watched as he stopped breathing. Off to his left, Mike Bryant walked up to the shotgunner he'd hit in the thigh. The injured man flopped about weakly. Blood was leaking in astonishing quantities from his twisted leg. Beneath the mask, his head shifted back and forth between Chris and Mike like a trapped animal's. He was making a panicked moaning noise.

'Look, you're going to bleed to death anyway,' Mike told him.

The Nemex shell punched him flat. The ski-masked head jerked about with the impact. A new rivulet of blood groped out across the asphalt from the torn wool and gore of the exit wound. Mike knelt and checked his handiwork, then looked up at Chris and grinned.

'Five to two, eh. Not bad for a couple of suits.'

Chris shook his head numbly. The Nemex hung at the end of his arm like a dumb-bell weight. He unlocked the opened breech, put the weapon away, fumbling with the holster. Post-drive shakes, setting in.

'This is nice.' Mike picked up the dead man's shotgun and hefted it with approval. 'Remington tactical pump. Fancy a souvenir?'

Chris said nothing. Bryant got up, tucked the shotgun casually under his arm. ''s okay, I'll talk to the police, get one for both of us out of evidence, when they've finished with it. Something to show to your grandchildren.' He shook his head, talking a little fast with the adrenalin crash. 'Fucking unbelievable, huh? Like something off a game platform. Ah. See you got Makin pretty good then?'

'Yeah.' Chris looked incuriously at where the other exec lay, still masked. Up close, you could see the wounds in his chest and belly. His whole body was drenched with the blood. 'Dead.'

Mike looked around judiciously.

'I think they all are. Oh, wait a minute.' He crossed to the man Chris had hit when he tangled with Makin. He crouched and put two fingers to the man's neck, shrugged. 'On his way out, I reckon. Still.'

He got up and pointed the Nemex down at the man's masked face. He was already turning away as he pulled the trigger.

'How did you know I'd be here?' Chris asked him.

Another shrug. 'Carla rang me this morning at home. In tears. Told me you'd had a row, you'd got out in the middle of the zones and now she couldn't get hold of you. I came in looking for you. Had to break into your office. Sorry about that, I was pretty worried. Anyway, I spotted that message from Liz. Thought I'd catch you up. Took a while, my ribs are still killing me.'

Chris looked at him narrowly. 'You just happened to be carrying twenty grand in cash?'

'Oh, that.' Mike grinned again and crossed to where the bundle of currency still lay on the street. 'Improvisation. Look.'

He tossed the money across, and Chris caught it awkwardly with his left hand. The notes were twenties. There was a thousand euros in the bundle at most.

'Best I could do on the spur of the moment. You really walk in from the zones last night?'

'Yeah.'

'Must have been some row.'

They stood amidst the carnage, the scattered weapons and spreading pools of blood, and very slowly Chris became aware that, amongst a small knot of people gathered at the end of India Street, Liz Linshaw was watching him.

He walked towards her.

'Do you have any idea how bad this looks?'

Louise Hewitt stood stiff legged at the head of the conference table and gestured at the projection. Blown-up surveillance camera footage ran grainy and silent behind her, Mike Bryant giving the coup de grâce to the two masked gunmen still breathing.

'Do you have any idea what this kind of *brawling* does to our image as a serious financial institution?'

Chris shrugged. His side was numb where the Shorn medic had dosed him with contact anaesthetic prior to digging out the shotgun pellets. The rest of him was past feeling very much of anything too. 'You should be talking to Makin. He started it.'

'*This is not a fucking playground, Faulkner!*'

'Louise, you're being unreasonable.' Mike Bryant met Philip Hamilton's eyes across the table and the other man looked away, towards Hewitt. Beside him, Jack Notley stared into the middle distance, seemingly oblivious to the storm building around him. 'Makin called this one, all the way down. If I hadn't been there, Chris'd be dead now and the blame'd be farmed out to zone gangwits. We wouldn't even know we had a loose cannon aboard.'

On the projection screen, Chris walked away from the bodies and out of shot. It was odd, watching himself disappear, back into the past of three hours ago and the confrontation with Liz Linshaw.

You set me up.

She took it like a slap. For the first time he could recall, he saw open hurt in her face. The sight of it licked the pit of his belly.

You fucking set me up, you bitch.

No. She was shaking her head. *Chris, I don't—*

And then Mike was there, and they both slid their masks back on. Passion sheathed. There was control, there were words that meant something factual, there was the long, verbal comedown. Explanations, talk and shots of rough, blended whisky in *Break Point* to combat the shakes. Sanity leaking into the nightmare aftermath like blood across asphalt.

I just got a call. This guy said he worked Driver Control, he knew what really happened to Chris on the M11, did I want to know too? Meet him here. Five grand in cash.

She brandished the money out of her wallet. Like proof of innocence.

306

When Mike went to the bathroom, she reached out across the cheap plastic-topped table and took Chris's hand in her own. No words, only a cabled look, eye to eye. Spinning sudden vertigo, and then the flush of the toilet through cardboard-thin walls, and their hands leapt apart like matched magnetic poles.

Louise Hewitt was talking to him, but he couldn't make it matter. He levered himself to his feet, faced her disbelieving fury.

'I've had enough of this shit, Louise. It's pretty fucking clear what happened here.'

'Sit down Faulkner, I haven't—'

'Makin couldn't hack the NAME account. I took it from him, and it hurt. He couldn't take me on the road, so he hired a gangwit kid to do what he didn't dare do himself. When that didn't work—'

'I told you to *sit dow*—'

He shouted her down. 'When that didn't *fucking* work, Louise, he hired some more sicarios and tried this. He couldn't beat me playing by the Shorn rules, so he broke them. And now he's dead. Everybody in fucking black.'

'Chris.' Notley's voice didn't seem to have raised much, but there was an edge on it that cut across the air like tyre screech. 'You don't talk to partnership like this. You're overwrought, but that's no excuse. Now get out.'

Chris met the senior partner's eyes, and saw the man who had almost shot him dead in his own office a week ago. He nodded.

'Fair enough.'

They watched him go in silence. Mike Bryant looked round the table again. He shook his head.

'This isn't right, Jack. I mean, it's a fucking mess. But Makin called it. He's been a fuck-up since he took over the NAME, he was way too impressed with himself from day one. I would have called him out myself, but what's the point. Anyone could have seen he'd blink first.'

Hamilton blinked. 'I beg your pardon?'

'You don't have to drive against someone to know you're better than they are, Phil. That's crude. Sometimes you just know what the outcome'd be, and that's enough. This kill-or-be-killed shit just gets in the way.'

The look ran between the partners like current. Up on the projector screen, the surveillance film had looped. The gun battle was starting again. Jack Notley cleared his throat.

'Mike, perhaps you could give us some time to discuss this from a partner perspective. We'll get back to you again on Monday morning.'

Bryant nodded. 'Sure.'

When the door closed, Louise Hewitt spun on Notley.

'Did you hear that? You know where that comes from, don't you. That's chess and bullshit neojap philosophy, courtesy of Chris bloody Faulkner. The man is a fucking toxin, Jack. He's the real loose cannon around here.'

'It doesn't show up like that in the numbers, Louise.'

'It's not *about* the numbers.'

'No?' Notley raised an eyebrow. 'Am I missing something here? Would you care to tell me what Shorn CI is about besides the numbers?'

'Don't be obtuse. It's about an ethic. A corporate culture. A way of *doing* things. And if we let that go, *this*,' she jabbed a finger at the surveillance film. Masked figures, collapsed like unstrung marionettes. Pools and snakes of blood. 'Is what happens. Structural breakdown, anarchy in the streets. It's axiomatic. Does anyone sitting round this table have any inkling why Nick Makin might have acted the way he did? Why he found it necessary, even believed perhaps that it would be acceptable, to breach Shorn etiquette like this? Think hard, Jack. Think about a certain major client, beaten to death in conference a week ago. Think about the way you rewarded Faulkner for that. Does anyone see a connection?'

For a fraction of a second, Jack Notley closed his eyes. When he spoke, there was a soft warning in his voice.

'I don't think we need to revisit that, Louise.'

'I think we do, Jack. You gave Chris a green light for behaviour beyond any acceptable limits. And Makin learnt the lesson, resulting in this mess. And meanwhile we've got Bryant, our best driver, talking like a fucking ombudsman. Any way you look at it, Jack, you've destabilised what we're about. And we can't afford that.'

'I wonder if Martin Page would see it that way?'

Hamilton and Hewitt traded a glance. Hewitt came to the table and seated herself carefully.

'Is that some kind of accusation?'

Notley shrugged. 'Let's just say that your talk of loose cannons is selective, Louise. Page was a junior partner. What you did to him ran counter at least to an unspoken *understanding* of how partnership works here.'

'I resent that, Jack. Page was a filed challenge.'

'Yes, a challenge without a vacant post to justify it. Executive brawling at partnership level. An act of pure, equity share greed.'

'Which you underwrote, as I recall.'

'Retrospectively, yes. Because back then, Louise, *you* were the loose cannon, and I admired you for it.'

Hewitt smiled thinly. 'Well, thank you. But I think there's a limit—'

'Oh, *shut up*. Don't talk to me about,' Notley gestured impatiently, '*destabilisation*, as if it's something we have some kind of choice about. As if it's something we can avoid. What we do here is *built* on instability. It's a fucking prerequisite.'

Philip Hamilton cleared his throat. 'I think what Louise means is—'

'Yes, I thought it was about time you weighed in, you little sycophant. *Christ*, you're beginning to sicken me, both of you.'

Notley stood up and strode to the head of the table. He stabbed the projector control with two folded fingers, and the wall behind him was abruptly blank. His voice was tight with leashed anger.

'Louise, I helped you climb to the top of this pile, and now you're up here all you want to do is surround yourself with low-threat colleagues like this bag of guts, and kick away the ladder in case anybody sharper gets to scramble up and *destabilise* things for you. Haven't you learnt *anything* on the way up? Either of you? You can't *have* stability and dynamic capital growth. It's textbook truth. Come *on*. What transformed the stock market back in the last century? Volatility. Competition. Deregulation. The loosening of the ties, the *removal of social security systems*. What's transformed foreign investment in the last thirty years? Volatility. Competition. Small wars. It's the *same* pattern. And what ensures that we stay on top of it all? Volatility. Innovation. Rule-breaking. Loose cannons. Christ, why do you think I hired Faulkner in the first place? We *need* that factor. We *have* to keep topping up with it. Otherwise, we all just turn back into the same fat-fuck, complacent, country-club scum that nearly sank us last time around. Sure, men like Faulkner are unstable. Sure, they keep you looking in your rearview all the time. *But that's what keeps us hard.*'

For a couple of beats, silence held the conference room. Nobody moved. Notley stared from Hewitt to Hamilton and back, daring them to dispute. Finally, Hewitt shook her head.

'It may make you hard, Jack,' she said with measured insolence. 'But to me it's just bad business. We have structures in place to ensure volatility and competition. I don't think we need to go courting chaos into the bargain. I'm making a recommendation this quarterly that we let Faulkner go.'

Notley nodded, almost affably.

'Alright Louise. If that's the way you want it. But understand this. We've been courting chaos since the day we signed on for Conflict Investment. All of us. It's what drives us, it's what gets results. And I'm not going to watch you sell that out, just because you've got comfortable. You go on record with that recommendation, I will find reasons to call you out. Do you understand me? I will drive you off the road.'

This time no one broke the silence. Notley leaned his neck hard to one side and they heard it click in the stillness.

'That will be all.'

When he had gone, Hewitt got up and went to stare out of the window. Hamilton pushed out a long breath.

'Do you think he means it?'

'Of course he means it,' said Hewitt irritably.

'So what are you going to do?'

'I don't know.' She came back to sit on the edge of the table. She looked down into Hamilton's face. 'But I'm going to need your help.'

THIRTY-NINE

Out in the corridor, Mike Bryant quizzed security. They told him Chris had taken a lift to the ground floor. *Seemed pretty pissed off,* admitted one of the guards. Mike called a lift of his own and bombed downward in pursuit.

He spotted Chris, already halfway across the sun-lit cathedral expanse of the lobby. The holos and fountains and subsonics were all switched off, and there was nobody about. In the Sunday afternoon emptiness that was left, the space felt suddenly steely and inhuman.

Mike cleared his throat and called across it.

'Chris. Hey, Chris. Wait up a minute.'

'Now's not a good time, Mike.' Chris flung it back over his shoulder, not stopping.

'Okay.' Mike jogged to catch up. Residual bruising across his chest made it painful. 'You're right, it's not a good time. So why don't we go and grab a drink somewhere.'

'I've got to get my car back from Hawkspur Green. And then check into a hotel.'

'You're not going home?'

'What do you think?'

Mike put out a hand, breathing heavily. 'What I think is, you need to drink some of that seaweed-iodine shit you like, and talk about this. And, luckily, I'm here to listen to you spill. Alright? Come on, I saved your life out there, Chris. At least buy me a drink. Alright?'

Chris looked at him. An unwilling smile bent his mouth. Mike saw it and grinned back.

'Alright. I'll get the car.'

They found a tiny antique pub called *The Grapes,* tacked onto the Lime Street edge of Leadenhall Market, catering mainly to the insurance crowd and powered down to a single barwoman for the Sunday trade. Like most city-based hostelries, it opened seven days a week because the simple fact that it was always open was worth something in itself. Brokers knew they could get fed and watered there whatever day they were working, and the knowledge stuck. There was no room for five-day amateurs.

311

Three – *or four?* – whiskies in, Chris had drowned his fury and was slumped on a stool, watching dust motes dance in the streams of sunlight that fell in through the windows opposite the bar. A faint, pervasive odour of alcohol seeped up off the polished wood counter. The Laphroaig sat on top of the cheap three fingers he'd taken in *Break Point*, the codeine tabs and no food to speak of. He felt like a mud-smeared windscreen.

'Look,' Mike was saying. 'It doesn't matter what Hewitt thinks. You took Makin down. That's what counts. Sure, it was unorthodox, but that's the point isn't it? It ups your don't-fuck-with-me stock through the roof. Builds you the killer rep.'

'Killer rep.' Chris stared into his glass. He coughed up a laugh and shook his head. 'You want to know something about me, Mike?'

'Sure.'

'My *killer rep* is a fucking accident.'

He saw how the other man's gaze narrowed. He nodded, knocked back the rest of the Laphroaig. Grunted, like letting go.

''s right. I'm a fucking fake, Mike. Hewitt has me, cross-hairs and centred. She always did. She's not wrong. I don't belong here.'

Mike frowned, finished his vodka and gestured to the barwoman.

'Same again. Chris, what are you talking about? You've been a fuel-injected killing machine since Quain, at least.'

'Ah! Quain.' Chris watched as the whisky rose two fingers in his glass. 'Quain, Quain, Quain. You want to know about Quain?'

'I already know about Quain. Chris, you left him smeared along thirty metres of asphalt. That's pretty open and shut. You ran him over five fucking times, man.'

'Yeah.'

He sat, remembering. Brilliant spring sunshine, and the crunching impact of his barely legal ten-year-old Volvo Injection against the smooth racing green flanks of Quain's Audi. The light had gleamed so hard off the bodywork, he'd had to squint.

And Quain spinning out, finally, into the barrier, jammed onto a snapped section of uprights. What Chris had been trying for all through the difficult latter stages of the duel, well past the point when he'd actually won. Quain gaping, middle-aged and fearful, through the smashed-in driver-side window as the Volvo backed up, preliminary to ramming. Gaping as Chris killed the motor and got out.

He felt his face twitch with the memory.

He seemed to make the walk between the two cars at an immense distance from himself. The turnover of his pulse throbbed in his own ears. No Nemexes back then. He walked right up to the window and showed Quain the thing in his hand. The recycled raki bottle, the soaked rag. Perfume of petrol as he waved it back and forth. Snap of the lighter and the pale flame in the sunny air. Quain started babbling.

Get out, Chris told him, surprising himself. The plan had been to burn Quain alive. The plan had been to tell Quain why, and then throw the bottle with enough force to shatter on the floor between his feet. The plan had been to watch Quain turned into a shrieking, flailing, flame-armed thing, to listen to the screams and—

Get out and run, you fuck.

And Quain did.

Crazed, maybe, with fear of what he saw in Chris's eyes, hypnotised by the blob of pale, dancing flame. Chris stood there and watched him go, groping about inside his own head for a reason. Something was happening in there, and he couldn't make out what it was.

He threw the bottle into the Audi anyway, as much in frustration as anything else. It shattered on the dash and the flames sprang up. The sight seemed to switch something back on inside him. He sprinted back to the Volvo, kicked it alive and floored the accelerator. Fishtail waltz as he hauled the wheel over and his gaze sharpened on the portly, lumbering figure ahead on the road. Quain must have heard the engine and known what it meant. He was making for the central reservation as the Volvo came up on his heels. It wouldn't have made any difference, Chris realised later. He would have driven straight through it to get to Quain.

He dropped a gear and the engine screamed. Quain looked back over his shoulder just before the Volvo hit. Chris saw his eyes. Then he was gone, a suddenly, impossibly aerodynamic body thudding and tumbling up off the hood, the windscreen, the roof. A flash of dark falling in the rearview as Chris braked the Volvo to a screeching halt.

It wasn't enough.

He never knew if Quain was dead when he reversed back over him the first time. But he saw what emerged under the front wheels as he pulled up five metres back from the body.

It still wasn't enough.

He did it again. And again.

Five times, before he realised it would never be enough.

'He killed my father,' he said.

And Mike Bryant, staring at him in the sifting dustlight. A look on his face Chris had never seen before. Stalled out, lost.

'Your father?'

Chris sighed. Loading up for the long, tedious climb of explanation. 'Not directly. Quain never met my father directly. My father worked for a reconstruction consultancy called IES – International Economic Solutions, but when you said it all together it sounded like *Yes*. Cute, huh? My mother said he used to.'

He clamped his mouth. Shook his head. Cleared his throat.

'Uh, they modelled admin systems, infrastructure, things like that. They were into central Africa, the Middle East. Pretty small, but hungry and hard on the roads, as far as that went back then.'

Mike nodded. 'Enough to just get there first, right?'

'That's what they say.' Chris stared at a ray of dusty light falling across the bar top. A faint scarring of overlaid glass rings showed up in the wooden glow. '2018, Edward Quain was a hotshot young gun in Hammett McColl Emerging Markets. Couldn't have been older than his early twenties. And he pulled off this cutting-edge piece of incursion for Hammett McColl in Ethiopia. Got backing for a major policy shift. Nothing dramatic by CI standards, this is more than thirty years ago, remember. But it was enough to bring down the government. A lot of high-ranking officials lost their jobs. And Quain's new team publicly reneged on a stack of external contracts. Happened overnight, literally. IES couldn't take the damage. They went under, bankrupted along with a dozen or so others, and about forty per cent of the low-end commercial sector in Ethiopia at the time. They say it precipitated the civil war.'

'Ah yeah, I remember this.' Mike snapped his fingers. 'The Ayele Protocol, right? Read about it in Reed and Mason.'

'Right. Quain walked away with a huge commission, Hammett McColl repositioned for regional dominance in the Red Sea zone, and my father woke up with a walletful of dead plastic he didn't know about. He got shot the same day, arguing with a supermarket security guard. His card wouldn't scan at checkout, they wouldn't take him seriously and it got.' Chris watched his knuckles whiten around the whisky glass with absent fascination, as if they belonged to someone else. 'Out of hand. My mother says, said, if he'd been dressed better that day, it would never have happened. Hated suits apparently, my old man. Dressed scruffy as he could, outside the office. Maybe they thought he'd stolen the card or something. They tried to throw him out, it got rough. Blam. Some fat over-the-hill fuck with a dick extension blew his fucking head off.'

He looked at the whisky glass. Let go of it abruptly and stared at the palm of his suddenly liberated hand.

'We lost everything. The house, both cars. Health insurance, savings. Stock options. My mother got rehoused in the eastern zones. My father's friends helped out as much as they could, but most of them were going under too. They were all at IES or working in related firms.' Chris picked up his drink again, knocked it back. 'And then, even that early, they say you could see the domino coming if you were paying attention. It was still nearly a decade off, the worst of it, but people were already running scared, just hanging on with whatever they had. And Quain had just seen to it that we had nothing.'

'You remember all this?'

'Not really, no. I was two when my father was killed. I was there but,' Chris shivered, dodging the dream. 'I don't remember it. I just remember growing up in the zones with this accent everybody hated. This vague sense that things were better once. *Before*. But I could have picked that up listening to my mother. No way you remember stuff from when you're two years old.'

'No. But.' Mike gestured helplessly. 'How the fuck did you. I mean, Quain. Didn't he see you coming, the day you joined HM? How did you even get into HM, come to that?'

'I changed my name. My father wasn't called Faulkner, it was my mother's maiden name. She died of thorn fever, when I was seventeen. I took her name, sold everything else we owned and cut myself a new identity. Got a gangwit datarat in Plaistow to fix my records. Probably did a shit job, the money I gave him, but it was what I could afford. I doubt it would have stood up to close scrutiny, but when you're from the zones who the fuck cares. You're just cheap, faceless labour. And by the time I got to Hammett McColl, I had five years of new identity behind me. I'd made a lot of money for Ross Mobile and LS Euro, I could drive. That's all the HM recruiters cared about.'

'Sloppy. Was that their own people?'

'No, contracted out. Some cut-rate two-room outfit off Ludgate Circus. They tendered for HM on straight cost. No duel requirement. Lowest offer wins.'

Mike shook his head. 'Fucking amateurs.'

'Yeah, but you know what. It wouldn't have mattered anyway. Quain wouldn't have recognised my father's name. Some guy he ruined twenty years ago, one name out of hundreds he probably didn't even know back when it happened, let alone two decades on. What are the chances?'

'Yeah, figures.' Mike puffed out his cheeks. 'Jesus, what a story. Does Carla know all this?'

'No. She knows I grew up in the zones, she knows my parents are dead, but we don't talk about it. I met her after Quain. I'd already buried it all. She used to ask, back when we started seeing each other. Think it might even have been some of the attraction for her, the zone connection. I told her I wasn't interested in looking back.' He stared down the receding perspectives of the memory. 'Snapped her head off whenever she asked. She stopped asking after a while.'

'Yeah, it's true. You never talk about it, do you.'

Chris shrugged. 'Nor do you. Nor do any of us. We're all too flat-out

315

fucking busy trying to make it big right *now* to talk about the past. You'd think none of us had parents, the way we live.'

'Hey, I've got parents. I see them pretty often.'

'Good for you.'

Mike shook his head again, a little blearily this time. 'Still can't believe it, man. It's like a fucking movie. All the way back from the zones to take down Edward Quain.'

Chris finished his drink. 'Yeah, well. Some of us have got what it takes, some of us haven't. Remember.'

'Ah, shit, Chris, I didn't mean *you*. I'm not saying everyone in the zones deserves to be there, you know that. If I'd known, you know, about your parents and stuff, I wouldn't have said—'

'No? You must have known my background, Mike. You said yourself, that first day I met you in the washroom, Hewitt was batting my details about before I arrived. And it's not a secret where I grew up. It's on the résumé.'

'What?' Mike squinted at him. 'Well, yeah, but I assumed. I don't know, accidental son of some slumming exec and a bargirl, a dancer or something.'

'Thanks.'

'Fuck, I don't mean. I mean, it doesn't mean anything, but I just assumed. It happens, you know. *Seen* it happen. Come close a couple of times, myself. I just figured, something like that, that's how you got your break at Ross Mobile, maybe a leg up into LS as well.'

'No.' Chris smiled tightly. 'I got Ross through an old friend of my father. Everything else I clawed down myself. Don't worry about it, Mike. You were right. Some of us have got what it takes, and what it takes is hate. I had enough hate to paint a towerblock. I grew up hating. It was like fuel. Like food. You don't need much of anything else when you've got hate.'

'Look—'

'And then one morning I woke up and I'd killed Edward Quain, and the world was still here. I had a job, I had a life, well, a life*style* anyway. Hammett McColl had just promoted me. I had money, a *lot* of money, for the first time in my life.' He tipped his empty glass horizontal. Looked into it and laughed. 'It seemed a little ungracious not to go on living.'

The two of them sat there in silence for a while. Finally, Mike shifted uncomfortably and cleared his throat.

'Chris.' He hesitated. 'You, uh, you want to stay at my place tonight?'

'No. Thanks, no. I've got to be alone for a while, Mike. There's stuff I need to sort out. I'll get a hotel. But thanks. And.' He waved vaguely. 'Thanks for, you know, saving my life and everything.'

Bryant grinned.

'Shit, I always owed you for Mitsue Jones. Just call it even.'

The hotel would not hold him.

He poured himself a whisky – *another fucking whisky* – and stared at the phone as if it were poisonous. His mobile was still switched off. No one outside of Mike knew where he was. He'd have to pick up and dial.

He picked up the TV remote instead, and zapped through the channels. Endless, mindless, brightly-coloured shit and an upbeat report just in from Cambodia. He recognised the editing.

He shut down the TV's painted window and went out on the balcony. Warm night air gusted over his face. A well-lit Kensington street angled past seven floors below. A couple walked along it, arm in arm. Laughter floated up. A cab idled by in the opposite direction, cruising for custom.

He retreated to the bedroom. He lay face up on the bed and stared at the perfectly moulded plaster ceiling. Tension itched down his limbs.

He prowled the suite and gnawed a thumbnail down to the quick.

He lit the laptop and tried to carry out simple database tasks.

He hurled the whisky glass across the room.

He grabbed wallet, Nemex, jacket, and he left.

She was waiting for him.

She must have heard the cab in the street outside. The door opened as he pressed the bell. She stood in the clothes she'd worn at *Break Point*, black leggings and a loose grey running top, face scrubbed clean of make-up, hair gathered back. They stood looking at each other, an arm's reach apart.

'I've got to talk to you,' he started, but she shook her head.

She reached for him as he crossed the threshold. It felt like falling. He was close enough to smell freshly drunk coffee on her breath, behind that the swirl of female scent mingled with orange blossom. The kiss was an open-mouthed collision that squeezed tears into his eyes, a mutual assault of tongues, of teeth tugging on lips and hands on clothing below. She was laughing excitedly into his open mouth as they clinched and his hands felt impossibly full of her body, unable to grasp the substance of it with enough force. He kicked the door shut and found a breast beneath the sports top, unsupported and surgically perfect – *the porn segment sprang through his mind like sweat* – hard under soft, a swath of stomach sprung with taut muscle, the hard length of one thigh and the lift of arse cheek above it. He could not settle on any of it.

Her leg thrust between his and ground upward against his prick. He was already hard. She bit him on the neck. Hands dragged him down the hall, past the kitchen and bathroom and left into an untidy bed-room. Cluttered bedside unit, a teetering pile of books and a glass of stale water. A pale blue quilt crumpled across an unmade bed. He drank it in and the new intimacy was a tiny itching in the pit of his stomach, an opening to an inner sanctum, built into his prior knowledge of the rest of the house. She let him go with a sudden motion as if he was hot, sank to the bed in front of him and peeled off her leggings in two single stripping motions. Fingers touched the mound beneath the white cotton thong she wore underneath, rubbing the groove up and down. She grinned up at him as she did it. Her free hand scrabbled across to the bedside table, ripped open a drawer and reached inside.

'No, wait.'

He shed jacket and shirt, dropped to his knees beside the bed and buried his face in the white cotton, breathing in the undiluted scent of her. She gasped and sank back on the folds of the quilt. The heated heart of flesh between her thighs was moist. He slid his hands up the insides of her thighs, fingers first, pulled aside the cotton and sank his tongue into her. A hard spasm and her hands came to grip the sides of his head. Her legs lifted and folded over his back like wings. She was panting.

When she came, she ground up hard against him with a deep grunt-ing sound, then flopped to twitching stillness. He shouldered his way gently out from under her legs and straightened up. In the drawer she had opened, he found the Durex can. He rolled its chilly length along the plain of her stomach, got another twitch as it touched her, then lodged it between her breasts and rolled it idly back and forth in the indelible cleavage surgery had given her. She raised herself on her elbows.

'So what do you want *now*?' she asked, mock tough.

'I want to fuck you, Liz.'

She seemed to consider that for a moment, head tilted slightly. Then she sat up, tugged her hair loose of its binding and set about unfastening his belt buckle. She liberated the engorged length of his prick from the cloth it was trapped in, handling it with greedy care and sliding it back and forth into her mouth. Then she gripped it at base between thumb and forefinger, picked up the Durex can and sprayed him steadily from end to end.

It was a long time since he'd needed to use the stuff, and the sudden, cold tightening of the instant membrane was a shock. He gasped and Liz Linshaw grinned again as she heard it.

'That's just for starters,' she said in the back of her throat and held up the can for his inspection. 'This is cocktail-laced. Expensive stuff. You wait 'til the contact sensitisers kick in. You're not going to last long.'

He reached for her and she scooted back on the bed, opening herself for him. He sank all the way into her with a groan, cupped one breast in both hands, working the flesh. He sucked in the nipple and it touched the roof of his mouth.

She was right. He didn't last long.

'Can you feel my heart?' she asked him, later.

He nodded drowsily against her chest.

'It's still beating like a fucking drum, Chris. That's with thinking about what you did to me. I want you to do it again.'

'What, right now?'

She laughed. 'Well, ideally yeah. But I can wait.' She craned her neck to look at his face. 'Are you staying the night?'

'If you ask me to.'

'Stay the night.'

'No, I got to go.'

'You bastard.' She slapped at his flank. 'That's not funny. I want you to stay, Chris. I want access to you.'

'You've got access to me. Look at me.' But beneath the comfortable humour, he felt a vague stirring of alarm. Not at what she wanted. At what he might want from her.

'So we're going to do this again?'

He thought about Carla. Pushed the thought away again. Let go.

'Yeah, we are. I'm living out of a hotel now, Liz. No more complications.'

And in the back of his head, something heard and lifted its throat to the sky, and laughed like a hyena.

Amidst the plinthed Grecian sculpture, Louise Hewitt sat on the edge of the grey-sheeted bed and stared past the white blast of a bedside halogen lamp. The room was silent around her. She had hung her jacket away with automated care on her way into the apartment, and now her shoulders slumped under the soft silk of her blouse. There was an unaccustomed ache in her throat.

She looked down at the bed and pressed her lips together. Then she lay sideways on the covers and lowered her face to the pillow. His scent came off the grey cotton and she clenched her eyes shut.

'Oh Christ, Nick,' she murmured, and her throat clicked as she swallowed. 'Didn't I tell you? Didn't I *warn* you?'

She lay there for a while, and a single tear leaked out from under her right eyelid. It trickled jerkily to the edge of her face and soaked into the pillow.

When the second and third tear slipped out, she sat up abruptly and wiped them off her face with the angry gesture of someone ripping off a mask. She cleared her throat, got up from the bed and went through to the study. She stabbed the datadown awake and seated herself before its soft, multi-coloured glow.

She worked.

FILE#5:
FINAL AUDIT

FORTY

There were times over the next few weeks when Chris had to forcibly remind himself that this was his own life he was leading.

Partly it was the hotel. There was something insulated about living out of a box of high-class services long-term, something that felt like wearing thin rubber gloves. Household tasks he was used to performing himself happened distantly, almost invisibly. He put out his dirty laundry and it came back again pristine, as if cleaned by elves. Fresh towels, and little bottles of soap and shampoo appeared daily in the bathroom by a similar magic. He ordered food and it came to his door from a kitchen he never saw, or he fed himself in one of the hotel's three internal restaurants. Either way, he was saved the tiny increments of physical and emotional effort involved in going outside to look for a place to eat.

At Shorn, he performed with a slightly numb, mechanical competence. The work piled up into account overload as Nick Makin's abrupt departure took its toll on everyone. He cut a path through it like someone working through dense bush with a blunt machete. Focus ahead, *swing*, grab, clear and step, focus ahead, *swing*. Occasionally he sagged, but habit kept him on his feet.

The pellet wounds in his side healed, fading rapidly from actual pain to inconvenience to vague memory. Dreams of Carla stubbornly refused to follow the same path.

Covert reports came in from the NAME via Lopez. Barranco had taken his first dose of Shorn beneficence – three hundred Kalashnikovs plus ammunition, thirty of the Aerospatiale plane-killers, an even thousand King grenades, all brought ashore in the dead of night on some Pacific beach, courtesy of a privatised Epsilon-class Russian attack sub and her demobbed crew. The best international bulk-by-stealth couriers money could buy.

On the other side of the globe, Nakamura played Cambodia the way Vasvik had told him they would. Planning for the military coup lurched into motion. Chris had the relevant local tools to hand – he'd mustered them almost absently – days before the indesp intelligence came through. He pretended to study the reports, phoned through pre-arranged authorisation codes to Langley an hour later, sat and waited.

Explosions bloomed across Phnom Penh like a rash. A colonel and his family in a car bomb. A general in a restaurant. An air force commander in a whorehouse, shot three times with an uncharacteristic precision that made Chris suspect the place was a protected Langley franchise of some sort. A couple of others, drive-by and car bomb respectively. The remainder got the message. The coup fell apart before it could properly gain momentum, and Nakamura recoiled. Word came down to Chris from on high. Notley was impressed.

Meanwhile, an ongoing investigation was launched into the mysterious disappearance of Nicholas Makin. No one outside the Shorn debriefing knew where he'd gone. His corpse was helicoptered out of Crutched Friars with the rest, still masked, still warm. No footage of faces, and no DNA trace – before they left, the rapid response crew Mike called had hosed down the bloody asphalt with chemicals that would defeat any tissue analysis. The firefight was written off as an overly ambitious gangwit incursion that had met with poetic justice. Carefully massaged media speculation arose that Makin had fallen solitary victim to the same gang before their luck ran out. Chris and Mike gave prepared statements and watched it all from the sidelines.

The media did its job, rather better than anyone had expected. Accurate detail dissolved rapidly in a splash of lurid full-colour, replayed from the surveillance cameras in Crutched Friars. The gunfighter chic of the thing caught and sold. *Comp Drivers In Eastwood-Style Bloodbath! Zone Gangs Reap High Noon Whirlwind! Police Commend Shorn Heroes!* Coverage went global, TV and the men's magazines went crazy. Chris and Mike got their souvenir Remingtons, handed over by the chief of corporate police in a white gale of erupting flashbulbs. Everyone grinning into the teeth of the media storm. It made the triumph against Mitsue Jones and her team seem like relative obscurity. One morning Mike came into work and found a call on his phone from a Hollywood agent. Studios, the agent said, were queuing up. Options, offers, amounts of money that made even Louise Hewitt blink. There was talk of a book tie-in. A game. Action figures.

Sign nothing, said Notley with characteristic avuncular tolerance. *Yet.*

Corporate police units went into the zones looking for associates and relatives of the four men who had died with Makin. They kicked in doors and broke heads, bullied and bribed and ascertained that no one knew anything worth telling. Arrests were made. The media stood up on its hind legs and applauded. *Shorn Leads Gang Crackdown! Law and Order Priority for Corporate Community! Drug Scum Will Be Stopped Says Shorn Partner! Safer Streets for Our Kids Promise Executives!*

Ten days in, the original events surrounding Nick Makin's death were gone. No one remembered anything but the quick-draw images of Chris Faulkner and Mike Bryant, outnumbered and outgunned, taking down five cold-blooded, cowardly, drug-dealing masked killers.

Reality blurred out in hype.

Chris gave interviews, looked into cameras. Fended off a spate of calls from the driving fanworld and the London Chamber of Commerce. Requests for after-dinner speaker engagements, pleas for worn pieces of the Saab's engine and offers of bizarre sexual services all fogged into a single drag on his attention. Messages piled up once more on the datadown from the same wolfish-looking women with Eastern European names, and from drive sites like *Road Rash* and *Asphalt Xtreme*. He read movie treatments and CI reports with the dazed sense that some time soon he might not be able to tell the difference. He rolled out the official Shorn line, dictated policy down phones. He handled Cambodia, the NAME. Parana. Assam. Makin's accounts in Guatemala, Kashmir, Yemen. More.

He took the Remington down to the firing range and took out some of the secreted stress on holotargets. There was a deep satisfaction to the scattered blast pattern it made that not even the Nemex could equal. He grew to like the weapon in a way he had never allowed himself with the pistol. He used the feeling like a drug.

In the evenings, in the anonymous seclusion of the hotel, he had Liz Linshaw, like a jagged sensory overload on the screen of his feelings. Sprawled elegantly naked across his bed, soaped slick in his shower, pressed against the walls of the room, legs wrapped around, tensed with orgasm, damp with sweat, grinning through her tousled hair.

Her too, he used like a drug. Like a materialised visitation from some soft-porn pay-channel reality the hotel had moored close to. When she wasn't there – about every third night, *just so we stay sane about this, Chris* – he masturbated thinking of her. She helped him sleep, helped him avoid overly conscious introspection when at the ragged end of each day he arrived back in the hotel and found himself wondering if you really could live out a whole life this way.

Eventually, Carla came to the hotel.

She called first. Several times. He had her screened out of his mobile and the office phone, but somehow she'd got the hotel out of Mike. The first time she called, he walked into it, head-on. He hung at the end of the phone, weightless, making monosyllabic responses. After a while, she cried.

He hung up on her.

He rang the switchboard and got them to screen and announce all further incoming calls. Then he called Mike, furious. He got an apology of sorts, but what the other man was really thinking came through underneath, loud and clear.

'Yeah, I know Chris. I'm really sorry. She's been calling for days – I just couldn't blow her off any more. She was upset, you know. Really upset.'

'I'm fucking upset as well, Mike. And I could use a bit of solidarity here. It's not like I go telling tales to Suki behind *your* back, is it?'

'You need to talk to her, man.'

'That's an opinion, Mike, and you're entitled to it. But you don't fucking make my marital decisions for me. Got it?'

There was a long pause at the other end.

'Got it.' Mike said finally.

'Good.' Chris cleared his throat, cranked down his tone a little. 'I'll see you tomorrow at eight, then. Cambodia briefing.'

'Yeah.'

' 'night, then.'

'Yeah. Goodnight, Chris.' There was a flat quality in Mike's voice that Chris didn't much like, but he was still too angry himself to care much either.

Liz emerged from the bathroom, naked, towelling her hair vigorously.

'Who was that?'

He gestured. 'Ah, Mike. Work stuff.'

'Yeah? You look pretty pissed off about it.'

'Yeah, well. Cambodia.'

'Anything I should know?'

He forced a grin. 'A lot of stuff you'd *like* to know, probably. But let's talk about Mars.'

She threw the towel at him.

'I'll get it out of you,' she promised, advancing.

The next morning on the way to work, Mike's tone came back to him and he wondered if the other man was going to have another go after the Cambodia briefing. He rehearsed angry rejoinders in his head as the cab swung around Hyde Park Corner.

He never got a chance to use them. It was the day Hollywood chose to come calling and all Mike wanted to talk about were the hallucinatory figures involved and the possibility that they might get to watch themselves immortalised on screen by Tony Carpenter or Eduardo Rojas.

Carla called a couple more times that week, and then, suddenly, she was at the front desk, asking for him. Mercifully, it was a night Liz Linshaw had chosen not to show up. He thought briefly, cruelly, about telling the desk staff to send her away, then caught a glimpse of himself

326

n a wall mirror and grimaced. He changed into something freshly
aundered, slipped on a pair of casual shoes and went down to face
er.

She was sitting on one of the sofas in reception, immaculate in faded
eans he remembered buying with her, boots and a neat black leather
acket. When she saw him, she got up and came to meet him, trying for
smile.

'So. I get an audience with the man of the moment. Feel good, being
amous again?'

'What do you want?'

'Can we go up to your room?'

'No.'

She looked elaborately around the quiet, well-bred bustle of the
obby. The hurt barely showed in her voice.

'Have you got someone up there?'

'Don't be a fucking bitch. No, I haven't got anyone up there. Jesus,
Carla, this isn't about someone else. *You* fucking left *me*.'

'So I've got to stand here while you shout at me?'

He swallowed and lowered his voice. 'There's a bar through there,
hrough that arch. We can sit in there.'

She shrugged, but it was a manufactured detachment. In the corner of
he bar, she sat and stared at him out of eyes that shone with unshed
ears. She'd been crying recently, he knew. He could tell. He felt a tiny
hawing at the edges of his anger at the knowledge, a tiny, aching
varmth. He crushed it out. A uniformed waitress appeared with an
xpectant smile. He ordered Laphroaig for himself, asked Carla
vhether she'd like something to drink, and watched the formality of
iis tone stab her through. She shook her head.

'I didn't come here to drink with you, Chris.'

'Fair enough.' He nodded to the waitress and she went back to the
bar. 'What did you come for?'

'To apologise.'

He looked at her for a long moment. 'Go on then.'

She managed a smile. Shook her head. 'You bastard. You've turned
nto a real bastard, Chris. You know that?'

'*You left me in the middle of the fucking zones, Carla*. At two o'clock in
he *fucking* morning. You've *got* some apologising to do.'

'You called me a whore.'

'And you called me.' He gestured helplessly, not remembering how
he row had stoked so high. 'You said—'

'I said I couldn't recognise you any more, Chris. It wasn't an insult, it
vas the truth. I don't recognise you any more.'

He shrugged. Ignored the tiny acid drip at the centre of his chest. 'So

327

why come here at all? I'm a write-off, I'm unrecoverable. Tender trash
So why waste your time?'

'I told you why I came.'

'Yeah, to apologise. You're not making a very good job of it.'

The Laphroaig came. He signed for it, sipped and put it down on the
table between them. He looked back up at Carla.

'Well?'

'I didn't come to apologise for leaving you in the zones.' He opened
his mouth and she made a slashing gesture to silence him. 'No, listen to
me, Chris. I'd do it again if you spoke to me like that again. You
deserved it.'

She stared away across the bar, assembling what she wanted to say
Absently, she reached across the table for the whisky tumbler, recog-
nised the automatic intimacy for what it was and stopped herself rigidly
She blinked a couple of times, fast.

'That's not what I have to apologise for. I have to apologise because I
should have left you a long time ago. I've spent the last year, the last two
years, I don't know maybe even longer than that, trying to turn you
back into the man I thought you were when we first met.' She smiled
unconvincingly. 'And you don't want to be that man any more, Chris.
You aren't that man any more. You've found something harder and
faster, and you like it better.'

'This is crap, Carla.'

'Is it?'

Silence. A tear broke cover under her left eye. He pretended not to
see it, reached for his whisky instead. She found a wipe in her jacket.

'I'm leaving you, Chris. I thought maybe. But I was right the first
time. There's no point.' She gestured at the hotel around them. 'You're
happier like this. Living on room service, locking out the rest of the
world. It isn't just the job you do any more, that fucking tower you run
your remote control wars from. It's everything. Twenty-four, seven,
insulated from reality. How long would you have gone on sitting in this
place, if I hadn't come here tonight? How long would you have shut me
out like everyone else?'

She got up abruptly. He sat staring straight ahead, out of the windows
of the bar to the street outside.

'You fucking left me, Carla. Don't try and turn it around.'

She gave him a bright, brittle smile. 'You're not listening to me,
Chris. I'm leaving you. I'll need a couple of weeks to get my stuff out of
the house—'

'And where are you going to go?' It came out ugly.

'I'm going to stay with,' she laughed a little. 'Not that it's anything to
do with you any more. I'm going to stay in Tromsö for a while. Until I

can get the divorce sorted out. I'm assuming you aren't going to contest it, you'll probably be happier than I am to get free. Give you plenty of room for your new penthouse playmate, whoever she is.'

'What the fuck are you talking about?'

'Oh, please. I'm not stupid, Chris. I saw the way the people at the desk looked at me when I asked for you. I hear the way they react when I try to call you. I'm not the only woman you've got coming here. I just hope whoever it is is worth what you're paying.'

He shrugged. 'Think what you like. Better yet, check the credit-card accounts. Spot all the charges to escort agencies I must be making. You never did have a very high opinion of me, did you?'

She shook her head, drew a hard breath that had tears in it. 'You don't know how wrong you are about that, Chris. You'll never fucking know.'

'Yeah. Whatever.'

She turned to go. Paused and turned back.

'Oh, yeah. You'd better come out and collect the Saab. Some time soon. I haven't touched it, but I'm not sure how long I can stand it sitting there in the drive while I know you're here fucking some moan-on-demand tit-job. My maturity's wearing pretty fucking thin.'

She walked away from him.

FORTY-ONE

Liz Linshaw came over the following evening, and walked bang into the aftermath. Chris was moody and snappish, and when they got into bed he needed a hand-crank start. They fucked, but it wasn't much fun. He went through the motions, wrestling irritably over choices and changes of posture, and only finally managed to lose himself in the pay-channel perfection of her body as he came. Scant seconds later, he hit the real world like concrete from fifty floors up. No post-coital warmth, no chuckling or smoothing of sweat-soaked skin. There was a raw hollow behind his eyes and in his chest.

They unplugged and lay apart.

'Thanks,' she said, staring at the ceiling.

'Sorry.' He rolled towards the juncture of her thighs. 'Come here.'

She pushed his head away. 'Forget it, Chris. Just tell me what's wrong.'

'You don't want to hear it.'

'Yes I do.'

He rolled onto his back again. He blew imaginary cigarette smoke at the ceiling. 'Carla came to see me,' he said finally.

'Great.' she sat up against the headboard, arms folded under her breasts. 'Fucking great. You seeing her again?'

'Told you you didn't want to hear it.'

She looked down at him, angry. 'You're wrong. I do want to hear it, I want to hear all about it. Every fucking detail. You're what I do in the evenings now, Chris. Anything that's going to ruin it this badly, you better believe I want to hear about it. Are you seeing her again?'

'Doubt it.'

He recounted the conversation in the bar, almost word for word. When he came to Carla's parting line, she grimaced.

'Nice.'

'Yeah.' Chris stared off into a corner of the room. 'Used to scare me sometimes, how she could get inside my head like that. Just read stuff out of me like I was a screen.'

Liz Linshaw's gaze twitched around. 'Excuse me?'

'I mean, the way she knew that—'

'That's what I am in your head? A moan-on-demand tit-job? Well, thanks a fucking lot, Chris. Thank you *very* much.'

'Liz, I'm not. That's not what I meant. It's.' He groped after some explanation of what he meant, the way she seemed to form an integrated part of the smooth-lined hotel-suite reality he was living. 'Christ, you're *beautiful*, that's what I was trying to say, too beautiful to be real, it seems like. Okay? And that must have been what she picked up on in my head. I mean, look, she was right about the tit-job, wasn't she.'

Liz cupped her breasts at him. The anger on her face robbed it of sexuality. 'You got a problem with these? Funny, because you didn't seem to earlier when your face was fucking buried between them. You know, Chris, this is me. I'm here for real, all of me. I'm not trying to sell myself to you as some piece of fucking merchandise.'

'No?' A little of his own anger was starting to seep back through the emptiness under his ribs. 'So why send me the edited highlights of your porn career? Good old airbrushed girl-on-girl action? You wouldn't call that merchandising the goods?'

She stared at him. 'What the fuck are you talking about?'

'Oh, come on Liz. You're trying to tell me you didn't do porn?'

'No, I did.' Something in her face had changed. 'Back when it was the best way I knew to make money. I just want to know how come you never told me you'd been jerking off to it.'

'Liz, you fucking *sent* it to me.'

'No, Chris. I didn't.'

'You're saying you didn't mail me a videoclip of you and some blonde bimbette on a, like, an exercise rack or something. You never sent that?'

She sighed and sank back against the headboard. Her gaze rolled out to the middle distance. She seemed to curl into herself.

'*Donna's Dominion*,' she muttered.

'Sorry?'

'*Donna's Dominion*. That's what it was called, that particular piece of classy erotic art. I was Donna Dread, gym training world dominatrix.' She smiled without much mirth. 'Pretty infantile stuff, huh?'

Chris gestured uncomfortably. He was pretty sure he was blushing. Liz Linshaw nodded.

'Got you hard, though. Right?'

'Uh.' He looked away.

She sighed again. 'Look, don't worry about it. Stuff's made to get you hard. As a male, you'd be practically dysfunctional if it didn't. Youthful tits are supposed to turn you on, and there you've got four of them on screen, all rubbing up against each other, and all blown up to hyper-real proportions. You might as well get embarrassed about four lines of uncut NAME powder keeping you awake all night. It's just another drug, Chris. Refined, maxed-up, bang-on-the-nail sex-chemistry trigger dust.' Another weary smile. 'So you liked me, huh?'

He cleared his throat. 'You, uh, were you really into, you know?'

'Girls?' She shrugged. 'Not really, no. I mean, get someone licking your clit for you, that's not unpleasant, whatever sex the person doing it is. Once you get used to the six or seven people watching you off camera, that is. And you'd be surprised how quickly you do get used to that. But no, I was never a try-out lesbian, not even a try-out bi. It's pure theatre, Chris. Just a job. Oh, yeah, and if you stick to girl-on-girl, your health insurance premiums go way down. Less risk, less general wear and tear on the works.'

'Why did you, I mean, how did you get into it?'

This time her smile seemed genuine. Her posture unwound. She shook her head, reached over the edge of the bed for her bag, and started going through it. 'Well I wasn't kidnapped into it by white slavers, if that's what you mean.'

She found a bent and crumpled ready-rolled spliff, a lighter. Sat back against the headboard again and lit up. She coughed and waved little eddies in the sudden cloud of smoke.

'You want some of this? No? Sure?' She pulled down a lungful of smoke, held it for a moment and let go. She looked critically at the embered end of the spliff. 'Thing is, you listen to some twisted evangelical fuck like Simeon Sands, you'd believe we *are* all sex slaves by any other name, kidnapped, trapped by drugs, victims of our own unclean, incest-aroused lust – I think guys like Sands like that one especially, you hear the way they trot it out. One hand on the pulpit, one hand below, eh.' She grinned crookedly. 'But it just ain't so, Chris. I mean, it isn't this other thing the industry wants to sell you either. You know, we're all dripping wet sluts, just can't wait to get our orifices stuffed. Forget that. You want clinical and jaded, go watch a porno shoot. It's work, Chris, pure and simple. More or less professional, depending on who you're working for, better or worse paid ditto. But no one ever put me under pressure to do stuff I wasn't happy with, and no one tried to stop me when I quit.'

'Do you think you were typical?'

Liz held down more smoke. Frowned, then let it up. Shook her head. 'Globally? No. I heard a lot of nasty stories coming out of Costa Rica and Thailand. Still do. But you don't need me to tell you about that, Chris. This is what you do for a living. Enterprise zones, political instability. Market forces, weak governmental structure, the poor get fucked. Literally, in this case.'

'Oh, right.' The casual way she'd said it stung, made him snappish. 'So everyone you worked with was smiling and happy were they?'

She plumed smoke, looked at him quizzically.

'No. Even in Copenhagen, you've got some fucked-up girls working the trade. That blonde I was with in *Donna's Dominion?* Renata something, I think she was Polish. She had some strange ideas, and those tits were just insane. She had to go to three different plastics guys before she found one who'd give her those implants and then she had on-and-off post-op trouble the whole time. So, yeah who knows? Maybe old Simeon was right in her case. Turned on to pornographic filth because her father abused her as a child. But, to be honest, I think she just wasn't very bright. Yeah, Chris, there are going to be women doing porn who were fucked up by abuse when they were kids, it makes sense. But most of the ones I worked with were just like me – uninhibited, maybe overly exhibitionistic media wannabes, marking time while they looked for their big break. I went out to Copenhagen, looking for work with the pirate 'casters out of Christiania. I got into Danish porn instead. It was easier, there was a lot more of it about than pirate work, and it was better paid. It was a couple of years, it felt weird and different and maybe taught me a few things about myself that I wouldn't know otherwise. And I saved a lot of money. End of story. And. Happy ending, yeah.'

'But you need to smoke that stuff to talk about it.'

The quizzical look again. 'Chris, you need to get a grip. You're telling me you've really got some kind of moral problem with my career as a porn doll a decade ago? For a man who works in international finance, you've got some fucking nerve.'

'I don't have a problem with it. And I didn't think you had a problem with what I do either.' Spite gleamed through. 'In fact, I thought it got you off.'

Her eyes narrowed. 'What?'

'Sure. You fucked Mike Bryant, now you're fucking me. Spot the connection. Hey, I'm not complaining, Liz, but take a look at your own fucking motivations. This is textbook passenger-seat passion. Let's be honest about it.'

She sat up abruptly, flicked ash off the spliff. 'Yeah, *that's* a good idea, Chris. Let's be honest. If you had a problem with me, you could have left me well alone.'

'Left *you* alone?' The injustice of it staggered him. It was like fighting with Carla, all over again. An opening well of curdled hurt. 'You came on pretty fucking strong to *me*, as I recall. At Troy's party. After the party, at *Regime Change*. You *called* me for that one.'

'Oh, yeah, well maybe you shouldn't have sent me a copy of your wife's flight times to Norway, then. Because you know Chris, as invitations go, that was pretty fucking blatant.'

Shock held him unstirring for a moment. She caught it, coiled back on the bed, face still tight with anger.

'What?'

'I. Liz, I didn't send you anything.'

'Right.'

'No, fucking *listen* to me.' He reached out for her with both hands. She gestured him away. Stared out of the window. 'I didn't send you that stuff. I didn't even know Carla was going to Tromsö until about an hour before you called me. I. Someone's fucking with us, Liz.'

Her gaze tracked warily back to him. She didn't turn her head. Her whole body was closed to him again, limbs folded defensively.

'I'm not a drive-site groupie, Chris.'

'Okay.' He held up his hands, palms out. 'Okay, you're not a drive-site groupie. Whatever you say. But I'm telling you, I never sent you those flight details. And you're telling me you didn't send me *Donna's Dominion*. So. Someone's fucking with us, right? It's got to be that.'

And he got her back. Limb by limb, line by line, the softening stole through her. The place in Carla he could no longer reach, the point of reconciliation abraded by years of impact along the same emotional front. She opened a little, turned to face him. Nodded.

A tiny shard of hope spiked him, unlooked for. A prickle across the underside of each eye and a sudden surge in the empty space he'd excavated in his own chest.

This time. He promised himself silently. *This one, this time, this woman. I will not fuck this one up.*

But the hyena was still out there, still prowling in silhouette on the sunset horizon of his thoughts.

And would not shut up.

FORTY-TWO

He got to work early, running on residual anger that still had no clear focus. The datadown rolled out its gathered screed of messages. Top of the line, *Irena Renko*, subject: *need loading fast*. It wasn't the first time he'd seen the name in the last week. Something snapped.

'For *fuck's* sake.' He hit reply, and listened to the dial.

'*Da?*'

'Listen to me, you stupid fucking natasha. I do not need your whore's services, now or ever. Just leave me the fuck alone.'

There was a pause, during which he nearly hung up. Then the accented voice came back, icy with controlled rage.

'Just who *fucking* you think you are talking to? Fucking suit cowboy, think you will talk to me like this. I am Captain Irena Renko, commander of free sub freighter *Kurt Cobain* talking to you.'

'I'm. Sorry?'

'You should fucking be sorry. Fuck your mother! Four days I am here in Faslane, awaiting second loading. Four days! My crew drunk in Glasgow bars. What for you waste my time like this?'

'I. Wait. The *Cobain?*' Chris flailed across the desk and hit the datadown deck. Details fled up into a new window. 'You're loading for the NAME? Military hardware.'

'No,' purred the woman at the other end. 'I am not loading, because I'm waiting four fucking days for cargo. Port Authority know nothing. I call Lopez, he also knows nothing. Normally, *Cobain*, she sails and fuck you all if this happens. But Lopez tells me, call you. You are sympathetic, he says. Not like other suits. Perhaps I have wrong man.'

'No, no. Captain Renko, you have the right man. I, I apologise for my tone earlier. There's a lot going on at this end.'

'Well, at this end is nothing going on. No delivery, no data about delivery. And mooring charge is costing me—'

'Never mind the mooring charge. I'll cover that, plus ten per cent for your inconvenience. Go get your crew, I'll get back to you.'

He cut the connection and stared across the office. The marbled chess board gleamed back at him, pieces frozen in a pattern that hadn't changed in weeks. He called Mike.

'Yeah, Bryant.'

Mike, listen, we've got a problem.'

'I'll say. I would have called you earlier, but I didn't see the Saab. Didn't know you were in.'

'It's still at home. I haven't been back for it yet.' A chilly quiet back down the line. 'Mike, I just heard from our couriers to Barranco.'

'We haven't got time to worry about the NAME right now, Chris. Didn't you catch the news this morning? Fuck, last night even.'

'No, last night I.' *I was kiss-and-make-up fucking your ex-mistress.* 'I went to bed early. Headache. And I'm coming from the hotel in cabs at the moment, I don't get the radio either. What's going on?'

'Some fucking junior Langley aide just came down with a bad dose of conscience. He's promised covert reports from the last two years to ScandiNet and FreeVid Montreal.'

'Oh, *fuck.*'

'Yeah. What I said.'

'Cambodia?'

'We don't know yet. This gutless wonder at Langley worked archive, so could be the Phnom Penh stuff is too recent to show up. But we can't rely on that. There's no telling what he's going to give them.'

'Can't we just have the guy wiped?'

'Oh, what do you think Langley are trying to do right now? Chris, he worked for them. He was on the inside. You don't think he's going to have covered himself? He's grabbed the discs and gone underground.'

'Okay, so get someone else, someone better than Langley. Special Air, or one of the Israeli contractors.'

'Same applies, Chris. First they've got to find the fucker. And meanwhile ScandiNet and FreeVid are leaking this fucking stuff like vindaloo diarrhoea. We're going to have the UN charter people all over us by end of the week at the outside.'

'Well, look.' Chris frowned. Something didn't fit here. 'Calm down. They don't have any power of access. All they can do is make a noise. We fight them in the courts, the whole thing boils down to two years' paperwork and legal wrangling. What are you getting so bent out of shape about?'

'It's bad for fucking business, alright. Leakage of any sort. Kind of publicity we don't need.'

'Yeah, well, speaking of bad for business, you'd better get onto your pal Sally Hunting. I've just had a Russian sub commander yelling at me because she's been waiting four days at Faslane for a NAME shipment that hasn't turned up.'

There was a beat of silence. 'What?'

'You heard. Barranco's Mao sticks have gone walkabout. No one at Faslane can find them.'

'That can't be.' There was an odd strain in the other man's voice.

'Can be. Is. Look, I'm going to ring Lopez in Panama. See if he knows anything. You get onto Sally, then call me back.'

Lopez wasn't answering. Chris hung up and was about to try again when the datadown lit with an incoming video call from Philip Hamilton. He frowned again and picked up.

'Yeah?'

Hamilton's soft features resolved on the screen. 'Ah. Chris. There you are.'

'Yeah.' Still the vague sense of something out of place. He'd had almost no dealings with the junior partner since he joined Shorn. Some of the Central American stuff he'd inherited from Makin brushed up against Hamilton's accounts, but—

'What can I do for you, Philip?'

'Well, Chris.' The junior partner's tone was silky. 'It's more a case of what I can do for you, I think. You've no doubt heard about the Langley crisis.'

'Yeah. Mike t—' He just stopped himself. 'I was just talking to Mike about it. Archive material, they reckon. Suggests the Cambodia stuff might not be included.'

'That's correct.' Hamilton nodded. His chins folded. 'In fact, we just got confirmation. Good news for everybody. Louise will probably forward it down to you shortly. But, ah, it seems there is one covert operation that will crop up, and unfortunately it has your name on it. I'm talking about the action you took against Hernan Echevarria's security forces in Medellín.'

Now the sense of wrongness was quick and jagged. Like the floor cracking apart under him.

He covered it with drawl. 'Yeah. So?'

'Well, I think under the circumstances, and given recent developments with the Echevarria regime, the best thing would probably be if you were removed from the NAME account, at least for the time being.'

Chris sat up. 'You can't fucking do that.'

'I *beg* your pardon?'

'What developments are you talking about, Philip? Last I heard, the Echevarria regime was a corpse walking.'

'Ah, yes.' Hamilton fingered his jowls. 'This also is new. Perhaps you'd better come along to the briefing this afternoon. I'd invited Mike, and assumed he could pass on detail to you later. But, yes, perhaps it's better if you're there. Main conference, two o'clock.'

Chris stared at him. 'Right. I'll be there.'

'Marvellous.' Hamilton beamed and cut the link. His face inked out, still smiling.

Chris tried Lopez again. Still nothing. He windowed up an indesp site he had the keys to and checked the Langley data. Nothing solid. The whistleblower's face grinned out of an employee file thumbprint that was five years stale. He looked young and happy, and blissfully unaware of what his just-acquired job was going to do to him a few years down the road.

Because they're going to fucking crucify you, son, Chris told the thumbprint silently. *They're going to take you apart for this.*

The datadown chimed. Audio call from Mike. He grabbed it.

'Talk to me, Mike. What's going on.'

'I don't know, Chris. I wish I did. Sally says the order still went through, but it's been diverted to some surface shipping contractor out of Southampton. Standard cross-Atlantic rate, she's getting a cashback bonus for the difference in cost.'

'*Surface?*'

'I know, I know. I don't get it either. It's not like Barranco can wander into Barranquilla docks and just sign for it.'

'That's—' He stopped. Abruptly, the spinning chaos of the last ten minutes locked to a halt in his head. He saw the sense.

'Mike, I'll call you back.'

'Wait, you—'

He snapped the line across, sat staring at the datadown for a full thirty seconds while the sudden weight in his guts settled. *Has to be*, he knew. *Fucking* has *to be*. He felt physically sick with the knowledge.

He placed another call to Lopez, got the busy signal and fired an override down the connection. There was a brief electronic squabble on the line, as Shorn's intrusion software fought with the Panama City net, then Lopez came through, still talking to someone else in furious Spanish.

'*—de puta, me tienen media hora esperando—*'

'Joaquin, listen to me.'

'Chris? *Como has podido—*' The Americas agent stopped as his language caught up with the change of call. 'Listen, Chris, what are you fucking playing at over there?'

'I don't know, Joaquin, I *don't know*. This shit only just landed on me, and I don't know what it is. Talk to me, man. I'm blind here. Tell me what's going on.'

'What's going on,' said Lopez, rage spurting from every syllable, 'is that you've sold me just like your fucking amigo Bryant. Arena challenge, Chris. That mean anything to you. I just got the word. Shorn-approved tender, I got some fucking favela-born sicario calling me out for a half per cent fee reduction. He's twenty years old, Chris. Priority challenge, two weeks' notice. Shorn-fucking-approved, man.'

'Alright, listen.' Chris felt the sudden clarity of drive time set in, the suspended icy seconds of adrenalin injection. 'Joaquin, listen to me carefully. That's not me. The tender, it's not authorised by me. I'm going to fix it for you, it's dead on the datadown. I promise you. You'll never have to fight. Meantime—'

'Yeah, you say that. You said—'

'Joaquin, fucking *listen* to me. I got you out of Bogotá in one piece, didn't I? I told you, I look after my people. Now, I don't have much time. I need you to get onto Barranco.'

'You want me to fucking *work* for you while—'

'*Fucking listen, I said.*' Whatever was in his voice must have got through. Lopez went quiet. 'This is life or death, Joaquin. You get onto Barranco, and you tell him to stay away from that delivery beach next week. Tell him the rest of the arms aren't coming, and most likely there'll be an army death squad waiting for him instead. Tell him I'm under fire as much as he is, and it'll take me time to sort it out. He's got to fall back to safe ground, and stay there until he hears from me. Have you got that?'

'Yeah.' Lopez was suddenly calm, as if the same adrenalin shiver had crept down the line and touched him with its time-warping cold. 'Got it. You're in the arena too, huh?'

'Yeah, looks that way.' There was a finality about the way his own words sounded in his ears. 'I'll get back to you as soon as I can.'

'Chris.'

He held off the disconnect. 'Yeah. Still here.'

'Chris, listen to me. You going into the arena, you stab low, man. Stab low, where they won't see it coming. And when you pull it out, you twist that fucker. Quadruples the wound. You got that?'

Chris nodded distantly. 'I got it, Joaquin. Thanks.'

'Hey, I'll be praying for you, man.'

Philip Hamilton cut a surprisingly impressive figure in presentation. Somehow the softness of the man disappeared, became confident bulk and the resonance base for a rich baritone voice that gave his words a longevity way beyond the moment of their utterance. His evidence was compelling, it was set up that way, but more powerful was the echo of what he said in the minds of his listeners. Chris looked round the table and saw heads nodding, Mike Bryant's included.

'Thus we convert,' Hamilton declared vibrantly, 'the uncertainty of change, the *certainty* of post-land-reform unrest, and the probable budget deficit of the classic revolutionary regime, at a stroke, into a return to the profitable status quo we have enjoyed in the NAME for the last twenty years. It seems to me, ladies and gentlemen, that there is really no question or choice here, only a course of action that common sense and market return dictate. Thank you.'

Applause rippled politely round the table. Murmured comments. Hamilton inclined his head and stood back a couple of steps. Louise Hewitt stood up.

'I think that's pretty clear, thank you, Philip, but if there are any questions, perhaps we could have them now?'

'Yes.' Jack Notley raised a hand with completely superfluous deference. Every exec in the room shut up on the instant, and pinned their gaze on the grizzled senior partner. Louise Hewitt folded herself back into her chair, and Philip Hamilton moved to take up the space she had left him. It was, Chris thought bitterly, choreographed tightly enough to be a *Saturday Night Special* dance act.

'Yes, Jack.'

'The Americans,' said Notley with heavy emphasis that earned a sprinkling of laughter. The old man's nationalist eccentricity was well known in the division. 'We know from Mike here's painstaking research that Echevarria junior has, shall we say, a predilection for our transatlantic cousins and they are, unfortunately, far closer to him, both geographically and culturally, than are we. I appreciate, Phil, that you're factoring in Calders RapCap with the liaison work, and obviously, Martin Meldreck, well he believes in a free market about as much as Ronald Reagan did.' More laughter, louder this time. 'So the secondary contractors he brings in will be exclusively US firms. That much is clear. My question is, will this be enough? Will it hold off Conrad Rimshaw at Lloyd Paul, for example? Or the Saunders Group, or Gray Capital Solutions, or Moriarty Mills & Silver? Francisco Echevarria has had close dealings with all these gentlemen, or at least their Miami officers, at one time or another. Can we be confident he will not bring them into play as soon as a budget review fails to please him?'

Hear fucking hear, sleeted through Chris. *Glad someone in this bunch of fucking sycophants spotted it.*

Hamilton cleared his throat.

'That's a fair concern, Jack. I think it's indicative that the firms you've just named, with the exception of the Saunders Group, are all fast, hungry players from the New York corner. Sure, they'll all bear watching. But the point with Calders is that they have the US state department's ear. That's long-term relationship – in the case of Senator Barlow, we're talking fifteen years, and there are others with ties almost as old. And of course, as you say, the secondary contractors Calders RapCap's people will bring in should have their own lobby network in place. If we combine all that pull with the influence we have on our own

340

Foreign Office here in London, I feel sure we're in a position to repel any prospective boarders.'

He got the laughter too. He beamed round the table.

'Any more questions?'

'Yeah, I've got a question for you.' Chris climbed to his feet, trembling slightly. He stared at Hamilton. 'I'm curious as to why *the fuck* you're throwing away a guaranteed regime change, with a leader who is guaranteed one hundred per cent proof against US involvement of any kind – in favour of this. Fucking. Carve up.'

Sudden slither of shock around the table. Gasps, shuffling, the shaking of wiser heads. At his side, Mike Bryant was looking up at him in disbelief.

'Ah. Chris.' Hamilton smiled briefly, like a comic to his audience just before the straight man gets it. 'Now before you go and get Mike's baseball bat, could I just point out that we're trying for a non-violent model here.'

A couple of sniggers, but battened down. Officially, no one below partner level was supposed to know what had really happened to Hernan Echevarria. Nick Makin would have talked, Chris knew, he would have made sure word got out, but just how far they could all go along with Hamilton's indiscretion was unclear. Once again, gazes sought Jack Notley for his reaction, but the senior partner's features could have been pale granite.

'You stupid fuck,' said Chris clearly, and the silence that followed it was absolute. 'Do you really think Vicente Barranco is going to be stopped by some pissant cokehead dressed up in his old man's uniform? Do you really think he'll just *go away*?'

He saw Louise Hewitt on her way to getting up. Saw Jack Notley lay a hand on her arm and shake his head almost imperceptibly. Philip Hamilton spotted the exchange as well, and his mouth contracted to almost anal proportions.

'Might I remind you, *Mr* Faulkner, that you are talking to a partner. If you can't show the proper respect in this meeting, I will have you removed. Do you understand me?'

Chris's eyes widened slightly, and an unpleasant smile floated onto his face.

'Try it,' he said softly.

'Chris.' Notley's voice cracked across the room. 'If you have anything to contribute, I'd like you to contribute it now, and then sit down. This is a policy meeting, not the Royal Shakespeare Company.'

Chris nodded. 'Alright.' He looked round the room. 'This is for the record. I know Vicente Barranco, and I'm telling you, if you try to fuck him over like this, he'll fade back into the highlands like he has before and he'll take the disenfranchised of the NAME with him by the thousand. And then, some day, maybe five years down the road, maybe next year, he'll be back. He'll be back, and he'll do what we were going to ask him to do in the first place, and when he's sitting in the Bogotá parliament chamber, and Echevarria junior is facing a firing squad somewhere for crimes against humanity, we'll find ourselves on the wrong fucking side. He'll go to someone else, maybe Nakamura, maybe the Germans, and he will *cut us out*. No GDP percentage, no enterprise zone licences, no arms trade, no supply side contracts, no commodities angle, *nothing*. We'll just have a roomful of angry Americans, and nothing to feed them with.'

More silence, glances up and down the table in search of where this was going. Chris jerked his chin at Hamilton and sat down.

Hamilton looked at Notley. The senior partner shrugged. Hamilton cleared his throat.

'Well, Chris. Thank you for that, ah, *academic* insight. Of course, I appreciate you taking the time to come and give your view on an account you're no longer working on, but let me just say, I think we can handle one disgruntled marquista and indeed there are already initiatives in place—'

Chris grinned like a skull.

'He won't be there, Hamilton. I already called Lopez, told him to steer Barranco well clear of the beach. When the *Cobain* doesn't show up, and junior's pet thugs do, either they'll find nothing, or better yet Barranco'll catch them in an ambush and slaughter them. After that, he'll fade like a fucking ghost.'

The room erupted before he finished. Uproar from the gathered ranks of execs, half of them on their feet, pointing and shouting, not all wholly opposed to Chris, it seemed, Hamilton yelling across the mêlée of voices, something about *fucking* professional misconduct, Notley bellowing for order. The door burst open and security rushed the room, wielding non-lethal weaponry. Louise Hewitt went to stop them, hands and voice raised to make herself understood above the noise.

In the midst of it all, Mike turned to Chris, face distorted with shock and anger. 'Are you fucking insane?' he hissed.

It took ten minutes to clear the conference room, and even then security weren't happy about leaving the partners with Chris. They'd heard their own set of rumours about the Echevarria incident.

'It'll be fine,' said Notley. 'Really, Hermione. I appreciate your diligence, but we're all colleagues here. Just tempers flaring, that's all. A bit of misplaced road rage. Just keep a couple of your people outside the door, that'll be fine.'

He ushered the guard captain out and closed the doors, then turned back to the table. In the places they had occupied when the room was filled, Chris, Mike, Louise Hewitt and Philip Hamilton sat staring at their respective patches of polished wood. Notley came back to the head of the table and stood looking at them.

'Right,' he said grimly. 'Let's sort this out, shall we?'

Louise Hewitt made an impatient gesture. 'I don't see anything to sort out, Jack. Faulkner's just admitted to gross professional misconduct—'

'Yeah, that's—'

'Chris, you will *shut up*,' roared Notley. 'You are not a partner, nor will you ever be if you cannot behave in a civilised fashion. Do as you're told and be fucking quiet.'

'Louise is right, Jack.' Hamilton's voice was soft and calm, at odds with the rage he'd shown earlier. He was back on comfortable ground. 'Warning Barranco has endangered a delicate piece of policy restructuring. At a minimum, it's cost us a possible bargaining chip with Echevarria. At worst, it's given succour to a terrorist who could provide us with insurgency problems for the next decade.'

'He was a freedom fighter last week,' muttered Chris.

Louise Hewitt turned a look of distilled contempt on him. 'Let me ask you a question, Chris,' she said lightly. 'Would it be fair to say that you've become *political* where the NAME is concerned? That you've been contaminated by local issues?'

Chris looked at Notley. 'Am I allowed to answer that?'

'Yes. But you'll keep your tone civil, and show some respect, is that understood? This isn't some basement fight club in the zones.'

'Yes, I understand that.' Chris jabbed a finger at Hamilton. 'What I don't understand is our junior partner's system of communication. Until this morning, I had no idea either that I had been relieved of duty on the NAME account, or that we were reversing our established client relationship.'

'Echevarria *is* the established—'

'Philip.' Notley wagged a finger at the junior partner. 'Let him finish.'

'In fact,' Chris saw the opening and accelerated into it. 'The client change was news to me until this meeting, which wasn't helpful. If I warned Barranco off, it was because I thought someone was running infiltration into the account—'

'Oh, please.' Louise Hewitt pulled a face. 'This is your job on the line, Chris. Surely you can do better than that.'

'This morning, Louise, I received a direct call from the captain of the sub freighter we're using to ship Barranco's arms. She's stuck in

343

Faslane, waiting for freight that isn't coming because *this*,' Chris indicated Hamilton, 'genius has had it rerouted to the NAME military. Only he didn't think to inform me of the fact, so all I can assume is outside interference. I act accordingly, I protect our client as best I can. I get slammed for it, when the real problem here is a lack of top-down communication.'

'You're lying,' said Hamilton angrily. He also had seen the loophole.

'Am I, Philip?' Chris turned to gesture at Mike Bryant. 'Ask Mike. He's been as much in the dark as I have, he knows all about the sub freighter call, because the two of us were both trying to work out what the *fuck* was going on this morning. Right, Mike?'

Bryant shifted in his seat. For the first time ever that Chris could remember, he looked uncomfortable.

Notley's gaze sharpened. 'Mike?'

'Yeah, that's right.' Bryant sighed. 'Sorry, Phil. Louise. Chris is right. You should have told us earlier.'

Hamilton leaned across the table, flushed. 'Bryant, you *knew* —'

'I knew there was a policy meeting, and yeah, from the hints you dropped, I guessed the way it was going. But there was nothing solid, Phil. And nothing about the shipments. You know,' a sideways glance at his friend, 'I didn't know what Chris was going to do, but I couldn't tell him for sure what was going on either. I can see why he would have played it the way he did.'

The room was still. A glance crackled between Hamilton and Hewitt. No one spoke. Jack Notley steepled his fingers.

'Is there anything else?' he asked quietly.

Louise Hewitt shrugged. 'Only that what we've heard is a pack of lies designed to hide the fact that Chris has gone political on us.'

'Anything *constructive*,' asked Notley, still more softly.

'Yes,' said Chris, thinking of Lopez, tossed into the arena and up against a twenty-year-old blade sicario who'd be savage with favela poverty and sight of a way out. Thinking of Barranco, machine-gunned to death on a darkened beach, blood leaking into the sand under a shattering of glass shard stars. 'I am *not* political. My reasons for backing Vicente Barranco have nothing to do with politics. And anyone who wants to call that into question can see me on the road.'

FORTY-THREE

'You are a lying motherfucker, Chris.' Mike Bryant paced back and forth in front of the BMW, furious. His feet crunched in the hard shoulder gravel. Off to one side, a breeze stirred the grass beside the motorway ramp. He stopped and jabbed a finger at Chris. 'You *have* turned political, haven't you. Fucking Barranco got to you, didn't he?'

Chris leaned on the still warm hood of the car, arms folded. The orbital stretched away below them, deserted as far as the eye could see in both directions. After the confines of the Shorn block, the sky over them seemed enormous. They'd driven for less than an hour, but it felt as if they stood at the edge of the world.

'Oh, give me a fucking break. You're accusing *me* of politics. A week ago, Barranco was the horse to back. Now suddenly, he's *unprofitable*? What is that, Mike? That's not political?'

'The numbers make sense,' said Bryant.

'The numbers?' Chris came off the hood of the BMW, taut with rage. 'The fucking *numbers*? That shit is *made up*, Mike. You can make the numbers tell you any fucking thing you want them to. What about the numbers that made sense *for* Barranco? What happened to them? What are we, economists all of a sudden? You want to draw me a fucking curve? *It's got nothing to do with reality, Mike. You know that.*'

Mike looked away. 'That fact remains, Chris. You're in way too close with Barranco. You've got to come off the account. Let Hamilton run with it, see what happens.'

'Great. And meanwhile what happens to Joaquin Lopez?'

'That's not *important*!' Bryant made fists, punched exasperatedly off into the wind. 'Fuck Chris, pay attention, will you. You can't get personal on this thing. It's just business. Lopez has been undercut, that's all there is to it. If this new guy can do the same work for a percentage point less commission, what the fuck are we doing still working with Lopez anyway?'

'It's a half per cent, Mike. And he's a twenty-year-old sicario, straight out of the favelas. How do we know what he'll do?'

'If he's hungry, he'll do well. They always do.'

'Oh, what the fuck are you talking about, Mike? You were at the briefing. This guy is cheap and aggressive, and that's all we know. He could be fucking illiterate for all the background Hamilton's shown us. This is a bad call, Mike. This isn't business, it's a fucking greed call. Can't you see that?'

'What I see, Chris, is that you're cruising for a fall.' Mike's voice softened, but it was the gentle tug of a steel tow cable, taking up slack. He moved in, stood close. 'I see why you're acting like this, but it's no good. You're out of control. You're unmanageable. And we can't afford that, not in any of us. I'm sorry about what happened to your dad, really I am.'

Chris flinched away. Mike caught his arm.

'No, I am. I'm sorry about the zones and your mum and everything that's happened to you. But that's the past, Chris, and it's over. It doesn't give you an excuse to fuck up everyone else's life around here. Now I'm telling you, *listen to me*, Chris, I'm telling you, you're off the NAME account. End of story. I'm the one that brought you aboard in the first place, and now I'm cutting you loose. It's not like you haven't got enough else to worry about. Fuck, Chris, why don't you go home? Talk to Carla, sort your life out.'

Chris shoved him away, both palm-heels into the chest. For a flashpoint second, both men almost dropped into a karate stance.

'I've told you before, Mike. I don't need marital advice from you.'

'Chris, you're throwing away the best—'

'*Shut the fuck up!*' The yell lashed out, fury etched with pain. 'What do you know about it, Mike, what the *fuck* do you know about it?'

'I know—'

Chris cut across him savagely. 'Try staying faithful to Suki for ten minutes, why don't you? Try acting like a responsible father and husband for a change. Get your dick out of Sally Hunting and Liz Linshaw and whoever else you're dipping it into these days. There. You enjoying this, Mike? Doesn't feel good, does it?'

'I'm not seeing Liz at the moment,' said Mike quietly. 'She's got a lot of work on. And I haven't fucked Sally Hunting in better than six years. You want to make sure of your facts before you start mouthing off.'

'I couldn't have put it better myself.'

They stood twitchily, facing each other across one corner of the BMW's hood. Very distantly, the sound came of a single vehicle on the orbital. Finally, Mike Bryant shrugged.

'Alright,' he said. 'If that's the way you want it. But what I said before stands. You're off the NAME account, you're—'

His phone queeped for attention. He grimaced and fished it out, pressed it impatiently to his ear. 'Yeah, Bryant. Out on the orbital, why? Yeah, he's right here.'

He handed the phone to Chris.

'Hewitt,' he said.

*

Louise Hewitt sat behind her desk, hands spread on its surface as if she might find built-in weaponry there to blast Chris into grease on the carpet. Her tone was chilly.

'Well, I'm glad you're back from your picnic in the country. There are a couple of things we need to clear up.'

Chris waited.

'Primarily, I'm concerned to get your files for the NAME transferred to Philip Hamilton's desk as soon as electronically possible. He'll need your Panama City contacts, the background data on Barranco, and any of the other insurgents you did work on for Hammett McColl.' She offered him a thin smile. 'Since we're now back in the business of helping the regime flatten its opponents, anything you have will be of some value.'

'Then maybe you should shut down the agency tender on Lopez. He knows the ground. That's value, right there.'

She looked him up and down, like a specimen of something she'd thought was extinct. 'Remarkable, Chris. Your capacity for inappropriate loyalty, I mean. Quite remarkable. However, I think we all agreed at the briefing that a clean break is essential. There's no telling what inconvenient loyalties Lopez himself may have. Perhaps he has, uh, *bonded* with Vicente Barranco as strongly as you have. The man is, by all accounts, quite inspiring.'

Nothing. He wouldn't give her the satisfaction.

'But I digress,' Hewitt said smoothly. 'In addition to the file transfer, I want you to prepare a formal statement of apology for your behaviour today. For posting on our intranet. First and foremost, that means an apology for your zone-mannered outburst in Philip's briefing, but it's not limited to that. There are other matters. I feel, and our senior partner concurs, that the apology had better also cover your failure to consult your colleagues before taking client-related decisions.'

'Notley said that?'

The thin smile again. 'He's not on your side, Chris, whatever you think. Don't make that mistake. Notley's concerned wholly with the success of Shorn Conflict Investment, with maybe a side interest in waving the Union Jack when he gets the chance. Call it a hobby. That's it, that's the whole story. At the moment, he still thinks you're a necessary component for the division to do well. Thus far, I've failed to persuade him otherwise, but I think, with your help today, he's coming around. I told you once you'd disappoint him, and I think we're closing on that.'

'That'd make you happy, would it?'

'What'd make me happy, Chris, is to take back our plastic from your lightly charred and broken corpse.' She shrugged. 'I'm unlikely to get that chance, of course. Policy doesn't allow us to duel across partner-employee lines. But I will, I think, live to see you booted out of Shorn and back to the riverside slum existence you so eminently suit. I've told you before, and it's becoming clearer by the day, you do not belong here.'

Oddly, the line made him grin. 'Well, you're not the only person who thinks that, Louise.'

It got him a sharp look, but Hewitt wasn't biting.

'Notley and I have also agreed that you'd better draft the apology to Philip's specifications. A first draft by this evening. That's a minimum requirement if you intend to continue with this firm. Philip's in uplink conference right now, with Echevarria. But he'll be done by six. Take it in for his approval then. You might like to add a verbal apology at the same time.' She looked at him, grim amusement curled in the corner of her mouth. 'A personal touch, say. A little bridge-building.'

He walked out, wordless. Louise Hewitt watched him go, and as the door slammed, the smile broadened on her lips.

It took him the walk to his own office to decide. Two flights of stairs and a corridor. He saw no one. He reached the door with his name on it, stood facing the metalled slab for ten seconds, and then turned away.

He was a dozen paces away and accelerating before it had properly dawned on him what he was going to do.

I look after my people.

He found his way almost absently, most of him thinking about Carla and how fucking delighted she'd be to see his life come tumbling down like this. The main door to the conference room was locked, but the entrance to the covert viewing chamber was on a code he knew. He let himself in. Peered through the gloom and the glass panel.

In the conference room, Philip Hamilton sat opposite a holo of Francisco Echevarria. The dictator's son was dressed in his usual Susana Ingram splendour. He looked hard and implacable against Hamilton's soft and light-suited untidiness.

'—are aware that you have friends in Miami, and we have no desire to exclude them from the proceedings. You should certainly speak with Martin Meldreck at Calders, who will, I'm sure—'

Enough. He coded himself through the connecting door, stood abruptly behind Hamilton. Echevarria's eyes widened as he stepped inside the pick-up field of the holoscanner and he knew that in the chamber on the other side of the world he had appeared, like a ghost at the feast.

Hamilton turned around in his chair.

348

'Faulkner.' He wasn't worried yet, just surprised. Anger edged his cultured tones. 'What the hell do you think you're doing, interrupting me with a client?'

Chris grinned down at him. 'You wanted a statement from me.'

'Yes. In due course. At the moment, I'm busy. You can—'

Chris hit him. Open-handed, swinging from the shoulder. It took Hamilton across the side of the head and tipped him out of the chair.

'First draft.' Chris grabbed him up by the hair and hit him again in the face, this time with a fist. He felt the junior partner's nose break. He punched him once more for security and let go. Hamilton slumped to the floor like a filled sack. He turned about, reached Francisco Echevarria with his eyes.

'Hello, Paco.' He got his breath back, straightened up the chair. 'You don't know me, do you? Allow me to introduce myself. I'm the man who beat your father to death.'

Echevarria's face tightened. 'Are you fuckin' crazy, man? You di'n kill my father.'

Chris settled into the chair. 'No, I did. The terrorist stuff was something we set up to cover what really happened. The CE—, those guys, they went with the claim because it gives them prestige. Your father was a sick fuck, and anyone killing him could claim they'd done a good day's work.'

'You gonna fuckin' die for that, man.' The dictator's son was staring at him, transfixed. 'You gonna fuckin' *die* .'

'Oh, please. *As* I was saying, there's no way the, that bunch, are well enough organised to do something like that on the streets of London and get away with it. So, as I said, *I* killed your old man. I beat him to death, in this very room, with a baseball bat. All part of a day's work for the Shorn corporation. Check with Mike Bryant if you don't believe me, I'm a colleague of his.'

Echevarria's voice came out strangled. ' *You—*'

'It's what we do here, Paco. Neoliberal commercial management. Global mayhem, remote-control death and destruction. Market Forces in action. If you don't like it—'

Hamilton charged him from the side.

He had time to be impressed – *fat fuck didn't look like he had it in him* – then the chair went over and the junior partner was on top of him, bloodied nose spattering down into his face, soft hands digging into the cords of his throat with surprising strength.

Chris wasted no time struggling. He got a grip on the little finger of Hamilton's right hand, curled it back and snapped it. Hamilton yelped and let go. Chris came up from the floor like a hinge and punched the partner in the throat. Hamilton lurched back, just on his feet, clutching at the point of impact. Somewhere on the other side of the world, Echevarria was yelling in Spanish. Chris got to his feet, stalked towards Hamilton. The partner's eyes widened. Chris threw a punch, Hamilton ducked and fended with a rusty boxing move, the other hand still at his throat. There wasn't much strength in it, and he came up panting. Impatiently, Chris repeated the punch, snagged Hamilton's wrist with an aikido hold he knew and jerked the partner off balance towards him. He punched low into the expansive gut, and as Hamilton spasmed, he grabbed him round the neck and yanked up and round.

It had the fury of the whole day behind it.

It snapped Hamilton's neck.

Chris heard the muffled crack, and as the partner went limp in his grip, the rage drained out of him. He let go and Hamilton hit the floor. He turned back to Echevarria and the suited aides who were crowding into the holocast around him. They stared at him like frightened children.

He cleared his throat. 'Now—'

Something cold and jagged slapped him. He blinked and raised one arm to look at the mass of silvery wire mesh that had come out of nowhere and wrapped around his side. He was starting to turn to the door behind him, when the stungun web sparked and went off with a smell like scorching plastic. The jolt flung him hard against the table, where he clung for a moment, staring.

In the open doorway, Louise Hewitt stood with the stungun still levelled and watched him collapse.

The last thing he saw was her smile.

FORTY-FOUR

The cell measured about three metres on a side, and smelled very faintly of fresh paint, thick pastel layers of which coated the walls. There was a comfortable steel frame bed against one such wall, a three-drawer desk under the window and an en suite bathroom capsule in one corner. Next to the capsule, plain white towels hung on a heated rack and next to that there was hanging space and boxed shelving for his clothes. The fixtures were good-quality wood and metal, and the window looked out over the river through glass that only betrayed its toughened qualities with the tiny red triangle logo in one corner. The whole place was no worse than some hotels Chris had seen on placement, and it was in considerably better condition than any of the rooms in Erik Nyquist's Brundtland estate apartment.

As far as he could work out, he was the only person in the block.

Guest of honour, he thought vaguely as he went to sleep the second night. *Full run of the facilities.*

The truth was, the corporate police didn't seem to know what to do with him. They'd taken his phone and his wallet on arrival, but beyond that basic security measure, they appeared to be making it up as they went along. They weren't used to holding executives for anything more serious than drunken affray or the occasional white-collar accounting misdemeanour. Most of their duties went the other way – investigation of crimes and apprehension of suspects where the victims were corporate but the criminals were not. Anyone of that stripe who made it to custody alive would be summarily handed over to the conventional police so that grubby business of state law enforcement could be set in motion.

Here, the victim was corporate but so was the offender.

Say what?

Murder, they were saying, but *hell, don't these guys off each other on the road practically every month.*

That's different.

It was confusing for everybody. In the ensuing vacuum, Chris was accorded a status somewhere between cherished celebrity and dangerous lunatic. The first role at least, he was learning how to play.

The days inched along, like slow, bulky files downloading.

He got meals in his cell at three appointed times daily, delivered on a tray by two uniformed officers, one of whom watched from the door while the other set down the food on the desk. An hour after each meal, the tray was removed by the same team, but only after all items of cutlery and crockery had been checked off on a palm-pad. Both men were friendly enough, but they never let the conversation get beyond pleasantries and they watched him warily all the time.

Impotence was two clenched fists and a fizzing wire through the head. Lopez, Barranco, the NAME account. *Nothing* he could do.

A different team, also all male, escorted him out of the cell for an hour's exercise after breakfast and lunch. They marched him along well-cared-for corridors and down a stairwell that let out to an internal quadrangle. There was a profusion of plants and trees planted in shingle beds, a complex step-structured bronze fountain and a high, angled glass roof covering a third of the open space. His escort left him alone in the quad, closed the doors and watched him from a glassed-in mezzanine gallery above. The first couple of times, he paced back and forth aimlessly, less out of any real inclination than from a vague sense of what was expected of him. Once he realised this, he stopped and spent most of his allocated hour sitting on the edge of the fountain, lost in the noise it made, knotted, hopeless plans to save Joaquin Lopez from the arena, and daydreams of driving the Saab.

When it became apparent he wasn't leaving any time soon, he got clothes. Three changes of good-quality casuals in dark colours and a dozen sets of cotton underwear. He asked the woman who came to fit him how she wanted him to pay, cash or cards and she looked embarrassed.

'We bill your firm,' she admitted finally.

He got no visitors, for which he was obscurely grateful. He wouldn't have known what to say to anybody he knew.

Between meals, the hours stretched out. He couldn't remember a time when less had been expected of him. One of his warders offered to let him have some books, but when the promised haul arrived, it consisted of a bare half-dozen battered paperbacks by authors Chris had never heard of. He picked one at random, a luridly violent far-future crime novel about a detective who could seemingly exchange bodies at will, but the subject matter was alien to him and his attention drifted. It all seemed very far-fetched.

He was asked if he wanted paper and pens and said yes, reflexively, then didn't know what to do with them. He tried to write an account of the events leading up to Philip Hamilton's death, as much as anything to get it clear in his own head, but he kept having to cross out what he'd written and start further back. When his first line read *my father was*

352

murdered by an executive called Edward Quain, he gave up. Perhaps inspired by the novel he was trying to read, he wrote an imaginary brief for the NAME account set five years into a future where Barranco had taken power and instituted wide-ranging land reform. It also seemed very far-fetched.

He started a letter to Carla and tore it up after less than ten lines. He couldn't think of anything worth telling her.

The week ended. Another started.

Shorn came for him.

He was on morning walkabout, cheated of his usual seat at the fountain by a persistent, heavy drizzle that drenched the exposed patio area and kept him penned under the glass roof. His escort had obligingly dragged a bench out from somewhere for him, and now he sat at one end of it and stared out at the curtain of rain falling a half metre away.

The plants, at least, seemed to be enjoying it.

The door to the quad snapped open and he flicked a surprised glance at his watch. He'd only been there twenty minutes. He looked up and saw Louise Hewitt standing there. It was the first time he'd seen her since she shot him with the stungun. He looked back at the rain.

'Morning, Faulkner. Mind if I sit down?'

He stared down at his hands. 'I guess they'll stop me if I try to break your neck.'

'Try to lay a fucking finger on me, and I'll stop you myself,' she said mildly. 'You're not the only one with karate training, you know.'

He shrugged.

'I'll take that as a yes, then.'

He felt the bench shift slightly as she lowered herself onto it at the other end. They sat a metre apart. The rain fell through the silence, hissing softly.

'Liz Linshaw says hi,' Hewitt told him, finally.

It jerked his head around.

'Well,' she amended. 'That's paraphrase. Actually, she says, *you fucking bitch, you can't hold him without charges this long, I want to see him*. She's wrong about that, of course. We can hold you pretty much indefinitely.'

Chris looked away again, jaw set.

'We don't plan to, though. In fact, your release papers should come through some time tomorrow morning. You can go home, or back to that expensive hotel fucknest you've been maintaining. Want to know how come?'

He locked down the urge to ask, to give anything. It was hard to do. He was hungry for detail from outside, for anything to engage the frantically spinning wheels in his head.

353

'So I'll tell you anyway. Tomorrow's Thursday, you should be out by lunchtime at worst. That gives you the best part of a day before you drive. We've posted for a Friday challenge, it's traditional at Shorn. Gives everyone the weekend to get used to the result.'

'What the fuck are you talking about, Hewitt?' The insolence shrouded the question enough that he could justify breaking his silence. 'What challenge?'

'The partnership challenge. For Philip Hamilton's post.'

He coughed a laugh. 'I don't want Hamilton's fucking job.'

'Oh yes, you do. In fact, you issued a formal notice of challenge just before you killed him. Citing unprofessional conduct over the NAME account, ironically enough.' She reached into her jacket and produced a palm-pad. 'I can show you it if you like.'

'No thanks. I don't know what shit you're cooking up, Hewitt, but it won't start. You know the policy, you told me yourself last week. No partner/employee crossover.'

'Well, yes, granted your actions were unorthodox. But, as you know, our senior partner is a big fan of policy-making by precedent. He's agreed that we can blur the distinction in this case. Apparently, he's had you in mind for partner status for quite a while. You *or* Mike Bryant, of course.'

And then it all came crashing down on him, like a slum clearance he'd watched as a kid. Explosions ripping through what he thought was solid from one side to the other, clean straight lines of structure tipping, curtseying and dissolving into a chaos of tumbling rubble and dust while a huddled crowd watched. He couldn't see the resulting wreckage clearly yet, but he sensed its outlines.

'Mike won't drive against me,' he said without conviction.

Hewitt smiled. 'Yes, he will. I've talked to him. More precisely, I've talked to him about equity, capital wealth, partner-safe status, professional versus unprofessional behaviour and the dangers of unmanageability. Oh, and the identity of your mystery hotel guest over the last couple of weeks.'

'The fuck are you talking about?' But as he said it, the sliding sense of despair was overwhelming, because he already knew.

'Don't be obtuse, Chris. I've got indesp microcam footage from Liz's house and the hotel too. Should have seen Mike's face when he saw *that* stuff.'

'Bullshit.'

'No,' she said almost kindly. 'I've been modelling this one for months, Chris. I mean, come on. Who do you think sent you Donna Dread's little performance in the first place?' She waited for a response, saw she was getting none and sighed. 'Okay, Linshaw was already leaning pretty hard in your direction, she's such a little tart with the driving thing anyway. But even so, I think I deserve some credit. If it weren't for me, you'd probably still be grinding through the same stale old fidelity numbers with your Norwegian grease monkey.'

Chris nodded to himself. The shock was still coming, in waves. 'You set me up with Hamilton, didn't you. You knew what I'd do.'

'It seemed likely.' Hewitt examined her nails modestly. 'To tell the truth, I wasn't sure I'd get a result this good. Putting you and Hamilton on a collision course was an obvious no-lose strategy, the Lopez/Barranco stuff looked likely to pull you in, you proved that with Echevarria senior. Little favour called in at the Langley end, tip you off the account and off we go. But even so, Chris, I was impressed . You really managed to fuck up beyond my wildest dreams. I don't know what you were thinking. If you *were* thinking.'

'You wouldn't understand,' Chris said distantly.

'No, I do understand. You're hooked on Barranco's shiny new dream – actually, it's a pretty grubby, old dream, but let's leave that – and some macho loyalty thing for Joaquin Lopez. I just wonder what you think trashing Hamilton was going to achieve.'

It was a ray of light, worth an almost-grin. 'You're wrong, Louise. Trashing Hamilton was incidental. He was just in the way. The point is, your deal with Echevarria is fucked. He'll never touch Shorn again.'

'Well, that remains to be seen. He's a smarter young man than you give him credit for, and if we can show him your charred corpse with Mike Bryant's boot on it, well, who knows?'

He folded his arms. 'I'm not doing it, Louise.'

'Oh, yes you are.' Her voice turned momentarily ugly. 'Because if you don't drive, then Phil Hamilton's death is just murder, and you'll be getting a swift ride to the organ bank. Those are your choices, Chris. Die on the road or die strapped to a gurney at St Bart's. Either way is fine with me.'

She leaned closer. Close enough that he could smell her perfume under the rain, clean and sharp and lightly spiced. Her voice was a serrated murmur.

'And whichever it is, Chris, when it happens, as you're going under, you just remember Nick Makin.'

Chris looked at her, not really surprised. 'Makin, huh?'

'That's right.' She sat back again. 'Makin.'

'So I called it from the beginning. Your toy boy got bumped for me, and you sent him to kill me.' He shook his head. 'Him and his gangwit proxies. That was brave of you.'

'There's no sent about it, Chris. He hated you for free. If anything,' she closed her mouth, looked away. She blinked. 'If anything, I tried to talk him down because I knew it wasn't necessary. I knew you'd fuck up sooner or later. And don't talk to me about brave, Chris. Not with Mitsue Jones shot through the head at close range while she was injured and trapped in wreckage. Not with the blood of an eighty-year-old man on your hands. You're no fucking different to me in the end.'

'No?' He spotted the weak spot and stabbed at it. He mimicked her savagely. *'Tried to talk him down?* Come on, Louise, if you'd wanted to stop Makin, you could have. He wasn't that strong. You let it happen because it suited the play. Tell yourself what you like in the wee small hours, but don't try and sell that shit to me. In the end, he was just another pawn.'

'Pawn. Ah, yes, the chess player.' Her colour was hectic again, but her voice had evened out. 'You know, I play a little chess myself, Chris. I never made a big splash about it, like some people, but I play. And it's a very limited game. In the end, it's just you and the other guy. That's not a good model for what we do, Chris. Not a good model for life in general. Of course it's very male, one-on-one combat, nice and simple. But it isn't real. You need to upgrade, play something like *AlphaMesh* or *Linkage*. Something multi-sided, something with shifting alliances.'

'Yeah, that sounds more like your speed.'

'It's the speed of the world, Chris. Look around you. See the chess players? Sure you do, they're the stupid third-world fucks sending out their pawns to kill each other over a fifty-mile strip of desert or what colour pyjamas God likes to wear. *We're* the *AlphaMesh* players, Chris. The investment houses, the consultants, the corporates. We shift, we change, we realign, and the game keeps flowing our way. We move around these horn-locked back-and-forth testosterone dickheads, we play them off against each other and they fucking pay us for the privilege.'

'Thanks for the insight.'

'Yeah well.' She got up to go. 'Here's another one. When Mike Bryant drives you off the road on Friday, Mr Chessman – and he will, because he's harder and faster than you – when that happens, just remember. You didn't lose to him, you lost to me.'

FORTY-FIVE

t rained on and off through the night and into the next morning. The
last of the showers sputtered out as Chris was eating breakfast, and
by the time he finished, the sky was brightening. His release order
came through about an hour later. The meal tray detail turned up,
looking unusually cheerful, and told him he could leave whenever he
wanted. They'd brought his phone and wallet, a small black carry-all
for his clothes, and the one who'd loaned him the books said he was
welcome to keep anything he was still reading. Chris said he couldn't
possibly.

Outside, the city was still damp from the rain, and the air smelled
rinsed. The weather had cleared the streets of people, leaving a forlorn
Sunday feel on everything. A moisture-beaded Shorn limousine was
waiting for him at the kerb, engine idling.

'We'll need to hurry, sir,' the chauffeur told him. 'The press release
said four this afternoon, but you never know. Even the corporate cops
have been known to leak. Always a price for drive data, eh?'

In the event, his cynicism proved unfounded. The drive to the hotel
was uneventful, and the chauffeur left him alone. Only once, as his
passenger was getting out, did the man's professional lacquer crack. He
waited until Chris started up the steps to the hotel, then climbed half
out of the driver-side door and leaned across the roof of the limo.

'Good luck, sir,' he said.

Chris turned to look at him. 'Not a Bryant fan, then?' he asked, not
quite steadily.

'No, sir. Didn't want to say anything before, in the car, in case you
thought I was brown-nosing. But I'll be watching you tomorrow, sir.
Betting on you too.'

'That's. Very kind of you.' The attempt at irony wavered away,
unnoticed. 'Any particular reason you're not backing Bryant?' *Because
he sure as fuck is a better driver than me.*

The chauffeur shrugged. 'Can't bring myself to like the man. 'course,
you didn't hear me say that, sir.'

'Say what?'

The chauffeur grinned. 'Like I said, sir. I'll be watching.'

Chris watched him drive away, gripped by a powerful desire to

exchange places with the man. *Secure service job, preferential housing*
likely as not. Modest means, a modest life and a probable future measured i
decades, not days. Look at him, not a care in the fucking world.

Suddenly, he felt sick.

When he got up to his room, the sense of unreality was complete
The only visible change since he left for work the day he murdere
Philip Hamilton was the absence of Liz Linshaw's sleeping form curle
into the bedclothes.

And the document pouch on the desk.

He ripped off the seals and skimmed through the paperwork
standard challenge documentation, agreement to waive normal lega
protection, itemised rules and references to the 2041 (revised) corporat
road charter. Duel envelope details, satellite blow-ups and recent roa
surface commentary from the relevant service providers. It was the M1
run, practically from his front door, down through the underpass an
up over the vaulted section, the Gullet, across the north-eastern zone
and down. The old favourite. No motorway changes, no ramps, jus
into the pipe and drive. Brutal, simple stuff.

In his jacket pocket, the mobile queeped. After ten days without th
phone, it took him a moment to realise what it was. He took it out
identified a video call from Liz and accepted.

'Chris.' She stared out of the tiny screen at him, a little haggar
around the eyes, he noticed, and couldn't help being slightly flattered
'Thank Christ for that, you're out.'

'You must be paying a lot for your tips.'

Her smile was strained. 'Tricks of the trade, Chris. Journalism, I
mean. You know what's happening, I take it.'

'Yeah, I got a full briefing yesterday. Has Mike been in touch?'

'Yeah.' She winced. 'Not a conversation I want to repeat.'

Chris tried to think of something vaguely intelligent to say. 'I guess
he was a lot more serious about you than he liked to show.'

'Yeah, and about you too, Chris. That's what really hurt, apparently.
As far as I could make out between the expletives.'

'Yeah, well.'

A long pause.

'Chris, are you really going to—'

'I don't really want to talk about it, Liz.'

'No. Right.' She hesitated. 'Do you want me to come over?'

Again, the pitching sickness in his stomach. The sheer fucking disbelief at what was going to happen. A rising, swelling bubble of fear.

'I, uh . . .'

'Fine. It's okay, I understand.'

'Good.'

The conversation fizzled for a few more seconds, then died. They said goodbyes that were almost formal, and he hung up.

He sat on the edge of the bed and looked at the phone for a while. Finally, he called Mike.

'Hello, Chris.' There was a flatness in Bryant's voice and eyes that told him everything he needed to know. He could have hung up there and then.

He gave it a shot.

'Mike, you can't be serious about this shit.'

'What shit is that, Chris? The trail-of-bodies-in-Shorn-conference-chambers shit? The political-alignment-with-terrorists shit? Or did you mean the fuck-your-best-friend's-woman shit?'

'Hey. You're married to Suki, not Liz.'

'Do the words *you don't fucking make my marital decisions for me* sound familiar?'

'Listen Mike, I'm coming in to the office. We're going to talk about—'

'No, we're not. I'm taking a half day today. Spending it with Suki, you'll be pleased to hear.'

'Then I'll come and see you there.'

'You do and I'll kick your fucking teeth down your throat on the doorstep.' Mike's top lip drew back from his teeth. 'You just stay where you are and fuck Liz a couple more times, while you've still got the chance. If you can get it up right now, that is.'

Chris snapped.

'Ah, fuck you then. *Asshole! I'll see you on the fucking road!*'

He hurled the phone across the room. It hit the wall and bounced, undamaged, to the floor.

He made one more call. Two, to be completely accurate, but when he called the house in Hawkspur Green, no one answered. He shrugged philosophically and dug Erik Nyquist's number out of the phone's memory. Leaking oil in a head-on collision. It could hardly hurt more than what he'd already swallowed.

The Norwegian was curiously gentle with him.

'She's not here, Chris,' he said. 'And honestly, even if she was, I doubt she'd talk to you.'

'That's fine, I uh, I understand. Uh, do you know if she's gone home? To the house, I mean. I tried her there, not to talk to, only to warn her I'm coming, I mean.' He heard the choppy stumbling of his own speech and stopped. He rubbed at his face, glad Erik didn't have videophone capacity. 'I'm going out to collect the Saab this afternoon. I didn't want to surprise her, you know, if she didn't want to, uh, to see me.'

'She hasn't gone to the house,' said Nyquist, and Chris knew then she was there, maybe standing next to her father in the cramped, damp-smelling confines of the hall, maybe off in the kitchen, back to it all, trying not to listen.

'Okay.' He cleared his throat of an unlooked-for obstruction. 'Listen, Erik. Tell her. When you see her, I mean, tell her she needs to stay resident in the UK for the next six months. Otherwise, uh, the terms of my will are invalidated. You know, the share options and mortgage insurance on the house? If she's gone, back to Norway, Shorn'll get the lot. So, uh. Makes sense for her to stick around, you know.'

There was a lot of silence before Erik answered.

'I'll tell her,' he said.

'Great.'

More silence. Neither man seemed ready to hang up.

'You're going to drive then?' Nyquist asked him finally.

Chris was relieved to find he could still manage a laugh. 'Well, let's just say the other options aren't great.'

'You can't run?'

'Shame on you, Erik. Run, from the filthy corporate monsters of Conflict Investment?' He grew abruptly serious, fighting the up-bubbling fear. 'There's no way, Erik. They've got me checked, filed and monitored. That fucked-up system you're always raging about. That system'll be locked up against any move I try to make. Plastic selectively invalidated, corporate police checking ports and airports. To put not too fine a point to it, if I don't roll out the wheels tomorrow, I'm a common criminal on my way to the jag gurney.'

Nyquist hesitated. 'Can you beat him? Carla says—'

'I don't know, Erik. Get back to me tomorrow afternoon, I'll have an answer for you.'

The Norwegian chuckled dutifully. Chris felt his own face take up the echo. He was suddenly, almost tearfully thankful for the older man's unhostile presence on the line. The instinctive male solidarity, the shoring up of his desperate bravado. He suddenly understood how badly he had failed to do the same thing for Erik at the crisis points in his father-in-law's life. How he'd taken the Norwegian's own cornered bravado at face value, failed to see it for what it was, berated him for it and cut him loose to suffer alone. With the realisation, something lodged in his throat.

'From what I understand,' Nyquist was saying, 'we'll all know by then. In fact we'll all be watching you crack open the champagne. The networks have been ad-screaming about full coverage since yesterday. Sponsored by Pirelli and BMW, they say.'

Chris's grin melted into a grimace. 'So. No prizes for guessing who *they* think's going to win, then.'

'Almost worth beating him just to piss them off, huh?'

'Yeah, that's right.' He could feel another bubble of fear coming up. He cleared his throat again. 'Listen, Erik. I've got to go. Things to do, you know. Got to get ready for all that publicity tomorrow. Interviews, fame, all that shit. It, uh, it isn't easy being a driving hero.'

'No,' said Nyquist very gently. 'I know.'

He signed the challenge documentation, got the hotel to courier it across to Shorn and sat waiting for receipt confirmation. He studied the route blow-ups and the surface reports with desultory attention, tried vaguely to imagine his way inside something resembling a strategy.

He could not focus on anything. He kept skittering off into daydreams. His thoughts slowed down, fragmented to useless shards.

He heard Carla's voice.

Even drunk, even like that, he's the best I've seen.

Hewitt's voice.

When Mike Bryant drives you off the road on Friday, Mr Chessman – and he will, because he's harder and faster than you – when that happens—

He remembered Bryant's driving. Bryant's chess playing. Headlong, full on, joyous in its savagery.

Bryant and the car-jackers. The boom of the Nemex, the tumbling bodies.

Bryant and Griff Dixon. Implacable, precise.

Bryant and Marauder, daring the gangwit forward, grinning into the possibility of it.

Bryant on Crutched Friars, walking empty handed into the duel against five men with *shotguns*.

He stared at it all, behind the curtain of his closed eyes.

And heard Hewitt again.

—Mitsue Jones shot through the head at close range while she was injured and trapped in wreckage—

—the blood of an eighty-year-old man on your hands—

You're no fucking different to me in the end.

He wondered if she was right.

Recoiled automatically as soon as he thought it.

Found himself lying face up on the bed an hour later, exploring the idea gingerly, like a broken bone or a gaping wound he didn't dare look at directly.

Caught himself, finally, hoping it might be true.

Because, in the absence of the consuming hatred that had driven him

361

after Edward Quain, he didn't know what else he could summon to keep him alive tomorrow.

He had the cab leave him at the end of the drive.

It felt strange to walk up the gravel S-curve and see the house emerge gradually through the trees. Just being there felt odd enough – he hadn't seen the place in weeks, and even then, before his life broke in half, he couldn't recall the last time he'd *walked* from the road. One weekend, one evening, out with Carla in the village maybe. Back at the start of the summer. He couldn't remember.

He reached the turning circle at the top, and the Saab was there, quiet and sequined with rain. He wondered if Carla had looked at it recently, wondered in fact when it had last been moved. He'd need to road-test it. Check it for—

A memory arrowed in past his defences – Carla under the Saab post test-drive, calling out questions about handling, while he stood with a whisky in his hand, watching her feet and answering. Warmth of shared knowledge, shared involvement.

He stared at the Saab, throat aching. The urge to get in and drive somewhere was overwhelming. He stood for a full twenty seconds, like a starving man faced with a large animal that he might just conceivably be able to kill with his bare hands and eat raw. He only moved when the straps on his bags began to cut deep enough into his palms to be painful.

Not yet.

He dumped the bags at the front door while he fished the recog tab from his pocket and showed it to the lock. Shouldered the door aside and moved across the threshold. Inside was cold with the lack of recent occupancy and everything had the skin-thin unfamiliarity of return home after long absence. He stood in the lounge, bags dropped once more at his feet, and Carla's departure came and hit him like a hard slap across the mouth.

She'd taken very little, but the holes it had left felt like wounds. The green onyx woman-form she'd bought in Cape Town was gone from its place by the phone deck. Two blunt little metal stubs protruded from a suddenly naked patch of wall where the flattened and engraved Volvo cylinder head from her mechanic's graduation had once hung. On the mantelpiece, something else was gone, like a pulled tooth, he couldn't remember what it was. The framed photos of her friends and family on the window ledge had been weeded out from others of Chris and Carla or Chris alone, and the remaining crop looked stranded on the white wood like yachts run aground. The bookshelves were devastated, the bulk of their occupants gone, the rest fallen flat or leaning forlornly together in corners.

He had no stomach for the rest of the house.

He unpacked his bag across the sofa, slung the Nemex and his recently acquired Remington into an armchair. The sight of the weapons brought him up short. He'd never brought the Nemex inside before this, he realised. Even when they went to the Brundtland that *fucking* night, he'd had to get it from the glove compartment of the Saab. It felt as alien now, perched on the soft leather of the armchair, as the absences where Carla had taken things away. It felt, in an odd way, like an absence of its own.

He picked up the shotgun, because it delayed the time when he'd have to go upstairs to the bedroom. He pumped the action a couple of times, deriving a thin satisfaction from the powder-dry *clack-clack* that it made. He lost himself in the mechanism for a while, put the thing to his shoulder and tracked around the room like a child playing at war, pausing and firing on the spaces Carla had left and, finally, on the image of himself in the hall entrance mirror. He stared for a long time at the man who stood there, lowered the Remington for a moment to get a better look, then pumped the action rapidly, threw the shotgun to his shoulder and pulled the trigger again.

He went out to the car.

Later, as evening was falling, he parked again and went back into the house for the second time. With darkness shading in outside and the lights on, the blank absence of things and Carla seemed less brutal.

He'd already eaten. He locked the door and went straight up to the bedroom. Carla had taken her scrubbed granite analogue clock from the bedside table and the only other time-piece in the room was on the dressing table, an old Casio digital alarm they'd bought together at some antique auction years back. Chris lay in the dark for a long time staring at its steady green numerals, watching the seconds of his life turn over, watching as the last minutes of the day counted down to zero and the new morning of the duel began.

He didn't sleep. He couldn't see the point.

FORTY-SIX

They were talking about him as he turned on the TV.

'—for a driver of that rank. It's not really what you expect, is it, Liz?'

'I think that depends, Ron.' She was resplendent in a figure-hugging black scoop-necked jersey, light make-up, hair pinned carelessly up. Looking at her made him ache. 'It's true Faulkner's form since Quain has been variable, but that doesn't necessarily make it *bad*. I know from interviewing him myself that he simply doesn't see blanket savagery as an asset.'

'Whereas Mike Bryant does.'

'Well, again, I think you're simplifying. Mike's form is more consistent, more conservative you might say, and yes, he certainly isn't afraid to go foot to the floor when it counts. But he's not cast in the same thug mould as, say, someone like Yeo at Mariner Sketch or some of the imported drivers we've got from Eastern Europe. That's savagery as a default setting. That's not Bryant at all.'

'You know them both quite well.'

She made a modest gesture. 'Mike Bryant was one of the main sources for my book, *The New Asphalt Warriors*. And I've been working with Chris Faulkner, among other drivers, on a follow-up. I hate to plug so blatantly, but—'

'No, no. Please.'

Mannered laughter.

'Well, then. It's called *Reflections on Asphalt – Behind the Driver Mask*, and it should, my workload permitting, be out some time in the New Year.' She grinned professionally into the camera. 'It'll be a great read, I promise.'

'I'm sure it will.' Face to camera. Pause, and. Cue. 'So now, let's go over to our live-coverage crew at the Harlow helideck. Sanjeev, can you hear me?'

'Loud and clear, Ron.' The inset screen sprang up. Maximised. Windswept backdrop, rotors and the location anchor sweeping dishevelled hair out of his eyes as he spoke.

'So what's the weather like up there?'

'Uh, looks as if the rain's still holding off, Ron. Maybe even some chance of sun later on, the forecast people tell me.'

'Good driving conditions, then?'

'Yes, it looks like it. Of course, we won't be allowed over the envelope until twenty minutes or so after the duel ends, but I'm told the roads have more or less dried out. And with the summer repairs on this stretch completed well ahead of schedule, this promises to be—'

He told the TV to sleep, finished his coffee and left the espresso cup standing on the phone deck. Brief existential shiver as he looked at it and realised it would still be there tonight, untouched, whatever happened on the road today. Wherever its owner was.

He shook off the chill and settled his jacket on his shoulders. In the hall mirror, he put on his tie with a languid, frictionless calm that was just the right side of panic. His hands, he noted, were trembling slightly, but he couldn't decide if it was fear or caffeine. He'd dosed himself pretty heavily.

He finished the tie, looked at himself in the mirror for what seemed like a long time, checked for keys and wallet, and went out to the car. He pulled the door of the house closed and breathed in, hard. The morning air was still and damp in his lungs.

Gravel crunched to his left.

'Chris.'

He spun, clawing at the shoulder holster. The Nemex came out.

Truls Vasvik stood at the edge of the house, hands spread at waist height. He smiled, a little forcedly.

'Don't shoot me. I'm here to help.'

Chris put up the Nemex. 'You're a little late for that.'

'Not at all. This is what I believe you English guys call the nick of time.'

'Yeah, right.' Chris shoved the Nemex back into the shoulder holster, spoiling the blunt gesture a little as the gun failed to clip in. He pushed a couple more times, then left it. Clicked the car key with his other hand and the Saab's lights winked at him as the alarms disabled. He stepped towards it.

'Wait. Chris, wait a minute.' Vasvik moved to block him, hands still held placatory at his sides. 'Think this through. Bryant's going to kill you out there.'

'Could be.'

'And – what? That's it? The great macho sulk? Kill me and be done with it. See if I fucking care. What does that achieve, Chris?'

'I don't expect you to understand.'

'Chris, I can get you out of here.' The ombudsman pointed. 'Back that way, through the woods. I've got a three-man team back there and a covered van. Sealed unit, medical waste documentation. It'll get us through the tunnel without checks. You get your million dollars, you get the job. All you've got to do is come with me.'

365

Out of nowhere, Chris found he could grin. The discovery made his eyes prickle, and put a ball of sudden, savage joy in the pit of his stomach.

'You've not been keeping up on current events, Truls,' he said. 'I'm globally famous these days. My face is right up there with Tony Carpenter and Inez Zequina. Everybody knows who I am. What kind of ombudsman is that going to make me?'

'Chris, that isn't important. We can—'

'What are you going to do then, give me a new face?'

'If necessary. But—'

'And the million dollars, well.' Chris tutted regretfully. 'That just isn't such a lot of money any more, Truls. I'm up for junior partner. That's equity. *Capital* wealth. Several millions, plus benefits.'

'Or cremation later today.'

Chris nodded. 'There's a risk of that. But you know what, Truls. The thing you guys will never understand. That risk is what it's all about. Risk is what makes winning worth it.'

'You aren't going to win, Chris.'

'Thanks for the vote of confidence. I'll see if I can live up to it. Now, if you'll excuse me—'

He stepped forward. Vasvik stayed where he was. Their faces were a handsbreadth apart. Eyes locked.

'Don't think I don't know what you're doing, Chris.' The ombudsman's voice was low and taut. 'You think this is going to pay off what you've done to Carla, and everybody else? Don't be a fucking child. Being dead doesn't solve anything. You've got to live if you're going to make a difference.'

Chris grinned again. 'Well, that's about as good a defence of cowardice as I've ever heard. I guess you need that, working where you do.'

He saw the flare in Vasvik's eyes.

'Yeah, that's it, Truls. Back the fuck off. Go file a report or something. You came and asked, and I turned you down.'

'You're a fool, Chris. You've pissed away your marriage, pissed all over your wife—'

The Nemex came out again, smoother this time, and he jammed it under Vasvik's chin.

'Hey. That's my fucking business.'

The ombudsman smiled with one corner of his mouth. He went on talking as if the Nemex wasn't there. '—and now you're going to piss your life away too. Just to make Carla Nyquist cry over your corpse.'

Through gritted teeth. '*I told you*—'

'And she will.' Vasvik saw the change in his face, and reached up for the Nemex. He curled his fingers around the barrel and pushed it away.

His eyes were icy with disgust. 'Yeah. She'll cry for the next ten years of her fucking life over you, Chris. But then, she would have done that anyway. Whatever happened. Whether you were dead like you're going to be, or just dead inside like you already are.'

Chris gave him a fixed little smile and stowed the Nemex again.

'Get out of my way.'

'My pleasure.'

Vasvik stood aside and watched him climb into the Saab. The engine woke with a rumble like distant thunder. Chris closed the door and put the car in gear. As he let out the clutch and the Saab began to crawl forward, something in the ombudsman's face made him crank down the window.

'Oh, yeah, Vasvik. Speaking of millions, I forgot. You heard they're going to make a movie about me?'

'Yeah.' The Norwegian nodded sombrely. 'I heard. Make a great ending if you and Bryant managed to kill each other both.'

Gravel crunched under the wheels. 'Fuck you.'

'No, really. I'd go and see it.'

He hit the turn for the ramp going too fast, ignored the bounce and accelerated down onto the motorway. Vasvik's offer was gone, like Vasvik himself, like conscious long-term thought, bundled up and flung out behind him, flapping on the road in the rearview. Over and out of reach. There was only the road ahead and his hold on the car around him. The Saab snarled throatily to itself as he picked up the centre lane and flipped on the comset.

'Driver Control.'

'This is Chris Faulkner, driver clearance 260B354R.' His voice was even in his own ears. He felt a quickening of the joy in the pit of his stomach. He felt armoured. 'Inbound on M11 for partnership challenge. I'm looking for the duel envelope.'

There was a brief pause. He wondered suddenly if any of the same crew that had worked the gangwit car-jack fiasco were on today.

'Got you, Faulkner. You're about twenty kilometres off the northern edge. We will advise when you breach. Leave the channel open.'

'Traffic?'

'Executive traffic has been disallowed until nine-thirty. You have two automated bulk transporters currently inbound within the envelope, moderate loads, and maintenance vehicles at junction eleven. Please note that collateral damage to said vehicles is not permitted within the duel protocol.'

'Noted. So where's Bryant, then?'

Another pause. You could hear the outrage.

'That information is classified under duel protocol. Please do not request it again.'

'Noted. The sense-of-humour failure, I mean.'

'Please also note that selective jamming is in effect within the envelope. You will be unable to receive outside transmissions other than our own.'

'Thank you, Driver Control. I have done this before a couple of times.'

He settled into his speed. The overgrown margins of the motorway flashed past on either side in a bumpy green blur. The asphalt fed thrumming under his wheels and fled in his wake. The sense of power grew, feeding off the caffeine and adrenalin. Dying suddenly seemed a long way off, a ridiculous rumour he didn't believe, something he wouldn't get round to.

Reality was the road.

He hit the duel envelope, tore through it at a hundred and sixty. Driver Control squawked the fact, whole seconds late. Peripheral glimpses of huddled vehicles on the bridge and ramps. Police lights, news crew vans and a rising boil of activity as the Saab slammed past them. He thought he felt the lenses of the cameras swing hungrily to follow.

No, you've just had way *too much coffee.*

A slightly hysterical laugh sat behind the thought. He forced it down and watched the hurrying perspective of the road, keyed up for the evening-blue flash of Mike's BMW. His speed sank to a more cautious hundred and thirty. The ghost of strategy floated up behind his eyes. Retained knowledge of the route from the blow-ups, sense of how Bryant drove.

Bryant! He grinned wolfishly. Folded away his misgivings, gave in to the pure hot flow of too-fucking-late-now.

Come on, you motherfucker. I took Liz off you, now let's see about that pretty blue car. Let's see about your plastic.

Lopez. Barranco. The men and women in the gunship-tortured highlands of the NAME. But most of all Bryant, Bryant and his craven fucking, keep-the-rain-off-me need for Hewitt and Notley and all the rest of it.

He mapped the faces over – Bryant into Quain. Just another murderous fucking suit. Just another—

The Saab hammered down towards junction ten. The first of the automated transporters blew up in his vision, nailed to the centre lane. Chime from the proximity alert, as he swung the Saab out and past. Gut-deep satisfaction as the car swayed and then straightened out under his hands. The high metal wall slid away on his left and he swung back in.

368

The road ahead—
Impact!
He was still swimming in the warm gutswirl of car control. Flash of
twilight blue in one wing mirror, metallic screech of impact from the
rear. Jolt of the crash, the seatbelt webbing grip across his chest. He
braked instinctively, remembered the transporter and slewed the Saab
hard right. The automated vehicle's collision alert split the air, blaring
banshee outrage above and behind him. He didn't have time to see if it
had braked. Mike Bryant's BMW shot past on the left, shedding speed
and hauling across to stay with the Saab. Forcing the duel, right here,
right now, right under the grille of the transporter.
He swam the blind spot, Chris knew numbly. Shadowed the automated
vehicle from the front until he spotted Chris in the depths of the wing-
mirror, falling back on the left as Chris overtook right, timing it on
instinct, pinning the Saab's blind spot as it emerged ahead of the
transporter, getting up close for the ram—
Even drunk, even like that, he's the best I've seen.
He's harder and faster than you—
Chris saw the BMW coming side-on and hauled over savagely. The
two cars met with a shriek. Flayed paint and sparks in the crushed air
between. Counterforce tried to push them apart again. Chris kept the
clinch, steering against the other car so the grating scream ran on like
nails down a blackboard. Bryant rode it, forcing him back and closer to
the central reservation. The BMW's greater weight was telling, the
plan loomed massively clear. Side impact at this speed would smash the
barrier down but not clear it. The wreckage would kick the Saab into
the air like a toy.
Options.
Behind them somewhere, the automated transporter came on, an
unknown quantity Chris didn't have time to look for.
Desperation crept out, flicker-tongued in his guts.
He floored the accelerator, but the BMW's nose already had him
blocked. Bryant had locked with careful malice, a half metre ahead of
neck-and-neck, enough to cut off any escape forward. Now, through
both side windows, he looked over at Chris and ripped a cocked thumb
across his own throat. He was grinning. The crash barrier—
Chris hit the brakes with everything he had.
The Saab staggered. Jerked free of the sparking, sandpapering fury on
its left flank. There was time for a flash glimpse of the transporter
coming up and he hauled hard left across Mike's rear, across the centre
lane and out of the automated vehicle's path. Another blaring of
machine rage and the transporter thundered past on his right cutting
off vision of the BMW and what it was doing. Chris gritted curses and

let them both go. Junction eight. His speed bled down to an unsteady ninety. Adrenalin reaction sloshed in his guts.

He caught a distant glimpse of the BMW disappearing down the incline towards the underpass.

It didn't take much imagination to work out what was coming.

He had about a minute, he reckoned. After that—

After that, somewhere down in the gloom of the tunnel, Mike Bryant would have executed his one-hundred-and-eighty degree crash-stop turn, would be barrelling back up the road towards him for the head-to-head chicken.

That old number. The Mike Bryant profile – fearless, headlong, savage. Conservative to the end.

Chris built speed. Cranked his nerves back up to drive tension. He passed the transporter again. Head buzzing with calculation.

Two outcomes for this. The head-to-head kills the duel, one way or another. Saab or BMW out of the game, turned too hard, too late and tumbled, into the path of the long-suffering transporter maybe, or maybe both cars, clipped against each other, tossed effortlessly apart with kinetic energy raging off at all angles, looking to shed itself in impact and flame. Or—

Or we both make it, and you're south, up and into the Gullet, no way to fight but slow down and let him ram you off into space like Hewitt did to Page, or try for the turn, a hundred and eighty screaming degrees on a vaulted highway only two lanes across.

He thought of this. He thought it out. Three-stage play, the crash barrier, the head-to-head, the end game in the Gullet.

And he knows you can't make that turn.

The BMW bloomed in the road ahead.

Up out of the tunnel ramp. *Very* fast.

He had time for a glance at the speedo, saw a hundred and something insane, doubled it in his head for Bryant's share of the speed, saw the BMW's armoured snout coming at him, rock steady and directly ahead—

He's harder and faster than you—

—and yelled, and hauled hard right.

The BMW flinched fragments of a second later. Flashed past.

Was gone.

Chris floored the accelerator and the Saab dived for the tunnel. Again, he had a minute at best. Not the time he needed, he'd have to make some more. The tunnel flew past in the hollow roar of the Saab's echoed passing. Up, out of the gloom and into sudden, watery sunlight. The Gullet flung itself down at him like a massive asphalt loading ramp. He rose to meet it, took the first curve at the very edges of his driving ability.

Felt his heart stumble as the Saab palpably gathered enough sideways momentum to skid. He dared not brake, there wasn't time. He needed the straight at speed. He unhinged the angle of the turn a miserly couple of degrees, slewed back across the double lane, fishtailing, muttering imprecations to the car. The Saab came back to him. He picked up the long rise-and-fall of the straight and ran for the next curve.

Almost to the end of the gut-tickling swoop, almost on the curve, he choked off his speed and threw the Saab into a shrieking, gibbering handbrake turn.

For one very long moment, he thought he'd fucked up. Thought he'd lose a tyre and then the car and plunge with it through the crash barrier into the zones below. The car slithered, tripped drunkenly across a badly mended pothole, screamed protest and tyre smoke he could suddenly smell—

And stopped.

Not the hundred and eighty. Just a ninety-degree sprawl across both lanes, blocking the Gullet like a bone in the throat.

Back along the straight, the BMW came over the rise.

He grabbed the shotgun from the passenger side footwell, threw open the driver side door and tumbled out of the car. Found his feet, found the BMW and cranked the action of the tactical pump.

Curiously, now that the situation was drawn, everything seemed very quiet. The Saab had stalled out in the turn, and the BMW's engine noise seemed almost inaudible past the distant ocean roar of his own pulse in his ears. The wind came and tugged at his hair, but gently. The sprawl of cordoned zone housing below seemed to be holding its breath.

He let Bryant come on for another second, then put the first shot into the driver-side half of the windscreen.

The familiar *boom* – he'd done a solid hour down in the armoury firing ranges, a final tuning of his earlier unexpected love affair with the long gun.

The BMW's windscreen cratered and crazed. He saw the splinter lines.

No discharge of projectile weaponry from a moving vehicle. The parchment-dry conclusion of the legal board of inquiry after the Nakamura playoff. *No substantial destruction to be inflicted with a projectile weapon. Provided these directives are adhered to—*

Bryant's windscreen was armoured glass. Even with the state-of-the-art vehicle shredder load the armourer had shown him, care of Heckler and Koch – *the* roadblock ammunition of choice for all your urban enforcement needs – even with that, at this range there'd be no *substantial* destruction.

He pumped the action, fired again. The spider-webbed screen resplintered, almost to opaque.

It was pushing the envelope, pushing it the way Jones and Nakamura had done, pushing it the way Notley liked.

The BMW came on. Behind the ruined screen, Bryant had to be almost blind. Chris pumped in another round, ran sideways to get the angle. Went after the leading tyre.

The shotgun kicked. The tyre blew into shreds.

No substantial—

The BMW slewed violently across the road, brakes shrieking protest, scorching rubber into the road and the wind.

Precedent, Chris. That's what counts.

In the elite, you don't get punished for breaking the rules. Not if it works.

The BMW careered past him, ploughed through the crash barrier and plunged over. It took less than a pair of seconds. Chris had time for one glimpse through the side window, Mike still fighting the wheel for control, then the big car was gone, and there was only the ragged gap in the barrier to mark its passing.

Breath held.

A flat, oddly undramatic metallic crump from below. Then nothing.

Done. Won. Finished.

Emptied out.

Nothing.

It coursed through him like current, that nothing. Emptiness, building to ecstasy. He threw back his head and screamed at the sky. It wasn't enough. He couldn't get it all out. He screamed until his throat felt ripped and his lungs locked up on empty. Until he gagged, finally, to a halt.

It wasn't enough.

Echoes rippled out across the cityscape below, chasing each other off towards the cluster of glass and steel towers on the skyline.

Overhead, even the clouds seemed to hurry away from the sound.

Behind them, the sky was a flawless, vacant blue. Against all the odds, it was going to be a beautiful day.

FORTY-SEVEN

ou bring back their plastic.

Stranded atop the marching pillars of the Gullet, listening to his own
ulse and the echo of his screams, Chris heard Hewitt's words with
allucinatory clarity. It was as if the woman was standing next to him in
he wind.

You go in and you finish the job. If you can, you bring back their plastic.

He peered down on the zone sprawl below. As far as he could tell, the
3MW seemed to have fallen through the roof of a decaying commercial
init. He scanned the surroundings in both directions and spotted his
ccess point. Fifty metres further along the Gullet, a caged staircase
wound down around one of the concrete support pillars and came out at
he end of a shabby residential street. It looked as if there might be a
oot passage through from the street to the commercial units. With luck
e could be in and out in ten minutes.

He jogged slowly along the road to the top of the staircase. There was
in ancient padlock on the rusting iron cagework. He levelled the shotgun, remembered the jagged vehicle-shredder load and thought better
of it. He reached for the Nemex and found an empty holster.

Fuck.

He remembered the way the gun had refused to clip in while he
talked to Vasvik. Remembered tumbling out of the Saab with the
shotgun. He looked back along the road to where the car was slewed.
No sign of anything on the asphalt, but it could have skittered away
under the belly of the vehicle. Or fallen while he was still inside.

*Well, that's it. You can't get down. Have to leave it for the clean-up squad.
Not like they'll take long to get here.*

The relief gusted through him. Duel etiquette forbade outside approach for a regulation fifteen minutes, except in medical emergencies.
But they'd reel the situation in on satellite blow-up, see the way it had
played out and be here pretty soon. All he had to do was sit at the edge
of the road and wait.

But he knew what Hewitt would say. Knew how the whisper would
run among the junior analysts on the floor below. *Yeah, sure, Faulkner's
some natty driver. But the way I heard it, no stones when it comes to the
consequences. Too soft to pick a corpse's pocket.*

Fuck it.

He locked on the Remington's safety, reversed the weapon and pounded at the rusted lock until it gave. Dull clank of metal on metal. Orange flakes of rust scattered around his feet. The lock snapped and hung, severed. He levered the cage door open and picked his way down the steps.

At the bottom, it was the same story. Another grilled iron door, another rusted lock, this time on the inside, as if a retreating army had fought a rearguard action out of the zones and up onto the highway. Weeds had grown up to shoulder height on the other side of the grille, effectively hiding the bottom of the staircase from outside view. From the inside, you could barely see the twinned row of black brick-terraced housing beyond. Chris craned his neck and stared through the nodding heads of the weeds, listening, trying to get some sense of whether there was anybody nearby.

Nothing stirred.

He started hammering at the lock. Slipped a couple of times, scraped his hand on the rusting iron. It was hard to manoeuvre the shotgun in the confines of the cage, hard to get a working angle. When he finally stepped out through the weeds, he was sweating and sticky inside his suit.

The street beyond was empty.

He scanned the frontages – the only motion was the flap of plastic sheeting over a broken upper window. A wrecked and rusted Landrover, one of the late models modified to burn alcohol, was beached on its axles about twenty metres down the street. It was skeletal, stripped of everything that would come off, the frame scorched molotov-cocktail black where rust had not yet crept in. He spotted the passageway a couple of houses beyond on the left and moved cautiously out into the street. Unrepaired potholes gaped in the cracked asphalt, some of them wide enough to take the whole front end of the Saab.

He moved a couple of steps at a time, painfully aware of the windows looking down on either side, pausing to listen every two metres. Belatedly, he remembered the Remington's safety and thumbed it off. Pumped out the last spent shell. The harsh metal noise it made shattered the quiet.

Suit and shotgun, he reasoned nervously. *It ought to keep the flies off long enough.*

He swung wide around the burnt-out Landrover, feeling slightly ridiculous as he covered the angles. He cleared the corner of the passageway. Moved down past high brick walls topped with broken glass. Detritus crunched under his feet. The passage came to an end amidst shallow mounds of weed-grown rubble and a clutch of leaf-canopied trees. He climbed the first mound with difficulty, burying his Argentine leather shoes to the ankle in little avalanches of sliding soil. From the top he saw the corrugated metal side of the commercial unit and a loading bay door, rusted open on empty square metreage beyond. In the gloom he could make out half of the BMW lying on its back. A qualified relief at his own navigational skills seeped—

Motion.

He whipped around, finger tightening on the Remington's trigger.

And snatched it away again, as if the metal was hot. On the down slope of the next mound, two children around four or five years old were playing a game with the slaughtered limbs and torsos of plastic dolls. They froze when they saw him, then scrambled to their feet and started shouting.

'Zek-tiv-*shit*, zek-tiv-*shit!* Zek-tiv-*shit*, zek-tiv-*shit!*'

He shook his head, lowered the shotgun and wiped a hand across his mouth. This close, the vehicle-shredder load would have—

'Zek-tiv-*shit*, zek-tiv-*SHIT!*' Elfin faces distorted with the force of the chant.

A woman's voice came from one of the houses, raised and harsh with anxiety. The children vectored in on it, looked at each other for a moment that was almost comical, and then darted away like spooked animals. They scrambled across the mounds of rubble and through a hole in a wall he hadn't seen. He was left looking at the plastic carnage of dismembered dolls.

Fuck. Fuck this. Fuck Louise Hewitt and her fucking plastic.

But he went on, over the rubble mounds, up to the loading bay door and through.

Inside, it was cold. Water dripped ceaselessly from the girder-laced roof and puddled along the lines of unevenly-laid concrete flooring. The BMW lay under the hole it had made, nose to the floor with the weight of engine and armour, back end in the air. There was a faint hissing from the front, and steam curled out through a gap where the hood had crushed out of true. Otherwise, it looked remarkably undamaged. The armouring had stood up.

Chris moved crab-wise to the driver-side door, hesitated a moment and then hooked it open. Bryant tumbled out like a bundle of unwashed clothes. Suit bloodied, eyes closed and mouth open. One arm trailed across the floor at an impossible angle to the rest of the body.

Nausea. The rising tide of delayed reaction from the duel. Chris pressed his tongue hard against the roof of his mouth and knelt beside the body. He stowed the shotgun under his arm and flapped back one side of Bryant's jacket. The wallet gleamed gold-cornered from the inside pocket. He took it between thumb and forefinger and tugged it free. Flipped it open. The photo of Suki and Ariana smiled up at him opposite Mike's racked plastic.

A hand closed around his leg.

Chris almost vomited with the shock. The shotgun clattered across the floor. He stumbled away from the car, broke the grip and saw. Bryant was still alive, eyes wide and staring up out of his inverted face. His good arm made feeble motions. His mouth opened and closed silently, like a landed fish. It was impossible to tell if he recognised Chris or not.

You go in and you finish the job. You don't take them to the hospital afterwards.

He remembered Bryant's gesture as the two cars ground against each other – the cocked thumb ripping across the throat. The grin. His mouth tightened and he picked up the Remington again.

You don't take them to the hospital, Chris.

You finish the job.

He stepped back and raised the weapon. Bryant saw it and flailed desperately about on the concrete. A broken moaning came out of his mouth. It looked as if he was trying to bring his working arm up to his shoulder holster and the Nemex, but he didn't have the strength. Chris clamped his mouth tighter, took another step back and levelled the shotgun. Jagged motion, quick, before he could give it thought. He'd stopped breathing.

Finish the fucking job, Chris.

He squeezed the trigger.

Nothing.

No click, no detonation, no kick. No spray of blood and tissue. The trigger gave soggily through half the pull and stuck. Chris pulled harder. Still nothing. He worked the action and jacked a perfectly good unfired shell out into the air. It hit the concrete and rolled away, cheerful cherry red.

Mike's face, pleading up at him.

Squeezed again. Nothing.

'Fuck.' It gritted out of him, as if he was afraid to be overheard in the empty warehouse. It still seemed to echo off the walls. 'Fuck, *fuck!*'

The padlocks – hammering at the padlocks until they snapped and came loose. He remembered the savagery he'd brought to the action, the haphazard angles he'd been forced to use in the cage at the bottom of the stairs.

He'd jammed the mechanism, jolted something, maybe broken something inside, irretrievably.

He stood looking at Mike Bryant. Wiped his mouth and swallowed.

376

Finish it. Fucking finish it.

He stalked closer, staring fascinated into the other man's eyes. Bryant gaped up at him, twitching. He made noises that sounded like the name *Chris*, the word *please*.

For some reason, it was enough.

'Fuck you, Mike,' he said quickly. 'You had your chance.'

He turned the injured man's head with one foot, reversed the Remington and jammed the butt of the weapon into Bryant's exposed throat. Leaned his full weight on the gun.

'Fuck you, Mike!' Now he was spitting it, bent over and glaring into Bryant's face. '*Fuck you!* Fuck you, all of you suited fuckers!'

It seemed to take forever.

At first Bryant only made choking sounds. Then, from somewhere, he found strength to get his undamaged arm up and grab the Remington around the trigger guard.

Chris kicked the hand away and stood on it. He was panting.

Mike's choking sounds grew frantic. He twisted his head against the concrete. He curled his trapped fingers around the edges of Chris's shoe, nails clawing at the Argentine leather.

Chris leaned harder. Tears sprang out in his eyes and streamed down his face. He lifted his foot and stamped down hard on Mike's hand. He heard the dry snap as one of the fingers broke. He leaned harder. His whole weight lifting on the braced shotgun, taking his body almost off the floor.

Something crunched. Mike stopped moving.

Afterwards, Chris could barely get himself upright. It was as if the shotgun had suddenly become indispensable, as if he'd been afflicted with a sudden muscular disease. He limped back from the corpse, trembling so violently his teeth chattered. He made less than a dozen steps. He bent suddenly double and, finally, threw up. A thin helping of vomit and bile – he'd barely eaten that morning, but what he had came up. He dropped to his knees in a puddle, retching.

The sound of boots through the wet.

He looked up, only vaguely interested, and saw the men. Big, blocky forms in the filtering light from outside, like knights in armour from some mediaeval fantasy.

He blinked to clear his eyes.

There were nine of them, dressed in the cordoned zone gangwit ensemble. Cheap, grimed clothes, loose canvas trousers, bulky padded jackets, shaven heads and workboots. Hands held crowbars, wrenches, sawn-off pool cues and a variety of other items too jagged to identify. Faces were scarred with streetfight souvenirs. Eyes watchful on the scene they'd just interrupted.

He got unsteadily to his feet. One of the men stepped forward. He was near two metres tall, heavily muscled under a sleeveless T-shirt scrawled red with the legend *I am the Minister for the Redistribution of Health*. The lettering was splattered to make it look bloody. His face was scarred from the corner of the left eye and down the cheek. It gave him an oddly mournful look.

'Finished, have you? Is he dead?'

Chris blinked and coughed.

'Who are you?' he asked harshly.

'Who are we?' Laughter rasped out, first from one throat, then building to a rattling echo off the metal roof. It died out as abruptly. The gangwit spokesman was swinging a short black-enamelled prybar softly and repeatedly into his left palm. His gaze seemed welded to Chris, playing up and down the clothes, the hair, the shotgun. He smiled and the scar tissue tugged at his face. 'Who are we? We're the fucking dispossessed, mate. That's who we are.'

There was no laughter to follow this time. The men had tautened, waiting for the leash to slip. Chris suppressed another cough and lifted the Remington as convincingly as he could manage.

'That's close enough. The police are on their way, and there's nothing to see here.'

'Yeah?' The spokesman for the group gestured at the BMW and Mike Bryant's corpse. 'From what we've seen so far, I beg to differ. This is prime time. *Mr Faulkner.*'

Chris pumped the action on the Remington.

'Alright, I said that's close enough.'

Mistake.

The unspent shell leapt in the air, hit the concrete and rolled towards the other man. For a moment, they both looked down at it. Then the gangwit looked back up at Chris and shook his head.

'See, that's a perfectly good round, mate. And to judge by your manner of execution back there a moment ago, I'd say—'

Chris flung the shotgun in his face and ran.

Back to the upturned BMW and Mike Bryant's corpse. He heard booted feet behind him, more than one pair. The gangwit's voice rang exasperated above the clatter.

'Well don't fucking stand there. Get him!'

He dived and landed on Mike in a kind of embrace. Scrabbled under the jacket, felt the butt of the Nemex in his hand. Proximity sense told him the first of his pursuers was almost on him. Shadows blocked out the light. The smell of old leather and cheap aftershave swamped him. A hand grabbed at his jacket.

He rolled free and came up with Mike's gun almost touching the gangwit's chest. He saw the man's eyes widen. A pool cue smashed down on his shoulder. He squeezed the trigger.

The Nemex thundered. The shot kicked the man off his feet and back across the concrete. He crumpled and lay still.

'*Toby!*' It was a howl of anguish. The gangwit spokesman. 'Fucking zek-tiv piece of *shit!*'

The second gangwit was two paces behind his fallen comrade, but the gun brought him to a dead halt. The others were converging, but now they stopped and began to back away, left and right. Chris got himself upright, grinning fiercely.

'That's right, back the fuck off.'

Something black whipped through the air and hit him a numbing blow across the elbow. The Nemex went off, firing wide into the concrete floor. Chris clutched at his arm and tried to bring the gun to bear as the spokesman, leaping in after the hurled prybar, hit him from the right. Below the elbow, his muscles were water. He snapped off a panic shot. It went wide. The gangwit snarled a grin and grabbed the arm, twisting. Chris felt his hand spasm open. The Nemex spun away, splashing into a puddle. He threw a punch left-handed and saw his opponent ride it with a streetfighter's impatient grunt. Desperate, he reached and grappled. The Minister for the Redistribution of Health punched him in the chest with shattering force. He collapsed backwards, fending weakly, tripping on Mike's corpse. The gangwit let him go, let him fall against the body of the upturned BMW and turned to scoop up his prybar. Stalked forward, still grinning. Chris saw the attack coming and rolled weakly left, along the BMW's flank. The crowbar arced down and clawed a long dint in the twilight-blue bodywork where he'd been. The metal screeched. Chris came off the car yelling, delivered a hooking left-handed punch to the Minister's temple. The gangwit threw up a block that didn't quite cover and staggered slightly with the impact. He grunted again, shook his head and whipped the crowbar round. Chris caught it across the side of the head.

Multi-coloured light rang in his skull. The ceiling waltzed by over-head. He reeled and fell. Something snagged his arm, he looked muzzily and saw the Minister had him, was holding him up. Comfortably.

'Fucking piece of shit *driver*,' the man was yelling in his face. 'Come into the fucking zones with your suit, will you?'

The crowbar slammed into his ribs. He screamed like a baby and twisted. There were others around him, holding him up for the spokes-man, cuffing him back and forth across the head.

'Come into the fucking zones, will you? *Hold him.*'

Another blow, another rolling tide of numbness. He thought he felt a rib crack this time. He yelled, but weakly. The grip on his arm let go and he slumped into a ring of supporting grasps. He saw a fist coming, heavy with dull metal rings. It split his vision apart, sent shards of it spinning away against a roaring darkness. He felt part of his face tear, felt blood streaming down into his collar.

'Show you what we think of—' the Minister was telling him between blows, but the rest was carried away on the roar in an opening tunnel of darkness.

Oddly, in the bottom of it all, he heard Carla.

So! You just want to fuck me and leave me. Is that it?

Her hands on him. She was smiling. For some reason he couldn't pin down, he wanted to laugh and cry at the same time.

I'm. Already sliding headlong into the dark. *Not going anywhere.*

But he was.

And a sound like distant thunder.

FORTY-EIGHT

Driver Control helicopters held the sky over the vaulted highway where Chris Faulkner had slewed the Saab to its shrieking sideways halt. Bright sunlight winked off underslung camera lenses and the clustered barrels of the gatlings. At a prudent distance beyond, news crew aircraft circled like sharks waiting for something to give up and die. There were police vehicles scattered up and down the stretch, equipment set up and armed figures hurrying about. Louise Hewitt stood talking to a ranking tactical-force officer and her mobile at the same time. She looked up and shielded her face as a new, twilight-blue helicopter drifted in through the black-and-green Driver Control machines and settled to the asphalt, twenty metres away. Jack Notley climbed down from the cabin, settled his suit a little more firmly on his shoulders in the gale of the rotors and strode towards her.

'I'll call you back,' she told the phone, and snapped it shut. 'And Captain, if you could just give me a moment.'

The officer saw who was coming and stepped back. Notley reached Hewitt and stared at her. 'Well?'

'I expect you've heard.'

'That's why I'm here.' Notley looked grim. 'What have you got?'

Hewitt shrugged and nodded towards the crane and winch system at the edge of the Gullet. 'We put in the tacs. Apparently they're bringing them both up now. Not a pretty sight, is what I was told.'

Notley looked away, up and down the stretch of highway. 'Four miles,' he said. 'Four miles from where Page went off. You realise that?'

'Four?' Hewitt frowned. 'Oh, *miles*, that's what, about six kilometres? Yeah, probably about that. And not far from where Barnes learnt to fly, come to that.'

'Yes.'

'Exciting stretch of road.'

The winch whined into action. Both partners turned to watch as it brought up a sheet-covered stretcher. Tactical-force corporate police swarmed around the load, swinging it in and lowering it gently to the road. The covering was white and blood had soaked through in small patches. A medic crouched, turned back the sheet and winced visibly. The winch swung back down. They watched the cable unwind.

'Going to be a lot of questions,' observed Hewitt when it stopped. 'Lot of precedent to be hammered out.'

Notley grunted. 'Good. Kind of thing that keeps us sharp.'

'Keeps the lawyers sharp, you mean. They're going to be arguing this one back and forth for months at our expense.'

'While we go ahead and get on with doing things anyway.'

'Ethics after the event.' Hewitt offered him a crooked smile. 'My favourite kind.'

Notley raised an eyebrow. 'Are there any other sort?'

The winch swung up again. More activity, another stretcher settling to the asphalt. More blood stains on white.

'Not in this world.'

'I'm glad—'

Amidst the weaving of the tactical-force uniforms, commotion. Uniforms milling. And Chris Faulkner, climbing off the stretcher like the living dead. Pushing his way clear. A ragged cheer floated over him like a banner.

Hewitt froze.

Notley blinked.

Then the senior partner was striding rapidly towards the new arrival, a grin broadening on his face. He only faltered as he got closer and saw the damage. Chris's face was a mask of blood and bruising. One eye swollen almost shut, ribbons of torn flesh around the mouth and both cheeks ripped, blood from a nose that looked broken. The way he moved under the abused and bloodied suit screamed cracked ribs.

'Chris! Jesus fuck, you're alive. I thought. You had me worried for a moment there. Congratulations!'

Chris stared at him. Stared past him, like the zombie he so closely resembled. Notley grabbed his shoulders.

'You've done it, Chris. You won. You're a partner at thirty-three years old. Fucking unprecedented. Congratulations! You know what this means?'

Chris looked sideways at him. Focused.

'What does it mean?' he whispered.

'What does it mean?' Notley was almost burbling. 'Chris, it means you're at the top. From here on up, there's *nothing* you can't do. Nothing. Welcome aboard.'

He thrust out his hand. Chris looked down at it as if the gesture didn't make sense. He made a coughing noise that it took Notley a moment to realise was laughter. Then he stared up into the senior partner's face and off past it again. The Saab. Hewitt.

'Uh, Chris—'

'Excuse me.'

He pushed past Notley, pacing a steady line for Hewitt. She saw him coming and tensed. A brief nod to the tactical captain, and the man was at her shoulder. Chris came to a halt a metre away, swaying a little.

'Louise,' he husked.

She manufactured a small smile. 'Hello, Chris. Well done.'

'This is for you, Louise.'

He held it out. The Shorn Associates card, Mike Bryant's name engraved and streaked across with new blood.

'I don't think now is—'

'No, it's for you.' Chris took another, sudden step in and tucked the card into Hewitt's breast pocket. He nodded to himself, already turning away. 'For you. Because that's the way we do things around here, right?'

Hewitt's smile was frozen on. 'Right.'

'I'll see you on the road, Louise.'

He walked away, dipping in his pocket for keys. The door of the Saab was still wide open. Driver Control personnel busied themselves around it, measuring and photographing. When he tried to get in behind the wheel, one of them barred his way.

'Sorry sir, we're not finished here ye—'

He backed up as Chris looked at him.

'Get. Out of my way.'

The man retreated. Chris eased himself into the seat, teeth clenching up as his hastily taped ribs grated with the move. The medics had shot him full of something warm, but the pain was still getting through in flinty little flashes. He sat for a while, breathing it under control. He thought it would probably be manageable.

He closed the door. Reached for the ignition.

The Saab fired up growling. Around him, up and down the Gullet, activity stopped at the sound. Heads turned. He saw people gesturing.

No one seemed interested in stopping him.

He moved his head, a little awkwardly. Coughed and tasted blood. Checked the rearview and cut a smooth circle in reverse, so the car was pointing southward, towards Shorn. He shifted gear, let the vehicle start to glide forward.

'Sir, wait.' Muffled through the seal of the closed doors and windows. A uniformed tactical hurried across and rapped on his window. He cranked it down and waited, foot light on the clutch, barely holding the Saab back. The tac hesitated.

'Uhm, sir, it's just. The shooting down there. Well, we arrived sort of in the nick of time, sir, so it was a bit rushed. Just trying to get them off you, you know.'

'Yes.' His voice still wasn't working properly. It had taken him whole minutes, lying there on the concrete, to make sense of the thunder, the screams of men dying and then the urgent voices of the tacs as they circled him. The ring of concerned faces peering down. 'Yes. Thank you.'

'Yes, well, uhm. Thing is, a firefight like that, you don't always get everyone dead centre, and now it looks like at least a couple are going to live. I, well, I assume you're going to be pressing charges, sir.'

'Yes, alright.'

'Well, I'll need a number for you, sir. For the statement. Obviously, we can get you at Shorn, but we like to provide a full personalised service in cases like this. Victim support, one-to-one interviews, we can come out to you any time. And I'm the officer assigned, so. Do you, uh, have a home number, sir?'

Chris closed his eyes briefly. 'No, not really.'

'Oh.' The tac looked at him for a moment, puzzled. 'Well, anyway. I'll get you at Shorn, then.'

'Yes.' He tried to curb a flooding tide of impatience. He wanted to be gone. 'Is that all you need?'

'Oh. Yes sir. But, uh, you know, congratulations. The duel and everything. My whole family were watching it. Well done. Fantastic driving. Uh, my son's a huge fan, sir.'

He fought down the urge to cackle. Hid it in a cough.

'That's nice.'

'I expect you'll be on the screen a lot the next few weeks. Probably even get an interview with that Liz Linshaw, eh?' The tac saw the look on his face and stepped back. 'Anyway, I'll. Let you go, sir. Thanks.'

'No problem.'

He let the Saab roll forward. People got out of the way. He moved past Louise Hewitt and then Jack Notley, gathering speed. By the time he passed the last of the uniforms and the parked police vehicles, he was closing on ninety. The Saab took the curve on a rising growl. He hit a pothole, but the suspension and the onset of the painkillers damped it out. He reached for the phone, jabbed it on. Winced only a little this time as his cracked ribs jarred. He placed a forward call to Joaquin Lopez in Panama, ten minutes ahead. Then he dialled Shorn's priority client operator and told them to get him Francisco Echevarria immediately.

They didn't like it. They didn't know if—

'Tell him it's a national emergency,' Chris suggested.

It took a couple of minutes, but Echevarria grabbed the call. He wasn't pleased. Chris got the impression the ride in the last week had been bumpy.

'Bryant? That you? Now fuckin' what? What national fuckin' emergency you talkin' about?'

'The one that's going to put you in front of a fucking firing squad, you piece of shit. This is Chris Faulkner.'

Strangled silence, then fury. 'You motherfuckin'—'

'Shut up and listen, Paco. I don't know what line of shit they've been handing you in my absence, but things just changed for the better. Mike Bryant is dead.'

'You're lyin'.'

'No, I'm not. I killed him myself. With my bare fucking hands. So I'm now junior partner at Shorn Conflict Investment, which means *executive* partner for the NAME account. Which means *you*, Paco. And I'm telling you, I'm going to have Vicente Barranco in the streets of Bogotá by the end of this fucking month. So if I were you, I would gather up as much of your father's stolen loot as you can get in a Lear jet, and I would fuck off out of the NAME right now, while you can still walk to the plane.'

Echevarria lost English in the storm of his fury. Spanish washed down the line, beyond Chris's ability to follow. He cut across it.

'You've got forty-eight hours, Paco. That's it. After that, I'm sending Special Air to put a bullet in your face.'

'*You cannot do this!*'

This time, Chris really laughed. Across the pain in his broken ribs, across all the pain. The drugs were numbing him nicely.

'You still don't get it, do you, Paco? From where I'm sitting, I can do whatever the fuck I want. Men like me, there's nothing you can do to stop us any more. Understand? *There is nothing you can do any more.*'

He killed the call.

Fed power to the Saab and watched as his speed climbed.

Gave himself up to the snarl of the engine, the spreading numbness of the drugs in his system, and the onrushing emptiness of the road ahead.

BOOKS CONSULTED

Chomsky, Noam — Rogue States: The Rule of Force in World
Affairs
— Profit Over People: Neoliberalism and Global
Order
Easterly, William — The Elusive Quest for Growth: Economists'
Adventures and Misadventures in the Tropics
George, Susan — The Lugano Report: On Preserving Capitalism
in the Twenty-First Century
Moore, Michael — Stupid White Men . . . and Other Sorry Excuses
for the State of the Nation
— Downsize This: Random Threats from an
Unarmed American
Morgan, Robin — The Demon Lover: The Roots of Terrorism
Pilger, John — Hidden Agendas
— The New Rulers of the World
Stiglitz, Joseph — Globalisation and its Discontents

Note: the views expressed in Market Forces *are in no way intended to
represent the views of any of the authors listed above.*